Yu Hua

CRIES IN THE DRIZZLE

Yu Hua was born in 1960 in Zhejiang, China. He finished high school during the Cultural Revolution and worked as a dentist for five years before beginning to write in 1983. He has published four novels, six collections of stories, and three collections of essays. His work has been translated into French, German, Italian, Dutch, Spanish, Japanese, and Korean. In 2002 Yu Hua became the first Chinese writer to win the prestigious James Joyce Foundation Award. His novel *To Live* was awarded Italy's Premio Grinzane Cavour in 1998, and *To Live* and *Chronicle of a Blood Merchant* were named two of the last decade's ten most influential books in China. Yu Hua lives in Beijing.

Allan H. Barr is the translator of a collection of short stories by Yu Hua, and his research on Ming and Qing literature has been published both in the West and in China. He is Professor of Chinese at Pomona College.

ALSO BY YU HUA

Chronicle of a Blood Merchant

To Live

The Past and the Punishments

CRIES IN THE DRIZZLE

CRIES IN THE DRIZZLE

A NOVEL

YU HUA

Translated and with a preface by

ALLAN H. BARR

ANCHOR BOOKS

A Division of Random House, Inc.

New York

FIRST ANCHOR BOOKS EDITION, OCTOBER 2007

Cataloging-in-Publication Data is on file at the Library of Congress.

Anchor ISBN: 978-0-307-27999-6

Book design by Jo Ann Metsch

www.anchorbooks.com

Printed in the United States of America
10 9 8 7 6 5 4 3 2 1

TRANSLATOR'S PREFACE

Yu Hua established his reputation in the late 1980s through a provocative series of short stories and novellas that placed him at the forefront of the literary avant-garde in China. *Cries in the Drizzle*, written when Yu Hua was thirty-one, was his first full-length work of fiction, and marked a new phase in his career, one that would soon produce two other memorable novels, *To Live* and *Chronicle of a Blood Merchant.* In China, *Cries in the Drizzle* is perhaps not quite as widely read as Yu Hua's subsequent books, and its international reception has also lagged behind those more popular titles. It is nonetheless a technically accomplished novel that prefigures several themes and situations of Yu Hua's later work. Set largely in provincial Zhejiang in the 1960s and 1970s, the place and time of the author's upbringing, it also comes closer than much of his fiction to his own life experience. With its searing and elegiac vision of childhood and adolescence in the Mao era, *Cries in the Drizzle* easily holds its own against Yu Hua's other novels, and in the judgment of some critics may even be his finest achievement to date.

When it first appeared in the Shanghai literary journal

Shouhuo in 1991, *Cries in the Drizzle* was entitled *Huhan yu xiyu* (Cries and drizzle). It was under this title that the book was published in Taipei in the following year, and that is how it is known in Taiwan to this day. In mainland China, however, the novel was soon renamed *Zai xiyu zhong huhan* (Crying out in the drizzle), in order to avoid confusing it with Ingmar Bergman's film *Cries and Whispers,* whose Chinese title sounds identical to the novel's original name. The text used in this English translation is that of the 2004 Shanghai reprint, which restores a word excised from early editions of the book.

I am grateful to Yu Hua, Zhang Yongqing, Li Hua, Jane Barr, and Catherine Barr for their advice at various stages. In transcribing Chinese personal names, I have followed the standard pinyin romanization system, with one exception. The name of the narrator's father I render as Kwangtsai rather than the conventional Guangcai, so as to distinguish more clearly the names of his three sons, which are quite different from his in Chinese.

CRIES
IN THE DRIZZLE

Chapter 1

SOUTHGATE

It was in 1965 that nighttime began to stir in me a nameless dread. I am thinking now of that evening when a light rain drifted down. In my bed I lay, a child so little you could have set me there as easily as a toy. The dripping from the eaves simply called attention to the silence that surrounded me, and the steady onset of sleep was but a gradual forgetting of the rain's patter. As I glided peacefully into slumber, it was as though a secluded path had appeared before me, opening a passage between trees and shrubs. Then from far away there came the sound of a woman's anguished wails. When those hoarse cries erupted so suddenly in the still of the night, the boy that I was then shivered and quaked.

I can see myself now, a startled child, eyes wide with fear, the precise outline of my face obscured by the darkness. The woman's cries persisted. Anxiously, I expected to hear another voice, a voice that would respond to her wails, that could assuage her grief, but it never materialized. I realize now why I was gripped by such intense disquiet: it was because I waited in vain for that answering voice. Surely there is nothing more chilling than the sound of inconsolable cries on such a desolate night.

A second memory comes hot on the heels of the first: three or four white lambs trotting across the grass by the riverside, a daytime image, a way of easing the agitation evoked by the previous memory. But I find it hard to decide just where I was when this sight left its mark on me.

Several days may have passed before I seemed to hear a voice that answered the woman's cries. It was late afternoon. A storm had just passed, and dark clouds filled the sky like billows of smoke. I was sitting by the pond behind the house, and out of the damp landscape a man I did not recognize walked toward me. He was dressed completely in black and as he approached his dark clothes waved like a banner under the gloomy sky. When this image began to close in on me it brought to mind the unmistakable sound of the woman's cry. Even from far off in the distance the stranger fixed me with a piercing gaze, and he continued to stare at me as he drew nearer. Just as I was about to panic, he abruptly changed direction, mounted the path on the edge of the field, and gradually moved farther and farther away, his loose black clothes flapping loudly in the breeze. Now, when I look back on the past from an adult point of view, I always linger long on this particular moment, puzzling over why it was that I interpreted the rustling of his clothes as a response to the woman's cries in the evening drizzle.

Then there is a morning I remember, a crystal-clear morning when I was scampering along behind some village boys, over soft earth and windblown grasses. The sunshine at that moment seemed to be a matter not so much of dazzling light as a warm color daubed on our bodies. Like the lambs on the riverbank we bounded along, running for ages, or so it seemed, until we arrived outside a dilapidated temple from which enormous cobwebs caught my eye.

It must have been a little earlier that one of the village boys had come tramping over from a spot far off in the distance. I still remember that his face was drained of color and his teeth were chattering. "There's a dead man over there," he said.

The body was lying beneath the cobwebs. It was the same man who had walked toward me the day before. Although I try now to recapture my feelings at that moment, the effort fails. My memory of that incident has been stripped bare of the reactions I had at the time, and all that is left is the outer shell: the associations it now carries simply reflect my current outlook. For me as a six-year-old the sudden death of a strange man could have prompted only a quiver of astonishment and would not have been the occasion for much hand-wringing. He lay faceup on the moist earth, eyes closed, with a relaxed and peaceful expression on his face. I noticed that his black clothes were stained with mud, mottled the way a country path is spotted with somber, anonymous flowers. It was the first time I had seen a dead man, and it looked to me as though he was sleeping. That must have been the extent of my reaction then: that dying was like falling asleep.

After that I dreaded the night. I saw myself standing at the entrance to the village and pictured the gathering darkness surging toward me like floodwater, engulfing me and then swallowing up everything else. I would lie in the dark for ages, not daring to fall asleep, and the silence all around simply intensified my terror. Again and again I would wrestle with sleep. My antagonist strove with all its might to seize me in its powerful grip, and I desperately resisted. I was afraid that once I fell asleep I, like the stranger, would never wake up again. But in the end I was always reduced to exhaustion, sucked helplessly into slumber. When I woke up the following morning and discovered I was still alive, the sunlight poking through the crack in the door, I was overjoyed to find that I had been spared.

When I think back to when I was six years old, one last scene comes to mind. Here again I see myself dashing along at full speed, and in my memory I relive the former glory of the boatbuilders' yard in town, and the day when their first-ever concrete boat was making its way down the river into Southgate. My big brother and I were running toward the riverbank. How bright was the sunlight of those bygone days, illuminating my still-young mother, her blue-checked headscarf fluttering in the autumn breeze; my little brother was seated in her lap, his eyes wide with wonder. My father, with that penetrating laugh of his, clambered barefoot onto the ridge between the fields. But what was that tall man in the army uniform doing there? He seemed to have arrived by chance at my parents' side, like a leaf blown into a thicket.

The riverside was packed with people. My brother showed me how to squeeze through their legs, and a clamor of voices enveloped us. When we finally crawled into a spot overlooking the river, we stuck our heads out between two grown-ups' trouser legs and gazed around like a pair of turtles.

The moment of highest drama was announced by an earsplitting din of gongs and drums and the cheers of the crowd assembled on the banks. The concrete boat was coursing toward us. Long ropes hung down its sides, with pieces of colored paper fastened to them like so many flowers blooming on a vine. A dozen young men on board were banging gongs and beating drums.

"Hey, what's that boat made of?" I called to my brother.

He turned his head and answered with a shout, "Stone."

"Then why doesn't it sink?"

"You idiot," he said. "Can't you see the ropes?"

It was at this point in my life that the burly figure of Wang Liqiang appeared in his military uniform, imposing on my memories of Southgate a five-year hiatus. He took me by the hand and led me off toward a steamboat with a piercing whistle. It would carry me down an endless river, to a town called Littlemarsh. I didn't know then that my parents had given me away and I was under the impression that this trip was going to be a pleasurable excursion. On the narrow dirt road I ran into my grandfather, now racked by pains and aches. I answered his troubled gaze with a complacent announcement: "I don't have time to talk to you now."

Five years later, as I returned alone to Southgate, I was to run into Granddad again on this same road.

Not long after I moved back home, a family from town by the name of Su came to Southgate to live. One summer morning the two boys of the Su family carried out a small round table and placed it in the shade of a tree. They began to eat breakfast.

This is what I saw then, when I was twelve. The two town boys were sitting there in their store-bought shirts and trousers while I sat alone by the pond in my homespun shorts. I watched as my fourteen-year-old brother led my nine-year-old brother toward our new neighbors. Like me, they were shirtless and dark as two loaches in the sun.

Just before this, I had heard my big brother say, over by the drying ground: "Come on, let's go and see what the townsfolk eat."

Of the children who had congregated on the drying ground, my little brother was the only one prepared to join him in this inspection of the newcomers. Striding ahead with his chin up, my big brother was boldness personified, while my little brother trotted along at his heels. Baskets of grass cuttings dangled from their arms and swung back and forth as they made their way down the road.

The two town boys laid down their bowls and chopsticks and watched warily as the visitors approached. My brothers did not pause, but marched past the table with a swagger, then looped around the townspeople's house and walked straight back again. Compared with the image struck by my older sibling, my little brother's effort to project authority came across as rather unconvincing.

On their return to the drying ground, my big brother said, "The townsfolk eat pickles, just like us."

"No meat?"

"No fucking good stuff at all."

My little brother corrected him. "There's oil in their pickles. We don't have any oil in ours."

My big brother gave him a shove. "Get out of here. What's so great about oil? We have oil at our house too."

"But it's sesame oil they've got. We don't have *that.*"

"You don't know shit."

"It's true—I could smell it."

The year when I turned twelve Wang Liqiang died, and I made my own way back to Southgate. Once there, I felt as though I was experiencing the life of an adopted child all over again. In those early days, I often had the strange sensation that Wang Liqiang and Li Xiuying had actually been my natural parents and that this home in Southgate was no more than a kind of almshouse. It was the fire that first stirred those feelings of estrangement, for at the very moment that Granddad and I were walking back to Southgate after our chance encounter, our house was going up in smoke.

This coincidence made my father look at me and Granddad

with intense suspicion in the days that followed, for all the world as if we were the ones who had started the blaze. If I happened to stand next to Granddad, he would erupt into howls of frenzied protest, as though he expected our newly erected cottage to burst into flames any second.

Granddad died the year after my return to Southgate. His departure from the scene allowed my father's paranoia about us to dissipate, but this did nothing to alleviate my plight. My big brother took his cue from my father and made no secret of his disapproval of me. Any time I made the mistake of appearing by his side, he would tell me to get lost. So I grew steadily more distant from my siblings, and as the village boys were always doing things with my big brother I became ever more remote from them too.

To compensate, I would immerse myself in nostalgia for my life in Wang Liqiang's home and for my childhood companions in Littlemarsh, recalling countless happy moments, yet assailed at the same time by sadder memories. As I sat alone by the pond, engrossed in reliving the past, my solitary smiles and copious tears left the villagers bemused. In their eyes I was fast becoming a freak. That's why later, when people got into rows with my father, I became a weapon in their arsenal, and they'd say that only defective genes could spawn a son like me.

In all the time I spent in Southgate, there was just one occasion when my big brother turned to me as a suppliant—the time he cut my head open with a sickle, leaving my face dripping with blood.

This was in our sheep pen. When his stinging blow struck my head, I wasn't at all clear what had happened, and what first caught my attention was the abrupt change in my brother's attitude. Only after that did I feel the blood coursing down my face.

He stood aghast in the doorway and begged me to wash the blood off. I shoved him aside and headed out of the village, toward the fields where Father was working.

The villagers were fertilizing the vegetables, and a faint odor of feces wafted on the breeze toward me. As I approached the vegetable plot, I heard several women give cries of alarm and dimly perceived my mother running toward me. When she arrived at my side she asked me a question, but I made no reply, carrying on doggedly toward my father.

In his hand he was holding a long ladle, which he had just lifted out of the honey bucket. He held it stationary in the air as he watched me walking toward him. I heard myself say, "It was big brother who did it."

He hurled the ladle to the ground, leapt onto the path, and set off for home at a rapid pace.

What I didn't know was that after I left, my big brother had cut my little brother's face with the sickle. Just as my little brother was about to open his mouth and bawl, my big brother explained why he'd done what he did and begged his forgiveness. In my case his entreaties had fallen on deaf ears, but my little brother was more receptive.

And so, when I returned home I was greeted not by the sight of my older brother taking his punishment, but by that of my father waiting for me under the elm tree, rope in hand.

Owing to my little brother's false testimony, the facts of the case had now taken on a completely new cast: it was only because *I* had cut *him* with the sickle that my big brother had bathed my face in blood.

Father tied me to the tree and gave me a thrashing that I will never forget. During the beating the village children stood around in a circle and watched with rapt attention while my brothers complacently maintained order.

After this episode I made two marks, one large, one small, on the last page of my composition book. I kept a record of every beating I suffered at the hands of my father and my big brother.

Now, so many years later, I still have that composition book, but its mildewy odor makes it impossible to reexperience the urge for revenge that animated me then. It evokes instead a vague sense of wonder, which in turn brings to mind the willow trees of Southgate. I remember that one morning in early spring I noticed with surprise that their withered branches were dotted with tender green buds. This lovely image, when it now reappears in my consciousness so many years later, turns out to be intimately linked with the composition book that is the symbol of my childhood humiliations. Perhaps that is how memory works, outlasting loves and hates to make its entrance unaccompanied and unencumbered.

Just as my family situation was going from bad to worse, something else happened that created an unbridgeable gap between me and the other members of my household and also destroyed my reputation in the village at large.

Adjacent to our private plot was a tract tended by the Wang family, which included among its members a pair of brothers, the strongest men in the whole village. The elder of the two was married, his older son the same age as my little brother. Arguments over private plots were commonplace in Southgate and I can no longer recall exactly what triggered this particular dispute. All I remember is that it was late in the afternoon and I was sitting by the pond watching my parents and brothers as they engaged in an unending altercation with the six members of the Wang family.

Our side appeared to be in the weaker position, or at least it was making less noise. This was particularly true of my little brother, who was still unable to enunciate swearwords as clearly as his opposite number in the Wang household. Practically everyone in the village was standing around watching, and a few came over in an effort to pacify the antagonists, only to be sent packing. Some time later I saw my father hurling himself at his adversaries, his fists flying. The younger of the two Wang brothers, Wang Yuejin, seized his wrist and with one blow sent him hurtling into the rice paddy. My father unleashed a string of curses and just as he tried to climb soggily to his feet, Wang Yuejin kicked him back into the field. Mother screamed and threw herself at Wang Yuejin, but he dodged to one side and gave her a shove that sent her headlong into the paddy as well. My parents floundered about clumsily, like chickens tossed into a lake. I bowed my head in distress at the sight of them thrashing around.

Later my big brother charged over brandishing the kitchen cleaver, my little brother hot on his heels grasping a sickle. My big brother aimed a blow at Wang Yuejin's buttocks.

A dramatic reversal of fortune ensued. Under the onslaught of my brother's cleaver, the Wang brothers, who had seemed so invincible just moments earlier, retreated to their house in alarm. My brother chased them right to their door, where the Wang brothers grabbed fish spears in an effort to fend him off. But when he recklessly threw himself at them, cleaver flailing, they dropped the fish spears and ran for their lives.

Inspired by his big brother's example, my little brother raised his sickle high in the air and gave a battle whoop, quite the intrepid warrior. But he had trouble keeping his balance as he ran and tripped over himself several times.

Throughout the whole confrontation I remained rooted to my spot next to the pond, and it was because of my detached role as spectator that the villagers—no matter whether they were my father's supporters or his detractors (the Wangs included)—came to the conclusion that in all the world there could not be another person as degenerate as me, and it is not hard to imagine what kind of reception I got from my own family. My big brother, on the other hand, was proclaimed the hero of the hour.

There was a period when I would make a point of quietly observing the Su family as I sat by the pond or cut grass for the sheep. The two town boys did not emerge from their house all that often, and the farthest they ever went was to the cesspit at the edge of the village, where they immediately turned back. One morning I saw them come out of the house and stand between the two trees in the front yard, pointing at something as they talked. Then they walked over to one of the trees, and the older of the two squatted down on his haunches while the younger climbed onto his back. The one carried the other over to the second tree, where they exchanged positions and the younger boy carried his older brother back to the original spot. They repeated this routine over and over again, and each time one threw his weight on the other's back I could hear their infectious laughter. The two brothers' laughs sounded very much alike.

Later on three bricklayers came from town, bringing two loads of red bricks. A wall was erected around the Sus' house, enclosing the two trees, and I never again saw the Su brothers playing the game that so captivated me. But I often heard laughter from the other side of the wall, so I knew they still played it.

Their father, a doctor, worked at the hospital in town. Often I saw him strolling along the road late in the afternoon, a man with clear skin and a gentle voice. Once, however, he didn't come home on foot as usual, but sped past me, perched on the saddle of one of the hospital's bicycles. I was heading home with a basketful of grass and was startled by the sound of a bicycle bell behind me. He was calling his sons as he rode past.

The two boys went into ecstasies as soon as they came out the door and raced joyfully to meet the bicycle, while their mother stood by the side of the lane, greeting with a smile the returning man of the house. The doctor loaded his two sons onto the bicycle and rode off along a path between the fields. They shrieked with excitement, and the younger boy, who sat in front, rang the bell incessantly. This spectacle made the village children green with envy.

When I was sixteen, in my first year of high school, I tried for the first time to come to terms with the word *family.* I hesitated for a long time, faced with the choice between my home in Southgate and Wang Liqiang's home in Littlemarsh, and the understanding I finally reached was inspired by the memory of that particular scene.

My first contact with the doctor occurred some time before the argument over the private plots. I had been back at Southgate only a few months then, and Granddad was still alive. After staying with us for a month, he had gone off to my uncle's house. Meanwhile I had come down with a fever that left my mouth parched dry. I lay in bed for two days, all in a daze. Our ewe was just about to lamb and the rest of the family was out in the pen, so I was alone in the house, listening groggily to the noises outside. My brothers' shrill voices were particularly audible.

Later my mother appeared by my bedside and said something or other, then went out. Next time she appeared Dr. Su was by her side. He placed the palm of his hand on my forehead, and I heard him say, "Must be a hundred and two."

After they left, the noise in the sheep pen went up a notch. Though the doctor had just laid his hand lightly on my forehead, it felt to me like a tender caress. Before long I heard the voices of the Su brothers outside; only later did I realize that they were delivering medicine.

Once I was on the mend, feelings of dependency began to stir. I had been close to my parents until I was six, when I left the village, and later, during my five years in Littlemarsh, Wang Liqiang and Li Xiuying had provided their care and support, but since my return to Southgate I had found myself suddenly abandoned and unprotected.

So around this time I would often stand by the roadside and wait for the doctor to pass on his way home from work. I watched as he approached, imagining the heartwarming things he might say to me, anticipating how his broad hand would pat me on the forehead.

But the doctor never paid me the slightest attention, and I realize now that there was no reason he should have given any thought to who I was or why I was standing there. He would brush past me, and if on occasion he threw me a glance it was only as one stranger looks at another.

Su Yu and Su Hang, the doctor's two sons, soon afterward were inducted into the ranks of the village children. My brothers were trimming grass from the bank of earth between the fields, and I watched as the Su brothers walked hesitantly toward them, debating some point as they went. My older brother, who in those days tended to think he could take charge of anything, waved his sickle at them and said, "Hey, do you want to cut some grass?"

In the short time Su Yu spent in Southgate, he came over to talk to me only once. I still remember his shy expression, the unmistakable timidity in his smile as he asked, "You're Sun Guangping's younger brother, right?"

The Sus lived in Southgate for only two years. The sky was overcast on the afternoon they moved out. The very last cart of furniture was hauled away by the doctor himself, with the two boys pushing, one on either side, and their mother brought up the rear, clutching two baskets full of odds and ends.

Su Yu died of a brain hemorrhage when he was nineteen. I didn't hear the news until the day after it happened. On the way home from school I passed the house where the Sus had lived and sorrow surged through my heart, bathing my face in tears.

When my big brother went to high school his behavior changed quite markedly. (I find I now recall rather fondly my brother at the age of fourteen. Though he was a real dictator, there was something unforgettable about his arrogance. Sitting on the bank, directing the Su brothers' grass-trimming activities—for a long time this was the image of him that was foremost in my mind.) Once he began to mix with the children from town, he became increasingly standoffish toward the village boys. As his town classmates became more regular visitors to our house, my parents felt that this reflected very well on them, and there were even some senior residents of the village who predicted that my brother would have the brightest future of any of the village children.

During this period two teenagers from town often came running out to the village early in the morning, shouting at the top of their lungs just for the heck of it. They yelled so much that they became hoarse, and their screeches made our hair stand on end. The villagers thought at first they were hearing ghosts.

This made a deep impression on my brother, and I once heard him say darkly, "Here we are, wishing we could be townsfolk, but it's entertainers that the townsfolk want to be."

My brother was definitely the quickest of the youngsters in the village to spot developing trends, for it was already dawning on him that all his life he would never be able to compete with his classmates from town; this was his earliest sensation of inferiority. But at the same time his friendship with the town boys was a natural extension of his customary self-regard: their visits unquestionably raised his standing within the village.

My brother's first love interest appeared when he reached the second grade of high school. He took a fancy to a strongly built girl, the daughter of a carpenter. Several times I saw him in a corner, taking a bag of melon seeds from his satchel and slipping it into her hands.

She would often emerge on the playground, munching our melon seeds, spitting out the shells with such gusto and expertise that you might have taken her for a middle-aged matron. Once, after she spit out a shell, I noticed that a long thread of saliva trailed from the corner of her mouth.

Around this time girls began to figure as a theme in conversations between my brother and his classmates. I sat by the pond behind the house, listening as they explored territory entirely new to me. Out of the window drifted brazen commentary on breasts, thighs, and other body parts, provoking surprise and arousal in me. In due course they moved on to their own experiences with girls. My brother kept quiet at first, but under pressure from his classmates he soon revealed his dalliance with the carpenter's daughter. So taken in was he by their vows of confidentiality that he let himself get carried away: it was obvious that he was exaggerating their intimacy.

Not long after that, the girl stood in the middle of the playground, surrounded by several other schoolgirls, all just as full of themselves as she was. She called him over.

My brother walked toward her nervously, for he may already have had some inkling of what was about to happen. It was the first time I saw him afraid.

"Did you say I have a crush on you?" she asked.

His face turned bright red. I did not stay to observe how my brother, usually so self-assured, now found himself reduced to helpless embarrassment. Encouraged by her classmates' chortles, the girl threw the melon seeds in his face.

My brother returned home from school very late that day and lay down in his bed without having anything to eat. I was dimly aware of him tossing and turning practically the whole night through. Still, he managed to swallow his pride and go off to school as usual the following morning.

My brother knew that the town boys had sold him down the river, but he never showed any signs of resentment or even allowed the faintest hint of reproach to appear on his face. Instead he continued to fraternize with them as before, for he would have hated to let the villagers see that his townie classmates had dropped him all of a sudden. But in the end my brother's efforts all came to naught. After they graduated from high school, the town boys were assigned jobs one after the other, thereby forfeiting the freedom to loaf around, and the time came when he found himself ditched.

Late one afternoon, when my brother's classmates were no

longer gracing our home with their presence, Su Yu arrived quite unexpectedly, the first time he had returned to Southgate since his family moved away. My brother and I were in the vegetable plot and only my mother was home, busy preparing dinner. When she saw Su Yu, she assumed he had come to see Guangping. Now, so many years later, I am still stirred by the memory of her standing at the edge of the village, calling him eagerly at the top of her voice.

My brother hopped onto the path and hurried home, but Su Yu's first words to him were, "Where's Sun Guanglin?"

My mother realized with astonishment that Su Yu had come to see me. My brother managed to take this in stride and he answered casually: "He's over in the vegetable patch."

It didn't occur to Su Yu that he should take a moment to chat, and without further ado he turned his back on them and headed for the field where I was working.

Su Yu had come to tell me he had been assigned a job at the fertilizer plant. We sat on the bank for a long time, gazing at the Sus' old house as the evening breeze began to pick up. "Who lives there now?" Su Yu asked.

I shook my head. I would see a little girl come out the gate, and her parents were often around, but I knew nothing about them.

Su Yu left as night fell. I watched as his stooping form disappeared on the road into town. Before the year was out, he was dead.

By the time I graduated from high school, the university entrance examinations had been reinstated. When I was admitted to college I had no chance to inform Su Yu as he had informed me about his job placement. I did see Su Hang on a street in town, but he and his buddies were on bicycles and they raced past me in high spirits.

I didn't tell my family that I was taking the entrance exam, and I borrowed the money for the registration fee from a classmate in the village. A month later, when I went to pay him back, he said, "Your brother already gave me the money."

I was taken aback. After I received the notice of my admission, my brother put together some things that I would need. By this time my father was already having his affair with the widow across the way; he would often slip out of her bed halfway through the night and slip into my mother's. He was too preoccupied to give much thought to family matters. When my brother told him my news, he simply said offhandedly, "What! They're going to let him stay in school? The lucky devil!"

My father realized that this development signaled my long-term absence from home, and this put him in excellent spirits.

Mother had a fuller understanding of things. In the days immediately preceding my departure she would often look uneasily at my brother, for what she had really been hoping was that *he* would go to university. She knew that graduation from college assured your promotion to an urbanite.

When I left, only my brother saw me off. He walked in front, my bedroll on his back, and I followed close behind. Neither of us said a thing. Touched by the efforts he had made during the previous few days, I was looking for an opportunity to thank him, but the silence that enveloped us made it difficult for me to broach the topic. Only as the bus was about to depart did I blurt out: "I still owe you one yuan."

My brother looked at me blankly.

"The registration fee, I mean."

Now he understood, and a doleful expression appeared in his eyes.

"I'll pay you back," I went on.

I watched him through the window as the bus lurched forward. My brother was standing underneath a tree, and I saw a stricken look on his face when the bus pulled away.

Not long after this, the land in and around Southgate was requisitioned by the county authorities for the construction of a textile mill, and the villagers were turned overnight into suburbanites. Although I was in faraway Beijing, I could easily imagine their excitement and anticipation. Even if some people ended up sobbing as they prepared to relocate, it seemed to me that their sadness was the inevitable sequel to the initial rejoicing. Old Luo, the storehouse janitor, shared with everybody one of his pearls of wisdom: "No matter how successful a factory may be, it will go bust eventually. You'll never be out of a job if you till the fields."

But years later, when I returned to my home district, I ran into Old Luo in an alley in town, and the old man, dressed in a dirty, tattered cotton jacket, said to me proudly, "I'm living off my pension now."

After I left Southgate for good, I never felt any attachment to my childhood home. For a long time I was convinced that memories of the past or nostalgia for one's birthplace really represent only a contrived effort to restore one's equilibrium and cope better with life's frustrations, and that even if some emotions arise these are simply ornamental. Once, when a young woman politely inquired about my childhood and hometown, I found myself enraged and retorted: "Why do you want me to accept a reality that I have already left behind me in the past?"

If anything about Southgate induces some nostalgia, it has to be the village pond, and when I heard that my birthplace had been appropriated for development, my first reaction was concern for the pond's future. That spot, which for me had been a source of comfort, would, I feared, just be buried and forgotten, the same way Su Yu had been buried and forgotten.

Some ten years later I went back to Southgate, returning alone one night to my home village. In its new incarnation as a factory, Southgate no longer projected a faint odor of night soil wafting on the evening breeze, nor could I hear the gentle swaying of crops. Despite all the changes I could still identify exactly where my old home once stood and the pond once lay. When I moved closer my heart couldn't help but skip a beat, for the moonlight revealed that the pond of my childhood was still there. As it came into view, an upheaval stirred within me. The memory of this pond had always offered me solace, but its appearance in the present now brought to life the very fiber of my past. Gazing at the refuse that littered its surface, I realized that the pond was more than just a provider of consolations; it served, rather, as an emblem of days gone by: far from fading in my memory, it still clung stubbornly to its place on Southgate's soil, an eternal reminder of what had been.

WEDDING

In those early days when I sat beside the pond, Feng Yuqing inspired endless yearning when she walked by, exuding youth and buxom beauty, wooden bucket in hand. As she approached the well she would move more cautiously. This circumspection in turn stirred an anxiety in me, a concern that she might lose her footing on the moss growing around the edge of the well. When she bent over to lower the bucket into the shaft, her braid would flop down over her chest and swing in an exquisite motion.

One particular summer—this was Feng Yuqing's last year in Southgate—I felt a different sensation as she walked by at midday. I caught a glimpse of her breasts quivering inside her floral blouse and my scalp went numb. A few days later, as I passed her house on the way to school, she was standing in the doorway, combing her hair in the first rays of the sun. Her head was slightly tilted to one side and the early morning sunshine bathed her sleek neck and caressed her shapely figure, while her raised arms clearly exposed to the daybreak breeze the lighter shade of hair in her armpits. These two scenes kept replaying in my mind, with the result that when I next saw Feng Yuqing I was conscious that I kept averting my gaze. My feelings for her were no longer as straightforward as they once had been, for budding desire was now bundled up with them.

I was surprised by something my brother Sun Guangping did one evening not long afterward. Now fifteen, he undoubtedly noticed her physical appeal earlier than I did. It was a moonlit night, and as Sun Guangping headed home with a bucket of water Feng Yuqing was walking in the direction of the well. In the instant when they passed each other, Sun Guangping's hand darted toward her breasts, only to rapidly withdraw. He then hurried homeward, while she was so shocked by his gesture that she stood there paralyzed, regaining her composure only when she saw me, at which point she continued on toward the well. I noticed that as she drew up the bucket she made a point of tossing her braid back over her shoulder whenever it fell over her chest.

For the next few days I was sure that Feng Yuqing would come to our house to lodge a complaint, or at the very least that her parents would. Sun Guangping often cast anxious glances out the door. But as time went on and the moment he was dreading never materialized, he gradually recovered his usual confidence. Once I saw him run into Feng Yuqing, and he gave an ingratiating smile while she simply brushed past him with a scowl.

Even my younger brother Sun Guangming was not immune to Feng Yuqing's charms. Ten years old, still clueless about sex, he greeted her once with a shout of "Big breasts!" He was sitting on the ground at the time, a grimy little boy toying with a scrap of brick. He gave a silly smile, and a thread of saliva dripped indiscreetly from the corner of his mouth.

Feng Yuqing, blushing, continued on toward her house, her head lowered. Her mouth was bent a little out of shape, and it was obvious that she was trying to stifle a laugh.

In the autumn of that year Feng Yuqing's life took a new turn. I remember it all so clearly: how, as I crossed the wooden bridge on my way home from school one lunchtime, I saw a profoundly altered Feng Yuqing, clinging tightly to Wang Yuejin and surrounded by a crowd of onlookers. To me this scene came as a great shock. The girl who was the focus of all my desires eyed the spectators with a pleading, anxious look. They gave no sign of extending to her the sympathy she deserved, for they were animated by curiosity more than anything else. Wang Yuejin, still in her iron grip, said to them facetiously, "Just see how shameless she is!"

The laughter of the audience had absolutely no effect on

Feng Yuqing, except perhaps to render her expression all the more sober and obstinate, and for a moment she closed her eyes. In that instant, a hundred thoughts ran through my mind. She was clinging to something that was not hers: it was just a matter of time before it would slip from her hands. When I gaze back at the past, it's as though I see her clutching not a man, but air. Feng Yuqing was quite ready to cast aside her natural reserve and forfeit her reputation in order to hold that vacuum in her arms.

Wang Yuejin tried everything under the sun, hurling abuse at her one minute, cracking jokes the next, but nothing he did succeeded in loosening Feng Yuqing's grip. He looked helpless and gave a sigh. "What a woman!"

Feng Yuqing never said a word in response to his insults. Perhaps she realized that she had no hope of winning the bystanders' sympathy, for instead she shifted her gaze to the river's restless flow.

"What the hell does she want?" Wang Yuejin bellowed, angrily tugging at her hands. She was gritting her teeth as she turned her head.

When this effort failed, Wang Yuejin lowered his voice and said, "Come on, tell me. What is it you want?"

She answered quietly, "Come with me to the hospital while I have a checkup."

She said this without any embarrassment, utterly serene, as though she felt reassured that she would achieve her goal. At that moment she glanced at me and I felt my body tremble under her gaze.

"You have to let go," Wang Yuejin said. "Otherwise there's no way I can take you anywhere."

Feng Yuqing hesitated for a moment, then relaxed her grip.

Wang Yuejin, free at last, immediately took to his heels, shouting back at her as he left: "You want to go—then go by yourself!"

Feng Yuqing frowned as Wang Yuejin made his escape, then took a look at the people standing around and saw me a second time. She made no attempt to pursue Wang Yuejin, but set off alone for the hospital in town. A few village kids, back home after school, followed her all the way to the hospital, but I did not go with them; I simply stood on the wooden bridge and watched as she receded into the distance. As she left, her braid, disheveled in the tussle, unraveled, and I saw how she deftly reorganized her long black hair, tying her braid as she walked.

Feng Yuqing, normally so bashful, now seemed completely poised, and her inner turmoil was reflected only in the paleness of her face. She let nothing throw her off balance, and when she registered at the reception desk, she asked for an appointment with a gynecologist as calmly as a married woman might. She answered the doctor's questions just as calmly, saying, "I need a pregnancy test."

The doctor noticed that she had checked the "Single" box on the medical form and asked, "You're unmarried?"

"That's right," she said, nodding.

The three boys from my village saw her go into the women's toilet, clutching a tea-colored glass bottle. When she emerged, her expression was grave. As she waited for the results of the urine test, she sat on the bench in the corridor like any other patient, gazing blankly at the laboratory hatch.

Only later, when she learned that she was not pregnant, did she slowly lose her composure. She walked over to a cement power pole outside the hospital, leaned against it, buried her face in her hands, and wept.

Her father, once a young man who could consume a couple of bottles of spirits in no time at all, now an old man who could still put away well over a bottle, stood outside the Wang residence that afternoon as the sun went down, stamping his feet and unleashing a string of curses. Carried by the evening breeze, his obscenities drifted through the whole village. But as far as the younger folk were concerned, all his swearing paled in importance compared with his single bitter complaint, "You went all the way with my daughter!"

Deep into the night, this line lingered like snot on the lips of the village children. When they spotted him, they would chant from a safe distance, "You went all the way with my daughter!"

Of the weddings I witnessed in Southgate, Wang Yuejin's was the most memorable. This powerfully built young man, once forced to run for his life from Sun Guangping and his kitchen cleaver, wore on that morning a brand-new Mao jacket, and his complexion was as ruddy as that of an official from town. He was getting ready to go across the river and fetch his new bride. Everyone in his family was running around, hectically engaged in the final wedding preparations, while he, already dressed in his smartest outfit, was the one person who seemed at a loss for something to do. As I passed his house on the way to school, he was trying to persuade a young man from the village to accompany him on the trip to fetch the bride, saying to him, "Nobody else will do. You're the only bachelor."

"I'm no virgin," said the other man.

Wang Yuejin's attempts to persuade him were offhand and perfunctory, and it wasn't as though the other man was unwilling to go—he simply wished to register a certain lack of enthusiasm.

On the village drying ground, two pigs were slaughtered and

several dozen grass carp met their end. Sprinkled with pig's blood and fish scales all morning, the ground had been swept clean by the time we came home from school and was now covered with twenty round tables. Sun Guangming's face was festooned with fish scales and he exuded a fishy odor. He walked over to Sun Guangping, saying, "Can you guess how many eyes I have?"

Sun Guangping adopted my father's dismissive tone: "Go wash your face." I saw him grab our little brother by the collar and haul him off toward the pond. Guangming's pride was cut to the quick, and in his shrill little voice he cursed: "Sun Guangping, I fuck your mom!"

The wedding party had set off that morning. Amid a discordant clamor of gongs and drums, this purposeful but undisciplined band crossed the river that would later take Sun Guangming's life and marched off to collect Wang Yuejin's bedmate.

When the chubby bride, who hailed from one of the nearby hamlets, coyly entered the village, she seemed to think that nobody knew how often (under cover of darkness) she had been a visitor during the preceding weeks, and she put on a bold and confident show of looking timid.

At the wedding feast Sun Guangming must have consumed over one hundred and fifty broad beans, with the result that he kept letting off the foulest farts, even when he was sound asleep that night. When Sun Guangping pointed this out to him the following morning, Sun Guangming had a fit of the giggles. He was pretty sure that he had eaten five fruit candies, but hadn't bothered to count all the beans. On the day before he died, my little brother would sit on the threshold and ask my big brother who else was going to get married soon, vowing to eat ten fruit candies this time around. As he said that, a dribble of snot was working its way toward his lips.

I often think of my little brother, who died so young, and his gritty performance that afternoon as he fought for the candies and beans. When Wang Yuejin's sister-in-law came outside, basket in hand, Sun Guangming was not the quickest to react, but he was the first to fall flat on his face. She dumped the basket's contents in front of the assembled children as though she were feeding hens, and a cascade of beans tumbled to the ground along with just a few dozen candies. As my older brother bent down, another boy accidentally kneed him in the face. Always hot tempered, Sun Guangping concentrated on clobbering his assailant, with the result that he missed out on the plunder. With Sun Guangming, it was a different story: he threw himself on the candies and beans and withstood no end of pummeling. Afterward he just sat there, his face streaked with mud, grimacing as he rubbed his head and his ears, and he told Sun Guangping that his legs were covered in bruises.

Sun Guangming came away with seven fruit candies and a full handful of broad beans. He sat there meticulously removing earth and gravel from his booty. Sun Guangping stood off to one side, glaring at the children who gazed enviously at his little brother, deterring them from grabbing the delicacies he had claimed.

Of these items, Sun Guangming allocated to his big brother a small bunch of beans and a single candy. As he took them, Sun Guangping said in an aggrieved tone, "That's all I get?"

Sun Guangming rubbed one of his chafed ears and looked at Sun Guangping uncertainly, then offered an additional candy and a few more beans. When his big brother showed no signs of leaving, in his piping tone he delivered the following threat: "If you ask for any more, I'll cry!"

The bride had entered the village at noon. Though this round-faced, round-bottomed girl kept her head bowed, it was clear from her smile that she was pleased with the match. The bridegroom, buoyed by satisfaction as well, appeared to have forgotten all about his tussle with Feng Yuqing several days earlier, and when he came walking up, brimming with good spirits, he raised his right hand and waved it clumsily in our direction. At that moment I rejoiced: no longer would Wang Yuejin besmirch the Feng Yuqing whom I so worshipped. But when my gaze shifted to the house where she lived, an indescribable distress welled up within me, for I saw that the object of my fantasies had her eyes fixed on where we were. Feng Yuqing was standing in front of her home, disconsolately watching the ceremony in which she played no part. Of all those present only she felt the sting of exclusion.

Later the wedding guests sat out on the drying ground, eating and drinking. My father Sun Kwangtsai had sprained his neck when sleeping, and was sitting there, one shoulder bared, like an outlaw hero of old. My mother, standing behind him, swigged a mouthful of celebratory liquor and spat it onto his back. Kneaded and massaged by Mother's hand until he swayed back and forth, he emitted moans of pain that made him appear touchingly vulnerable, but this didn't get in the way of his doing some serious drinking. As he lifted his chopsticks and transported a large chunk of meat into his mouth, Sun Guangping and Sun Guangming stood off to one side, their mouths watering. Sun Kwangtsai constantly turned his head to shoo away his sons. "Get lost!" he said to them.

They ate from noon straight through to dusk, which was

when the climax to the wedding took place. It was then that Feng Yuqing appeared unexpectedly, a rope in her hands. Wang Yuejin didn't see her approach because he was busy clinking glasses with another fellow from the village. By the time somebody tapped him on the shoulder, Feng Yuqing was standing right behind him. He instantly turned pale. I remember how a hush fell over the drying ground, which only seconds earlier had been buzzing with noise. The result was that, even from my distant observation post, I could clearly hear Feng Yuqing's words. "Stand up!" she said.

Wang Yuejin performed a replay of the panic he showed that day Sun Guangping pursued him with the cleaver. He rose to his feet as slowly as an old man. Feng Yuqing walked off with the stool he had been sitting on and set it down underneath a tree beside the drying ground. In full view of the assembled audience she clambered onto the stool. Under the autumn sky she stood tall, her figure, with its upturned curves, unutterably beautiful to my eyes. She tied one end of the rope to a tree branch.

That was when Old Luo yelled, "She's going to kill herself!"

Feng Yuqing, from her elevated perch, looked at him in seeming astonishment, then deftly looped the rope so that it formed a noose big enough to accommodate a human head. She jumped off the stool with a flourish and made a solemn exit.

On her departure, the drying ground once again buzzed with noise. Wang Yuejin, pallid and trembling, began at last to curse, but his outrage lacked conviction. I expected that he would go over and remove the rope, but instead he sat down on a stool that someone lent him and did not stand up again. His bride, who had put two and two together, was at this point distinctly more collected than he was. She sat there, eyes straight ahead, and her only action was to down in one gulp a bowl of spirits while he sneaked furtive glances at both her and the rope. Later his older brother removed this ghastly decoration, but it continued to prey on his mind and things continued in uneasy limbo for some time. The rope had come to the village just like a movie brought by a mobile projection team, introducing itself into the wedding to stunning effect, throttling the life out of the wedding while it was still in its prime.

Before long the bride was drunk. She gave a spine-chilling cry, rose unsteadily to her feet and announced, "I'm going to hang myself!" As she stumbled over to where the rope had once hung, she was firmly held back by Wang Yuejin's sister-in-law, a mother of two. "Hurry up and help her inside," she shouted at Wang Yuejin.

As the bride was hustled into the house, she continued to yell stubbornly, "I'm going to hang myself!"

It was quite some time before Wang Yuejin and his friends reappeared. No sooner were they out of the house than the bride herself emerged, now brandishing a cleaver, which she pressed against her throat. People couldn't tell if she was crying or laughing, and all they heard was her shout, "Just watch me!"

Feng Yuqing sat on her doorstep, viewing these events from a distance. I will never forget her meditative look, her head slightly tilted, her chin cupped in her right hand, as the breeze blew her hair back and forth in front of her eyes. It was as though she was not so much watching this chaotic scene as looking at herself in a mirror. At that moment Feng Yuqing no longer cared about the wedding she was witnessing; she was perplexed about where her own life was taking her.

A few days later, a peddler appeared. A man in his forties, dressed in gray, he set down his load in front of Feng Yuqing's house. Speaking in an alien accent, he asked Feng Yuqing, standing in the doorway, for a bowl of water.

Village children gathered around in a circle and watched him for a while before dispersing. It must have been sheer happenstance that had brought the peddler into the village, for it was too close to town to be a worthwhile business destination for him. Nonetheless he sat there in front of Feng Yuqing's house until nightfall.

I walked that way several times that afternoon, and each time I could hear him describing wearily, in a hoarse voice, the hardships of his nomadic life; he looked pained even when he smiled. Feng Yuqing sat on the threshold with her chin in her hand and listened raptly to his stories, an opaque expression on her face. Only now and again, as though by accident, did the peddler turn his head to look at her.

That evening, as the village lay bathed in moonlight, the peddler left Southgate. His departure coincided with the disappearance of Feng Yuqing.

PASSINGS

One lunchtime that summer my little brother, Sun Guangming, who had learned how to swagger from my older brother, walked toward the river to catch snails. In my mind's eye I glimpse the scene once more. Dressed in shorts, he picks up his basket from the corner of the room and steps outside. The sunlight beats down on his bare back, so tanned that it seems to be glistening with oil.

A blurry picture appears before my eyes, as though I can see time in motion. Time becomes visible, a translucent gray whir, and everything has its place within that dark expanse. Our lives, after all, are not rooted in the soil as much as they are rooted in time. Fields, streets, rivers, houses—these are our companions, placed like ourselves in time. Time pushes us forward or back, and alters our aspect.

When my little brother left the house that fateful summer day, his leave-taking was entirely routine—he must have left the house a thousand times before in just the same way. But because of the outcome of this particular departure, my memory has altered the particulars of that moment. When I traverse the long passage of memory and see Sun Guangming once more, what he was leaving then was not the house: what he exited so carelessly was time itself. As soon as he lost his connection with time, he became fixed, permanent, whereas we continue to be carried forward by its momentum. What Sun Guangming sees is time bearing away the people and the scenery around him. And what I see is another kind of truth: after the living bury the dead, the latter forever lie stationary, while the former continue their restless motion. In the stillness of the dead, we who still roam can see a message sent by time.

A village boy, eight years old that year, waited outside the door for my little brother, basket in hand. I had noticed subtle changes in Sun Guangming. No longer did he tag along behind my big brother, for he preferred now to rub shoulders with other boys of seven or eight who were beneath Sun Guangping's notice, thereby enjoying the same kind of prestige among the village children that my older brother was himself accustomed to command. As I sat by the pond, I often saw kids who were still unsteady on their legs clustered around Sun Guangming as he bustled about self-importantly.

That day I watched from the rear window as my little brother walked toward the river in my father's huge straw sandals, throwing up clouds of dust as he proceeded along the path, his angular behind and tiny head propelled forward by his oversize footwear. As he reached the house so recently vacated by the Su family, he balanced the basket on the top of his head with the result that his body, normally so unruly, suddenly acquired a stiff and erect posture. Sun Guangming hoped to maintain this balancing act all the way to the river, but the basket would not cooperate, tumbling into the rice field adjoining the path. He simply glanced back briefly before continuing his advance. His eight-year-old companion clambered down into the paddy and retrieved the basket. Sun Guangming walked complacently toward his demise, while the boy behind, who would have many more years to live, carried a basket in each arm and trailed wearily in the footsteps of his ill-fated mentor.

Death did not elect a direct approach but established contact through this intermediary. While Guangming stuck close to the riverbank as he foraged for snails, the other boy, unable to resist temptation, made a rash plunge into a spot where the water was deeper. In a second he lost his footing and tumbled headfirst into the river. As he struggled he gave a desperate cry, a cry that was to be my brother's ruin.

Sun Guangming drowned trying to save him. It would be going too far, of course, to present this as an act of heroic self-sacrifice. My little brother had not reached a level of such lofty virtue as to be willing to exchange his own life for someone else's. It was his authority over the other boy that prompted his action. When death threatened his sidekick, he jumped to the conclusion that saving him would be easy.

The rescued boy was unable to recall what actually happened, and all he could do was stare dumbfounded at his questioners. Several years later, when people raised the topic with him, he seemed unconvinced that the accident had ever occurred, as though the story was all cock-and-bull. If one of the villagers hadn't witnessed the incident, people might well have thought that Sun Guangming drowned all by himself.

When it happened, the villager was crossing the wooden bridge. He saw how Sun Guangming gave the boy a shove and how the boy splashed his way frantically to the bank, leaving Sun Guangming to struggle in the water. When my brother stuck his head out for the last time, he gazed at the blinding sun with his eyes wide open, maintaining that posture for several seconds before he sank beneath the surface. Several days later, after my brother's burial, I sat by the pond at midday and attempted to look straight at the sun, but the glare forced me to avert my eyes. So I discovered a difference between life and death: a clear view of the sun is inaccessible to the living—only people who are about to die can see the sun as it is.

When the horrified onlooker came running over, I did not yet realize what had happened. His cries exploded in the air like shards of glass. Sun Guangping had been peeling a sweet potato with his sickle and was just about to eat it. He flung the tool aside and charged out the door. As he ran he called my father, who dashed from the vegetable plot, and the two of them raced toward the riverside. My mother also appeared on the road, and the scarf that she was clutching in her hand fluttered as she ran. I heard my mother's piercing wails and somehow they gave me the impression that even if my brother was still alive, he would die all over again.

I had always worried about some kind of disaster affecting our family. My eccentricity in operating outside the family circle was already taken for granted by the villagers, and as far as I was concerned it was better this way, better to be forgotten. If something went wrong at home, on the other hand, this would make me stand out and again be the object of people's attention. So as I watched the villagers run toward the river, I felt a huge pressure bearing down on me. It would have been perfectly natural for me to have run to the riverside too, but my fear was that this would give both my family and the villagers the impression that I was actually rejoicing over misfortune. My best option at this point was to keep well out of the way, and only late that evening did I finally return home. At nightfall, when I went down to the riverside, the river gently murmured as it tossed a little flotsam about on the current, and the water's babble was just as soothing as it had always been. The river that had just swallowed up my little brother seemed as placid as ever. I saw village lights in the distance, and the breeze brought a hubbub of voices to my ears: my mother's intermittent wails, accompanied by sympathetic sobs from other women. There in the background was a scene of grief and lamentation, while in the foreground the river, fresh from its lethal exploit, behaved as if nothing had happened. It was at that point that I realized that the river was itself alive: it swallowed up my brother because it needed another life to supplement its own. The wailing women and grieving men off in the distance likewise needed other lives to enhance theirs. They were harvesting vegetables that had been happily growing just a moment ago, or they would slaughter a pig, taking lives just as offhandedly as the river flowing past me.

Sun Kwangtsai and Sun Guangping dove into the river, and between them they brought Sun Guangming up to the surface. They found his body under the wooden bridge, and when he was dragged onto the bank his face was the color of grass. Sun Kwangtsai, though already exhausted, grabbed Sun Guangming by the feet, slung him headfirst over his shoulder, and took off down the path on the run. Sun Guangming's body swayed violently on Father's back, his head knocking rhythmically against my father's shanks. My big brother ran along behind. On that summer day three bodies seemed to merge into one as they raced down the path, enveloped in clouds of dust. Behind them came my mother, still sobbing, still clutching her scarf, and a swarm of villagers.

As my father ran, his head gradually lolled back, he breathed more and more heavily, and his pace slowed. Finally he came to a complete stop and called Sun Guangping. My big brother slung Sun Guangming's body over his back and set off again at a smart pace. Sun Kwangtsai, now falling behind, shouted in short bursts: "Run . . . Don't stop . . . Run!"

My father had seen drops of water falling from my little brother's downturned head and he thought Sun Guangming was perhaps coughing up water, not realizing that my little brother was already gone.

After running some thirty yards or so, Sun Guangping began to stagger but Sun Kwangtsai kept on shouting, "Run! Run!"

In the end Sun Guangping collapsed on the ground and Sun Guangming tumbled down beside him. Sun Kwangtsai picked up his son once more and set off again at a running pace. Though he swayed from side to side, he was able to maintain an astonishing speed.

By the time Mother and the villagers arrived at our doorstep, it was already clear to my father that his son was dead. Utterly spent, he knelt on the ground retching. Sun Guangming's body lay sprawled underneath an elm tree whose leaves shielded it from the fierce summer sun. Sun Guangping was the last to arrive, and when he saw Father retching he fell to his knees not far away and followed suit.

At this moment, only Mother was expressing grief in a normal fashion. As she shrieked and sobbed, her body bobbed up and down. My father and brother, their retching over, remained on their knees, dumbly watching her ululations.

My dead brother was laid on the middle of the table, an old straw mat underneath him and a sheet on top.

As soon as my father and brother recovered, the first thing they did was to go to the well and fetch a bucket of water. Taking turns, they drank the whole bucketful and then each grabbed a basket and headed into town to buy bean curd. As he left, Father, grim faced, told the bystanders to take a message to the family of the boy whose life had been saved: "I'll go and see them when I come back."

That evening the villagers sensed that something bad was likely to happen. When my father and brother returned and invited everyone to the wake, practically all the villagers went. Only the family of the rescued boy failed to make an appearance.

It was after nine o'clock that evening that the boy's father finally arrived. He came alone, without any of his brothers in attendance, prepared, it seemed, to bear all the consequences himself. He entered the room with all due ceremony, knelt in front of the body, and knocked his head on the floor three times. Then he stood up and said, "I can see everyone is here." He acknowledged the presence of the production team leader. "Team Leader is here too. Sun Guangming died rescuing my son, and I am deeply grieved. There is nothing I can do to bring Sun Guangming back to life. All I can do is give you this." He groped in his pocket and thrust a wad of bills in Sun Kwangtsai's direction. "This is a hundred yuan. Tomorrow I will sell everything in the house that is worth anything and give all the proceeds to you. We're neighbors, and you know how little money I've got—I can only give you as much as I have."

Sun Kwangtsai stood up and found a stool for him, saying, "Please sit down."

My father began to speak in impassioned tones, like a town official. "My son is dead, and nothing can bring him back to life. No matter how much money you give me, it cannot compensate for the loss of my son. I don't want your money. My son died saving someone else's life. He is a hero."

Sun Guangping elaborated on this theme with equal fervor. "My brother was a hero, and my whole family is proud of him. We don't want anything you could give us. All we want is for you to spread the word so that everyone knows about my brother's heroic deed."

Father rounded things off by saying, "Go into town tomorrow and have the radio station broadcast the news."

Sun Guangming's burial took place the following day. He was buried between the two cypresses behind our house. During the funeral I kept my distance. Isolation and neglect had practically negated my existence as far as the village was concerned.

Under the hot sun Mother's wailing cries pierced the air for the last time; the grief of my father and brother were not clearly visible to me from where I stood. Sun Guangming was carried out, wrapped in the straw mat, while the villagers stood in clusters along the road from the village to the burial ground. My father and my big brother laid Sun Guangming in his grave and covered him with earth. This was how my little brother officially terminated his stay in the world.

That evening I sat by the pond behind the house, gazing at the hump of my brother's grave in the quiet moonlight. He lay a ways off but somehow I felt he was sitting right next to me. In the end both of us had put a distance between ourselves and our parents, our older brother, and the village folk. We had taken separate paths, but the outcome was much the same. The only difference was that my younger brother's departure seemed much more decisive and carefree.

My alienation had kept me away from the scenes surrounding his death and burial, and I was anticipating that I would now be the object of even more forceful censure at home and in the village. But many days passed and nobody said or did anything different from before, which took me rather aback until I realized with relief that I had been utterly forgotten. I had been assigned to a position where I was recognized and at the same time repudiated by everyone in the village.

On the third day after the funeral the radio station publicized the heroic exploits of Sun Guangming, a young boy who had sacrificed himself to save another. This was the proudest moment for my father. During the three days leading up to it, whenever there was a local news broadcast Sun Kwangtsai would grab a stool and sit down right next to the radio. Now that his long wait had been rewarded, he was so exhilarated that he ambled about like a happy duck. That afternoon, when people were taking a break from work, homes throughout the village echoed with my father's resounding cry: "Did you hear?"

My older brother stood under the elm tree by the front door watching my father, his eyes gleaming. Thus began their splendid but short-lived days of glory. They felt sure that the government would immediately send someone to call on them. This fantasy originated at the district level, but in its more elaborate forms went all the way to Beijing. Their most impressive moment would come on National Day, when as the hero's closest kin they would receive an invitation to join the dignitaries at Tiananmen. My brother proved more astute than my father, for although his mind was filled with equally vacuous illusions, a fairly realistic thought occurred to him as well. He alerted my father to the possibility that my little brother's death might well elevate them to some kind of official status in the county. Though he was still in school, there was nothing to stop him from being groomed for public office. My brother's comments brought some substance to my father's dizzying fantasies. Sun Kwangtsai rubbed his hands with glee, scarcely knowing how to contain his excitement.

So elated were they that father and son shared their highly unreliable notions with the villagers on a variety of occasions. Thus it was that reports of the Sun family's imminent departure soon spread around the village, the most unnerving version of the story being that we might well be moving to Beijing. These speculations in turn were relayed back to my family, and one afternoon I heard my father gloating to my brother, "No smoke without fire! If this is what the villagers are saying, it must mean that the officials will soon be here." My father had broadcast his own fantasies to the villagers and then used the ensuing gossip to reinforce his own illusions.

As he awaited the new title of "Father of a Fallen Hero," Sun Kwangtsai decided his home needed a makeover. Such a disorderly household, he realized, might compromise the government envoys' assessment of our credentials. The makeover began in the clothing department: with money he had borrowed, my father had a new outfit made for each of us. This made me an object of attention, and how to deal with me became a real headache for Sun Kwangtsai. More than once I heard him say to my brother, "It would all be so much simpler without him in the way."

After ignoring me for so long, my family now acknowledged my existence, only to discover that I was a millstone around their necks. Nonetheless, one morning Mother came up to me, a set of new clothes under her arm, and asked me to put them on. Absurdly, we all wore the same color. Accustomed as I was to going around in tattered old clothes, I felt ill at ease the whole day through in this stiff new outfit. After gradually having faded from the consciousness of my neighbors and classmates, I once again was noticed. When Su Yu said, "You're wearing new clothes," I was thrown for a loop, even though he delivered this line so calmly as to make me feel that nothing was wrong.

A couple of days later my father realized that his approach had failed to reap the expected dividends. He now felt that thrift and fortitude were the family virtues that ought to be showcased, and the most threadbare clothes in our possession emerged from hiding. My mother sat bent over under the oil lamp for a whole night, and the following morning we donned clothes with patches all over, like scales, and like four ridiculous fish we ventured out to greet the new dawn. When I saw my brother set off reluctantly for school, for the first time I felt that there were moments when he and I had the same reaction to things.

Sun Guangping lacked Sun Kwangtsai's unswerving confidence in the arrival of good fortune. He was the butt of so many jokes for wearing his ragged clothes to school that he refused to go on wearing them, even if their continued use should qualify him to become emperor. My brother thought up a compelling justification for his abandonment of this costume, telling my father, "To wear the kind of clothes that one could find only in old China is an insult to the new communist society." This remark left Sun Kwangtsai quite rattled, and for the next several days he was constantly explaining to the villagers that we had just one purpose in dressing as we did and that was "recalling the bitter to think of the sweet": "When we think of the miseries of the old society, we are all the more aware of how wonderful life is in the new society."

The government representatives, so eagerly awaited, failed to show even after a month had passed. As a result, public opinion shifted, and this boded ill for my father and brother. Now, in the slack season, the villagers had more than enough time to get to the bottom of things, and they realized that all the reports they had heard ultimately emanated from my family. My father and brother came to be seen as comic figures and were made the target of their banter. Everyone would ask Sun Kwangtsai or Sun Guangping, in tones of exaggerated solicitude, "Did the officials come yet?"

The fantasy shrouding my family began to come apart at the seams. Sun Guangping was the first to retrench. With the ruthless practicality of youth he felt, sooner than my father, that none of it would ever materialize.

In the first few days of his disenchantment, Sun Guangping

seemed glum and subdued, and often he just stayed in bed. Since my father remained firmly ensconced in the fantasy world, relations between the two of them became increasingly distant. Father had developed the habit of sitting by the radio with a foolish expression on his face, saliva dribbling from his half-open mouth. Sun Guangping clearly was tired of seeing him making such an ass of himself and once he said with exasperation, "Stop thinking about it!"

This had the effect of infuriating my father, who jumped up, spraying spit and cursing, "Get the fuck out of here!"

My brother came back with a stinging retort: "Try saying that to the Wang brothers."

My father screamed like a child and threw himself at Sun Guangping. He didn't say he was going to kill him, but rather: "Let's have it out!"

Were it not for Mother, whose tears and diminutive figure were the only obstacles in the way of these two raging males, our home, already so ramshackle, might well have ended up a complete ruin.

As Sun Guangping marched out the door, his face livid, he happened to see me and said, "The old man can't wait to get in his coffin."

My father was in fact quite isolated by this time. He and my brother had lost the sense of fellowship that had prevailed in the wake of my little brother's death, and it was now impossible for the two of them to sit together feverishly picturing their wonderful future. Sun Guangping's withdrawal left Father by himself in the fantasy world, and he alone had to contend with the dreadful thought that the government representatives might never show up. Just as Sun Guangping grew increasingly impatient with

Father, Sun Kwangtsai likewise was on the lookout for opportunities to pick a fight with him. For a long time after that row, they were either looking daggers at each other or treating each other with coldness.

My father paid close attention to the little dirt road at the entrance to the village, on tenterhooks for the arrival of the government envoys in their formal wear. His secret was soon discovered by the village children, and often boys would run up to our front door and shout, "Sun Kwangtsai, the men in suits are here!"

The first few times he was thrown into a tizzy, as jittery as an escaped convict. I watched as he raced pale faced to the village entrance, then came back, utterly deflated. The last time that he was duped was during the onset of winter, when a nine-year-old boy ran over, shouting, "Sun Kwangtsai, lots of men in suits are coming!"

Sun Kwangtsai rushed out, clutching a broom. "I'm going to have the hide off you, you little bastard!"

The boy took off right away, and when he had reached a safe distance he shouted back, "If I'm lying, then my mom's a bitch and my dad's a dog!"

This oath, so disrespectful to his parents, left Sun Kwangtsai a bundle of nerves as he returned to the house and paced to and fro, wringing his hands and talking to himself: "If they really are here, what are we going to do? I've made no preparations."

So anxious was he that he made another dash to the edge of the village, only to see empty fields and sparse, lonely trees. I was sitting by the pond, and watched as Father stood dumbly at the village entryway. He hugged his chest to shield himself from the gusting wind, and after a while he squatted down and began rubbing his knees. As dusk fell at the waning of the year, Sun Kwangtsai crouched there shivering, his eyes fixed on the track that wound its way toward him from the far distance.

Father clung to his dreams until, with the approach of Spring Festival, he had no choice but painfully to abandon them. From every house in the village came the sound of rice flour being pounded into New Year's cake, but our home, rent with divisions as it was, showed not the faintest sign of a holiday approaching. Finally Mother summoned up the courage to ask him, "What are we going to do for New Year?"

My father had been sitting dejectedly by the radio. After deep thought he said, "It looks like the officials are not coming."

I began to notice that Father was sneaking glances at my big brother, and it was clear that he was eager they be reconciled. On the last day of the lunar calendar he finally spoke up. Sun Guangping had just finished dinner and was about to go out when Sun Kwangtsai called him back. "There's something I want to talk to you about."

The two of them went inside and began to confer in whispers. When they emerged, both wore grim expressions. The following morning, the first day of the Chinese New Year, father and son set out to visit the family of the boy whose life had been saved.

Now that he had lost hope of becoming a hero's father Sun Kwangtsai drew inspiration from the prospect of monetary gain. He demanded that the family provide compensation for Sun Guangming's death, to the tune of five hundred yuan. Shocked by this exorbitant figure, the boy's kinfolk told their visitors that there was no way they could pay that kind of money. They reminded them that it was New Year's Day and asked them to please postpone discussion of the matter until another time.

The two guests insisted that the sum be paid immediately;

otherwise they would smash all their furniture. Sun Kwangtsai said, "We're already doing you a favor by not demanding interest."

Although I was nowhere near, the noise of the quarrel carried so far that I knew exactly what was happening. Later I could hear further commotion as my father and brother wrecked their house.

Two days later, three men in police uniform arrived in the village. We were having lunch, and some little boys came running up to the door, shouting, "Sun Kwangtsai, men in uniforms are here!"

When my father rushed out, broom in hand, he saw the three policemen walking in his direction and immediately put two and two together. "Are you here to make an arrest?" he bellowed.

This was Sun Kwangtsai at his most majestic. "Who do you think you are dealing with?" he shouted. Pounding his chest, he cried, "I am the hero's father." Then he pointed at Guangping. "That's the hero's brother." Then at my mother: "That's the hero's ma." He glanced at me, standing off to one side, but offered no comment on my status. "So just who do you plan to arrest?"

The policemen were not the least bit impressed and simply asked coldly, "Which of you is Sun Kwangtsai?"

"I am!" cried Father.

"Come with us," they said.

All along my father had been looking forward to the arrival of men in suits, but it was men in police uniforms who greeted him in the end. After he was led away, the production team leader came to see us, along with people from the house that had been vandalized, and announced to my brother and mother that we had to compensate them for their losses. I went over to the pond behind our house and watched our possessions being carted off.

Items that had been purchased with such difficulty after the fire now became other people's property.

A fortnight later, when my father was released from jail, he was as white and shiny as a baby fresh from its mother's womb. In the past so coarse and slovenly, he now walked toward us as delicate and dainty as a town official. He would declare to all and sundry that he was going off to Beijing to protest the treatment he had suffered, but when people asked him how soon he would be leaving he told them that he needed to wait three months until he could cover his travel expenses. But three months later he had still not set off for the capital. Instead he had clambered into the bed of the widow whose house was diagonally opposite ours.

The image of the widow that lingers in my mind is of a woman in her forties, sturdy, full throated, striding rapidly along the path between the fields in her bare feet. Her most notable trademark was that she always tucked her blouse inside her trousers, with the result that her large bottom was invitingly conspicuous. For the widow to wear her clothes that way made her stand out, because in those days even an innocent young girl would not have dared so openly to flaunt her waist and buttocks. The widow had no waist to speak of, but the sway of her fleshy bottom conveyed a potent allure. Her chest failed to provide a comparable visual interest, replicating instead the flatness of the concrete streets in town. I remember Old Luo saying that the flesh on her chest had all moved to her behind. "That has its advantages," he added. "If you pinch her ass, you're getting to squeeze her tits too."

When I was young, as people knocked off in the afternoon, I would often hear the widow making a generous offer to some young man of the village: "Come over to my place tonight."

The answer was always the same: "Who the hell wants to go to bed with you? That thing of yours has gone all slack."

At the time I didn't understand what was meant, and only as I grew older did I begin to know more about the widow's happy life of sensuality. Then I heard the following joke. A man climbs through the window one night and gropes his way to the foot of her bed. Amid sounds of frantic panting and moans of ecstasy the widow is heard to murmur, "Not now, I have company." As the latecomer slips away, she delivers a piece of sound advice: "Come a bit earlier tomorrow."

This joke actually did make a point—namely that after dark the widow's bed was seldom anything less than fully occupied. Even on the most sweltering summer night the sound of the widow's groans would float over to the drying ground where the villagers were trying to cool off. This supplied Old Luo with more grist for his mill: "Such a hot night, too—she's really a Model Worker."

Tall and fit as she was, the widow liked to sleep with young men, and in my mind's eye I can still picture her shouting lustily to the village women from her end of the field: "Young guys have lots of stamina, they're clean, and no bad breath."

But when the former production team leader, then in his fifties (later to die of tuberculosis), arrived outside her bedroom, she received him with equal alacrity. At times she had to defer to authority, after all. Later on, her looks began to fade and she put out the welcome mat for middle-aged men more generally.

It was at this point in time that my father Sun Kwangtsai, as though motivated by some philanthropic impulse, clambered into the widow's now more lonely wooden bed. It was an afternoon early in the spring when my father entered the widow's house, bearing a large sack of rice on his back. She was sitting on a stool sewing shoes and she watched him out of the corner of her eye as he came in.

A grin on his face, my father dumped the bag of rice at her feet, then made as if to enfold her in a bear hug.

She stuck out an arm to repel his advances. "Hang on a minute there! I'm not so easily bought," she said. She reached out a hand and felt around in his crotch.

"Well?" said my father with a leer.

"It'll do," she responded.

After leading a respectable life for so long, my father found that his inhibitions had been weakened by the shattering of illusions and the tricks that life had played on him. From now on Sun Kwangtsai would often go about sharing his newfound wisdom with the village youths, saying in the smug tones of a man of experience, "While you're still young, you should make the most of it and sleep around as much as you can. Everything else is a scam."

When he clambered so confidently onto the widow's ornate antique bed, this did not go unnoticed by Sun Guangping. Father's brazen visits to the widow's home provoked great chagrin on his part. One day, after my father had wined and dined to his satisfaction and was preparing to set off for the widow's house to digest his meal, my brother spoke up. "You should have had enough by now, surely."

My father didn't let this faze him in the slightest. "You can never have enough of *that*," he said.

So day after day Sun Kwangtsai would march briskly into the widow's house, emerging some time later a good deal worse for wear. Moved by a morbid curiosity, I stealthily observed my mother and tried to gauge her reaction to events. My mother, who said little but whose hands and feet were perpetually in motion, bore the humiliation in silence, as though it was a matter of complete indifference to her. I wondered what went through her mind late at night, when Sun Kwangtsai would leave the widow's side and clamber into her bed. Here my thoughts would linger, and though my speculations were fueled in part by malice, I felt sorry for her at the same time.

What happened later made me realize that Mother's nonchalance was simply a cover for her burning indignation. Her hostility to the widow, to my mind, demonstrated the narrow-mindedness of women. Inwardly I admonished my mother over and over again: it should be Father you resent, not the widow. When he climbs out of the widow's bed and makes his way over to you, you should refuse him. No matter what happened, she would never reject him, but always let him have what he wanted.

Mother's rage finally exploded one day when she was fertilizing the vegetable patch. The widow was walking along the path between the fields, looking very pleased with herself, and her manner instantly made Mother tremble all over with long-suppressed rage. She swung the dung ladle in her hand, and filthy water splattered over the widow's smug figure. The widow's voice rang out like a trumpet. "Are you blind?"

Beside herself with anger, Mother cried out in a voice shaking with emotion: "The town's the place for you! You can lie down on the sports ground there and have the men line up to fuck you."

"Hah!" The widow gave as good as she got. "What makes you think you have the right to say that? Shouldn't you go on home and give yourself a good wash? Your man says that thing of yours stinks to high heaven!"

When these two sharp-tongued women laid into each other

with such crude obscenities, quacking like two noisy ducks, the village—usually rather quiet at lunchtime—was thrown into disarray. After some further exchanges, my mother, forgetting how thin and frail she was, charged fearlessly toward the widow and attempted a head butt.

Just at this moment Sun Kwangtsai happened to arrive back from town, a bottle of spirits swinging behind his back. All he saw at first, off in the distance in the vegetable patch, were two women wrestling with each other, hair all over the place, and this spectacle tickled him no end. After advancing a few steps and recognizing the combatants, my father, flustered, climbed onto a path between the fields and tried to beat a retreat. One of the villagers blocked his escape route, saying, "You'd better go and sort it out."

"No way!" My father shook his head vigorously. "One's my wife and the other's my mistress, and I can't afford to get on the wrong side of either of them."

By this time my mother had already been knocked off her feet and her adversary's large bottom had pinned her to the ground. When I saw this from my distant vantage point I was stricken with heartache. After all the humiliation Mother had suffered she had finally blown her top, only to suffer further ignominy.

Several of the village women, who perhaps found this one-sided contest too embarrassing to watch any longer, ran over and dragged the widow off. She swaggered home victoriously, nose in the air, saying as she went, "What a nerve! That'll teach you to provoke me."

Back at the vegetable patch my mother burst into tears and wailed: "If Sun Guangming were still alive, he wouldn't let you get away with this!"

My older brother, who had at one time brandished the cleaver so gallantly, was nowhere to be seen. Sun Guangping had shut himself in his room. He was perfectly aware of what was happening outside, but refused to get involved in what was to him a pointless squabble. Mother's weeping only intensified the shame that he felt for his family and did not stir him to indignation on her behalf.

In her defeat, the only champion Mother could imagine was my little brother, now no longer with us. It was the one straw that she could clutch at in her moment of despair.

My older brother's unresponsiveness I first interpreted as a reluctance to show his face when our family scandal was gaining such wide publicity. After all he was no longer the Sun Guangping of the private plot fracas. He had sunk into a deep gloom and his dissatisfaction with our home life was more and more evident in everything he did. Although he and I were still at odds with each other, our shared discontent made it possible for us to feel a subtle empathy at times.

Not long afterward—shortly before I left Southgate—I watched as late one evening a figure emerged from the widow's window and sneaked into our house. I recognized the arrival right away as Sun Guangping. Then I realized there was another reason he had been so passive during the altercation between Mother and the widow.

The day that my brother saw me off to the bus station, he carried my bedroll on his back, and Mother accompanied us as far as the entrance to the village. She stood there in the morning breeze and watched us walk away—a little lost, it seemed, as though still unsure what to make of the hand that fate had dealt her. When I looked at my mother for the last time I realized that her hair was streaked with gray. "Good-bye," I said.

She showed no reaction, and her gaze seemed to be directed elsewhere. In that moment a warm feeling surged over me, for this image of my mother tugged at the heartstrings. But as I walked on, her fate seemed to change into a breath of wind and dissipate at once, leaving no trace behind. My feeling at the time was that I was never coming back. But, like Sun Guangming, I forsook her in a less callous fashion than my father and Sun Guangping, who not only deserted her but went to bed with her archrival, the widow. Unaware of that second betrayal, Mother was still devoting herself heart and soul to the family.

After I left, my father went full speed ahead in his campaign to be an utter scoundrel. At the same time he began to perform a deliveryman's duties, transferring a number of items from our house to the sturdy widow's, thereby lubricating their relationship and keeping things ticking over nicely. His show of loyalty was rewarded by a comparable demonstration on her part, for around this time her omnivorous tendencies moderated and she became quite abstemious. Now rounding on fifty, she was no longer inspired by the same lust that once used to sweep all before it.

Having lost the courage that he had at fourteen, Sun Guangping took his cue from Mother and swallowed his rage, watching in silence as my father did as he pleased. When Mother, much distressed, told him about this or that item that had been removed from our home, he would say consolingly, "We can always buy another one."

As a matter of fact, Sun Guangping never harbored much resentment against the widow, and actually felt some gratitude.

Those nights he made his way in and out of her rear window left him on tenterhooks for a long time afterward, and it was his nervousness on this score that explains why he could be no more than a spectator to my father's misdeeds and never once interfered. The widow, as it turned out, told no one about their affair, but this may simply be because she had no idea which young man it was who was sneaking in to see her. She was not in the habit of questioning the men who had designs on her body and could identify her visitors only in cases like that of Sun Kwangtsai, who bedded her in full daylight.

By the time Sun Guangping graduated from high school and returned home to work the land, his self-confidence had sunk to a new low. In the first few days he often just lay in bed, staring into space. His dazed look told all. Given my own mood at the time, I had no trouble figuring out that his most ardent wish was to leave Southgate and start a new life. More than once I saw him stand at the edge of a field, gazing as though in a trance as an enfeebled old man, his face lined with wrinkles, his body caked in mud, trudged across the farmland. I noted the misery in my brother's eyes. This grim sight struck a chord in him, making him wonder about the latter stages of his own life.

Once he had come to terms with reality, Sun Guangping soon became aware of a vague but persistent craving for a woman. It was a need quite distinct from that which the widow had satisfied. What he needed now was a woman who would stand by him and take care of him, a woman who could put an end to those nights of restless agitation and bring him contentment and peace of mind. So he got engaged.

The girl was quite average in looks. She lived in a two-story house in a village nearby; below the rear window of her house flowed the river that had claimed my little brother's life. As her family had been the first in the area to put up a house of more than one story, reports of their wealth had spread far and wide. Sun Guangping did not have his eye on their money, for it was just a year after the house went up, and he knew that they still had loans to pay off and would not be in a position to offer an impressive dowry. Rather, this match was a gift presented by the village matchmaker, a woman who despite her bound feet hopped about as briskly as a flea. That afternoon when the matchmaker came walking over, her face wreathed in smiles, Sun Guangping knew what was about to happen, and knew too that he would agree to whatever was proposed.

My father was excluded from the negotiations preceding the engagement, and it was the widow, not Mother, who informed him of the outcome. On hearing the news, he realized at once that it was his responsibility to conduct an inspection. "What does she look like, this girl who's going to be sleeping with my son?" he asked.

Sun Kwangtsai set off at a brisk pace that morning, beaming happily as he walked, leaning forward with his hands clasped behind his back. He could see the fiancée's imposing home from quite some distance away, and the first thing he said to her father was, "He's a lucky bastard, that Sun Guangping."

My father sat down in the girl's house as relaxed and at ease as if he was sitting on the widow's bed. Coarse language flowed from his lips as he conversed with her father. Her brother slipped out, bottle in hand, and brought it back full to the brim with spirits. Her mother set to work in the kitchen, and the noise of her preparations made my father's juices flow. He had already forgotten that the purpose of his visit was to inspect my future sister-in-law. Her father, however, had not.

He raised his head and called a name that Sun Kwangtsai forgot as soon as he heard it. The daughter, my might-have-been sister-in-law, called back from the second floor, but she was clearly reluctant to show herself. Her big brother ran up the flight of stairs and returned a few moments later with a smile on his face. He told Sun Kwangtsai, "She won't come down."

My father showed himself to be a broad-minded man, saying airily, "That's all right, no big deal. If she won't come down, I'll go up."

He poked his head into the kitchen for a moment and then went up to view the young lady. I think I can say with certainty that he tore himself away from the kitchen only with great reluctance. Not long after he had gone upstairs, the family down below heard a bloodcurdling shriek. Father and son remained glued to their seats in astonishment while the lady of the house rushed out of the kitchen in alarm. As they puzzled over what could possibly have precipitated that scream, Sun Kwangtsai came down the stairs with a big grin on his face, muttering, "Not bad. Not bad at all."

From upstairs could be heard sobs so muffled it was as though they had been buried under a deep layer of cotton.

My father sat down unconcernedly by the table and as the girl's brother dashed upstairs Sun Kwangtsai said to her father, "Your daughter is really well put together."

His host nodded uneasily, at the same time scanning Sun Kwangtsai's face with suspicion. "Sun Guangping is so damn lucky!" my father went on.

No sooner did he say that than the girl's brother careened down the stairs and with one enormous blow knocked Sun Kwangtsai to the ground, along with the chair he was sitting on.

That afternoon Sun Kwangtsai returned to the village with his face all black and blue, and the first thing he said to Sun Guangping was, "I canceled that match for you." My father was outraged. "Those people are so unreasonable!" he cried. "I was just trying to look out for my son and make sure the girl was in good health. Can you believe how bad they beat me up?"

The reports that came from the neighboring village offered a different interpretation of the incident, according to which my father's first gift to his future daughter-in-law had been a breast massage.

My mother spent the whole day after the visit sitting by the kitchen stove, wiping away tears with the hem of her apron. Sun Guangping did not, as the locals were expecting, come to blows with Sun Kwangtsai, and his reaction was simply not to speak to anybody in the village for several days in a row.

In the two years that followed, my brother was never again to see the matchmaker approach him, her face wreathed in smiles. During that period he would think of his father only in bed at night, gnashing his teeth. Sometimes, as dawn approached, his thoughts would turn to his brother, far away in Beijing. I would often receive letters from him in those days, but they said nothing of substance and their vacuous contents made me realize how empty he felt.

When he turned twenty-four Sun Guangping married a Southgate girl. Yinghua's only family was her father, confined to bed after a stroke. The pond played a role in their union. Late one damp afternoon Sun Guangping looked out through the rear window and saw Yinghua washing clothes there. She was crouched down in her patched clothes, so overwhelmed by the hardships of life that she had constantly to wipe her tears away. The sight of her shivering in the chilly winter breeze triggered the same kind of heartache that his own plight inspired in him. The couple reached an understanding without the help of the matchmaker, who made a point of ignoring them.

Sun Guangping's marriage took place a year or so after he glimpsed Yinghua at the pond. The wedding arrangements were so skimpy that the older villagers were reminded of how a landlord's hired hands used to get married in the old days. Though meager, the wedding was not without its comic aspects, since the bride waddled about with a big belly. Before sunup the next morning Sun Guangping borrowed a flatbed cart and took Yinghua to the obstetric ward in the town hospital. For newlyweds, morning in the bridal chamber is normally a time of blissful cuddles, but Sun Guangping and Yinghua had to brave the piercing cold and rush into town to tap on the doors and windows of the hospital, still locked tight at that hour of the day. Two o'clock that afternoon, protesting furiously, a boy later to be named Sun Xiaoming came into the world.

Sun Guangping had entangled himself in a web of his own design. After his marriage he was duty bound to provide for his bedridden father-in-law. At this point in time, Sun Kwangtsai had not yet completed his career as a deliveryman, but to his family's relief he had restrained some of his impulses and was no longer in the habit of ostentatiously transferring property from our house to the widow's home. He did, however, reveal a new talent, an aptitude for pilfering things on the sly. Sun Guangping's financial and domestic difficulties continued for some years before his father-in-law—embarrassed, perhaps, at being such a burden—closed his eyes one night and never opened them again. For Sun Guangping, the greatest challenge was not his father-in-law's infirmity or his father's thievery but the period following Xiaoming's birth. During that time he was seldom seen just walking around the village, for he was in a blur of constant motion, scurrying from the fields to Yinghua's house, then to his own home, as nervous as a rabbit.

His father-in-law's death came as a relief to Sun Guangping, but a peaceful life remained far out of reach. Not long afterward Sun Kwangtsai was up to his old tricks again, reducing Yinghua to tears for a full three days.

This was in the summer of the year that Xiaoming turned three. As my father sat on the threshold and watched Yinghua fetch water from the well, he saw how the flowers imprinted on her shorts tightened and then loosened over her fleshy buttocks, and how her thighs gleamed in the sunlight. Worn out by the widow and by his advancing years, my father now had as little vitality as the dregs of an herbal medicine, but Yinghua's robust figure triggered in him a recollection of his exuberant energy of yore. This memory was not summoned up through mental effort as much as by a quirk of his withered body, which suddenly saw a revival of his once so irrepressible lust. As Yinghua walked over, bucket in hand, my father flushed and gave a loud cough. Although villagers were walking by not far away, the incorrigible lecher put his hands on the big red flowers on Yinghua's shorts and on the flesh underneath. My nephew heard his mother give a shocked screech.

Sun Guangping had gone to town that day, and when he came home he found his mother hunched up on the doorsill, tears streaming down her face, muttering to herself, "Such a sin!" The next thing he saw was Yinghua perched on the edge of the bed, sobbing, her hair in disarray.

Sun Guangping did not need to be told what had happened. As the blood drained from his face, he marched into the kitchen and emerged with an ax glinting in his hand. He walked over to where Yinghua was weeping and said to her, "You're going to have to look after Ma and the boy."

When the meaning of this sank in, Yinghua burst out into wails of anguish. She clutched at his jacket and said, "No, don't! Don't do that!"

My mother threw herself on her knees in the doorway, stretching out both arms in an effort to block his way. Eyes wet with tears, she said gravely to Sun Guangping in a hoarse, wavering voice: "If you kill him, it's you who'll suffer."

Her expression brought tears to his eyes. "Get up!" he shouted. "If I don't kill him, how can I ever show my face in the village again?"

My mother remained stubbornly on her knees and tried a different tack: "Think of your little boy. It's not worth it, going that far."

He gave a bitter smile and said to her, "I can't think of any other way out of this."

The outrage suffered by Yinghua made Sun Guangping feel that he had to have it out with Sun Kwangtsai once and for all. For years now he had been putting up with the losses of face that his father had inflicted upon him, but Sun Kwangtsai's latest affront had forced them, he knew, into a collision course. In his rage he saw with total clarity that if he failed to take a stand it would be impossible to hold his head up among the neighbors.

Everyone in the village was milling around outside that afternoon. In the dazzling sunlight and the glowing eyes of the spectators, Sun Guangping recovered the bravado he had exhibited as a fourteen-year-old. Ax in hand, he strode toward my father.

Sun Kwangtsai was standing under a tree in front of the widow's house, and he watched, perplexed, as Sun Guangping approached. My brother heard him say to the widow, "Can this joker really be out to kill me?"

Then he shouted at Sun Guangping, "Son, I'm your dad!"

Sun Guangping maintained a grim silence and a look of determination. As he came ever closer, a note of alarm crept into Sun Kwangtsai's voice. "You've got only one dad. If you kill him, that's it."

By this time Sun Guangping was almost upon him, and Sun Kwangtsai could only mutter in panic, "He really does want to kill me!" So saying, he took to his heels, crying out to nobody in particular, "Help!"

A hush fell as my father, now in his sixties, set off on a run for his life. He grew increasingly exhausted as he ran along the narrow road into town, with Sun Guangping, brandishing the ax, hot on his tail. Sun Kwangtsai gave incessant cries for help, but his voice sounded so different from normal that Old Luo, standing at the entrance to the village, asked other onlookers, "Is that Sun Kwangtsai yelling?"

It was quite an achievement for my father to maintain such a blistering pace at his age. But he slipped and fell as he was crossing the bridge, and ended up sitting down there and bursting into tears, crying as lustily as a newborn babe. This was the shocking sight that greeted Sun Guangping when he reached the bridge. Tears had made my father's face as gaudy as a butterfly, and snot dribbled down his lips. He cut such a sorry figure that my brother suddenly felt that chopping his head off made no sense at all. Usually so decisive, for once he was rendered irresolute. But with the throng of villagers around him he knew he had little choice but to put the ax to use. I am not sure what led him to pick my father's left ear, but there in the afternoon glare he grabbed hold of this appendage and lopped it off as cleanly as one might snip through a bolt of cloth. My father's blood spilled out and within a few seconds it encircled his neck like a crimson kerchief. Sun Kwangtsai was so immersed in his own loud weeping that he did not realize the nature of his injury. Only when he grew alarmed by how many tears he seemed to be shedding and stretched out a hand to wipe his face did he see his own blood. He gave a cry of horror and fainted.

As my brother walked home that afternoon, his body was rent with shivers. On this sultry summer day he clutched his arms as tightly as if he was exposed to subzero temperatures. When he threaded his way through the crowd of villagers, they could clearly hear his teeth chatter. My mother and Yinghua blanched as they watched him approach, and both women saw black spots in front of their eyes, as though a horde of locusts was descending. Sun Guangping smiled faintly and went inside. He rummaged through the storage cabinets, looking for his padded jacket. By the time Mother and Yinghua were back in the house, he had already put it on. He was sitting on the bed, his face streaming with perspiration, while the rest of his body continued to shake uncontrollably.

A fortnight later, Sun Kwangtsai, his head swathed in bandages, had a scribe in town write a letter and send it to me in Beijing. This missive, along with much flattery and many endearments, emphasized his role in rearing me and closed with an injunction to seek redress on his behalf from the top officials in Zhongnanhai. The absurdity of this idea left a deep impression on me.

In fact, when my father wrote to me, Sun Guangping had already been arrested. As he was taken away, my mother tugged at Yinghua and blocked the policemen's path. She burst into tears and cried out to them, "Take us instead! Two of us for one of him—isn't that a better deal?"

Sun Guangping served two years, and by the time he came home Mother was already ailing. On the day of his release, Mother stood at the entrance to the village with five-year-old Sun Xiaoming. When she saw Sun Guangping and Yinghua walking toward her, all of a sudden she spat blood and fell to the ground.

After this, Mother's condition deteriorated and she tended to wobble as she walked. Sun Guangping wanted to take her to the hospital for treatment but she flatly refused, saying, "I am going to die anyway. The money's not worth spending."

When Sun Guangping insisted on carrying her into town piggyback, Mother wept tears of rage and pounded his back with her fists, saying, "I'll hate you till the day I die!"

But Mother calmed down after they had crossed the wooden bridge, and as she clung to Sun Guangping's shoulders a girlish, bashful look began to appear on her face.

Mother died shortly before the Spring Festival that year. One winter evening she began to cough blood, and once it started, it wouldn't stop. When she first felt her mouth fill with blood, she did not spit it out, unwilling to soil the floor and give Sun Guangping more work. Though normally unable to rise from her bed unassisted, Mother still managed to get up and grope around in the darkness for a basin to set next to her bed.

The following morning, when Sun Guangping came into
room, he noticed that Mother's head was drooping over the
the bed and that dark red blood had accumulated in

leaving the sheets untouched. When he wrote to me later, he said the air outside was thick with driving snow. Her breath reduced to the merest wisp, Mother spent the last day of her life in bitter cold. Yinghua held vigil at her bedside the whole time, and Mother's expression as death grew near seemed peaceful and serene. But in the evening, this woman, hitherto so taciturn, began to rave with startling vigor. Sun Kwangtsai was the target of all her expostulations. Although she had not offered the slightest protest when he was shifting our household property into the widow's possession, her deathbed rants revealed that she had taken these losses very much to heart. In her final moments she cried over and over again, "Don't take the chamber pot away, I need it!" Or, "Give me that basin back!" She listed every one of the items that he had filched.

Mother's funeral was somewhat more lavish than my little brother's had been. She was buried in a coffin. Throughout the whole proceedings my father was assigned the same position that I had once occupied, banishment outside the family circle. Just as I had earlier been the object of reproach, Sun Kwangtsai became the butt of criticism because of his lack of involvement in the funeral, even though his relationship with the widow was now tacitly accepted. When he saw the coffin being carried out of the village he asked a villager in confusion, "The old woman is dead?"

They noticed he was drinking spirits nonchalantly in the widow's house all afternoon. But later, in the middle of the night, the locals heard a piteous wailing coming from outside the village. My brother recognized the sound as that of my father grieving by Mother's grave. After the widow fell asleep he had surreptitiously made his way to the burial site, and grief made him forget how loudly he was wailing. Not long afterward my brother heard the widow's voice. Her scolding was followed by a clear order: "Get back here!"

Father, sobbing, tramped back to the widow's house, his steps as hesitant as those of a lost child. Now that her once unquenchable libido had dissipated, the widow recognized Sun Kwangtsai as her official sleeping partner.

In the last year of his life Sun Kwangtsai exhibited a limitless devotion to liquor. Every afternoon, rain or shine, he would go into town to buy a bottle and by the time he got home it would already be completely drained. I can imagine what a romantic figure my father must have cut as he walked along the lane, swigging spirits. Whether making his way through clouds of dust or squelching his way through mud puddles, encouraged by the alcohol, my father, stooped and bent though he was, was as exhilarated as a boy who sees his sweetheart's hair waving in the breeze.

It was his limitless devotion to liquor that did my father in. On that particular day he changed his normal routine and instead chose to do his drinking in a small tavern in town. Walking back home in the moonlight, completely sozzled, he stumbled into the cesspit at the entrance to the village. As he fell, he did not give a shout of alarm but only muttered, "Don't push."

When he was discovered the next morning, he was lying facedown in the muck, covered with little white maggots. He could not have chosen a filthier place in which to lay himself to rest, but he was quite unaware of that in his final moments and had every reason to wear a contented expression, given that he died in such a painless fashion.

After Sun Kwangtsai had fallen into the cesspit that night,

Old Luo, another famous drunkard, passed that way in a besotted haze. When, by the light of the moon, his eyes rested blearily on Sun Kwangtsai, he failed to realize that it was a dead man floating on the manure soup. He squatted down beside the cesspit for a few moments and asked himself, "Whose pig is this?"

He stood up and shouted, "Whose pig has fallen into . . . ?"

Old Luo clapped his hand over his mouth and said to himself conspiratorially, "No shouting. I'll fish it out and keep it for myself."

Still completely in alcohol's grip, Old Luo nipped home as effortlessly as if treading on air, fetched a rope and a bamboo laundry pole, and just as briskly returned. First he used the pole to steer the corpse to the opposite side of the pit; then he made his way over there, got down on his knees, and tied the rope around Sun Kwangtsai's neck. He said to himself, "Such a skinny pig! Whose can it be? Its neck's no thicker than a man's."

He stood up, coiled the rope over his shoulder, and began to pull. "It seems on the lean side when you poke it," he said with a chuckle. "But it's plump enough when you have to drag the thing."

It was only after Old Luo had hauled the body up on the bank and bent down to untie the rope that he realized what he had retrieved. Sun Kwangtsai lay there grinning at him. Old Luo was startled at first, but then he was so angry that he punched him on the face several times and let loose a string of curses. "Sun Kwangtsai! Sun Kwangtsai, you old dog! Even when you die, you try to fool me into thinking you're a pig."

Then with one swing of his leg Old Luo kicked Sun Kwangtsai back into the cesspit. The impact of the body's entry spattered him with filth. As Old Luo mopped his face he said, "Fuck! No end to your tricks."

BIRTH

In the autumn of 1958, on the way to Southgate, a young Sun Kwangtsai ran into Zheng Yuda, future director of the commerce bureau. Late in life, Zheng Yuda described the scene to his son Zheng Liang. He was in the throes of lung cancer then and his lungs wheezed as he told the story, but even so Zheng Yuda was moved to throaty laughter by the memory of what had happened.

As a member of a rural supervisory team, Zheng Yuda was going to Southgate to check how things were being done. The young Zheng Yuda was dressed in a gray Mao suit, with a pair of Liberation gym shoes on his feet; his hair, parted in the middle, rippled in the breeze that blew over the open fields. My father was wearing a traditional-style jacket; his canvas shoes were Mother's handiwork, made by the light of their oil lamp.

A couple of weeks earlier Sun Kwangtsai had transported a boatload of vegetables to a neighboring county for sale. Then, in a flash of inspiration, he decided that a bus ride was an experience he deserved to enjoy, so he returned that way on his own, leaving two other villagers to scull the empty boat back.

Approaching Southgate, ruddy-faced Sun Kwangtsai caught sight of Zheng Yuda in his formal wear. The town official struck up a conversation with the farmer.

In the fields random and chaotic signs of prosperity were emerging. Small furnaces constructed out of dark bricks dotted the rice paddies. Zheng Yuda asked, "Are the People's Communes a good thing?"

"You bet," said Sun Kwangtsai. "Meals are free."

Zheng Yuda's eyes narrowed. "What a thing to say!"

Then Sun Kwangtsai asked Zheng Yuda, "Do you have a wife?"

"Of course."

"Slept with her last night, did you?"

Zheng Yuda was unaccustomed to fielding this kind of inquiry. His face stiffened and he said sternly, "Don't talk nonsense."

Sun Kwangtsai continued blithely, "It's been two weeks since I last slept with my wife." Pointing at his crotch, he said, "This fellow here is mad as hell!"

Zheng Yuda turned his head away and paid him no more mind.

They parted company at the entrance to the village. Zheng Yuda carried on toward the houses in the center while my father headed for the vegetable plots around the edge, picking up speed as he went. My mother, along with a few other women, was hacking at weeds with a hoe. Her young face glowed with health, like a red apple, and her blue kerchief was spotless. The breeze carried her silvery laugh to Sun Kwangtsai's ears, stoking the fire in his loins. He spotted her now, her back swinging rhythmically as she hoed, and hailed her with an eager shout. "Hey!"

My mother turned around and saw her randy husband standing on the path. She returned his greeting. "Hi!"

"Come over here."

Blushing, Mother removed her scarf. As she began to walk in his direction, she patted dust off her jacket. Her unhurried movements infuriated my father, who yelled, "I am dying for it! Run, can't you?"

Amid the laughter of the other women, Mother ran toward him, her body swaying.

My father's patience could not possibly last as far as their house, and as soon as they reached Old Luo's place at the entrance to the village, its door ajar, he called inside, "Anyone home?"

Having established that the house was unoccupied, he slipped in. Mother, however, stayed outside. My father found this maddening, "Come on in!" he cried.

Mother hesitated, "This is somebody else's house."

"Come in, will you?"

Once she had entered, my father quickly closed the door and moved a bench from a corner into the center of the room. "Get your pants off," he said.

My mother bowed her head, lifted the hem of her jacket, and began to unfasten her belt. But after some time she said apologetically, "There's a knot I can't untie."

My father stamped his foot. "You're driving me crazy."

She bent her head again and tried once more to loosen the knot, her face filled with contrition.

"Okay, okay, let me do it."

My father squatted down and tugged at the belt with all his might. He succeeded in ripping off the belt, but in doing so pulled a muscle in his neck. Though in a paroxysm of lust, he still found time to clutch his neck and yelp with pain. My mother hurriedly started to massage the sprain, but he yelled in rage, "Lie down, damn it."

She lay down meekly, raising one leg and letting it dangle in the autumn air as her eyes continued to rest uneasily on his neck.

Still rubbing the injured spot, he clambered on top of her, intent on performing his lubricious mission right there on the bench. Some of Old Luo's hens clucked enthusiastically, as though eager to be part of the action and resenting Sun Kwangtsai's monopoly of the goodies. They congregated around his feet and pecked at his toes. At this moment, when he would normally be focusing all his attention on one thing, my father was forced to expend effort on waving his feet to drive away these pesky fowl. Once knocked aside, the chickens rapidly regrouped and continued to peck at his toes. He vainly shook his feet and, as the critical moment approached, he cried in exasperation, "To hell with them!"

A series of ecstatic moans ensued, followed by uncontrollable giggles.

After it was all over, my father left Old Luo's house and went in search of Zheng Yuda. Mother went home, clutching the top of her pants, in need of a new belt.

When my father found Zheng Yuda, he was sitting in the party committee office listening to reports. My father beckoned him mysteriously. When Zheng Yuda came out, my father asked him, "Quick, wasn't it?"

Zheng Yuda did not understand. "What was quick?"

My father said, "I already had it off with her."

Communist Party cadre Zheng Yuda immediately assumed a severe expression and reprimanded him in a low voice. "Get out of here!"

It was only when he retold this story late in life that Zheng Yuda realized its comic aspects, and he expressed a tolerant, understanding attitude to my father's behavior that day. "What can you do?" he said to Zheng Liang, "That's peasants for you."

My parents' coupling on the bench that day marked the starting point of my life.

I came into the world during the busy season, when the rice was being harvested. My delivery happened to coincide with a time when hunger had driven my father, toiling away in the rice paddies, into a desperate fury. He later forgot about his stomach pangs, but he could clearly recall how angry he had been. My earliest knowledge of the circumstances of my birth came courtesy of my father's drink-soaked mouth. One evening when I was six years old he recounted the details without the slightest embarrassment. Pointing at a chicken that was strutting about nearby, he said, "Your ma squeezed you out as easily as that hen lays an egg."

Because my mother was nine months pregnant by then, she did not go out to harvest the rice, even though it was the busy period when everybody was up at the crack of dawn. As she was to put it later, "It wasn't that I didn't have the energy, it was just that I couldn't bend down."

But Mother did take on the responsibility of taking my father's lunch out to him. Under the dazzling sunlight Mother would waddle along, a basket under her arm, blue-checked scarf around her head, arriving in the fields at noon. To me, the thought of my mother trudging slowly toward my father with a smile on her face is very touching.

The lunchtime when I was born, Sun Kwangtsai wearily raised himself up dozens of times to scan the path, but my full-breasted, big-bellied mother just never appeared. Seeing the other villagers finish their lunch and pick up their work where they had left off, Sun Kwangtsai, tormented by hunger, stood at the edge of the field, furiously spewing obscenities.

Mother did not make her appearance until after two that afternoon. The blue-checked scarf was still wound around her head, but her complexion was pale and her body wobbled under the basket's weight.

My father, by now practically fainting, may have been vaguely aware that there was something different about my mother as she edged toward him, but he was in no mood to think about that, and as she came closer he bellowed at her, "You like to see me starve, don't you?"

"It's not that," said Mother weakly. "I had the baby."

It was only then that my father noticed that her rotund belly had shriveled.

Mother could bend at the waist now, and although this cost her fragile body a high price in pain she still managed to take the food out of the basket with a smile, at the same time saying to him softly, "The scissors were a long way away and it wasn't easy to pick them up. After the baby was born it needed a wash. I was going to bring you lunch ages ago, but I started getting cramps even before I left the house. I knew I was about to deliver and tried to fetch the scissors, but I was in such pain I couldn't get over there and—"

My father had heard enough of this tiresome recital and cut her off in midstream. "Boy or girl?"

"It's a boy," Mother said.

Chapter 2

FRIENDSHIP

After the Su family moved away from Southgate, I saw little of Su Yu and Su Hang until I entered high school, when we resumed contact once again. I found to my surprise that the two brothers, bosom friends during their Southgate days, were as remote from each other at school as I was from Sun Guangping, and not at all alike.

Though on the frail side, Su Yu behaved very much like an adult. He had outgrown his blue cotton clothes and once, when he was not wearing socks, his trouser legs were so short that I could clearly see his ankles when he moved. Like the other boys, Su Yu did not bother taking a satchel to school but simply tucked his textbooks under his arm. Where he differed from his classmates was that he never swaggered along in the middle of the road but instead walked circumspectly off to one side, his head lowered.

At the beginning it was not Su Yu who caught my attention but rather Su Hang, with his glossy well-groomed hair. When he whistled at female classmates, his hands in his trouser pockets, I was captivated by his debonair style. He would sometimes hold up a yellowing volume and softly read to us from it. "Do you want a girl? The price is very reasonable." To us other schoolboys, so poorly informed about sex, he embodied a style we associated more with unemployed youths.

At that point I had a particular dread of being alone and hated having to stand around on my own in some corner during the break between classes. When I saw Su Hang laughing loudly amid a bunch of classmates in the middle of the playground, I moved in his direction, but with some diffidence, country boy that I was. I hoped desperately that Su Hang would greet me with a holler: "Hey, I know you!"

When I went up to him he made no effort to recall our association in Southgate, but neither did he tell me to go away, so with a glow of pleasure I understood this as his accepting me. And he did accept me to the extent that he let me hang around with him and his friends as they joked and shouted in the playground. In the evenings, on the darkened streets, he would share his cigarette with us. We roamed restlessly through the town, and when a girl appeared we would join him in a chorus of groans, which although uttered seemingly in pain actually gave us a lot of pleasure. "Hey sister, why are you ignoring me?" we would say.

As I nervously delivered this greeting, overwhelmed by a sense of impending doom, I experienced at the same time an excitement I had never known before.

What we learned from Su Hang was that to go out after dinner was more fun than staying home, no matter how severely we might be punished at the end of the evening. He also educated us about the kind of girl that we should admire, emphasizing that we could not judge girls in terms of their academic achievements, but should base our selection of love interests on the size of their breasts and buttocks.

Although these were his criteria for evaluating the local talent, he himself was smitten with the skinniest girl in the class. She had a round face and two perky little pigtails, but apart from her dark eyes we could not for the life of us see what was so attractive about her. Su Hang's infatuation left us bemused, and one of us was moved to question his choice: "But what about her chest? There's nothing there! And she's got no tush to speak of, either."

Su Hang responded in the voice of experience. "You need to think ahead. Within the next year her boobs and her butt will fill out nicely, and then she'll be the prettiest girl in the whole school."

Su Hang's approach to courtship was simple and direct. He wrote a note full of compliments and endearments and slipped it inside the girl's English textbook. In English class that morning, she suddenly gave a yelp that made us quake and then burst into a long wail that hung in the air, like a note played on the organ. Su Hang, whom I thought bold and dauntless, turned white as a corpse.

But after leaving the classroom Su Hang quickly recovered his customary cool. When we got out of school that morning, he walked over to the girl, whistling nonchalantly, and accompanied her out the gate, making faces at us as he did this. The poor girl was again reduced to tears. At this point one of her friends, a well-built girl, came to her defense. She thrust her way in between them, quietly but indignantly cursing him. "You lowlife!"

Su Hang spun around and blocked her way, not so much angry as excited that she had provided an opportunity to show his mettle. We heard him cry menacingly, "Say that again!"

She was not intimidated, and said, "Lowlife, that's what you are!"

We would never have guessed that Su Hang would raise his

fist and hit her right between her ample breasts. She wailed in anguish, then ran off crying, her face in her hands.

When we joined Su Hang, he was gleefully rubbing the index and middle fingers of his right hand. He told us that when he punched the girl those two fingers felt something silky soft, a marvelous sensation denied the other three digits, which was why he was not bothering to rub them. "An unexpected bonus, really an unexpected bonus," he sighed.

I owed to Su Hang's teachings my earliest conceptions of female anatomy. One evening in early spring a bunch of us were walking with him through the streets. He told us that his parents had a large hardbound volume in which there was a color picture of a woman's pudenda.

"They have three holes," he said to us.

His tone evoked an air of mystery that was heightened by the occasional pounding of footsteps farther down the street, and I found myself short of breath. I was both frightened and attracted by the unfamiliar knowledge that he was imparting.

A few days later, when Su Hang brought the hardback to school, I was confronted with a difficult choice. Naturally I was just as excited as the other boys, but when classes had finished and Su Hang got ready to open the book I fell into a complete funk. With the sunlight blazing down, I lacked the courage to engage in an activity that seemed to me so ill-advised. So when Su Hang said that someone had to keep watch by the doorway, I gratefully undertook this commission. In my post outside the classroom door I was assailed by desire, and the gasps from inside the room—some long, some short—made my pulse race.

Having missed this opportunity, I found it difficult to get a second chance. Although Su Hang was later to bring the book to school quite regularly, it never occurred to him that he should let me have a look. I knew that I had no standing in his eyes, being just one classmate out of the many in his entourage and the most insignificant of them to boot. And besides, I was never able to overcome my shame and did not take the initiative to make any such request. It would be another six months before the color photo was revealed to me by Su Yu.

Su Hang was sometimes so daring as to take one's breath away. As time went on, he felt it was no fun just to show the photo to other boys. One day he actually went over to a female classmate, book in hand, and the next thing we saw was her fleeing in panic across the playground and bursting into tears by the perimeter wall. Su Hang returned to us, laughing heartily. We warned him anxiously that she might report him, but he was not in the least perturbed, reassuring us, "No chance of that. How could she possibly say anything? Can you see her saying, 'Su Hang showed me a picture of . . .'? She wouldn't be able to go on. There's nothing to worry about. Relax."

Afterward, the fact that there were no repercussions whatsoever proved Su Hang's point. His success in this adventure triggered even more bold exploits during the subsequent summer vacation. At lunchtime one day in the middle of the agricultural busy season, Su Hang walked idly along in the sunlight accompanied by a classmate named Lin Wen. I can imagine them expressing their preference for one girl or another in the crudest language possible. Lin Wen had attained his status as Su Hang's best friend during this period by using a mirror to peep at girls in the toilets. This brazen act had not enabled him to see anything of significance, but this is not to say he learned nothing from it. When Su Hang was contemplating testing the mirror's efficacy,

Lin Wen, the voice of experience, counseled against it, saying, "With a mirror in the toilet, a girl can see a boy clearly enough, but there's no way that a boy can get a clear view of a girl."

Immersed in topics such as this, they walked the countryside, and when they entered a village the only sound they heard was a whir of cicadas, for at this time of day all able-bodied people were in the fields harvesting rice. As they strolled under the trees, the topic at hand inflamed them more than the summer heat itself, and the sun-baked scene before them seemed reminiscent of a disaster zone, brought to ruin by desire run amok. When this restless pair saw smoke rising from the chimney of a cottage, Su Hang crept over and took a peep through its window, then signaled to Lin Wen to do the same. Lin Wen's pleasurable anticipation did not last long, because when he sidled up to the window the scene that met his gaze left him disappointed: all he saw was an old woman in her seventies, tending a fire beneath the stove. But he noticed that Su Hang's breath had become labored and heard Su Hang ask him tensely, "Do you want to see the real thing?"

Lin Wen now understood what Su Hang had in mind. Pointing at the old woman, he asked in astonishment, "You want to see hers?"

Su Hang smiled with some embarrassment. "Let's do it together," he proposed eagerly.

Despite the enterprise he had shown by testing the utility of mirrors in toilets, Lin Wen was not immediately persuaded. "Such an old woman?" he queried.

Blushing, Su Hang quietly exclaimed, "I know, but it's the real thing!"

Lin Wen could not bring himself to participate directly in

the proposed inspection, but Su Hang's excitement stirred a tremor within him, and he said, "You go ahead. I'll keep watch for you."

When Su Hang looked back and shot him an awkward smile just before climbing inside, Lin Wen knew that his was the more interesting vantage point.

Lin Wen did not stand right next to the window, for he was perfectly able to imagine how Su Hang would throw himself on the old woman. He concentrated instead on his mission as sentinel, taking a few steps back to assure a fuller view of any villager's approach.

He heard the sound of a body hitting the ground, followed by some shocked groans. At first the old lady must not have known what was happening. Once she did realize, Lin Wen heard a hoarse voice saying heatedly, "You bastard, I am old enough to be your grannie!"

This comment made Lin Wen chuckle. He knew that Su Hang was already halfway there. Then he heard her cry, almost penitently, "What a disgrace!"

She was not strong enough to withstand Su Hang's assault, and in her frail condition righteous anger could give way only to self-pity. Just at this moment—too soon for Su Hang—Lin Wen saw a man heading in their direction. Naked to the waist, sickle in hand, this apparition scared the daylights out of Lin Wen, and he rushed to the window only to see Su Hang kneeling on the floor, desperately tugging at the old woman's trousers, while she rubbed her shoulder (sprained, perhaps) and muttered something incomprehensible. At Lin Wen's warning, Su Hang rushed over and dived out the window with the furious energy of a rabid dog. Then they both raced madly toward the river. Su Hang kept throwing glances behind him, each time seeing a man with a sickle bearing down upon him. As Lin Wen fled for his life, time and again he heard Su Hang's despairing cry, "Can't! Not going to make it!"

As they dashed along the road toward town, through the midday heat, they threw up clouds of dust and their lungs protested furiously. Nauseated and caked in mud, they finally returned to safe territory.

Of my high school teachers, the music instructor, with his cultivated manners, made the deepest impression on me. He was the only teacher who spoke to the class in standard Chinese, and when he sat down in front of the organ to teach us a song I was captivated by his voice and demeanor. For a long time I would gaze at him in delight, and he became my ideal adult. What is more, he was the least snobbish of teachers, favoring all his pupils with the same smile. I still remember the first time he taught us. A songbook under his arm, dressed in a white shirt and dark blue trousers, he came into the classroom and told us solemnly, in the precise tone of a radio announcer: "Music begins where language disappears."

My classmates, accustomed to hearing uncouth provincial teachers talking in local dialect, found this hilarious.

In the spring of my third year in high school, around the time that the color photograph was attracting so much attention, Su Hang, already regarded as a major headache by the school staff, used his crudity to make the music class an occasion for ridiculing the music teacher. He took off his gym shoes and laid them on the windowsill, then stuck both feet up on his desk. The foul smell issuing from his nylon socks permeated the entire room. In the face of this rudeness, our music teacher continued to sing lustily, his resonant voice creating a counterpoint to Su Hang's stench, exposing us to a collision between beauty and squalor. Only when the song was over did the music teacher push back from the organ, rise to his feet and say to Su Hang, "Put your shoes on, please."

But this admonition succeeded only in reducing Su Hang to a paroxysm of mirth. Rolling about in his chair, he twisted around to us and said, "Can you believe it? He said *please*!"

The music teacher, as courteous as ever, said, "None of that nonsense, please."

This time Su Hang laughed even more wildly. Coughing ostentatiously, he patted his chest and said, "There he goes again with that *please* of his! This is cracking me up. Isn't he a riot?"

The music teacher was livid. Striding over to Su Hang's desk, he picked up his shoes from the windowsill and tossed them out the window. But as he turned around, Su Hang zipped over to the organ in his stocking feet, grabbed the songbook, and chucked it out of the window too. The music teacher was so stunned that he could only watch dumbly as Su Hang clambered out the window and then climbed back in again, shoes in hand. He returned the shoes to their perch on the windowsill, rested both feet on his desk, and gazed coolly at the music teacher, braced for action.

In the face of Su Hang's boorish behavior, the music teacher, so much admired by me, was utterly defenseless. He stood by the dais, his head slightly raised, and for a long time he said nothing at all. His face wore such a desolate look, you might have thought he had just received word of a death in the family, and it was ages before he finally said, "Could somebody go and fetch the songbook?"

After class, when many other boys crowded around Su Hang to hail his triumph, I did not join them. Somehow I felt a sense of loss, having just witnessed my role model being so easily humiliated.

It was not long after this that Su Hang and I went our separate ways. In actual fact, only I was aware of the rupture in our relations. All along he had regarded me as completely dispensable, and when I no longer joined the crowd clustered around him in the middle of the playground I alone was conscious of this change. Su Hang seemed unaware that I was now absent from his throng of adherents. He was in as high spirits as ever, whereas I now found myself alone. But I realized with surprise that the feelings I had experienced when I stood next to Su Hang were identical to my current sense of isolation. The only reason I had attached myself to Su Hang was to put on a show and try to look cool. Later, when I mentally reproached my brother Sun Guangping for sucking up to classmates from town, I sometimes would reflect ruefully that I had done much the same thing myself.

Now that I think about it, I am actually rather grateful for the beating that Su Hang administered that afternoon with the willow branch. But how shocked I was at the time—I had no idea that Su Hang would suddenly grab a branch and lay into me. A bunch of girls happened to be walking nearby, among them three whom Su Hang had fancied in the past. I could understand Su Hang's motive but I found it difficult to accept the way he chose to show off. At first I thought he was joking: he flogged me the way a carter might flog a recalcitrant mule, and I forced a smile and tried to get out of his way. But he persisted, and lashed me so fiercely across the face that my cheeks were stinging. When I saw that the girls had stopped and were looking on in wonder, my heart burned with shame. Intoxicated by his power, Su Hang kept turning his head and whistling at them, at the same time shouting at me to lie down. I knew why he wanted to hit me, but I neither lay on the ground nor seized hold of the willow branch, and instead headed off in the direction of the classroom. My classmates stood cheering as Su Hang pursued me and landed further blows on my back. I made no effort to resist but just kept on going. That afternoon my eyes blurred with tears of chagrin.

But in fact this humiliation made it possible for me to establish relations with Su Yu several months later. No longer did I claim to have lots of friends; I returned instead to solitude and began an independent life as the true me. Sometimes I found the experience so lonely that it was hard to overcome the emptiness inside, but I thought it better to maintain my self-respect than to gain superficial friends at the expense of shame. It was then I began to notice Su Yu, whose solitary manner as he walked down the side of the street made me sense a bond between us. Though still a teenager, Su Yu already projected an adult air of having lots of things on his mind, for he had yet to dispel the specter of his father's liaison with the widow back in Southgate. As I furtively took note of Su Yu, he likewise was quietly paying attention to me. I found out later that my utter indifference to my classmates had engaged his sympathy.

It did not take me long to realize that Su Yu found me intriguing. Often he would raise his head and look at me as I walked, silent and alone, along the other side of the street, while our classmates marched up the middle in groups of four or five, talking at the top of their voices. But Su Yu's carefree life in Southgate had left a deep impression, discouraging me from trying to forge any ties with him. Besides, the fact that I had no friends made it difficult for me to imagine that a boy two grades above me would come forward and greet me so cordially.

It was not until the term was about to end that Su Yu suddenly spoke up. We were walking down either side of the street, and when I looked over at Su Yu he surprised me by coming to a stop and smiling at me. Then—a moment I will never forget—he blushed with embarrassment. This self-conscious boy, so soon to become my friend, called out "Sun Guanglin."

I just stood there. I can no longer retrieve my precise emotions at that moment, but I know that I looked at him intently. Bunches of schoolchildren were walking along between us, and only when a gap appeared did Su Yu walk across and ask, "Do you remember me?"

When I first approached Su Hang, what I had been hoping was precisely that he would say something like this, but in the end I heard these words from his brother instead. Tears nearly came to my eyes as I nodded and said, "You're Su Yu."

After this exchange, if we happened to run into each other at the end of the school day it seemed natural to stay together. Often I would see Su Hang not too far away, watching us with a bemused expression. After a while we did not feel ready to head off in different directions when we reached the school gate, and Su Yu began to walk me partway home, as far as the wooden bridge that led to Southgate. He would stand there and wave to me after I crossed to the other side, then turn around and disappear into the distance.

A few years ago, when I made a return visit to Southgate, the old wooden bridge had been replaced by a new concrete structure. I stood in the winter twilight, recalling things that happened that summer. My nostalgic gaze gradually obliterated the factory, the now-bricked-over riverbank, and the concrete bridge I stood upon. I saw once again Southgate's fields and the muddy bank covered with green. The concrete slabs beneath my feet turned back into the wooden boards of earlier days, and through the slits between the boards I watched the river flow.

In the chill winter wind I remembered the following scene. Late one summer afternoon Su Yu and I stood on the bridge together for a long time, and as he gazed sheepishly toward Southgate his eyes reddened in the sunset. In a tone as serene as the dusk itself, he spoke of a tranquil moment during his time there. It had been so hot one night that he couldn't bear to let down his mosquito net, so his mother sat by his bedside, fanning him and driving away mosquitoes; only after he had fallen asleep did she close the net around him.

When Su Yu first told me about this incident, I felt a pang, for by then it was almost unthinkable that I would receive any affection from my family.

Su Yu had had a nightmare later. "I seemed to have killed someone. The police were looking for me everywhere, so I ran back to the house to hide. But when my parents came home from work and found me, they took a rope and tied me to the tree in front of the house so that the police could come and take me away. I cried and cried, begging them not to do that. But they just kept cursing and cursing."

Su Yu's wails woke up his mother. When she roused him from his dream, he was in a cold sweat and his heart was pounding. "What on earth are you crying about?" she scolded. "Are you out of your mind?"

The contempt in his mother's voice plunged Su Yu into despondency.

When the young Su Yu told this story to the younger me, probably neither of us could make much sense of it. More than ten years after Su Yu's death, as I stood alone with my memories on the bridge to Southgate, it dawned on me that Su Yu, such a sensitive soul, must always have oscillated between happiness and despair.

SHIVERS

When I was fourteen, under cover of darkness I discovered a mysterious activity that gave me a wonderful sensation. At the moment of climax, rapture arrived on the coattails of apprehension. After this, when I encountered the word *shiver*, I understood it in a sense different from the purely negative connotation ascribed to it by my peers, and perhaps more akin to what Goethe intended when he wrote, "To shiver is mankind's finest lot."

During those long evenings when I first scaled the thrilling heights, only to enter a world of utter emptiness and discover a wet patch on my underpants, I could not help but feel anxious and bewildered. My initial sense of alarm did not trigger guilt as much as a fear that I had fallen prey to some physiological disorder. At first I assumed the moisture was caused by an escape of urine, and what embarrassed me, in my ignorance, was not the shamefulness of my action but rather the idea that at my age I might still wet my bed. At the same time I was in a panic because I wondered if I might be ill. Nonetheless, such was my craving for this momentary wave of pleasure that I couldn't stop myself from repeatedly undertaking the maneuvers that would culminate in that ecstatic shudder.

When I left the house after lunch one day, the summer I was fourteen, and walked toward the school in town, my face went pale under the dazzling sun, for at this very hour I was intending to perform the disgraceful deed in order to solve the mystery of my nocturnal emissions. Given my age at the time, I was no longer able to let everything happen in accordance with what were held to be correct principles, and my inner desires began silently to control some of my words and actions. For days now, I had been dying to know exactly what had been discharged. At home, I couldn't carry out my scheme, and my only recourse was to pay a visit to the school toilets at lunchtime, when nobody else would be there. Later on the memory of those ramshackle toilets made me cringe, and for a long time I couldn't help but despise myself for choosing the most sordid venue in which to engage in the most sordid activity. Now I refuse to indulge in that kind of self-reproach, because my opting for the toilets simply reflected the fact that in my youth I had no place to hide. My choice was forced on me by circumstances.

I prefer not to describe the grim ambience of the school toilets; just to recall the buzzing of flies and the din of cicadas in the trees outside is enough to make me tense. I remember that after leaving the toilets I felt completely drained as I walked across the sun-bleached playground. With my most recent discovery confusion had given way to bafflement. When I walked into the classroom opposite I was thinking I might lie down in the empty room, but to my alarm I saw a girl doing her homework there, and her serene expression instantly drove home to me the weight of my sin. I dared not enter the classroom, but stood miserably next to a window in the hallway. I had no idea what I should do next and felt as though the day of judgment was nigh. When an old cleaning woman went into the toilet I had just vacated, bucket in hand, I began to tremble.

Later I grew more accustomed to the sensation, and when darkness fell I was no longer so fearful of sinning. It had become apparent to me that self-reproach was ineffectual in the face of temptation, and night always accorded leniency and consolation. As I wearily drifted off to sleep, the sight that often met my eyes was a brightly colored jacket fluttering gently in a light gray sky, and the austere soul that had been wont to put me on trial disappeared in the distance.

But in the morning, when I started my walk toward the school, heavy chains dragged me down. As I approached the school and saw female classmates, so neat and tidy, I could not help but blush. The healthy life embodied in the sunlight by their gay laughter seemed to me the most wonderful thing in the world, and my tainted condition stirred in me a disgust with myself. What I found hardest to bear was the way their glowing eyes skimmed over me from time to time, because now all I felt was anxiety, and I was no longer able to enjoy the happiness and excitement of being warmed by a girl's glance. At moments like that I always vowed to reform, but with night I would return to my old ways. My self-contempt expressed itself through weak avoidance, and I would slip out to some empty spot at the intervals between classes and stand there blankly. I kept away from Su Yu, on whom I had become increasingly dependent, for I felt I didn't deserve such a good friend, and when I saw Su Yu (who was completely in the dark about my ordeal) approaching me in a friendly way, I was so distressed I scuttled off in the other direction.

My life organized itself into two parts, day and night. During the day I felt upright and fearless, but once night arrived my resolve quickly collapsed. The speed with which I fell into desire's embrace never ceased to astonish me. In those days my heart was in turmoil. I often felt that I was being torn in two, my dual identities glaring at each other like archenemies.

At night, as desire ran rampant, I increasingly felt a need of a female image for inspiration. I didn't really want to sully anybody's honor, but the urge was just too compelling. I chose a pretty girl in my class named Cao Li. She wore shorts to school that summer and other boys more physically advanced than me quite lost their heads over her, hot in their praise of her exposed thighs. I, on the other hand, still lacked a true awareness of the female body and was quite taken aback when I heard their muttered comments. It was incomprehensible to me that they did not single out her face for accolades, for at the time I felt she possessed a peerless beauty and was completely infatuated with her captivating smile. At night she became my fantasy companion. Although my attention to her physical assets was not nearly as down-to-earth as the other boys', I noticed her thighs too, and their sleek luster made me quiver. But it was her face inspired my most fervent admiration. The sound of her voice, from wherever it came, was always tantalizing.

And so after nightfall, in my imagination, lovely Cao Li would appear by my side. In these moments I never had any improper designs on her body, for we would simply walk along a riverbank which we had all to ourselves. I made up the words she said and imagined the looks she gave me, and at my most daring I could even fashion a scent that emanated from her flesh, the smell of a meadow at daybreak. My only unseemly fantasy was that of stroking her hair as it stirred in the breeze. Later, when I prepared to caress her cheek, my nerve failed and I cautioned myself: No, you're not to do that.

Although I successfully prevented myself from stroking Cao Li's adorable face, with the arrival of daylight I still felt I had behaved indecently toward her, and as soon as I stepped inside the school I grew uneasy. I chose not to let my eyes rest on her, but I had no way of imposing similar control over my hearing, and the sound of her voice might wing its way toward me at any moment, making me happy and miserable all at the same time. Once she was tossing a paper ball toward one of her girlfriends, and it accidentally hit me instead. She just stood there, not knowing what to do, and then sat down amid the laughter of our classmates. Her face turned crimson as she bent her head to organize things in her satchel, and that flustered look stirred me to the core: if a trivial paper ball could embarrass her so acutely, then my nocturnal fantasies about her had to count as really filthy. But it was not so long afterward that I was to see a dramatic change in her.

Over and over again I vowed to cease my secret injuries to Cao Li, and on a trial basis I would fantasize about dating another girl, but it never took long before Cao Li's image took her place. Despite my best efforts I could never break free from her grip, and my only comfort was that no matter how often I molested her in my imagination she remained as beautiful as always, and when she ran across the playground her figure was just as vital and touching.

As I sank deeper and deeper into this quagmire of self-indulgence and self-laceration, Su Yu, who was after all two years my senior, noticed my haggard face and my strange insistence on avoiding him. Not only was seeing Cao Li a source of distress, encounters with Su Yu also left me acutely embarrassed. His cultured manner as he walked across the sunny playground evoked purity and an unruffled calm, and my dirty secrets had deprived me of the right to enjoy his company. After class I did not venture over to the older boys' classroom to look for him as I had earlier done but made my way to the pond next to the school, enduring in silence and solitude all these problems I had created for myself.

Su Yu came over to the pond on several occasions. The first time he asked me what was wrong with such obvious concern that it brought me to the verge of tears. I said nothing and just went on watching the ripples on the surface of the pond. After that, if Su Yu came over he would not say a word, and together we would stand there quietly waiting for the bell to ring, when we'd head back to school.

Su Yu had no way of knowing what torments I was having to endure, and my manner made him suspect that perhaps I had begun to get tired of him. So he became more cautious in his approach and no longer came over to the pond to check on me. Close friends for so long, we found a barrier now lay between us and estrangement quickly ensued. Sometimes if we ran into each other on the road to or from school we both appeared nervous and ill at ease. I noticed that Zheng Liang, the tallest boy in the whole school, was now beginning to appear by Su Yu's side. The two would stand at the edge of the playground, and Zheng Liang would chat amiably with the more refined Su Yu, punctuating their conversation with his loud laugh. I watched in misery as Zheng Liang occupied the place that was rightfully mine.

I tasted to the full the bitterness of losing a friend, resentful that Su Yu had bonded so quickly with Zheng Liang. At the same time, when we ran into each other I was stirred by the expression of perplexity and hurt in Su Yu's eyes, and there was sparked in me a fervent desire to reestablish my old friendship with him. But as long as I was bogged down in my nightly sinning I felt it impossible to set about restoring our relationship. Daylight plunged me into a mood of unspeakable dread; under the blazing sun I always hated myself and Su Yu's remoteness simply intensified my self-contempt. So one morning I made up my mind to confess to him how low I had sunk. I wanted to do this partly to impose a real punishment on myself and partly to demonstrate my loyalty to him. I could perfectly well imagine Su Yu's shocked reaction to my revelations, for he could not possibly anticipate the extent of my wickedness.

But the morning I summoned up courage to call Su Yu over to the pond and was able to maintain this bold stance long enough to tell him everything, Su Yu showed not the slightest sign of alarm, instead saying earnestly, "What you're talking about is masturbation."

His attitude astonished me. There was a smile of embarrassment on his face as he told me evenly, "I do it too."

Tears seemed to spill from my eyes and I heard myself saying with vexation, "Why didn't you tell me that before?"

I will never forget that morning beside the pond with Su Yu. In the wake of his admission, daytime recovered its beauty. The grass and trees nearby gleamed in the sun and when some boys burst out laughing over some joke or other, Su Yu pointed at them and said, "At night they do it too."

One evening not long afterward, at the tail end of winter, Su Yu and Zheng Liang and I were walking along a quiet street—the first time I was with Su Yu after dark. I remember I had both hands in my pockets, through habit ingrained by the winter cold, and it was only when I realized that my palms were breaking into a warm sweat that I asked Su Yu in surprise, "Is it spring already?"

I was fifteen that year, and to be going around with two friends considerably older than me was a memorable experience. Su Yu was on my right, his hand on my shoulder. Zheng Liang—my companion for the first time—was on his right. When Su Yu introduced me, Zheng Liang did not think any the worse of me for my shortness and even seemed pleased, saying to Su Yu, "Did you think I don't know who he is?"

Zheng Liang made a deep impression on me that evening. He had a way of swinging his arms as he walked, and in the moonlight his tall figure conveyed an air of complete self-assurance. It was on that occasion that the three of us quietly addressed the topic of masturbation. Su Yu, normally so laconic, was the one who started things off, and I was quite taken aback when he calmly broached the subject. It is only now, when I recall this scene after an interval of so many years, that I understand Su Yu's intentions. At the time I had yet to shake off all the baggage I had accumulated, and Su Yu brought the issue out in the open to help me put it in perspective. And it is true that only after this did I become truly relaxed about it. Now, as then, I feel there was something touching about the conspiratorial tone of the confidences we shared.

Zheng Liang's attitude was matter-of-fact. "If you can't sleep at night, it really does the trick," he said.

Recalling how cruelly I had been punishing myself just a few days earlier, I shot him an admiring glance.

Although on that particular evening he put me entirely at ease, a casual remark of his somewhat later on created a new matter for concern. Zheng Liang, quite unaware that he was revealing his own ignorance, said to me, "That stuff is like water in a thermos—there's only so much of it in you. People who use it up quickly exhaust their supply by the time they're in their thirties, whereas people who save it up still have some when they're eighty."

This comment sent me into a tizzy. Given my overindulgence during the preceding weeks, I thought it very likely that my stocks had been drained dry, and I was worried sick at night when I contemplated my future. As fear gnawed away, my romantic yearnings failed to reignite those fantasies that once kept me in their thrall and instead I became increasingly resigned to a life of loneliness. One evening I imagined myself as a doddery old man plodding alone through the winter snow, and I felt heartsick over my wretched lot.

For many nights after this I continued my nocturnal activities—not to satisfy physical urges but to determine the status of my bodily functions. Successful experiments gained me only momentary reassurance, for panic followed hard on their heels. I was well aware of the risks I was taking with each effort at verification and that the very last drops of fluid had just been discharged. Then I would bitterly regret the proof I had just completed. But within days anxiety about the prospect of internal depletion would stir me to renewed testing. My physical growth took place against the backdrop of a wan complexion, and often I would stand next to the pond in Southgate, looking at my reflection. I saw my emaciated chin and lackluster eyes drifting helplessly in the water, and faint ripples made me see a face covered in wrinkles. Especially when the sky was overcast I could clearly make out the gloomy features of a man grown senile before his time.

It was not until I was twenty years old that I learned the truth of the matter. I was at the university in Beijing at the time and happened to make the acquaintance of a poet who then enjoyed a considerable reputation. He was the first celebrity I had known and his offhand, distracted manner inspired me regularly to take a two-hour bus trip to reach the other side of town, just to enjoy a few minutes of conversation with him. After three such visits he was still vague about what my name was, but his friendliness and his scathing mockery of fellow poets more than compensated for this indignity. Though prone to holding forth at great length, he was also capable of listening attentively to my own scattered opinions while regularly correcting what he saw as erroneous views.

At the home of this forty-year-old bachelor I would encounter women of various stripes and hues, a reflection of the poet's catholic tastes. After our relationship developed, I once rather gingerly suggested that perhaps it was time for him to get married. This intrusion into his privacy did not seem to irritate him, for he answered casually, "What's the point of getting married?"

This put me on the spot. Out of concern for him as a man I much admired, I blundered on, "You don't want to use all that stuff up prematurely."

This bashful remark left him incredulous. "How on earth could you think like that?" he asked.

So then I repeated what Zheng Liang had said that evening years earlier. His reaction to this account was a roar of laughter, and I still remember vividly the sight of him doubled up on the sofa, splitting his sides with mirth. Later he invited me for the first time to stay for dinner, a meal that took the form of two packets of instant noodles purchased from the convenience store downstairs.

The poet did get married when he was forty-five, to a woman in her thirties whose striking good looks were paired with a remarkably fierce temper. The poet, formerly such a free spirit, now found himself the cat's-paw of fate. Like a child in the hands of a stepmother, when he left his apartment the only money he had in his pocket was his round-trip bus fare. Control of the purse strings was just one of her areas of expertise. He often came over to my place, bruises all over his face, seeking temporary refuge, the reason being simply that a certain female had called him up. A few days later he would insist that I accompany him back home as he prepared to make an official apology. I said to him, "Don't look so dejected. You've got nothing to be ashamed of. You didn't do anything wrong."

But he smirked and said, "Better to confess my errors."

I remember how his pretty wife, from her perch on the sofa, said to her husband as he came in the door, "Take the garbage out!"

Our poet lifted the bulging basket of trash, a beam of pleasure on his face. He was wrong to assume that performance of this chore would secure him a clean bill of health, for on his return she gave me my marching orders, and after the door had closed behind me, I heard her launch forth like a parent lecturing a child. As his wife, she was of course fully aware that the object of her reprimands was a gifted poet. So it was that I heard a tirade that left me quite dumbfounded, so wide was its lexical range, incorporating references to classical poetry and contemporary political jargon, pop lyrics, and goodness knew what else. At intervals in between I heard her husband's pious utterances: "That's well put" or "You've set me straight on that."

As the wife's voice grew ever more passionate, she was no longer censuring her husband as much as she was carried away by a pure love of invective. I hated to imagine what it would be like to be under her thumb on a daily basis: even if one could endure the black eyes and bloody noses, it would be hard to put up with her verbal incontinence.

Her most extreme measure was to decorate their apartment with her husband's letters of repentance, pledges to reform, and statements of self-criticism, as though they were some kind of design element that would impress her husband's friends when they visited. When she first stuck them up, his face was ashen, but with time he was able to pretend it was no big deal. "A dead pig's not afraid of being scalded with hot water" was his comment.

"Forget about the physical abuse," he once told me. "She's making an emotional wreck out of me too."

"Why did you marry her in the first place?" I asked.

"How was I to know she was a shrew?"

Along with other friends I urged him to get a divorce, but he ended up reporting our advice to his wife, holding nothing back. His betrayal resulted in an identical outcome for each of us, a threat-filled phone call from his wife. The curse placed on me was that I would die on the street on my twenty-fifth birthday.

In the spring of that year when I turned fifteen, I was dressing after a shower one lunchtime and discovered that my body had undergone a peculiar change. I noticed that some long hairs had appeared in my groin, which added a new layer of agitation to the inner turmoil generated by my nocturnal activities. Uninvited guests, these slender intruders had all of a sudden sprouted on my smooth skin. I stared at them stupefied, uncertain just how I should view their arrival, though I had the fearful sensation that my body had lost its carefree simplicity.

As I headed off for school through the sunlight, everything around me was just as it had always been—my body alone had changed. Something ugly was hiding in my underpants, making me feel that my feet were unbearably heavy. Although I hated those hairs I had to keep their existence a secret, because I could not deny that they were a part of me.

Soon after, hairs started springing up on my legs, too. I noticed this in the summer, when I no longer wore long trousers, and when I walked to school in my shorts the hairs' obvious and inescapable presence made me feel hideously exposed. All it took to make me squirm was for a girl to glance in their direction. Even if I had uprooted the most flagrant offenders by the following morning, I was always worried that Cao Li would already have seen them.

The tallest boy in my class had legs densely covered with dark hairs but walked around casually all the same, flaunting them to the whole world. I went through a phase when I often felt anxious on his account, and if I noticed girls' eyes fixed on his legs my concern for him only accentuated my own sense of unease.

Shortly before the start of the summer vacation, I came back to school early after lunch, but was deterred from entering by the sound of girls talking and laughing loudly inside. (Even now, if it is all women or all strangers in a room, I find it an intimidating experience to go in on my own. With so many eyes resting on me all at once, I am nervous and flustered.) I meant to walk away immediately, but I heard Cao Li's voice and her laughter kept me rooted to the spot. Next thing, I heard the others ask her which boy she liked most, a question that startled me with its boldness. What surprised me even more was that Cao Li was not the least embarrassed. There was a clear note of relish in her voice when she told them to guess the answer.

So tense was I that my breathing became labored. The girls came out with a whole string of potential candidates, including Su

Hang and Lin Wen, but my name was conspicuously absent and I was mortified at having been overlooked. At the same time, Cao Li's total rejection of these possibilities gave me some fleeting hope. But soon a voice named the classmate with the hairy legs and Cao Li immediately responded in the affirmative. The girls greeted her admission with simultaneous peals of laughter, and amid the hilarity one voice chipped in, "I know what it is you like about him."

"What's that?"

"The hair on his legs."

For a long time I would puzzle in vain over the explanation Cao Li herself gave. She said that of all the boys in the school he looked the most grown-up.

I quietly edged away from the classroom door and Cao Li's wanton laughter pursued me all the way down the corridor. What I had just heard did not sadden me as much as shock me. In that moment, as never before, life had revealed to me a state of affairs that seemed utterly counterintuitive. The lanky schoolboy who couldn't care less about the hair on his legs would hand in essays littered with miswritten characters and there wasn't one teacher who didn't single him out for ridicule, but this very same student had gotten the thumbs-up from Cao Li. Precisely what I regarded as ugly was alluring to her. I walked all the way to the pond next to the school and stood there for a long time watching the sunlight and the foliage that floated on the water's surface, and my deep disappointment with Cao Li slowly evolved into self-pity. For the first time in my life a beautiful dream had been shattered.

A second disillusionment was brought home to me by Su Yu, and involved the secrets of the female body. By now I had a long-standing desire for the opposite sex, but I was still in the dark about women's anatomy. I had specially earmarked my purest notions, using them to construct in a vacuum my image of Woman. This specter had appeared at night in the shape of Cao Li but never emerged as a genuinely sexual being, and in the evenings I would content myself with glimpsing female figures of matchless beauty who were dancing in the dark.

It all started with that hardback volume on Su Yu's father's shelves. Su Yu was quite familiar with his father's library, but it was through Su Hang that he became aware of this particular title. Ever since leaving Southgate the Su family had lived in one of the apartment blocks for hospital staff, with Su Yu and Su Hang on the first floor and their parents on the second; the one chore the brothers were assigned was to mop the floors each day. In the first few years Su Hang took responsibility for mopping downstairs, for he was unwilling to carry the mop up to the second floor, with all the extra work that would entail. But later on Su Hang abruptly told Su Yu that he would take charge of cleaning upstairs. He did not provide any explanation, for he was already accustomed to ordering his older brother about. Su Yu accepted Su Hang's suggestion without comment, this minor change striking him as of no consequence. After Su Hang took charge of the second floor, two or three classmates would drop in every day and help Su Hang with the mopping. So it was that Su Yu downstairs would often hear a flurry of furtive comments from upstairs, as well as a puzzling assortment of whistles and sighs. Su Yu burst in on them one time and thereby learned their secret.

After this, when Su Yu and I met, there was often a morose look on his face. Like mine, his conception of women was constructed around fantasy, and he was thrown off balance when suddenly confronted by the banality of real life. I remember that one particular evening we strolled quietly along the road and later stood on the newly completed concrete bridge. Su Yu, deep in thought, stared at the moonlight and lamplight on the water and then said to me awkwardly, "There's something you need to know."

That night I gave a little shiver under the moonlight, for I knew what I was about to see. My examination of the color photograph had been delayed until now; how bitterly I had regretted my offer to stand guard that day.

The following morning, I sat upstairs in the Sus' house in a dilapidated rattan chair and watched as Su Yu picked the book off the shelf. He showed me the color plate.

My first reaction was, How lurid and gross! Once confronted with this photograph, the image of femininity that had formed in my mind collapsed in ruins. Instead of the beauty I had so anticipated, a grotesque sight met my eyes; there was something malignant about this tasteless illustration. Su Yu stood beside me, his face just as pale as mine. He closed the book, saying, "I shouldn't have shown it to you."

The color plate had the same effect on me as it had on Su Yu, severing my attachment to an illusory perfection and thrusting me headlong into unvarnished reality. Although I persisted with my beautiful visions for a little longer, I was conscious that they were vaporizing.

When I started thinking about girls again, I found I had lost my original innocence, for the color plate had reoriented me toward practical physiology. I started to have all kinds of fantasies. Though I had a dreadful feeling that I was rapidly becoming decadent, raw desire made my resistance crumble. As I grew older the way I looked at girls changed drastically, for I began to pay attention to their buttocks and breasts, no longer susceptible only to winsome eyes or a cute expression.

The autumn when I was sixteen, the film projection team from town visited Southgate for the first time in six months. In those days it was a big event for country folk to watch a movie in the evening and people from adjacent villages came hurrying over before dark, clutching stools in their hands. For years now the production team leader had been accustomed to planting his seat firmly in the center of the drying ground. I will never forget how he used to make his entrance. Just as night fell he would appear, brandishing the kind of long bamboo pole normally used for hanging out laundry, and swagger across the drying ground. After he sat down, he would lean the pole against his shoulder and if anyone in front of him obstructed his line of vision he would hold out the pole and give that person a tap on the head, to preserve his unimpeded view.

Children generally sat on the other side of the screen and watched the characters fire guns or write letters with their left hands. When I was little, my place had been in this juvenile section, but I ruled out such a viewing position now that I was sixteen. On this occasion the person immediately in front of me was a young woman from a nearby village, whose name I never knew.

It was so packed that I had to squeeze in behind her and peer over her head to see the screen. At the beginning I was quite relaxed, but the smell of her hair kept wafting over me, making me more and more unsettled. As people behind us pressed forward, my hand brushed against her buttocks; this brief contact electrified me. Temptation, when it comes one's way, is hard to resist: suppressing my inhibitions, I gave her a second little pat. When she did not react, this strengthened my nerve and I pressed my palm against her buttocks, ready to take to my heels should she begin to stir. But she stood as stiff and still as if she were carved out of wood. My hand could feel her warmth, and the part of her that I was touching seemed to get hotter and hotter. When I gently adjusted my position, she still made no response. I turned my head to look around and saw that the man behind me was a good bit taller than me. Emboldened, I pinched the young woman on the bottom, making her giggle. This sound was particularly noticeable, as it was emitted during the film's most tedious sequence, and it instantly deflated my courage. I squeezed my way out of the crowd, trying to assume a pose of nonchalance. But panic took over before I had gone very far and I bolted for home, where my heart continued to thump even after I had thrown myself down on my bed. Whenever steps approached our house I trembled all over, convinced that she must be coming with a backup to apprehend her molester. After the movie was over, the random patter of feet made me more agitated still, and long after my parents and my older brother had gone to bed I worried that the young woman might yet track me down. Only sleep rescued me in the end.

I could find no outlet for my desires, and Su Yu was in the same boat. The difference was that Su Yu's sexual frustrations at least distracted him from the anxieties that beset him during his stay at Southgate. Now, when I look back, the happy childhood that I associated with Su Yu from my pond-side observation point was actually just as unreliable as the breezes that blew across the water. I was vaguely aware at the time of his father's entanglement with the widow, but I had no idea of the full extent to which Su Yu was affected. In fact, just as my family's antipathy to me was growing daily more obvious, Su Yu had begun to suffer insecurities of his own following that act of his father's.

When the Sus moved to Southgate the widow was still in full flower, and she made no effort to conceal her interest in Dr. Su. For it was at this stage, before her vigorous appetite began to wane, that she developed a tendency one associates more with men—a taste for novelty. The guests she had received previously were all peasants with mud on their legs, and the appearance on the scene of Dr. Su struck her as a refreshing change. With his glasses and the whiff of ethyl alcohol that clung to him, this man of culture was an utter revelation, making her realize that however many visitors had honored her carved bed with their presence, they had all been patterned from a single mold. The doctor's arrival in the village excited her no end, and she would say to everyone she met, "These intellectuals are so adorable!"

To be fair, one has to point out that during those days she was so infatuated with the doctor she must have observed at least two weeks of celibacy, no longer accepting every volunteer who came along. She knew that doctors are particular about hygiene and didn't want to make things difficult. Her faked illness provided the occasion for seducing him. As he walked to her house to perform the examination, he had no idea that he was headed for a trap, and even when he stood by her bed and she looked doe-eyed up at him he failed to note the warning signs. In his usual even tone he inquired about the nature of her malady, and was told she had a bellyache. He asked her to pull back a corner of the quilt so that he could take a look at the problem area. Instead she kicked the quilt to one side, offering herself for his inspection in her birthday suit. This unexpected move took him completely by surprise. He found himself gazing at a female body in impressive physical condition. His wife's figure was not at all in the same league.

"You didn't . . . ," he stammered, "you didn't need to take it all off."

"Come to me," she said in an imperious tone.

The doctor could have taken to his heels, but instead he slowly backed away and shuffled toward the door. It was hard to say no to the widow's lusty body.

She jumped to her feet, and between her strength and his lack of resistance she found it an easy matter to maneuver him onto her bed. During the act that followed she heard him muttering again and again, "I am letting my wife down. I am letting the boys down."

The doctor's incessant self-reproaches did not hinder his participation in their activity, and everything took its normal course. Afterward the widow told people, "You have no idea how bashful he is. What a sweet man!"

Nothing else happened between them, but for a long time afterward the villagers often saw the widow made up like some girl from Xinjiang, her hair twisted into little braids, pacing back and forth near the doctor's house playing the coquette. The doctor's wife would sometimes come out and look at her, then go back inside, without any words being exchanged. A few times she managed to intercept the doctor as he came down the road, and the villagers would see the doctor flee in embarrassment before her doting smile.

One evening in my second year at junior high, Su Yu pensively related to me the events of one other evening. His father's brief lapse had not created such a big stir as to seriously disrupt family life, but something untoward did ensue. One day their parents came home unusually late. Their mother was the first to return, well after dark, but when he and his brother went to greet her she ignored them. Instead she rummaged around in a trunk for some clothes, put them in a bag, and went off carrying the bag. Their father returned soon afterward. He asked them if their mother had come home at all. Told that she had, he went out again. They waited till midnight on empty stomachs, but with no sign of their parents' return had no choice but to go to bed. When they woke up the next morning, their parents were in the kitchen preparing breakfast, just like any other day.

I could detect uneasiness in Su Yu's voice that night. In the aftermath of his father's escapade, Su Yu, sensitive and impressionable as he was, was easily thrown off balance simply by witnessing, say, a man and a woman having a personal conversation. Even though his parents had been careful to cover up his father's indiscretion, the facts of the matter gradually had become plain to him. Observing the carefree manner of his classmates, he would feel envy of them and esteem for their parents. It never crossed his mind that their parents might also be involved in some hanky-panky, and he was convinced that only his family could generate such a scandal. On occasion he even indicated that he felt a little jealous of me, although he was well aware of my miserable status in my family. As he looked at me with admiration, he did not know that my father, Sun Kwangtsai, was that very moment marching triumphantly into the widow's house with the foot basin that my grandmother once used slung over his shoulder. In the face of Su Yu's benign envy, I could only blush with shame.

In his last year in high school, as Su Yu approached full physical maturity, it became difficult for him to resist his burgeoning desires, urges whose intensity I was to feel to much the same degree when I entered high school. One summer lunchtime this yearning for the opposite sex led him on the path toward what we regarded at the time as fearful ruin. He happened to be walking along a quiet alleyway when he saw a full-breasted young woman approaching. He gave an involuntary shiver and in that moment his self-control was vanquished by the sheer force of his sexual need. As he walked in a daze toward her, he had no idea that he would end up putting his arms around her, and only when she shrieked in terror, pulled herself away, and ran off did he gradually realize what he had done.

Su Yu paid a heavy price, sentenced to a year of reform through labor. The day before his departure, he was led onto the rostrum next to the school playground with a wooden placard suspended from his neck, on which was written "Su Yu, Hooligan." I watched as several classmates I knew well strode onto the rostrum, each clutching a sheet of writing paper, and delivered stern condemnations of Su Yu's crime.

I learned what had happened very late in the game. At morning recess on the day after the incident, I was on my way to Su Yu's classroom as usual when some older boys called out, "When are you making your first prison visit?"

I had no idea what they meant. When I got to the window and glanced toward Su Yu's desk, Zheng Liang saw me and signaled grimly. He came out and said, "Su Yu's in trouble."

That's when I heard the whole story. Zheng Liang asked me tentatively, "Do you hate Su Yu?"

Tears spilled from my eyes, for my heart went out to my friend. "I could never hate Su Yu," I told him.

I felt Zheng Liang's hand on my shoulder. As we began to walk, the boys who had jeered at me earlier yelled again, "When are you guys off for your prison visit?"

"Just ignore them," Zheng Liang murmured.

At the west end of the playground I saw Su Hang. Together with Lin Wen he was busily sharing his worldly wisdom with other boys my age. Su Hang was unperturbed by his brother's disgrace and loudly declared, "I don't know what we've been fucking doing all this time! While we were fooling around, my brother goes off without a word and feels a woman up. I'm going to cop a feel myself tomorrow."

Lin Wen chipped in, "Su Yu has shown what he's made of now. We're novices by comparison."

Two weeks later, Su Yu stood on the stage, his head shaved. Those tight, short clothes of his clung to his puny frame, and under an overcast sky he looked too weak to withstand a gust of wind. Even though I knew this was coming, I was still shocked to see Su Yu reduced so quickly to such a pitiful state. The way he stood there, head bowed, threw me into a welter of confused thoughts. I peered through a crowd of heads in an effort to catch Zheng Liang's eye and I noticed that he likewise was looking over his shoulder to see how I was reacting. At this moment only Zheng Liang felt my anguish, and our eyes were seeking out each other's support. When the denunciation session ended, he made a sign and I ran over. "Let's go," Zheng Liang said.

Su Yu had been led off the stage in preparation for being frog-marched around the town. Many of our classmates followed in his wake, laughing and joking, excited by all the drama. I noticed Su Hang, who not long before had been so impervious to his brother's misfortune. Now he walked by himself, a hangdog look on his face, clearly upset by what had happened at the denunciation meeting. When the parade turned onto the main street, Zheng Liang and I pushed our way to the front of the crowd. Zheng Liang cried, "Su Yu!"

Su Yu walked on unhearing, his head down. Zheng Liang flushed and a look of distress crossed his face. I called out too, "Su Yu!"

Immediately I felt blood surging to my cheeks. With everyone's eyes on me all of a sudden, I felt terribly self-conscious. This time Su Yu turned his head and gave us a relaxed smile.

We were bewildered by that smile of his, and it was not until later that I understood what lay behind it. Despite Su Yu's seemingly terrible plight he himself felt that pressure had been lifted from his shoulders. Afterward he was to tell me, "I understood how it was my father came to do what he did."

In the wake of Su Yu's disgrace, the conduct of Zheng Liang and me—particularly our final farewell—was excoriated by our teachers, who ordered us to write self-criticisms. As they saw it, since we not only were not indignant about Su Yu's hooligan act but actually offered him our sympathy, this proved that we were ourselves would-be hooligans. On the way home from school once, I heard some girls behind me commenting, "He's even worse than Su Yu."

We refused to write self-criticisms, no matter how the teachers threatened us, and when Zheng Liang and I met we would proudly say to each other, "Better to die!"

But not long afterward, Zheng Liang came to me looking dejected. I was shocked by his bruised and swollen face. "My dad did it," he told me. Then he said, "I have written a self-criticism."

I was appalled. "You have let Su Yu down," I told him.

"I had no choice," Zheng Liang replied.

I spun on my heel and as I walked away I said, "I will *never* write one!"

Looking back on it, I see that if I was brave then, it was

because I was under no pressure at home. Sun Kwangtsai was absorbed by his aerobic exercises in the widow's carved bed, while my mother was quietly nurturing her animosity toward her rival. Only Sun Guangping knew what I was going through. But by then he was saying little; the day that Su Yu came to grief was the very day that the carpenter's daughter threw the melon seeds in his face. That time the older boys taunted me, I noticed my brother in the distance, watching me in a preoccupied way.

During this period, I was gripped by unquenchable rage. In the wake of Su Yu's departure, everything around me became hateful, infuriating. Sometimes, sitting in the classroom, I would look at the window glass and wish that it would shatter. Once, an older boy yelled to me in a provocative tone, "Hey, how come you still haven't made that prison visit?"

His big grin struck me as so despicable that, trembling with anger, I raised my fist and slammed it into his face.

His body swayed, and then I received a stinging blow to the head and slumped to the ground. As I tried to get to my feet, he kicked me in the chest, inflicting a sharp pain that made me want to vomit. Then somebody else flung himself at my tormentor, only to be knocked down too. It was Su Hang. I was startled to see Su Hang intervene in a fight that wasn't his. He got back on his feet and lunged out, grabbing the other boy by his waist. The two fell to the ground in a tussle. Su Hang's entry into the fray raised my fighting spirit and I seized hold of our opponent's flailing feet while Su Hang gripped his arms. I bit his leg and Su Hang planted his teeth in the boy's shoulder. He squealed with pain. Su Hang and I looked at each other and—perhaps through sheer excitement—we both burst into tears. How loudly we wept that afternoon, at the same time butting our heads against the older boy's pinioned body.

Because of Su Yu, a bond was formed between Su Hang and me, if only fleetingly. Su Hang sported a little switchblade, and he and I would roam the school with ferocious looks on our faces. He vowed to me: The next person who dares to say anything bad about Su Yu is going to have a taste of this.

As time went on maybe attitudes changed. At any rate, nobody seemed to think about Su Yu for very long and we were never provoked again, so we had no further opportunity to develop our friendship. Just when we viewed the world with unrelieved hostility, the world suddenly grew more civil. Hatred united Su Hang and me, and as hatred dissipated our friendship withered on the vine.

Not long after this, Cao Li's affair with the music teacher became public knowledge. Cao Li's weakness for mature men had led her straight into his arms. When I first heard the news, I was dumbfounded. Although my own sense of inferiority had forced me to accept that I could never be the right match for Cao Li, she was, after all, a girl whom I had fancied and of whom I was still fond.

Urged to make a clean breast of it, Cao Li wrote a long confession. The math teacher was among the first to read it, and when he ran into the Chinese teacher on the staircase, he handed it on to him with a leer. The Chinese teacher, who was having a smoke, seemed unwilling to endure even a moment's delay, for he took the document out of its envelope and started reading right there on the stairs. His eyes bulged, and he forgot all about the cigarette in his hand; when it burned down to his fingers he simply gave a shiver and dropped it on the floor. But when Su Hang quietly slipped behind him, he somehow sensed his intrusion and emitted a series of disapproving grunts and snorts designed to drive the boy away.

Su Hang had managed to read only a single sentence, but it was enough to keep him in ecstasies the whole afternoon. He glibly reported the fruits of his spying to every single person he met, including me.

"'I couldn't sit down afterward.'" He went on exultantly to explain. "That's what Cao Li wrote. Do you know what that means? Cao Li has had that thing of hers well and truly unsealed."

For a full two days, "I couldn't sit down afterward" was constantly on the lips of the boys in school, and the girls greeted this incantation with hearty laughter. At the same time, in the staff room, the chemistry teacher—a woman—voiced strenuous disapproval of Cao Li's graphic confession. Shaking the hefty manuscript till it rustled and flapped, she cried indignantly, "Isn't this just going to give people ideas?"

Her male colleagues, who by now all knew stem to stern the details of Cao Li's trysts with the music teacher, sat very properly in their chairs, gazed poker-faced at the chemistry teacher, and said nothing.

At the end of the school day, Cao Li had finished answering the teachers' questions, and she looked calm and composed as she went out the school gate. I noticed that she was wearing a black scarf around her neck that fluttered in the breeze along with her hair. Her face, slightly upturned, took on a rosy, diaphanous quality in the cold air.

A mob of schoolboys led by Su Hang had gathered at the

gate to await her appearance, and as she approached they shouted in unison, "I couldn't sit down afterward!"

I was standing not too far away. I watched as she was swallowed up by their laughter, and then I observed the sharp edge of her personality. She came to a halt among them and turned her head ever so slightly as she said with loathing, "A bunch of hooligans, that's what you are!"

My classmates were reduced to a shocked silence, never having expected that Cao Li would have the spirit to fire back. She was quite far off in the distance before Su Hang finally pulled himself together, directing a string of insults at her receding back: "Fuck! You're the hooligan. A hooligan and a harpy too."

Then I saw Su Hang turn to his pals, amazement all over his face. "And she says that *we* are hooligans!"

The music teacher went to prison, and when he regained his freedom five years later was banished to a school out in the countryside. Cao Li, like the other girls, went on to marry and have a child. But the music teacher has remained single. He lives in a tumbledown cottage and walks a muddy path to teach the local youngsters how to sing and dance.

I went home a few years ago and caught a glimpse of him when my bus pulled over at a little village stop. The elegant music teacher of yesteryear had aged, and his gray hair blew about every which way in the cold wind. He wore an old black padded overcoat streaked with mud, and as he stood next to a crowd of country folk only his scarf gave a hint of the poise he once possessed and made him look different from the other people. He was standing outside a steaming-hot shop that sold stuffed buns, waiting politely in line. Actually, he was the only one standing in line, for everyone else was trying to push their way to the front as he stood stiffly in his place. I could hear him saying in his mellow voice, "Stand in line, please."

After Su Yu came back from reeducation, I was not able to see him as much. Zheng Liang had already graduated by that time and the two of them were often together. I could see Su Yu only if I went into town in the evening. As before, we did not say much when we were together, but I felt that Su Yu had gradually become more distant toward me. He still had that rather shy manner of speaking, but he was no longer so discreet in his choice of conversational topics. He told me quite bluntly what his sensation was when he put his arms around the young woman. A shadow of disappointment passed across his face as he told me that in that instant he realized that a real female body was quite different from what he had imagined. He said, "It felt pretty much the same as when I put my arm on Zheng Liang's shoulder."

As he said this, Su Yu gave me a piercing look and I turned away in shame. I was stung by his remark, which sparked in me a jealousy toward Zheng Liang.

Later I realized that I was really at fault. When Su Yu came back from the camp, I never once asked him about his experience there, fearful that this would upset him. But it was precisely my caution that aroused his distrust. More than once he guided the conversation in that direction, but I would hastily change the subject. One evening when we had been walking along the riverbank for some time, Su Yu suddenly came to a halt and asked me, "Why do you never ask me about my time in the camp?"

In the moonlight Su Yu looked stern, and with him staring at me so intensely I was too taken aback to respond immediately.

Then he smiled desolately and said, "As soon as I got back, Zheng Liang asked me about it, but you never have."

"It didn't occur to me to ask," I said awkwardly.

"In your heart you look down on me," Su Yu said in a sharp tone of voice.

Although I denied this, Su Yu turned around resolutely, saying, "Good-bye."

As Su Yu walked away along the bank, his back stooped, I was grief stricken at the thought that he was terminating our friendship. To me this was unbearable. I rushed to catch up and shared with him the story of how I pinched the girl at the film show. "I always meant to tell you about it," I said, "but I didn't dare."

Su Yu's hand rested on my shoulder as I so much hoped it would, and I heard him say gently, "In the camp, I was always so worried that I had lost your respect."

Later we sat on the stone steps leading down to the river, and the water lapped around our feet. We sat there in silence for a long time before Su Yu said, "There's something I want to tell you."

I glanced at him in the moonlight. He paused, and looked up at the sky. I too tilted my head back and gazed at the starry night. The moon was gliding toward a cloud, and we watched quietly as it drifted across the void. The moon drew nearer to the cloud, illuminating its dark borders, and disappeared inside. Su Yu went on, "You remember what I told you a few days ago—the feeling I had when I put my arms around that woman?"

In the darkness, Su Yu's face was indistinct but his voice was clear. When the moon pierced the cloud its light suddenly exposed his face, and he broke off to look up at the sky once more.

Then the moon sidled up to another cloud and slipped out of sight again. "It wasn't like putting my arm on Zheng Liang's shoulder," Su Yu said. "It was like putting my arm on *your* shoulder. That was what I thought."

Su Yu's face suddenly brightened and in the returning moonlight I saw him smile. His smile and bashful voice warmed me and sustained me that evening when the moonlight came and went.

THE DEATH OF SU YU

Su Yu, who always woke so early, suffered a cerebral hemorrhage one morning and fell into a coma. His mind, though weakening, forced his eyes partially open, sending out to the world through their feeble glance a final cry for help.

My friend used his life's fading light to gaze at the room in which he had lived so many years. It was a narrow and confining space in which to catch one's ultimate glimpse of the world. He was vaguely conscious of Su Hang's figure, still sleeping soundly in his bed, like a boulder blocking his exit. He was falling into a bottomless crevasse, but it seemed as though a luminous glow somehow held him loosely in its grip, slowing the pace of his descent. The brilliant sunshine outside was drawn to the blue curtains, making them glimmer with light.

After Su Yu's mother woke, she came tramping down the

stairs. The sound of her footsteps triggered in Su Yu's failing life a fleeting throb, a longing for normality. When she picked up the empty thermos and discovered that Su Yu had not gone to the teahouse as usual to fetch hot water, she lost no time in registering her dissatisfaction with him. "Oh, for heaven's sake!"

She didn't even look at my friend as he struggled for survival.

The second person up was Su Yu's father. He had not yet washed his face or brushed his teeth when his wife told him to fetch the hot water. He gave a yell. "Su Yu, Su Yu!"

Su Yu heard a powerful noise coming to him from somewhere far away. His sinking body rose rapidly, as though a breeze propelled him up toward the surface. But he was unable to respond to the rescue call. His father strode over to his bed and fixed his gaze on him. Seeing that Su Yu's eyes were slightly ajar, he chided him. "Hurry up! Get out of bed and go fetch the water."

Su Yu was incapable of answering and all he could do was look at his father in silence. The doctor had always been irked by Su Yu's uncommunicativeness and now he found his demeanor exasperating. He went into the kitchen, picked up the thermos, and said heatedly, "Where did this kid learn his manners, huh?"

"Oh, he got them from you, no?"

Everything disappeared, and Su Yu's body started sinking once more, like a pebble tumbling down through the air. Suddenly a beam of light shone in and stopped him in his tracks, but the brightness was instantly extinguished and Su Yu had a feeling of being hurled beyond its reach. When his father left, thermos in hand, it was as though the room had plunged into a fog. The noise his mother made in the kitchen was like a boat's sail far off in the distance, and Su Yu felt that his body was floating on some watery substance.

By now Su Yu could not distinguish among the different sounds in the kitchen. When his father came back, the sunlight from outside briefly shone in through the door and his body was momentarily uplifted. His parents' conversation and the clatter of bowls and chopsticks caused him to linger in a field of gray. My friend lay becalmed in the quiet, just before the point of no return.

After they had finished breakfast Su Yu's parents passed by his bed, but they didn't give him another glance before going off to work. When they opened the front door, my friend once more was boosted by the sun's rays, only for the door to close again immediately.

Su Yu lay forever in the gloom, feeling his body slowly sinking as his life wearily approached its end. His brother slept right through till ten o'clock. When he got up, he went over to Su Yu's bed and asked him in surprise, "So you're sleeping in late today too, are you?"

Su Yu's eyes were already dim. To Su Hang, his expression was baffling. "What are you playing at?" he asked.

He turned and went into the kitchen, where he began a lengthy process of brushing his teeth and washing his face. Then he ate his breakfast. Like his parents, he crossed the room without giving his brother a second glance and opened the front door.

That was the last flood of light to enter the room, and it triggered a fleeting recovery of consciousness. Su Yu sent his brother a mental cry for help, but all that happened was that Su Hang closed the door behind him.

Su Yu's body finally found itself in an unstoppable fall that accelerated and turned into a tailspin. A stifling sensation held him in its grip for what seemed like an eternity, and then all of a sudden he attained the tranquility of utter nothingness. It was as though a refreshing breeze was blowing him gently into tiny pieces, as though he was melting into countless drops of water that disappeared crisply, sweetly, into thin air.

Su Yu was dead by the time I arrived. Noticing that the door and the windows were shut, I stood outside and called, "Su Yu. Su Yu!"

No sound came from within. I assumed that he must have gone out and I went away, crestfallen.

THE LITTLE COMPANION

In my last year at home, walking back to Southgate from school one afternoon, I came across three boys fighting outside a pastry shop. A small boy with blood dripping from his nose clung tightly to the waist of an older boy who was trying his best to pull the other's hands away, while the third boy stood to one side and shouted threateningly, "Are you going to let go now?"

Although little Lulu saw me approaching his jet black eyes gave no sign that he was appealing for help, and instead conveyed a total indifference to the prospect of impending punishment.

The boy who was being held said to his friend, "Hurry up and get him off me!"

"I can't pull him off. You need to shake him off."

So the other boy swiveled around in an effort to dislodge

Lulu. Lulu's feet left the ground but his hands maintained a tight grip on his adversary. He closed his eyes to avoid feeling dizzy. Despite spinning around several times, the boy failed to get rid of Lulu and succeeded only in tiring himself out. Panting, he cried to his buddy, "Get . . . him . . . off!"

"How?" The other boy was just as powerless.

At this moment a middle-aged woman emerged from the pastry shop and shouted at the children, "What, you're still at it?"

She turned to me and said, "They've been fighting for two hours already, can you believe it?"

The captive boy said in his own defense, "He won't let go of me."

She began to reproach them. "You two shouldn't gang up on a smaller boy."

"He hit us first," the other boy replied.

"Who are you trying to kid? I could see perfectly well that you two were bullying him."

"Well, he was the first to start hitting."

Lulu looked at me again with his dark eyes. It seemed never to have occurred to him that he needed to tell his side of the story, as though what the other boys said was of absolutely no interest to him. All he did was look at me.

The middle-aged woman gave them a push. "I don't want you fighting in front of my shop. Clear off, the lot of you."

The pinioned boy began, with great difficulty, to edge forward; Lulu hung to him grimly, his feet scraping along the ground. The other boy brought up the rear, with their two satchels in his hand. Lulu was no longer looking at me but was craning his neck around to look at his own satchel, which lay in the pastry shop doorway. When they'd gone some ten yards or so, the pinioned boy came to a halt, wiped the sweat off his forehead, and said to his buddy in annoyance, "Come on, get him off me, will you?"

"There's no way. Try biting his hand."

The boy bent down and bit Lulu's hand. Lulu's dark eyes closed and I knew he had to be in a lot of pain because he pressed his head tightly against his adversary's back.

After a few moments the pinioned boy raised his head and continued to threaten him feebly with some unnamed reprisal. "Are you going to let go or not?"

Lulu opened his eyes and twisted his head to check on his satchel.

"Shit, this kid is too much!" The other boy raised his foot and gave Lulu a fierce kick in the buttocks.

The pinioned boy said, "Squeeze his balls. That should do it."

His buddy looked around and, noticing me, he muttered, "No, I can't do that."

Lulu was still looking back and when a man approached the pastry shop, he shouted, "Don't step on my satchel!"

This was the first time I heard Lulu speak. His piping voice made me think of the gaily colored butterfly bows in a young girl's hair. The pinioned boy said to his buddy, "Throw his satchel into the river."

The other boy went over to the shop doorway, picked up the satchel, and crossed the street to the concrete balustrade next to the river. Lulu watched him anxiously. The boy laid the satchel on the balustrade and said, "Are you going to let go or not? If you don't, I'm going to toss it in."

Lulu released his hands at last, and then he stood there with his eyes fixed on his satchel, unsure what to do. The freed boy picked up their two satchels from the ground and said to his friend, "Give his back to him."

The boy flung the satchel on the ground and gave it a kick for good measure before running to join his friend.

Lulu shouted at them, "I'm going to tell my big brother! He'll settle accounts with you."

Then he went to fetch his satchel. I could see that he had fine, delicate features, but the blood dripping from his nose left a trail of red spots down the front of his white T-shirt. He squatted down next to his bag, took out his textbooks and pencil case, and placed them back in proper order. As he squatted there in the twilight, his small figure made a touching sight. After rearranging things to his satisfaction, he stood up, clutching his satchel to his chest, and with a corner of his shirt rubbed away the dust that had settled on it. I heard him muttering to himself, "My big brother's going to settle accounts with you."

He raised his hand to wipe away his tears and then went off, sobbing quietly.

After Su Yu's death, I once more was alone. Sometimes when I ran into Zheng Liang we would stand about and exchange a few words. But I knew that the sole connection between him and me—Su Yu—had disappeared, and so our relationship was expendable. When I saw Zheng Liang walking around in high spirits with his new pals from the factory, this only confirmed my assessment.

I often recalled how Su Yu would wait for me by the riverside, his head bowed, lost in thought. His death had transformed friendship from a wonderful anticipation of what would soon be to something fixed in place by what had been. I started to cultivate a stoop, slouching along the riverbank just as Su Yu did when he was alive, and I began to enjoy the action of walking, a love he had bequeathed to me. As I strolled along, I could reach back into the past and exchange a knowing smile with the Su Yu who once was.

That was how I spent my last year at home, and that was my inner life as I approached adulthood. It was the year that I met Lulu.

It was three days after that fight that I found his name. I was walking down a street in town when I saw him dashing across the sidewalk, his satchel clasped to his chest, with five or six boys about the same age in hot pursuit, crying, "Lulu, Lulu" and "You stupid idiot!"

Lulu turned around and yelled, "I hate you!"

After that, he ignored their shouts and stalked off. His rage was so out of proportion to his size that his body seemed to teeter under its weight, and his little bottom swayed as he disappeared among the pedestrians.

At the time I did not realize that a close friendship could develop between Lulu and me, despite the impression he had made. But that changed when I witnessed Lulu's next face-off. This time Lulu was up against seven or eight boys his age who were shouting madly, like a bunch of excited flies, as they rained blows down on him. The result once again was Lulu's defeat, but this did not stop him from shouting at them with a victor's confidence: "Be careful my big brother doesn't beat you all up!"

The boy's antagonism to everybody and his friendless isolation struck a chord within me. From that time on I began to pay real attention to him. As I watched his boyish gait, a warm feeling coursed through my veins. It was as though I was seeing my own childhood self unrolling before me.

One day as Lulu came out of the school gate and headed off down the sidewalk, I couldn't help but call him back. "Lulu."

He stopped, turned around, and studied me carefully, then asked, "Did you call me?"

Smiling, I nodded.

"Who are you?" he asked.

This abrupt inquiry took me by surprise; my being older did me no good at all. He walked away and I heard him muttering, "Why are you calling me, if you don't know me?"

The failure of this first approach was discouraging, and after this I began to be more circumspect when I watched Lulu leaving the school. At the same time I sensed with pleasure that I had provoked his interest, and he would often turn around and throw me a glance as he walked.

This impasse before we became friends seemed like a replay of the situation between Su Yu and me a couple of years earlier. We would both be surreptitiously watching each other, but neither of us would say a word. But one afternoon Lulu walked straight up to me, his dark eyes glowing with a winsome sparkle, and hailed me. "Uncle."

The sudden greeting startled me. He went on, "Do you have anything for a kid to eat?"

Before this, it had seemed so difficult for us to have any kind of genuine interaction, but Lulu's question made this become a reality in no time at all. Hunger, you could say, was what initiated our friendship. But I was embarrassed, because although now almost eighteen years old—old enough to count in his eyes as an "uncle"—I had not a penny in my pocket. I could only ruffle his hair with my hand and ask, "You haven't had lunch?"

The boy saw that I could not help him stave off his hunger pangs, and he bowed his head and said softly, "No."

"Why haven't you eaten?"

"My mom wouldn't let me."

He said this with no tone of reproaching his mother, just as a dispassionate fact.

Without realizing it, we had begun to walk, I with my hand on his shoulder. I thought of Su Yu, now so far away, and how he would put his hand on my shoulder as we started one of our intimate rambles. Now I was treating Lulu with the same affection that Su Yu had extended to me. We strolled down the street, next to people who had no interest in us.

Later Lulu raised his head and asked me, "Where are you going?"

"Where are *you* going?" I asked him.

"I'm going home."

"I'll walk you there," I said.

He put up no objection. My eyes began to mist, for I glimpsed the phantom of Su Yu standing on the wooden bridge that led to Southgate, waving his hand in farewell. What I experienced at that moment must have been the feeling that Su Yu had when he saw me home.

We entered a long, narrow alley. When we reached a rundown two-story house, Lulu's shoulder slipped from my grasp, and he climbed the staircase, his whole body swaying. Halfway up he looked back at me and waved just as an adult would do, saying, "Thanks, see you."

I waved back as I watched him go up the stairs. Soon after he disappeared from view, I heard a female voice raised in anger, and there was the sound of something hitting the floor. Lulu reemerged on the landing and ran back down the stairwell, pursued by a woman who hurled a shoe at his retreating back. It missed him and rolled down by my feet instead. On seeing me, the woman adjusted her hair, which had worked itself loose in all the uproar, and stormed back inside.

I was taken aback by the sight of the woman upstairs, because I had seen her before. Her features, though cruelly altered by the passage of years, were unmistakably those of Feng Yuqing. The shy young girl was now a mother, self-assured and unconstrained.

Lulu, who just a minute ago had been fleeing his mother's onslaught, to my surprise came over to retrieve the shoe and then went upstairs again to return it. He clutched it tightly against his chest, the same way he would hold his satchel, and walked toward his punishment, his little body swaying. Feng Yuqing could be heard yelling, "Get out of my sight!"

He came downstairs with head bowed, looking hard done by. I went over and ruffled his hair, but he brushed aside my gesture of sympathy. With tears in his eyes he stomped off toward a clump of bamboo.

Our friendship quickly blossomed. Two years earlier, I had experienced the warmth of friendship thanks to Su Yu, my senior in years, and now when I was with little Lulu I often felt as though I were Su Yu, gazing at me as I once was.

I enjoyed my talks with Lulu, and even if he didn't fully understand a lot of what I said, the way he looked at me so attentively, his dark eyes gleaming with admiration, made me feel that I enjoyed the complete, unconditional trust of another human being. After I had finished saying something and shot him a smile, Lulu would open a mouth yet to accumulate a full set of teeth and beam at me with equal pleasure, no matter whether he had really taken in what I told him.

Only later did I realize that Lulu in fact had no siblings, but I kept quiet about that so that he would not feel I had noticed his invention. In forlorn, friendless moments, he turned to a fictitious brother for support. I understood how much he needed imagination and hope, for they were equally vital to me.

Just as I had been jealous of Zheng Liang on Su Yu's account, Lulu was jealous of him on mine. In fact, that time when Zheng Liang greeted me in the street he did not look so delighted to see me as to give Lulu much cause for complaint. Never having been more than a casual acquaintance, he simply came over to say a few words of greeting, and now that he had so many new pals his own age he made no effort to conceal his astonishment that I was with such a small boy as Lulu. While we chatted, Lulu was left out in the cold, and he soon announced in a loud voice, "I've got to go."

He went off by himself, obviously nettled. I brought my conversation with Zheng Liang to an abrupt close and caught up with him. But his displeasure continued for at least another twenty yards, for he turned a deaf ear to what I was saying and then delivered a warning in his crisp little voice, "I don't like you talking with him."

Lulu's exclusive and high-handed attitude to friendship threw me off balance any time we ran into Zheng Liang after that, and often I would pretend not to have seen him and hurry off. I did not find this confining, for I knew very well that Zheng Liang and I had no claims on each other; his friends were young factory workers who wore fashionable clothes and had cigarettes dangling from their mouths, talking loudly as they walked down the street. Lulu was my only companion.

Practically every day, when classes finished I would stand outside Lulu's primary school and wait for him to emerge. Despite his tender age, he was perfectly able to keep his feelings in check, and he never seemed overly excited to see me but would greet me with a composed smile. Only on one occasion—when I did not stand in my usual place—did Lulu betray some emotion: a look of anxiety appeared on his face as he came out the gate and failed to see me right away. He stood rooted to the ground, as though transfixed by shock, and with disappointment and uneasiness written all over him he looked around in every direction but toward where I was standing. Even as he dejectedly headed my way, he kept craning his neck to scan the crowd. Finally he saw me watching him with a smile on my face, and he cast restraint to the winds and ran to my side. When he clasped my hand in his, I found that his palm was damp with sweat.

But my friendship with Lulu did not last very long. He was always at odds with other children, and now, for the third time, I saw him in a ferocious fight. As he walked toward me from the school gate, a group of boys were making fun of him. "Lulu, where's your big brother? You don't have a big brother, do you? A big smelly fart is all you have." And they waved their hands in front of their noses, grimacing as though they smelled something nasty. I watched as Lulu, livid, walked toward me, his thin shoulders shaking with rage. He had almost reached me when he suddenly turned around and charged the pack of boys, crying shrilly, "I'm going to teach you!"

He threw himself on them, hands and feet flailing. At first I could see him laying into a couple of boys, but then the others joined in and there was a general melee. When I next saw Lulu, the other boys were no longer beating him. He scrambled to his feet, his face covered in dust, bruises all over, and ran at them again, fists flying, so they all surged around and he became a punching bag once more. Shocked by the sight of Lulu's dirty, blood-streaked face, I rushed forward, giving one boy a good kick in the rear and grabbing another by the collar and pushing him away. These two boys quickly took to their heels when they saw I was getting involved, and the rest soon followed. After running off to a safe distance, they shouted at me indignantly, "What do you think you're doing, hitting us little kids?"

I ignored them and went over to Lulu (on his feet now), heedless of whatever protests other spectators might make, and said to him loudly, "Just tell them *I'm* your big brother."

But Lulu looked so shocked that my feeling of noble munificence was immediately deflated. His face reddened and he went off by himself, head lowered. I watched in confusion as his diminutive figure disappeared into the distance; he never once looked back at me. The following afternoon I waited outside his school entrance for a long time, but he never appeared; he left through a side gate. Later, if I happened to see Lulu, he would nervously avoid me.

So I understood at last that in Lulu's mind his big brother had a very special place. I remembered a story that I had told him, randomly cobbled together by my threadbare imagination, a tale of how Daddy Rabbit battled fearlessly with a wolf in order to protect his son Little Rabbit, but in the end was killed. Lulu listened raptly, and when he later asked me to tell him another story I came out with much the same yarn, but replaced Daddy Rabbit with Mommy Rabbit. Once again he was entranced. Later still I changed the would-be protector to Brother Rabbit, but before I'd finished telling the story, Lulu, knowing that it would end with the brother's destruction, jumped up, tears streaming down his face, and rushed off crying, "I don't want to hear this!"

After I saw Feng Yuqing, I often recalled that time when she clung to Wang Yuejin on the wooden bridge, showing the same stubborn determination that I saw in Lulu when he held that older boy in his viselike grip. In that respect, mother and son had so much in common.

A sizable portion of Feng Yuqing's life—from that moonlit evening when she vanished from Southgate until the day she appeared anew before my eyes—for me will always remain unknown. With Lulu, when I cautiously broached the topic of his father, he would look away and excitedly point out something quite boring, like ants or sparrows. I could not tell whether he truly knew nothing at all or was deliberately evading the issue. In the search for Lulu's father, I could only go back to a distant memory, the middle-aged man with the unfamiliar accent, sitting on the steps outside Feng Yuqing's house.

Later I heard that Feng Yuqing had returned on a concrete boat, along with some peasants from out of town. At dusk one day, carrying a worn old duffel bag in one hand and leading a five-year-old boy with the other, she carefully stepped across the gangplank onto the shore. I imagine that her expression then was as bleak as the darkening sky; heartless fate left her standing awkwardly on the bank, her eyes full of uncertainty.

Feng Yuqing did not go back to Southgate, but settled in town instead. A man of fifty, recently widowed, rented out a couple of rooms to her. The first evening, when he stealthily climbed into her bed, she did not refuse him. At the end of the month, when he asked her for the rent, she replied, "I gave it to you the first night."

That perhaps was the beginning of Feng Yuqing's career in the sex trade. At the same time she took a job cleaning plastic sheeting.

Feng Yuqing had completely forgotten me or, more likely, she had never really registered my existence. One afternoon before Lulu got out of school, I came by the place where they lived to find Feng Yuqing out in the empty lot in front of their house, where several clotheslines hung between the trees. Wearing a plastic apron, she tramped toward the well with a stack of dirty tarps clasped to her chest. When she lowered a wooden bucket into the shaft, it was with none of her old energy, and her hair had been cropped, the long braid that she once had sported now forever a memory left by the well in Southgate. She began to scrub the tarps, and the sun-baked afternoon resounded with the incessant rasp of her brush. Immersed in this mechanical repetition, Feng Yuqing turned a blind eye to me, though I was standing not far away. The difference between a girl and a woman was encapsulated in the contrast between the Feng Yuqing of Southgate days and the Feng Yuqing who made this her living now.

Then she rose and walked toward me, clutching a tarp the size of a bed sheet, and as she approached the clothesline she shook the tarp so brusquely that I was sprayed with water. She seemed to notice, because she shot me a glance just before she tossed it over the line.

In that moment I had a clear view of her face, now ravaged by time, its wrinkles all too apparent. When her glance skimmed over me, it so lacked animation it was like a cloud of soot floating in my direction. Then she turned back toward the well, exposing her sagging buttocks and thickening waistline. At that point I slipped away, saddened not by Feng Yuqing's having forgotten me, but by my first glimpse of beauty's pitiless decline. The Feng Yuqing who stood combing her hair in the sunlight outside her home would, after this, always be blanketed with a layer of dust.

So two different jobs occupied her, one by day and one by night. Her night job made her vulnerable to professional rivalries, and the intervention of the police forced a different kind of life upon her.

By that time I had already left my hometown. Fate had finally smiled on me, and I had gratefully begun a brand-new life in Beijing. At the beginning, I was so enamored of the capital's broad boulevards that when I stood at a crossroads in the evening, the tall buildings on every side made me feel that the intersection was as spacious as a plaza. Like a lost sheep drawn to the green grass on a riverbank, I could hardly tear myself away.

On just such a night, policemen burst through the door of that ramshackle apartment in my hometown, catching Feng Yuqing completely naked, along with an equally naked client of hers. Lulu, who had been sleeping soundly seconds earlier, was woken by the bright lights and loud accusations, and he opened his big dark eyes to look with perplexity at these sudden developments.

After dressing, Feng Yuqing said to her son, "Close your eyes and go to sleep."

So Lulu lay back down and closed his eyes. But he failed to follow his mother's instructions in full, for he did not go back to sleep. He heard all that was said, he heard the steps descending the stairs, and he suddenly became afraid that his mother might not come back.

During the interrogation at the Public Security Bureau, Feng Yuqing, normally so sparing with her words, proved quite eloquent. Calmly she said to them, "The clothes you wear, they're issued by the state, and your paychecks too. So long as you're taking care of state business, you're doing your jobs all right. But my vagina belongs to me—it's not government issue. Who I sleep with is my affair, and I can look after my own vagina perfectly well, thank you very much."

At dawn the following day, when the gatekeeper at the Public Security Bureau opened the gate, he found that he was being watched somberly by a handsome young boy, his hair dampened by the early morning mist. Lulu told him, "I'm here to collect my mom."

Though he claimed to be nine years old, he cannot have been more than seven. Feng Yuqing clearly had been hoping that he could make a contribution to the household income as early as possible, for when he was six she reported his age as eight, so that he could be admitted to primary school. Today he got the idea into his head that he would fetch his mother and take her home.

Before long, he realized that this goal was beyond his reach. He found himself facing no fewer than five police officers, who tried to cajole him into revealing the details of Feng Yuqing's career as a prostitute. Shrewd little Lulu saw through them straight away. "You're trying to fool me by making everything sound so nice. I'll tell you something," the boy said vehemently, "I'm not going to tell you anything!"

Lulu learned that not only would his mother not be coming home, she would be sent to a labor reform camp instead. Tears spilled from his eyes, but he still stayed remarkably calm and protested sharply, "You can't send my mom away."

Then, his tears welling up, he waited for them to ask why not. But none of them did, so he had to explain to them himself. "If you send my mom away, who's going to look after me?"

Lulu used his own abandonment as the ultimate threat; when he was waiting outside the gate he had already seen this as his trump card. He felt sure that in the face of this they would have no choice but to return his mother to him, but of course they did not give a second thought to a threat coming from a little boy like him. His attempt at intimidation did nothing to save his mother, and its only effect was that he was placed in a shelter.

When his mother was sent off to the camp, he was not informed. Practically every day Lulu would go to the Public Security Bureau and demand to see her; he drove them up the wall. Finally they told him: Feng Yuqing was now at the Seven Bridges labor camp, and if he wanted to see her he would have to go to Seven Bridges. He committed this name to memory. At the same time he was so shocked by the news that he just stood there crying. When they tried to usher him off the premises, he said, "Take your hands off me. I'll make my own way out."

As he turned around, he wiped away his tears with both hands, and he sobbed as he went off down the corridor, his shoulder brushing against the wall. Then he realized there was something he had forgotten to say, so he went back inside and told them with withering scorn, "Just wait till I'm grown up, and I'll make sure you all get sent to Seven Bridges!"

Lulu spent only a week at the shelter, in the company of a twenty-year-old blind man, a sixty-year-old alcoholic, and a woman in her fifties. These four misfits lived in a dilapidated courtyard on the west side of town. The alcoholic was always thinking about a woman named Fenfen with whom he slept when he was young, and he'd spend the whole day relating their exploits to the sightless but still vigorous blind man. His account was laced with erotic overtones: according to his description, Fenfen was a real peach. When he talked about how his fingers would caress Fenfen's sleek thighs, he would get quite carried away, unleashing a string of lascivious groans that left the blind man not knowing what to do with himself. Then the alcoholic would ask the blind man, "You've handled flour, right?"

Hearing an answer in the affirmative, the alcoholic elaborated with relish. "Fenfen's thighs were as smooth as flour."

The pale-faced woman had to put up with this kind of thing practically every day, and after protracted exposure to such prattle she developed delusions, becoming convinced that the alcoholic and the blind man were conspiring to do her an injury. When Lulu first arrived, she nervously called him over and pointed at the two men in the next room, whispering, "They want to rape me."

She would go to the hospital every morning, hoping that the doctors would be able to identify her illness so that she could be admitted to the hospital for treatment and escape the violation that was being plotted. But every day she would return despondently to the shelter.

Lulu spent a whole week in this company. Every morning he would go off to school with his satchel on his back, and return at the end of the day all black and blue and caked with dust. His injuries were contracted not from defending his imaginary brother, but because he was standing up for his very much alive mother. He had already decided what he wanted to do, but he did not share his plan with anyone else. In the shelter he learned the location of Seven Bridges by briskly quizzing the woman and the alcoholic. Early one morning he quietly rolled up his sleeping mat, tied it with a piece of string, and hung it on his back, then picked up his satchel and Feng Yuqing's big duffel bag and headed off for the bus station. He was full of confidence about his itinerary. He knew how much the ticket would cost and he knew there was no stop at Seven Bridges. To purchase the ticket, he handed over the five-yuan note that his mother had given him, and then, tightly clutching the remaining three yuan and fifty cents, walked over to a little shop next to the station, intending to buy a Front Gate cigarette to bribe the driver. What he found out was that it cost two cents to buy one cigarette, and only three cents to buy two. My little friend stood there in a quandary. In the end he decided to take out three cents and buy two cigarettes.

That morning on the verge of summer, Lulu sat in the bus heading toward Seven Bridges, holding in his left hand the remaining money, wrapped in a handkerchief, while his right hand gripped the two cigarettes. It was the first time he had ever been on a bus, but he was not in the least thrilled by the novelty of this experience and gazed solemnly out the window. At frequent intervals he checked with the middle-aged woman sitting next to him how far it was to Seven Bridges. Later, when he learned that Seven Bridges was just ahead, he left his seat and moved the duffel bag and bedroll to the doorway. Then he turned to the driver, passed him a cigarette now soaked with perspiration, and pleaded, "Uncle, could you please let me off at Seven Bridges?"

The driver took Lulu's gift, glanced at it, and then tossed the sodden cigarette out the window. Lulu noted the driver's disdainful expression and bowed his head in vexation. He now planned on walking back from the stop following Seven Bridges. But, as it turned out, the driver did stop the bus and let him off at Seven Bridges. It was almost midday now, and Lulu could see a high wall not far away, the barbed-wire netting on top confirming that this was indeed the labor camp. With the bedroll on his back, carrying a duffel bag that was practically his own size, he set off under a blazing sun.

When he got to the front gate, he saw an armed soldier on

guard there. As he walked up to him, he eyed the cigarette in his hand. Mindful of how the driver had thrown his out the window, he dared not try the same thing with this cigarette, so he just smiled bashfully at the young guard and said, "I'm going to stay with my mom." Pointing at the bedroll and the duffel bag, he said, "I brought all our stuff."

It was afternoon by the time Lulu saw his mother. The guard had passed him on to someone else who delivered him eventually to a man with a beard. The bearded man led him to a small room.

That is how Feng Yuqing, dressed in her black prison uniform, saw her battle-scarred son. The realization that her little boy had made his way to see her all by himself brought tears to her eyes.

Despite the rigors of the journey, Lulu, far from being tearful, told her excitedly, "I've quit school. I'm going to study on my own."

Feng Yuqing buried her face in her hands and wept, and this made Lulu cry too. Their meeting was very brief, and within a short time a man came to take her away. Lulu hurriedly picked up the bedroll and the duffel bag, planning to go with his mother. When he found his advance blocked, he cried sharply, "What's wrong?"

The man told him he had to leave. He shook his head emphatically, saying, "No, I'm staying. I want to be with my mom." He cried to her, "Tell him I'm not leaving!"

But when she turned around, it was to tell him he could not stay. He dissolved into a flood of bitter tears, and he wailed to his mother, "I brought the bedroll too, so that I can sleep under your bed. I won't take up any room!"

In the days that followed Lulu began living an outdoor life.

He laid the bedroll out underneath a camphor tree, used the duffel bag as a pillow, and lay there reading his textbooks. If hungry, he would take the money his mother left him and go to the snack shop nearby to have something to eat. Always on the alert, as soon as he heard the thud of well-regulated footsteps he would drop his book and sit up, opening his dark eyes wide. When a line of black-garbed prisoners trotted past, hoes on their shoulders, a head would turn to look at him and Lulu's rapturous gaze would meet his mother's eyes.

Chapter 3

FAR AWAY

It's been said that my grandfather Sun Youyuan was a man in a rage, but you need to bear in mind that it was my father who said that. Sun Kwangtsai was a father skilled in evading responsibility and fond of imposing crude discipline, and when a patchwork of welts began to appear on my skin and he was panting from the effort of laying into me, he would invoke the memory of my grandfather, saying, "If it were my dad, he would have beaten the life out of you ages ago."

My grandfather had passed away by then, and my father (like other people at the time) was in the habit of sticking *tyrant* or other such fearful epithets on the tombstones of the dead, while projecting himself as civilized and cultivated. My father's words must have had a certain effect, for when the pain wore off I could not help feeling some gratitude to him. What he said, after all, indicated that he did place some value on my life.

After I reached adulthood and began to create in my mind a more accurate image of my grandfather, I found it difficult to imagine him as a man in a rage. Perhaps my father was trying to console me by reminding me what hard lessons he had learned in *his* childhood, as though he were saying, "Compared with the beatings I used to receive when I was young, what you're getting doesn't count as much at all." If I could have seen things in that light, then my self-esteem would have survived intact even if my body took a beating. But pain made me lose my wits, and apart from howling like a beast I could think of no other way to react.

In the old days it never ceased to surprise people that my grandfather showed such respect for the woman in his life, but this was his way of expressing—however unconsciously—his gratitude to destiny. My grandmother had been pampered and coddled as a child. At sixteen she was married off, riding a bridal sedan chair and wearing tiny embroidered shoes, but within two years she was forced to leave that grand mansion, slumped drowsily on the back of a pauper. My destitute grandfather led her to a Southgate overgrown with weeds. Her dazzling heritage so overshadowed Sun Youyuan as to make his own life seem dismal and gloomy by comparison.

My grandmother, who died when I was three, maintained habits that were quite out of keeping with my home environment at the time, as a way of demonstrating that the prosperous and respectable life that she had once enjoyed had not entirely disappeared. Despite our poverty we would light a charcoal fire in the cold of winter, and she would spend the whole day huddled beside it, her eyes almost shut, a blank expression on her face. Before she went to bed she would always bathe her feet in hot water, and after a soaking those misshapen little feet of hers would gradually take on a rosy hue, an image that has printed itself indelibly on my memory. Those feet had never stepped into a rice field, even though she had slept with a peasant for over thirty years. Her indolent, aristocratic air somehow succeeded in wafting unimpeded for decades through our tumbledown house. My grandfather, so prone to fly off the handle (according to my father), in my eyes stood humbly, his hands at his side, before Grandmother's foot basin.

On a winter morning when she should have risen from her bed my grandmother failed to wake. She died so unexpectedly, without the slightest warning, that my grandfather was immobilized with grief. If he ran into anybody in the village he would greet them with a timorous smile, as though some kind of family scandal had occurred, rather than his wife passing away.

In my memory the following scene takes shape. My grandfather Sun Youyuan is standing among billowing snowflakes, dressed in a black padded jacket that has no buttons; it is so filthy it has acquired a dull sheen. He is not wearing anything underneath, and has tied the jacket shut with a piece of string; the skin of his chest is exposed to the winter cold. Stooping, both hands in his sleeves, he lets the snow fall and melt on his chest. As he tries to smile, his eyes redden; tears tumble down his face—a vain attempt to communicate his grief to my insensible heart. I faintly recall him saying to me, "Your grandma was ripe for picking."

My grandmother's father must have been the least distinguished rich man of his day. My grandfather, with a poor man's deference, never wavered in his esteem for this father-in-law, whom he had once had the privilege of meeting. In his twilight years, as his teeth dwindled in number, Sun Youyuan would often regale us with accounts of my grandmother's former high station, but it was the sighs of admiration—to us so meaningless—punctuating his reminiscences that made the biggest impression on us.

When I was little I could never understand why Granddad's father-in-law always had to have a ferule in his hand, rather than the string-bound book that I imagined he should have been holding. (Sun Kwangtsai, after all, could impose discipline too—though it was a broom that he clutched in his hand, he was simply using a different instrument for much the same purpose.) This ominous figure applied all the harshness of the old society, using his own pedestrian knowledge to educate his two equally mediocre sons and even, through a wild stretch of imagination, hoping that they would bring honor on their ancestors. Nor did he neglect the upbringing of his daughter, making a ritual out of practically every waking moment of her life. My poor grandmother did not view her submission to him as a surrender of the most basic freedoms, but in a spirit of blind happiness complied strictly with her father's rules on when to get out of bed, when to begin embroidering, what posture to adopt when walking, and so on. Later she inherited her father's prestige during her marriage to my grandfather, and in Sun Youyuan's quaking presence my grandmother savored to the full her own superiority. My grandfather was enveloped all his life by her short-lived wealth and status. The only respect in which she carried herself with modesty was that she always made a point of sitting sideways opposite my grandfather. Her father's admonitions had been so forceful that she continued to be constrained by them long after she had in effect made her escape from his control.

He prided himself on his rigor, and when it came time to select a husband for his daughter his gimlet eyes immediately came to rest on a man much like himself. On the day that Grandma's first husband appeared stiffly before him, his daughter's fate had already been settled. This fellow, who had to think things over carefully before making the simplest remark, from my perspective today seems practically retarded, and compared to my destitute but vigorous grandfather he was a complete nonentity. But he pleased my grandma's father, and his satisfaction in turn directly influenced my grandma, for every time she mentioned him to my granddad a look of admiration would appear on her face. My granddad was a secondary victim, for the reverence with which he hung on her words made this fellow in a long gown become the yardstick by which he measured his own inferiority.

The feebleminded fiancé, dressed in his silk finery, entered self-consciously through Grandmother's vermilion door, his waxed hair combed to perfection. He raised the hem of his gown with his right hand, crossed the courtyard, and walked into the reception room, skirting a large square table to appear in front of Grandma's father. And that was all it took for him to secure approval for the marriage. When Granddad told me all this, I had just turned six and was about to be placed in other people's care, and his account failed to stir very much interest on my part, just a faint degree of surprise. All you had to do was walk through an open door, make a turn, and a bride was yours for the taking. Well, I could do that too, I thought.

The extravagance of my grandmother's wedding was inflated in her imagination after thirty or more years of poverty, and then reported to me through the unreliable medium of my grandfather. So it was that my head resounded with the din of gongs and drums and a particularly loud horn, and in my mind's eye the entourage carrying the trousseau was so long it trailed completely out of view. My grandfather always stressed that the bride was conveyed in a large sedan carried by eight porters, but at six years of age I could hardly have taken in just how magnificent that was. Granddad's description was so vivid that it created a chaotic impression in my mind, and the worst thing was that the sound of the horn, which Granddad imitated most effectively, was as unnerving to me as the howl of a dog in the night.

My grandma was sixteen that year, and her face was like an apple about to fall from the tree, but she applied a thick coating of rouge to it all the same. As she was welcomed in from the sedan chair that afternoon, her face gleamed in the sunlight as brightly as an earthenware pot.

The dourness of the groom took my grandmother by surprise. Throughout the ceremony he wore what he considered to be a sedate smile, a smile so fixed and immobile that it could have been smeared on with paint. This fellow with his artificial grin did not maintain his gentlemanly profile in the latter part of the evening's activities. Once the candles had been lit in the nuptial chamber, the groom proved amazingly deft, and after a moment of shock my grandmother discovered that she was not wearing a stitch of clothing. He wasted no time with preliminaries, but did everything that could be expected of him without a word having passed his lips. When he woke the following morning he found that the bride had disappeared into thin air, and searched around frantically until he finally thought to have a look in the wardrobe. She was crouched there, stark naked, trembling from head to toe.

But he was a decent fellow. That, at least, was my grandma's final appraisal. I find it hard to imagine, but after traumatizing the bride on her wedding night he then delved deeper into his bag of tricks and provided the solace she needed. In the two years that followed, she greeted each night with equanimity and acquitted herself well. My grandfather Sun Youyuan claimed that her first husband was a man who knew how to treat a woman, but I suspect this is an image reconstructed by my grandmother over many years of remembrance. So continually did she harp on the past that no amount of meekness and humility on Sun Youyuan's part could gain much appreciation from her.

In the summer my grandma's mother-in-law sat in the reception room, wearing a black silk dress, fanned by a maid dressed in cotton. She maintained a grave demeanor as she discussed the illnesses that afflicted her. She could not tolerate the slightest moan in the house, not even her own, for she believed such sounds to be just as pernicious as the outbreak of unruly laughter. My grandmother found herself immersed for long stretches of time in her mother-in-law's accounts of her various pains and aches; you can imagine what a joyless atmosphere prevailed. But psychologically my grandmother was not so profoundly affected by the prevailing gloom, for her father had already administered an education that was not all that different in tone. The deadness of family life was relieved only in the evening, when her husband's brief fervor in bed invested the proceedings with a certain animation. But my grandmother felt perfectly at home and took it all in stride, and until she clambered onto my grandfather's back she could barely have imagined that a family might operate any differently. In the same way she had no clue that her face was really very pretty, and it took my grandfather's constant reassurance and earnest compliments to finally convince her of this point, something that her father, husband, and mother-in-law had always kept tightly under wraps.

I cannot shed much more light on my grandmother's life in that household, for their experiences, like they themselves, are long dead and gone. But in the first few years after my grandmother's death, loneliness and sorrow filled Granddad with enthusiasm for her past, and when a light shone in his gray eyes my grandmother came alive again in his retelling of her story.

The turning point in my grandmother's destiny came on a fine, clear morning. She was young and beautiful then, not the wizened old lady I saw later. Although she herself possessed a staidness compatible with the family into which she had married, she was only eighteen, and a young woman who spends her days in a dark mansion is easily drawn to the singing of birds outside. Dressed in a red tunic, with embroidered slippers on her feet, she stood on the stone steps. The early morning sun lit up her healthy complexion, and her delicate hands hung charmingly by her sides. A pair of perky sparrows chirped on a tree in the courtyard and unveiled a little repertoire of actions that she found captivating. In her ignorance, she did not realize that they were engaged in courtship, and was deeply touched by their intimacy and ardor. Her absorption in the wonderful mood of that morning rendered her completely unaware of her mother-in-law's ponderous steps approaching. As the sparrows continued to posture and preen, the unsmiling mother-in-law could not allow her impropriety to continue one minute longer, and frightening words suddenly resounded in my grandmother's ears. The old lady said to her coldly, "Time to go inside."

My grandmother was never to forget the shock she experienced at that moment. When she turned around, it was not just the usual dourness that confronted her; she saw instead, in her mother-in-law's keen and complex gaze, her own uncertain future. She was smart enough to realize immediately that the splendid little show put on by the sparrows must actually be a very shady piece of business. She returned to her room with a premonition that she was now in deep trouble, and her heart thumped in her chest with the awareness that the very course of her life had been thrown into doubt. She listened as her mother-in-law shuffled into another room, and soon other, sprightly footsteps approached, those of a maid. The maid entered the study and summoned her sleepy husband.

A silence ensued, as though nothing whatsoever had happened, but my grandmother's unease expanded by degrees, and with time a certain element of anticipation combined with her misgivings. She suddenly looked forward to the punishment coming sooner rather than later, for suspense could only make her more nervous.

At dinner my grandmother sensed right away that misfortune was about to befall her, for her mother-in-law was unusually nice to her and on occasion became quite red around the eyes, while her husband seemed doleful. Her mother-in-law had her stay behind after the meal and launched into a lengthy disquisition, reviewing their impeccable family history, emphasizing that—whether in terms of scholarship or government service—theirs was a heritage of which their posterity would be proud. What is more, their ancestors had produced a paragon of female chastity, the recipient of an official honor from a Qing emperor who had a soft spot for women. Here she really hit her stride, and waxed so lyrical on this subject that she could hardly drop the topic. In the end, however, she got to the point and told my grandmother she should get her things together. She could hardly have made it more obvious: a bill of divorce was on its way.

For my grandmother it was an unforgettable night. Her remote husband for once expressed affection for her, not by saying anything to her, but (according to what she later told my grandfather) by showering her with caresses—Granddad did not mention tears. It was perhaps on account of this evening that she always remembered him, and so later, as described by my grandfather, this dissolute character took on the virtues of a man who knew how to look after a woman.

My grandmother's mother-in-law lived at the tail end of the old order, and was not as despotic as her progenitors, for she did not tell her son what to do but gave him a choice, even though she knew all along what his choice would be. The next morning my grandmother rose early; her mother-in-law, even earlier. When her husband arrived in the reception room, he resumed his customary aspect, and my grandmother was hard put to find in his expression any trace of the previous night's sorrow. They had breakfast together. What was going through her mind in those moments? Still so young, she felt completely lost. Disaster was about to overtake her, there was no question about that, but before its arrival my grandmother felt dizzy, and everything in front of her swayed in an inchoate blur.

Then all three of them left the house, and my grandmother's mother-in-law, in her black clothes, led them to the highway. She instructed my grandmother to go west, while she for her part headed east. At this time the din of the Japanese war machine was steadily growing closer, and scattered clumps of refugees could be seen moving along the road. The matriarch committed to upholding the family's honor headed off toward the sunrise, while my grandmother set out in the other direction and the sun's first rays illuminated her back. As he had his last glimpse of her receding figure, her husband was stricken with grief, but his decision to follow his mother east was unhesitating.

My grandmother carried a heavy bundle on her back; inside were her clothes and jewelry, as well as some silver dollars. Her face exhibited a ghastly pallor; in the thirty years that followed, it would never again be rosy pink. The morning breeze blew her hair into disarray, but she did not have time to notice this as she was sucked into the flow of refugees. Joining them was perhaps a comfort to her, because it obscured her status as a divorced woman, and the helpless misery on her face could be seen on other faces too. My grandmother was like a leaf swept along in the current; she lumped together her misfortune and the others' exodus. It was unthinkable that she return to her father's home and throwing in her lot with the horde of evacuees took the edge off her agonized consideration of her future.

My grandmother, who had been raised in such a sheltered environment, now found herself on the road during a full-blown war, but the trauma she suffered was quite unrelated to the outbreak of hostilities. Her darkest moment came when she ran into a man identifiable now only as a butcher. My grandmother recognized him as such on the basis of the pork grease and raw stench that his body exuded. In the decades that followed, she would tremble and shake at the smell of uncooked pork. This brute ravished my grandmother as briskly as if he were chopping meat.

In the war-torn twilight my grandmother had unwisely parted from the throng of refugees and gone down to the river to wash her now weather-beaten face. The figures moving along the highway grew sparser, then faded from view altogether while she squatted by the riverside, lost in sentimental musings. She had to face the butcher alone. Beneath the darkening sky she kneeled at his feet, the sound of her entreaties quivering in the evening breeze like her body itself. She opened her bundle, offering its contents to him in exchange for her honor. The butcher gave precisely the kind of boisterous laugh that her mother-in-law abhorred. "Sure, I'll take these things off your hands," he said to her, "but I'm going to fuck you too."

The day my grandmother sat in her sedan chair, soon to become someone's wife, my grandfather, twenty-three-year-old Sun Youyuan, was on his way to a place called Northmarsh Bridge along with his father, the famous Stonemason Sun, and a team of apprentices. They were going to build a large stone bridge with thirty arches. It was a morning in early spring, and my great-grandfather had rented a wooden boat to carry him and his assistants down the broad river. He sat at the stern, smoking a pipe and watching his son with a twinkle in his eye. Sun Youyuan stood at the prow, his jacket open, his chest flushed red in the cold breeze. The bow gently rose and fell, cleaving the river like a knife and propelling the water into rapid retreat.

That winter an official in the Republican government had announced his intention to return home and visit his family. Years ago, after setting fire to the house of some moneybags, he had swum across this wide river when fleeing the area, and had later gone on to make his fortune. Now, as he prepared to go home in a blaze of glory, the county administrator could not possibly expect him to swim across the river one more time. So some Republican silver dollars were transferred to the hands of my great-grandfather. He knew it was an important assignment and enjoined his subordinates: "This time it's a government bridge we're building, so I'm expecting your best effort."

They arrived at their destination, which despite its name had no bridge at all. My great-grandfather was in his fifties then, a man with a lean build and a loud voice. He walked back and forth along the riverside, beginning the job in a seemingly offhand manner; close behind him walked my energetic grandfather. As he surveyed the local topography, my great-grandfather constantly looked back and—just as my great-grandmother might yell at chickens in her yard—barked out instructions to his apprentices. From time to time my grandfather would pick up a handful of soil and squeeze it between his fingers or test it with his tongue. After they had finished assessing the lay of the land on both banks and drawing up plans, Great-grandfather told the apprentices to put up a construction shed and start extracting stone, while he and my grandfather slung tools and provisions over their backs and headed into the hills.

Their mission was to extract the dragon-gate stone. These two ancestors of mine scurried across the slopes like feral cats, tapping away with their hammers and for three whole months giving the hills no rest. In those days, a stonemason's skill found its fullest expression in the dragon-gate stone, the keystone that at the culmination of the whole project was placed at the very center of a bridge, joining the two sides; it could not afford to be one inch too big or one inch too small.

My great-grandfather was the smartest pauper of his age; compared to my grandmother's father, he was dynamic and accomplished. He had spent his life roaming far and wide; he possessed both an artist's free spirit and a peasant's stolidity. My grandfather, whom he had sired and reared, was a remarkable man in his own way. The two of them extracted from the hills a square dragon-gate stone, and on its facade they carved a relief of twin dragons vying for a pearl; two stone dragons, their bodies writhing in the air, fought fiercely for the spherical stone pearl in the center. They were not the kind of masons content simply to lay a slab across a ditch; the bridge they were about to construct would be so exquisite that it would lord itself over their posterity.

After three months of work, having quarried all the stone required, the apprentices went into the hills to fetch my two ancestors. On a sweltering summer day my great-grandfather sat erect on the dragon-gate stone as the eight apprentices lugged it down from the hills on their shoulders. He was naked to the waist, puffing away at his pipe, contentment apparent in his squinting eyes, but he was not in the least triumphant, for this was all perfectly routine as far as he was concerned. My ruddy-faced grandfather Sun Youyuan marched steadily alongside, crying every few paces, "Here comes the dragon-gate stone!"

But this was not the most stirring moment. That came later, well into the autumn of that year, when the day finally came to close the gap in the middle of the bridge. Decorated archways were set up at the two ends, their colored bunting flapping in the wind like tree leaves; there were deafening peals of music and clouds of incense; a noisy hubbub rose from the ranks of country folk who had flocked to the scene from many miles around. Not a single sparrow was to be seen, the frightening din having driven them all to seek anxious refuge on trees far away. It has always surprised me that Sun Youyuan, having witnessed this splendid scene, could in his final years be so awed by my grandmother's wedding. Compared with this, her wedding was a nonevent.

It would never have occurred to my great-grandfather that his career would take a nosedive at this particular juncture. He had always been able to depend on his wits and his skills as he made his way in the world, but here in Northmarsh Bridge he came upon a cropper. He had in fact noticed that the soil was porous and that the bridge was subsiding. But he was a bit too confident, a bit too fixed in his judgment, thinking on the basis of past experience that some settling was inevitable. However, as the completion date grew closer, the rate of subsidence increased. By overlooking that point, my great-grandfather condemned himself to a miserable old age.

Although it was to end a fiasco, the sight of the eight apprentices carrying the dragon-gate stone onto the bridge was inspiring at the time. They marched proudly up to the apex and their work song died away. As they carefully lowered the dragon-gate stone toward the breach, the music hushed and the spectators went completely quiet. That was when my great-grandfather heard a grating scrape rather than the resounding clunk that he had anticipated, and knew, sooner than anybody else present, that disaster had struck. He had been watching from the decorated arch, and the unanticipated crisis left a smile frozen on his face. When that awful jarring noise reached his ears, he sprang to his feet, like a fish about to go bottom up—as my grandfather was later to tell us—with the whites of the eyes exposed. But he was after all a veteran of many adventures, and before the crowd had cottoned on to just what was amiss he had already come down from the decorated arch and walked away with his pipe pressed against his back, as though he was heading off to a tavern. He made straight for the hills, leaving his son and the team of apprentices to shoulder the disgrace.

The dragon-gate stone was tightly wedged inside the breach, and though the eight burly youths turned red in the face in their efforts to raise it out of its awkward position, it remained lodged there, immobile. As a wave of hisses swept over them, their eight faces shone like pig livers in the scorching sun. The dragon-gate stone lay tilted like a seesaw, unadjustable, unremovable.

I don't know how Sun Youyuan managed to get through that terrible afternoon. By making his getaway as he did, my great-grandfather came across too much like a petty thief. Sun Youyuan had to bear a double shame: while just as disconsolate as the apprentices, he also suffered the ignominy of being my great-grandfather's son. It was a complete disaster—just as bad, my grandfather told us, as if a house had collapsed on top of their heads. He was in all the worse a situation because he happened to be one of the eight porters. He gripped the balustrade but found himself unable to take a single step forward, as drained of strength as though someone had squeezed him in the crotch.

It was after dark when my great-grandfather returned. Although he had been too mortified to face the local spectators earlier in the day, he still managed to project a superior air in front of his son and the apprentices. The old man, masking his inner turmoil, lectured his dispirited audience in a rasping voice. "Don't pull such long faces. I'm not dead yet. A new start can be made. I remember how things were when I started out . . ."

In expansive, inspiring tones he reviewed his stirring past and painted for his disciples an even more splendid future. Then all of a sudden he announced, "We're disbanding."

He turned on his heel and strode away as the apprentices stared and gaped in shock. But when he reached the entrance to the construction shed, my great-grandfather, who was so fond of taking people by surprise, spun around and issued a piece of confident advice. "Remember your master's words: so long as you've got money in your pocket, you won't have to sleep in an empty bed."

In that bygone era, the old man found it very easy to impress himself. When he decided to leave that very night for the county seat so that he could present his apology to the local administrator, he felt that he was displaying an integrity worthy of legendary heroes, and when he told my grandfather that a man has to take responsibility for his actions the tremor in his voice came entirely from his own sense of exaltation. Seeing his father transported by the ambition to convert failure into glory, Sun Youyuan himself felt a foolish surge of pride.

But my great-grandfather's morale slumped after he had taken only a few steps, for he made the mistake of looking back at the stone bridge. He could not help himself, because the upturned dragon-gate stone glinted in the moonlight, like a wild dog baring its fangs in a bad dream. As my granddad watched, the old man's silhouette seemed to tremble and totter. Under a chilly moon my great-grandfather began his wearisome trek down that little country road, assailed by a persistent sense of failure. Far from marching gallantly into the county jail, as Sun Youyuan claimed was the case when he related this episode to us later, he looked even more feeble than a sick man trundled into the hospital at death's door.

For a long time Sun Youyuan was inspired by his father's heroic spirit, despite its fraudulence. He did not change his profession as his father had urged, and after a number of apprentices had packed up their belongings and left for home, he and the seven other bearers of the dragon-gate stone stayed on. Sun Youyuan vowed to salvage the stone bridge, and after his father's departure he applied his own acumen to telling effect. First he led the seven apprentices out and directed them to dig sixteen holes underneath the arch, and then he had them cut sixteen wooden stakes. After inserting the stakes into the shafts, the eight young men swung sixteen hammers and struck the stakes in a ferocious frenzy. Bystanders may well have thought they were lunatics, for they banged away there for a full four hours. In deference to their puny but strenuous efforts, the huge bridge ever so slightly rose, and eventually my grandfather heard an encouraging scrape, followed by a thunderous boom, and he had achieved his goal. The dragon-gate stone now snugly and securely filled the breach.

My grandfather was so elated that he bounded down the road, tears streaming down his face, calling my great-grandfather at the top of his lungs. He ran a full fifteen miles in one go, all the way to the county town. When my great-grandfather emerged befuddled from jail, he saw his son soaked from head to toe as if he had spent the whole night in the rain, though there was a baking sun in a clear blue sky. My grandfather had expended practically all his bodily fluids in making his dash, and he was able just to call "Dad . . ." before he collapsed to the ground with a thump.

My great-grandfather bore the imprint of his era's frailty, and even though he could draw comfort from his son's redemption of the Northmarsh Bridge debacle he found it impossible thereafter to recover his former vigor. With the ponderous steps of an old peasant, my demoralized great-grandfather plodded toward my great-grandmother, who when young had been quite a beauty. In their twilight years these two old folks began, for the first time in their lives, to spend day after day in each other's company.

Meanwhile my grandfather, the proud and self-assured Sun Youyuan, led a team of masons just like his father before him, and carried on the business established by his forebears. But his glory days were fleeting; as the last generation of traditional stonemasons, they encountered only indifference from the age in which they lived. Besides, many stone arched bridges already spanned the rivers in the surrounding area, and given their predecessors' skilled craftsmanship it was too much to expect that all these structures would simply give way overnight. Sun Youyuan's hungry crew traversed the waterlands of Jiangnan, clinging to their naive hopes. The only opportunity that came their way allowed them to construct a small stone-paved bridge—a crooked bridge, at that. But it gave Sun Youyuan the chance to observe his future father-in-law's scholarly bearing.

A group of peasants had pooled together funds to engage their services, and my grandfather by now was too hard up to be picky. At one time the Suns had specialized in arched bridges of impressive scale, but things had now reached such a parlous state that Sun Youyuan readily accepted the commission to build a little slab bridge. They selected a place where two highways intersected as the best site to build the foundation, but a large camphor tree on the other bank hampered construction at one end. My grandfather waved his arm and told them to cut the tree down, not knowing that its owner was the father of his wife-to-be.

Liu Xinzhi was known near and far as a man of property; he was to go through his whole life not knowing that his ultimate son-in-law was a pauper. A licentiate under the imperial examination system, he was much given to pontificating about the scholar's obligation to be first to worry about the world's problems and last to enjoy the world's pleasures. But when he heard that there was a plan afoot to fell his family's camphor tree, he was just as incensed as if they were proposing to dig up the ancestral tombs. Oblivious of his reputation for profound learning, he unleashed a string of barnyard curses at the people who had come to consult him.

Sun Youyuan, his hands tied, had no choice but to build the foundation at a slight angle to the line of the bridge, and after three months the crooked bridge was completed. Now that the job was finished, the sponsors invited Liu Xinzhi, Old Master Liu, to bestow a name upon it.

That was the morning that my grandfather saw his father-in-law. He watched with awe as Liu Xinzhi emerged, dressed in silk, and walked at a snail's pace toward him. Somehow this pretentious licentiate appeared even more imposing to Sun Youyuan's eyes than an official in the Republican administration. Years later, as my grandmother's bed partner, he looked back on the scene that day, recalling how the decadent Liu Xinzhi still managed to impress him in his robust youth.

My grandmother's father maintained a scholarly posture all the way to the bridge, but once he got there he promptly announced that it was beneath his notice, saying sharply, as though he had been insulted, "Such a lousy crooked bridge, and you ask me to think of a name for it!" And he went off in a huff.

My grandfather carried on crisscrossing the country north and south. He and his team trudged long distances amid the gunfire of Nationalists and Communists, through scenes of famine; in such times as these, who would think of raising money to have them demonstrate their skills? Like a band of beggars, they tried to drum up business everywhere they went. My grandfather was stirred by an ambition to build bridges, but he lived at the wrong time, in an era infatuated with destruction. In the end his motley crew had little choice but to compromise their initial innocence and take on any work available, even cleaning corpses and digging graves, for only by such means could they ensure that they themselves did not die by the roadside. In that dire hour, Sun Youyuan somehow managed to induce them to follow him on his aimless and futile travels; I have no idea what kind of blandishments he used to persuade them. Finally one night, mistaken for Communist guerrillas, they were fired upon by Nationalist troops, and these stonemasons, so steeped in out-of-date ideals, were forced to go their separate ways, alive or dead.

At that time my grandfather and his band of paupers were sleeping on a riverbank. After the first wave of shots rang out, Sun Youyuan was unscathed, and he propped himself up and yelled, "What do you think you are doing, letting off firecrackers?" Then he saw that the face of an apprentice next to him had been shot to pieces, reduced in the moonlight to a gruesome mess, like an egg that has been smashed on the ground. My bleary-eyed grandfather took to his heels and ran, yelling and screaming as he tore along the bank. But he soon hushed when a bullet whistled through the crotch of his pants. "Damn it," he thought, "my balls have been blown away!" He continued to run for his life all the same. When he had run a good ten miles, he felt that his crotch was completely soaked through. It didn't occur to him that it could be drenched with sweat and he felt sure that he was losing all his blood, so he came to a stop and reached in a hand to press down on the wound. In so doing, he brushed against his testicles. At first he was startled, thinking, "What the hell is this?" But more careful examination confirmed that the family jewels were intact and unharmed. Later he sat down under a tree, toying with his sweaty testicles for a good long time and chuckling away. Only when he was absolutely sure of his own safety did he give any thought to the band of apprentices on the riverbank. The memory of the youngster's shattered face reduced him to tears and wails.

For Sun Youyuan to try to keep the family business afloat was clearly no longer an option. At the age of twenty-five, he felt the same bleak hopelessness that had beset his father on his retirement. As Spring Festival approached, wearing the careworn expression of an old man, my young grandfather stepped onto a dust-blown highway and set off for home.

My great-grandfather had fallen seriously ill after he

returned home the previous year, and though my great-grandmother spent all their savings she was unable to return him to his former vigor and had to pawn everything of value in the house. Eventually she found herself bedridden too. On the last day of the year, when my grandfather returned home ragged and penniless, his father had already breathed his last, and his mother lay sprawled next to his lifeless body, on the verge of death. Racked by illness as she was, she could greet her son's return only with a rasping, hurried breath. My grandfather had brought poverty back to a poverty-stricken home.

This was the darkest hour in my grandfather's early years. By now there was nothing left in the house worth pawning and during the holiday season no way to sell his labor to earn rice and firewood. At his wits' end, braving a piercing wind, he ran toward town on the morning of the Chinese New Year, his father's body over his shoulder. He had come up with the idea of leaving his dead parent at the pawnshop, and as he ran he constantly apologized to the corpse on his shoulders, at the same time racking his brains to think of an excuse that would make him feel better. My great-grandfather's body had lain frozen for two days and two nights in the drafty thatched cottage, and was then carried by my grandfather for ten miles through the howling north wind. When he set it down on the counter of the pawnshop in town, it was as stiff as a board.

Tears welling up in his eyes, my grandfather threw himself on the mercy of the pawnshop proprietor, explaining that it wasn't that he was an unfilial son, but there was simply no other recourse open to him. He told the pawnbroker, "My dad is dead, and I have no money for his burial; my mom is alive, but ill in bed at home with no money for treatment. Do a good deed, will you? I'll redeem my dad in a few days' time."

The pawnbroker was an old man in his sixties; he had never in his life heard of using a corpse as collateral. Covering his nose with his hand, he waved him away. "No, that won't do, I'm afraid. We don't accept gold bodhisattvas here." On the first day of the New Year he wished to strike a propitious note, and so he elevated Great-grandfather to the rank of a priceless treasure.

But my grandfather, refusing to take no for an answer, persisted with his entreaties, and so three clerks came forward and shoved my great-grandfather down off the counter. He fell as rigid as a flagstone, hitting the ground with a resounding thud. Sun Youyuan hastened to pick his father up and inspected him fearfully to see if any damage had been done. A spray of cold water then descended on his head, for without waiting for him to leave the shop the clerks had begun to clean the counter soiled by the unwanted pledge. This incensed Sun Youyuan, who swung a heavy fist in the face of one, knocking him to the ground with the force of a pellet hurled from a slingshot. My grandfather used his enormous strength to overturn the counter, but when several more clerks descended on him, cudgels flying, the only thing he could think of was to raise his father's corpse aloft, to ward off their blows and take the battle to them. In that chilly morning he brandished the rock-hard carcass and turned the pawnshop upside down. Brave Sun Youyuan gained strong support from his father's cadaver, beating the clerks till they did not know what to do. None of them dared to touch the corpse for fear of incurring a whole year's worth of bad luck, and the superstitions of the day, combined with Sun Youyuan's audacity, ensured that he encountered practically no resistance. But when my grandfather swung his father around and lashed out at the ashen-faced proprietor, it was Sun Youyuan's turn to be horrified, for in so doing he knocked his father's head against a chair. An awful noise awoke him to the realization that he had committed a monstrous sin, using his father's remains as a combat weapon. His father's head had been knocked askew, and after a moment of shock my grandfather hoisted him onto his shoulder, dashed outside, and set off at a run through the icy wind. In the end he did, like a proper son, weep bitter tears—he was sitting under a winter elm then, cradling my damaged ancestor. It took a great deal of effort to twist his father's head back into its original position.

Sun Youyuan buried his father, but he had not buried poverty, and in the days that followed he could only dig up some herbs and boil them in a broth for his mother to drink. These were little pink and green plants that grew at the foot of the wall—motherwort, though Sun Youyuan did not know that. He was overjoyed to find that his ailing mother, after drinking the broth, was able to get out of bed and walk around. My slapdash grandfather found this a revelation, thinking naively that he now understood the true state of affairs, that those miracle-working physicians actually had no special skill at all, that there was nothing more to it than harvesting a pile of herbs and medicating a patient the same way you would feed a sheep. So he abandoned the idea of going to town to work as a laborer, and after being a mason all his life he decided he would now devote himself to health care.

Sun Youyuan was excited about the prospect. He knew that when starting out one needed to make house calls and interview patients; once his reputation was established he could sit at home and have the afflicted come to him for treatment. He threw a basket of herbs on his back and began an itinerant life, going from door to door, yelling like a rubbish collector in that ringing voice of his, "I'll swap my cures for your diseases."

His innovative sales pitch attracted much interest, but his ragtag appearance left people unsure how seriously to take him. In the end a family engaged his services; the first (and last) patient of my grandfather's career was a boy with acute diarrhea. Sun Youyuan took a casual look at the ailing child, and without bothering to take his pulse or ascertain his symptoms he reached into his basket for a handful of herbs, which he handed to the boy's father with instructions to cook them into a soup. While the family eyed the herbs doubtfully, Sun Youyuan made a quick exit, picking up his refrain, "I'll swap my cures for your diseases."

When the boy's father followed him out of the house, quizzing him in earnest perplexity, it astonishes me that Sun Youyuan still managed to tell him with supreme self-confidence, "That's right: he takes my medicine and I take his illness away."

No sooner had the poor boy drunk the herb soup than he vomited and excreted copious amounts of green fluid, and within two days he had breathed his last. The result was that one afternoon my great-grandmother was treated to the alarming sight of a dozen men rushing furiously toward her house.

My grandfather maintained his composure. He told his frightened mother to go back into her room and closed the door behind her, and then he went out to meet the visitors with a welcoming smile on his face. The father and other relatives of the deceased child had come to make Sun Youyuan pay with his life. Though confronted by their livid and intransigent faces, Sun Youyuan still tried to disarm them with specious platitudes. They were in no mood to listen to his rambling and ridiculous speech and closed ranks tightly around him, with several shiny hoes aimed at his shiny shaved head. Having survived a hail of Nationalist bullets, Sun Youyuan was unperturbed, and he informed them complacently that he didn't care if there were a dozen of them—even if there were twice that number, he would still beat them till they were covered all over with bruises. For Sun Youyuan to make such exaggerated claims when he was staring death in the face left them quite dazed. My grandfather untied the buttons of his jacket and said, "Let me just take this off, and then we can get on with it."

So saying, Sun Youyuan thrust a hoe aside, walked back up to the house, pushed the door open, and coolly kicked it shut. After that, no further sound was heard from him; the avengers outside were rolling up their sleeves, unaware that my grandfather had already jumped out the back window and fled, and they continued to stand there, gearing up to do battle with their terrible foe. Only after waiting a while longer with no sign of Sun Youyuan did they sense that something had gone awry, and kicking the door open they found the house completely deserted. Then they saw my grandfather, with his mother on his back, fleeing down the road and already well off in the distance. My grandfather was no country bumpkin, after all; his improvised escape shows that he was more than just dauntless, he could be wily too.

It was not so difficult for Sun Youyuan to sling my great-grandmother over his back and take to his heels, but now that he had started running, it was not so easy to stop. He mingled with the streams of refugees just as my grandmother had done, and on several occasions he clearly heard the sound of Japanese guns at his back. Being the devoted son that his era expected him to be, he could not bear to see my great-grandmother lurching down the road in her bound feet, so he carried her on his back the whole way, sweat pouring down his face, panting for breath, following the refugees as they fled helter-skelter along dust-swirled roads.

His only respite came one evening when, reduced to a state of near-total exhaustion, he detached himself from the throng, set my great-grandmother down under a withered tree, and went off in search of water. Successive days of arduous travel had so worn out my feeble great-grandmother that she fell into a heavy sleep as soon as she lay down, and on that chilly moonlit night she was savaged by a wild dog. As a child, I found it hard to get my mind off this nightmarish scene: somebody falls asleep, and then—a bit here, a piece there—they are devoured by a wild dog; I could not imagine anything more gruesome than that. By the time my grandfather returned to the tree, my great-grandmother had been horribly mangled. The wild dog stuck out its long tongue and licked its nose, staring at my grandfather ferociously. His mother's shocking appearance made Sun Youyuan howl like a lunatic. He forgot for a moment that he was human, and he bared his teeth just like the wild dog and made a lunge toward it. It was my grandfather's roar that frightened the animal most, and it turned tail and fled. Sun Youyuan, in a towering rage, set off in pursuit, but the curses he rained down on the vile creature must have slowed his pace. Eventually, when the dog had completely disappeared from view, my grandfather returned to his mother's remains, rattled and tearful. He knelt at her side and punched himself viciously in the face, his piercing wails filling the night with gloom and dread.

After burying his mother, Sun Youyuan found his confidence at a historic low. Sick at heart, he randomly followed the swarms of refugees, though his mother's death had rendered his flight suddenly meaningless. That's why when my grandfather first saw my grandmother by a tumbledown wall a brook babbled in his heart. By this time all traces of my grandmother's lofty pedigree had been erased; she sat bedraggled on a bank of wild grass and saw my grandfather's haggard face with blurry eyes, through disheveled hair. Reduced by hunger to utter debility, before long she slumped on my grandfather's back and fell asleep. Young Sun Youyuan thus acquired a wife and brought to an end his life as an aimless vagabond. So long a victim of poverty and undernourishment, Sun Youyuan now strode forward with my grandmother on his back, his face glowing with hope.

IN THE FLICKERING LIGHT

After Grandfather sprained his back, an uncle suddenly impinged on my consciousness. An utter stranger to me, he apparently lived in a small market town and did a job that involved people opening their mouths and his reaching in and pulling out their teeth. According to reports, he shared a street corner with a butcher and a cobbler. My uncle inherited the medical career that my grandfather had once pursued in such absurd fashion, but he was able to sustain it indefinitely, which shows that his medical technique differed from my grandfather's utter hogwash. By the side of a noisy street he opened his broad oilcloth umbrella and sat down underneath it, as though he were out fishing. As soon as he donned his white gown with its motley collection of dirty blotches, he could claim to be a medical specialist. The small table in front of him was piled with several pairs of rusty pliers and several dozen bloodstained teeth. These pulled teeth served effectively as a vehicle for self-promotion, advertising the high sophistication of his dental arts and drumming up business from customers with loose teeth.

When Granddad walked past us one morning without a word, a blue bundle over his back and a shabby umbrella in his hand, my big brother and I were taken aback. He said nothing to my parents as he left, and they gave no sign that there was anything unusual about his departure. My brother and I leaned up against the back windowsill, watching him shuffle off. It was Mother who told us, "He's gone to see your uncle."

In his final years my grandfather's plight was like that of a rickety old chair that is abandoned and can only wait quietly for the advent of the fire that will consume it. On the day Granddad came to grief my brother Sun Guangping had been given a satchel, an accessory that, owing to the fact he was older than me, he received well before I did. That moment still glimmers in my childhood memory. Late one afternoon, on the eve of the start of the school year, my father Sun Kwangtsai sat on the doorsill, puffed up with unjustified pride, loudly instructing my older brother what to do if the kids in town got into an argument with him: "If there's just one of them, hit him; if there's two, scoot back home."

Sun Guangping, then eight years old, gazed at Sun Kwangtsai with a look of mindless awe; it was during these years that he most idolized his father. His deferential expression inspired my father to patiently explain the reasoning behind this injunction, unconscious of what nonsense he was talking.

For a clodhopper, my father was very smart, and quick to pick up whatever fashion was in vogue. The first time my brother headed off for school with his satchel on his back, Sun Kwangtsai stood at the entrance to the village and issued a final reminder. It was comical to see a grown man like him imitate the tone of a bad guy in a movie. "Password?" he barked out.

My older brother had a natural gift for putting things in a nutshell. When he turned around to deliver his response, he did not repeat his father's fussy and complicated instructions but called simply, "Beat one, flee two."

In the midst of that gleeful exchange my aging grandfather slipped past silently, holding a length of cord: he was going up the hill to collect firewood. Seen from behind, he looked so tall and strong. I was sitting on the ground, and his forceful steps sprinkled dust over my face, blurring the jealousy I felt toward my brother and the unthinking excitement of the moment.

My grandfather's misadventure was intertwined with my big brother's jubilation. At that stage, more than twenty years ago, my younger brother and I were still happy just to forage for snails at the edge of the pond. But Sun Guangping, on his first day back from school, was all set to show off what he had learned. I'll never forget how he swaggered home with his satchel over his shoulder, then swung the satchel around so that it hung over his chest and put his hands behind his back. The latter gesture clearly was designed as an imitation of his teacher. He sat down next to the pond and pulled his textbook out, first letting the sunlight catch it, then reading it with great concentration. My little brother and I watched dumbfounded, the way two hungry dogs, their stomachs rumbling, might watch a bone flying through the air.

It was at this precise moment that Sun Kwangtsai came lumbering up, with an ashen Sun Youyuan on his back. My father was fuming. He set Sun Youyuan down inside on his bed, and as soon as he came out of the house he started muttering, "It's just what I was afraid of, that somebody would get sick. Now we're really screwed! One more mouth to feed and one less pair of hands at work—that's twice we lose out."

After taking that tumble on the hill my grandfather was laid up in bed for a whole month, and though later he was able to get up and walk about, his back was so stiff that full movement was beyond him. Having lost the capacity to engage in labor, he would greet the villagers with a smile even more timid than the one he wore when my grandmother died. I can still picture the tremulous look on his face as he told them, "I can't bend down."

One could hear self-recrimination in his voice, as well as an eagerness to justify himself. His fate was forever altered by this sudden handicap, and he began a life of dependency. In the few months leading up to my departure from Southgate, the old man, once so hale and hearty, rapidly grew sallow and emaciated, as though a makeup department had been working on him. It was clear that he had become an encumbrance, and thus was inaugurated the arrangement whereby his sons took turns looking after him, and I finally learned that I had an uncle. After a full month at our house, Granddad would set off along the dirt track into town. He needed to take a boat from there, I believe, to reach the place where my uncle lived. A month later, right around dusk, his figure would shamble into sight again in the distance, on that same road.

At such moments, my big brother and I would race exuberantly toward him. Our little brother could only stand at the edge of the village and watch us as we ran, a smile of vicarious excitement on his face. Sun Youyuan's eyes would brim with tears, and his hands would tremble as he ruffled our hair. In reality, our mad dash was inspired by sibling rivalry, not by any great delight at Granddad's return. The umbrella in his hand and the bundle on his back were what triggered our enthusiasm: whoever was first to grab the umbrella was the undisputed champion. Once, I remember, my brother seized the bundle as well as the umbrella, and then marched along on Granddad's right, proud as a peacock. I, on the other hand, was heartbroken to be completely empty-handed. On the short walk home I kept complaining to Granddad about how unreasonable my brother was. "He's got the bundle too!" I sobbed, "He took the umbrella, and then he took the bundle!"

Granddad did not correct this injustice, as I had hoped. His misunderstanding of our motives brought tears to his eyes, and I can still remember how he wiped them away with the back of his hand. My little brother, then four, was always on the lookout for ways of turning things to his advantage, and seeing Granddad so tearful he ran home as fast as he could, shrilly announcing to our parents: "Granddad's crying." Though he, like me, came back empty-handed, he had found something to make up for it.

Given my tender age before I left home, I could not possibly feel the extent of the humiliation Granddad suffered. But now that I think about it, my father was always in a foul mood during the month that Granddad was with us. In our cramped little house he would often howl as loud as a winter gale. If he pointed at Sun Youyuan and cursed him by name, then I would be in no doubt that Granddad was bearing the brunt of his rage, but at other times I would watch my father warily in case he was suddenly to aim a kick at me. When I was young my father was an unpredictable fellow.

During his time at our house my grandfather was so self-effacing that he practically disappeared. He would sit for a long time in an inconspicuous corner, silently idling away what little life he had left. But when meals were served he would appear on the scene as quick as lightning, often startling us three boys. My little brother then had an opportunity to show off, putting his hand to his chest and looking agitated, so as to underscore what a fright he'd been given.

Examples of Granddad's spinelessness remain etched on my mind. On one occasion when Sun Guangming went looking for him, my little brother—still unsteady on his feet—fell down and started wailing. Not only that—he started cursing too, as if he had somehow been tripped. Not yet able to enunciate very well, he did his best to swear with great conviction, though it all sounded like a puppy's yapping to me. Granddad, however, was so anxious that his face went pale, fearful that Sun Guangming would carry on crying right until my father came back from the fields at the end of the day, and knowing that Sun Kwangtsai would never pass up an opportunity to fly into a rage. One could see in Sun Youyuan's eyes a dread that disaster was about to strike.

After his accident Sun Youyuan seldom mentioned our grandmother, talk of whom made us uncomfortable. Instead he became accustomed to recalling for himself the days that he spent with her. He, after all, was the only member of the family who would have been able to savor the memories of their lives together.

When Sun Youyuan sat in a bamboo chair recalling his pretty young bride (once so well-to-do), his pallid face seemed all the more expressive, for its creases and furrows would start to undulate. I would often sneak a glance at the smiles that fluttered over his face like grasses in a breeze, smiles that strike me as poignant when I think about them now. But for me at the age I was then, I was simply astonished that someone could smile all by himself. When I shared this discovery with my big brother, who was down by the riverside catching shrimp, he ran home at a speed faster than I could manage, his excitement proving how right I was to be amazed. When we two grimy little boys arrived by Granddad's side, a smile was still playing delicately on his face. My brother acted with a boldness that was almost beyond my imagination, and his loud cries of protest jerked my grandfather out of his reveries. Granddad quivered from head to toe, as though struck by lightning; his mysterious smile vanished and his eyes filled with apprehension. My brother, still so immature, assumed a mantle of severity as he scolded Granddad: "How can you smile when you're on your own? Only loonies do that." Then he waved his hand dismissively: "In the future, you're not to smile by yourself, is that understood?"

Granddad, now clear on this point, gave a humble and deferential nod.

In his final years Sun Youyuan tried to get on the right side of everyone in the family, but given that he was our senior, his self-abasement could hardly win our respect. For a time I was pulled in two directions. On the one hand, I urged myself to follow Sun Guangping's example and throw my weight around with Granddad. For a child to issue orders to an adult, after all, is stirring stuff. But at the same time I was swayed by Granddad's kindly gaze, and when we exchanged glances, the warmth in his eyes made it impossible for me to flaunt some spurious authority. I could only leave the room in low spirits and go off in search of Sun Guangping, whose feistiness I admired.

After Granddad framed my little brother—and so cold-bloodedly, too—I abandoned altogether any idea I might have had of bullying Granddad. From that time on my grandfather was for me a sinister, forbidding presence.

It all stemmed from a simple accident. As my grandfather rose from his corner one day, he happened to give the table a jolt and a bowl was knocked to the floor. I was close enough to see how Granddad froze in horror. He stood with his back to me, staring at the shards of china that now lay scattered at his feet. When I try now to recall the image of him standing there, I see only a hazy shadow. But I do remember that he came out with a long string of shocked whispers; never since have I heard anybody talk as rapidly as he did then.

Sun Youyuan did not clear away the broken pieces as I was expecting him to do. By now I was six, an age when I could dimly sense that something awful was going to happen, something involving my father, who was due to come home any minute. I had no idea how fearsome he would be when he lost his temper this time, but I knew that to a man as strong as him, shaking a fist was as easy and natural as it was for my mother to shake out her scarf. I stood there as Granddad sat down again in his corner, seemingly unperturbed, having made no effort to conceal the damage. His calm demeanor only intensified my unease. My young eyes veered uncertainly between the shattered bowl and my grandfather's face, and then I fled in alarm, as though I had stumbled on a snake.

As I had feared, Sun Kwangtsai was driven to new heights of manic anger by the loss of the bowl. Perhaps he was secretly hoping that Granddad was indeed the culprit, so as to justify the abuse he was always tempted to heap on him. His face flushed, Sun Kwangtsai shouted and screamed tirelessly like a child. His anger caught us three boys in its slipstream, reducing us to shivers as though we were being buffeted by a gale. When I glanced timidly at Sun Youyuan, he shocked me by standing up and meekly telling my father, "Sun Guangming broke it."

My little brother, fidgeting at my side, did not take this in at all. There was alarm on his face, to be sure, but that came from Sun Kwangtsai's menacing expression. When my father, now boiling with rage, asked him, "Did you do it?" my little brother was scared speechless, and it was not until Sun Kwangtsai roared out this question a second time, pressing toward him threateningly, that I finally heard him speak up in his own defense: "It wasn't me."

My little brother slurred his words. Right up until the day he died, he was prone to mumble. His response further inflamed my father, who was no doubt bent on making the most of this opportunity to blow off steam. He practically exploded, "If it wasn't you, how did the bowl get broken?"

My little brother looked utterly bewildered. Questioned thus, he could only shake his head in confusion. He was just too young; though able to issue a simple denial, he did not understand that testimony was needed to support his case. Worst of all, he was suddenly distracted by a bird outside and ran out the door to investigate. For my father, this was an intolerable provocation. Seething with fury, he yelled, "Come back here, you little son of a bitch!"

Although Sun Guangming knew enough to be frightened, he did not realize the gravity of the situation. No sooner was he back in the house than he pointed outside and gave what seemed to him a perfectly reasonable explanation for his exit. "There was a little bird!" he told Sun Kwangtsai, his eyes wide. "It was just there!"

My little brother's tender face took the full force of my father's flailing hand. He flew through the air and landed with a thump on the floor, where he lay in total silence for what seemed like forever. My mother, no less frightened than me by my father's rampages, cried out in alarm and ran to his aid. Then at last Sun Guangming started to bawl. Just as he did not know why he had been slapped, he did not seem to know why he was crying either.

My father's rage began to recede. He banged on the table and yelled, "What the hell are you crying about?"

Then he went outside. Inflamed by his own anger but softened by Sun Guangming's wails, he chose to give way. As he went out, he continued railing, "Wastrels! I have a house full of wastrels. The oldest one claims his back hurts just from walking and the youngest one is a full fucking four years old but still talks in a mumble like he's got a ball in his mouth. Each one is worse than the last. The way they're going, this house is heading for ruin."

He capped this with a self-pitying coda: "Fate is so unkind to me!"

Events had unfolded so quickly: my father left before I had time to recover from the shock of what had happened. When I turned to glare at my grandfather, I found him still standing there, shaking like a leaf. Probably I had been too confused to immediately come to my little brother's defense: a six-year-old perhaps has slow reactions—or at least I did. But afterward this incident kept haunting me like a shadow in the moonlight. Although I wanted to expose Granddad, I could never bring myself to do so. Once, when nobody else was around, I did approach him. He was sitting in his sun-dappled corner, eyeing me in his usual benign way. But at that moment his affectionate gaze only made me shudder. With all the courage I could muster I said, "It was you who broke the bowl."

Granddad calmly shook his head and at the same time smiled at me indulgently. His smile was like a mighty fist arcing toward me, and I had to force myself not to turn around and flee. In an effort to conceal my alarm I shouted, "It was you!"

My accusation, however just, failed to wrest a confession from Granddad, and he responded serenely, "It wasn't me."

Granddad's tone of unshakable confidence made me begin to wonder if I was the one who had got things wrong. As I stood there uncertainly, he again gave me one of his terrifying smiles. My spirits crumbled and I hurriedly beat a retreat.

With the passage of days it was all the more difficult to blow the whistle on Granddad, and at the same time I realized that he stirred in me an indefinable phobia. If I ran home to pick something up and discovered that Granddad was watching me from his corner, I would tremble all over.

Through the depredations of my grandmother during the previous three decades, Sun Youyuan had lost his youthful energy, and now he had become a timid and servile old man. But as he deteriorated physically, his mental acuity sharpened. In the flickering light of old age Sun Youyuan recaptured the shrewdness and intelligence of his youth.

My father liked to scold Granddad over the dinner table, for it was at such moments that he was confronted with the most disagreeable evidence of the economic losses he was sustaining. Amid my father's bluster my grandfather would bow his head and assume an expression of anxiety. But this did not affect the pace of his eating, and the chopsticks in his hands conveyed food from plate to mouth with startling rapidity. He turned a deaf ear to Sun Kwangtsai's abuse, or seemed to treat it as a condiment that enhanced the pleasure of the meal. Only when the bowl and chopsticks were removed from his grip was he forced to stop. Sun Youyuan would then keep his head bowed and his eyes stubbornly glued to the dishes left on the table.

So it was that later on my father had Granddad sit on a low chair from which he could see the dishes on the table but not the food inside them. By then I had already left Southgate. My poor grandfather could only lay his chin on the table and stare as the others transferred food to their bowls. My little brother, being so short, suffered much the same inconvenience, but he could always count on my mother to help him. Sun Guangming liked to test the limits, and time and again he would stand up on his stool, rejecting his mother's help, and cater to his appetite through his own efforts. The silly boy would then incur a penalty quite out of proportion to the crime. In those days my father was not the least inclined to be lenient, and even for such a small thing he would subject my little brother to a pummeling, at the same time announcing, like a tyrant, "If anyone stands up again at the dinner table, I'll break their legs!"

Sun Kwangtsai's real goal in punishing my little brother so harshly was to cow his father into submission, as Granddad perfectly well knew. He sat meekly in his little chair, and for Sun Kwangtsai it was most gratifying to witness the old man's discomfort as he raised his chopsticks high in the air and struggled to pick up morsels from this awkward angle.

But my grandfather, like a rodent that digs a hole in a dike, found insidious ways of countering his son's malice. Having managed to shift the blame for the broken bowl onto my little brother, now he had his eye on him once more. Of course, it was only Sun Guangming who shared Granddad's discontent with the height of the table. But my little brother was conscious of this problem only during meals, for the rest of the time he was rushing madly all over the place like a wild rabbit. It was my grandfather, fixed for long periods in his corner, who had all the time in the world to figure out how to address the issue.

Over a period of several days, whenever my little brother came close to him, Sun Youyuan would mutter darkly, "The table's too high."

These repeated murmurings inspired my brother, now nine years old, to stand between Granddad and the table and look back and forth between the two for some time. A light in his eyes told my grandfather that the little chap had ideas turning over in his mind.

Sun Youyuan, who understood my brother's psychology so well, coughed loudly—to cover up his own scheming, perhaps, for he was quite prepared to wait for Sun Guangming to come up with a plan.

Apart from his habit of slurring words, my little brother was strong in other areas. With his budding intelligence and the destructive urge typical of his age he immediately saw a way to address the table-height issue. He cried to Granddad triumphantly, "Saw it down!"

My grandfather assumed a look of astonishment, at the same time throwing my brother an admiring glance that surely encouraged him. Carried away by his own ingenuity, he said, "Saw a bit of the legs off."

Sun Youyuan shook his head. "You wouldn't be able to handle the saw," he said.

My little brother, in his innocence, was unaware that he was being led toward a trap. Provoked by Granddad's condescension, he cried out, "I'm strong!"

Sun Guangming felt that words alone were not enough, so he ducked underneath the table, lifted it up on his shoulders and shuffled a couple of steps forward, then slipped out again and declared, "I'm *very* strong!"

Sun Youyuan shook his head once more, as a way of letting Sun Guangming know that his hands were not as strong as the rest of him, that he still wouldn't be able to saw off the table legs.

When it first occurred to Sun Guangming that the legs could be sawn down, he was content simply to have identified this solution in the abstract. Sun Youyuan's doubts about his strength were the impetus to put the idea into practice. That afternoon my little brother indignantly ran out of the house, heading for the home of a carpenter in the village in order to prove to Granddad that he could indeed put a saw to the table legs. He found the master of the house sitting on a stool, with a cup of tea in his hands. My little brother greeted him warmly. "How are things going?" Then he went on, "If you're not using your saw, you'll let me borrow it, won't you?"

The carpenter could not be bothered with him and waved him away. "Off you go, get out of here! Why the hell should I lend it to *you*?"

"I knew you wouldn't," Sun Guangming said. "But my dad said you would. He said he helped you when you were building your house."

Ensnared by Granddad, Sun Guangming had laid a snare for the carpenter. The carpenter asked him, "What does Sun Kwang-tsai want it for?"

My little brother shook his head. "I don't know."

"All right, take it," the carpenter relented.

With the saw over his shoulder my little brother went back

home, where he knocked it loudly on the ground and asked Sun Youyuan in a piping voice, "Now do you admit I can do the sawing?"

Sun Youyuan shook his head, saying, "You can saw off one leg at most."

That afternoon my little brother, so smart and so foolish, the sweat pouring down his face, sawed a length off all four table legs, turning round from time to time to ask Sun Youyuan, "Am I strong or not?"

My grandfather did not provide any direct encouragement, but he was careful to keep a look of amazement on his face the whole time. Just that was enough to motivate my little brother to finish sawing all four legs. Once he had completed the job, Sun Guangming did not have much chance to feel proud of himself, for my grandfather heartlessly revealed thc awful fate that now awaited him, saying, "That's a terrible thing you've done! Sun Kwangtsai is going to kill you."

My poor little brother was scared speechless, only now realizing what appalling repercussions were going to ensue. He looked at my grandfather with tears in his eyes, but Sun Youyuan simply rose to his feet and hobbled into his room. My little brother slipped out of the house and nothing more was seen of him until the following morning. Not daring to go home he spent the night in a rice field, fighting off the pangs of hunger. My father ran him to ground easily enough, standing on the raised path between the fields and spotting in the green expanse a patch where the rice had been flattened. Having howled with fury all night long, Sun Kwangtsai was still in a towering rage. He beat my little brother until his bottom was like an apple hanging from a tree, equal parts green and red, and it was a month before he was able to sit down on his stool again. Meanwhile, at mealtimes, my grandfather no longer needed to reach so high with his chopsticks. Only after this mutilated table was destroyed in the fire, on my return to Southgate when I was twelve, did the family no longer have to bend down low to eat their meals.

Once I rejoined the household, that old fear of Granddad—if it still lingered in my mind at all—soon mutated into self-pity, and as my own position at home grew more precarious, his presence turned out to be enormously comforting. I came to dread the prospect of some mishap affecting the family, knowing that I would be made a scapegoat whatever happened, and so with time I understood why, years earlier, Granddad had felt impelled to pin the blame on my younger brother. During this period my father would often bare his scraggly chest, exhibiting his protruding ribs to the villagers, and spell out plainly why there was so little meat on his bones, all because "I've got two worms eating away inside me." Granddad and I were like two unwelcome guests steadily burrowing a hole in his grain ration.

After my little brother sawed the table legs, there was to be yet another trial of strength between my father and Granddad. Although my father maintained his bluster till the end, he had suffered a psychological defeat. So after I returned to Southgate I no longer saw my father openly cursing or scolding Granddad as he had been so wont to do earlier. His resentment of Granddad was now expressed only in the most ineffectual way. He would sit on the doorsill and ramble on like an old biddy, muttering to himself mournfully, "People are so much more trouble than sheep. Sheep's wool you can sell, the dung is good fertilizer, and the meat makes a fine dinner. With a relative to support, you're really up shit creek. He's got no wool, and eating him is too big a risk—who would bail me out if I ended up in the slammer?"

Sun Youyuan's composure in the face of such humiliations left an indelible impression on me. He always looked upon these assaults with a kindly eye, even a smile. After I grew up, on occasions when I thought of him, that touching smile of his was the first thing that came to mind. My father dreaded his smile and would quickly turn away, as though anxious to fend off an impending attack, and only after he had put some distance between them and he was all by himself would he start cursing. "He grins like a dead man, but he's perky enough as soon as he starts eating."

Though now befuddled with age, Sun Youyuan gradually became aware of my tenuous position at home, and he made a point of keeping me at arm's length. That autumn, as he squatted at the foot of the wall sunning himself, I went up to him and quietly stood there for some time, hoping he might say something to me, but his aloof expression made it impossible for us to break the silence. Later, when he heard the faint sound of people knocking off work in the fields, Sun Youyuan stiffly got to his feet and shuffled back into the house. He was afraid that Sun Kwangtsai would see us two undesirables together.

The fact that Granddad and I came home just as the fire was in full swing made Sun Kwangtsai look at us with suspicion for a long time afterward, as though we had somehow brought the fire back with us. In the wake of the conflagration, if Granddad and I ever happened to be in the same place, to my alarm I would hear my father pounding his chest and stamping his foot, shouting hysterically, "My house, my poor house is heading for destruction again! If these two are together, fire can't be far away."

When I was almost seven, as I was leaving Southgate with Wang Liqiang in his army uniform, I ran into my grandfather, just back after spending a month with my uncle. I didn't realize then that I had been given away and thought I was simply going off on an excursion. My big brother, knowing that I had now dropped out of the sprint competition, did not run to meet Granddad, but stood listlessly at the entrance to the village. His dispirited air made me all the more proud to be leaving in the company of a man in uniform. That's why when I saw Granddad I was so full of myself that I said, "I don't have time to talk to you now."

As I slipped past my grandfather with my nose in the air, I made a point of kicking up some dust. Now I remember the expression on his face. When I looked back to catch a last glimpse of my big brother, Granddad's ponderous bulk blocked my view, and so it was he who commanded more of my attention. Granddad stood there, looking at me fretfully, as though with misgivings. Of what destiny had in store for me, he knew as little as I did, but on the basis of his own life experience he had reason to doubt that my buoyant mood was warranted.

Five years later, when I returned alone to Southgate, a fateful coincidence brought Granddad and me together at a moment when black clouds were encroaching on the red glow of sunset. By that time we no longer recognized each other. The five years preceding had given me a heavy burden of memories to carry, squeezing my recollections of the more distant past into an obscure corner. Although I could recall my family's faces, their features had grown indistinct, like trees at twilight. Just as my memories had been rapidly multiplying, Granddad was in the opposite situation: infirmity and old age had begun to cruelly ravage his past, and he lost his way on the most familiar road. When he ran into me, he was like a drowning man who sees a plank floating in the water; it was only by sticking close to me that he managed to make it back to Southgate. We and the fire appeared on the scene simultaneously.

The day after our return to Southgate, Granddad left for my uncle's home once again, and this time he stayed for two months. By the time he returned we had already put up the thatched cottage. I cannot imagine how the old man, with his memory deficit and his incoherent speech, managed to make it there and back. He died in the summer of the next year.

Despite having been reduced to servile self-abasement for so long, just before his death Sun Youyuan surprised everyone by recovering his youthful energy, and there was something splendid about the last chapter of his life. Just as the end grew nigh, he summoned his final flickering strength to vie with heaven itself.

That year, when the rice in the fields was almost ready to be harvested, day after day of steady rain caused consternation among the villagers. Standing water was clearly visible in the paddies, covering the earth like a sheet of plastic. The heavy ears of grain drooped lower and lower, gradually approaching the silently rising rainwater. I'll never forget the faces of the helpless farmers as disaster approached, for they looked as desolate as if they were in mourning. Old Luo, the storehouse caretaker, sat the whole day on the doorsill wiping his tears, and issued a pessimistic forecast to the villagers: "This year we're going to have to go begging."

Old Luo had a phenomenal memory. He could navigate a smooth course through the torrent of history and was able to tell us that the waterlogged fields were a mirror image of those in 1938 and 1960, leading us to believe that we would indeed be beggars soon.

Sun Kwangtsai, who was usually busily engaged in one dubious activity or another, was now as quiet as a sick chicken. But sometimes he would come out with something even more shocking than Old Luo. He told us, "When things get bad, we'll just have to eat dead people."

Some of the older residents surreptitiously brought out clay bodhisattvas, set them on their altar tables, kowtowed to them, and prayed to Buddha, imploring the bodhisattva to exercise his powers and save the rice crop. It was at this juncture that my grandfather came on the scene like a guardian angel. One afternoon, abandoning his customary position in the corner, he suddenly rose to his feet, picked up his ramshackle umbrella, and went out. I assumed he was planning to go early to my uncle's. He walked falteringly, but his face, pasty for so many years, now shone with a healthy glow. Raising his oilskin umbrella, tottering along through the wind and rain, he visited every house in the village, delivering in a drone the following message, "Throw your bodhisattvas outside and give them a good soaking. That'll put a stop to the rain in no time—you'll see."

The households with Buddhist leanings were shocked by my grandfather's audacious proposal. My father was amused, at least at first. After days of being down in the dumps Sun Kwangtsai gave us a smile, and pointing at my grandfather as he staggered around in the rain he said to us, "The old man can still tough it out."

Only when several old folks hurried over in alarm and begged Sun Kwangtsai to put a stop to Sun Youyuan's impious canvassing did he realize that it was all getting out of hand. I couldn't help but feel anxious for Granddad.

Sun Kwangtsai went up to his father and yelled at him savagely, "Get back home!"

To my astonishment Granddad showed no signs of his usual fear. His stiff figure swiveled ponderously in the rain, and he took a long hard look at Sun Kwangtsai. Then he raised his finger and pointed at him. "*You* go home," he said.

My father was outraged at my grandfather's temerity. "You stupid old fart, you're tired of living, aren't you?" he cursed.

But Sun Youyuan repeated slowly, with emphasis on every word, "You go home."

My father was flummoxed. Standing there in the rain, he glanced around helplessly, and there was a pause before he finally said, "Shit, he's not scared of me anymore."

The village production team leader, as a member of the Communist Party, felt that worship of the bodhisattva had gone on quite long enough; he had a responsibility to curb this superstitious practice. With three militiamen in tow, loudly touting the principle of man's capacity to triumph over nature, he went from door to door in a hunt for effigies. He used his incontestable authority to intimidate the weak-kneed villagers, warning them that anybody who tried to harbor a bodhisattva would be punished as a counterrevolutionary.

So that morning there was an uncanny convergence between the Communist Party's methods of dispelling superstition and my grandfather's approach of seeking divine intervention by punishing the bodhisattva. I must have seen at least a dozen clay bodhisattvas tossed out into the rain. My grandfather reprised his role of the previous afternoon, clutching his shabby umbrella and stumbling around from door to door, circulating his latest bulletin. Now that his teeth had all fallen out, his words undulated incoherently in the rain, as with a reassuring smile he told people, "The bodhisattva can't take more than a day of soaking. When he's had enough, he'll ask the Dragon King to stop the rain. Tomorrow will be dry."

My grandfather's confident forecast did not become a reality. The following morning Sun Youyuan stood underneath the eaves watching the billowing rain, his wrinkled face crumpled up with grief. I saw him stand there for a long time, and then, quivering, he turned his head upward, and for the first time I heard him bellow. It had never occurred to me that Granddad could express himself with such violent rage: Sun Kwangtsai's erstwhile tantrums were mere trifles compared to what Sun Youyuan came out with then. My grandfather turned to the sky and yelled, "God, you bastard! Why don't you get your cock out and fuck me, if that's what you want?"

But then all of a sudden my grandfather looked lost. His mouth seemed to be frozen open, as if he were dead. His whole body tightened and he stood rigidly for several moments. Then he went limp and burst out wailing.

What was curious was that at midday the rain stopped. The old folks were awestruck. As they watched chinks gradually appear in the clouds and the sun shine down at last, they could not help but recall the crazy behavior of Sun Youyuan earlier, which they had then regarded as sacrilege. These credulous villagers began to feel with wonder and trepidation that Sun Youyuan possessed the bearing of an immortal, and his ragged clothes made them think of the legendary mendicant priest Master Ji. In fact, of course, had the Communist Party member and team leader not commandeered the militiamen and conducted the search, the villagers would never have thrown their bodhisattvas out in the rain. But at the time nobody was in the mood to give the production team leader any credit, and the notion that Sun Youyuan might be an immortal spread like wildfire through the village for the next three days. Eventually even my mother wondered if there was some truth to it. But when she cautiously sounded my father out on this question, Sun Kwangtsai said, "What a load of crap."

My father was a confirmed materialist. He said to my mother, "It's his sperm that made me. If he's an immortal, then I've got to be one too, no?"

FADING FROM VIEW

Just before he died Sun Youyuan wore an expression very much like that of a water buffalo as it waited to be slaughtered. Though such an imposing animal in my eyes, the buffalo lay on the ground with legs splayed, meekly allowing itself to be trussed. I was standing off to one side of the village drying ground and my brothers were standing right at the front. The commentary of my little brother, who pretended to understand more than he actually did, drifted like dust through the morning air, interspersed with Sun Guangping's scoffing, "You don't know shit!"

At first I was no smarter than my little brother, believing that the water buffalo didn't know what was going to happen to it. But then I saw its tears, the tears it shed after being trussed up; they sprayed the concrete floor like raindrops in a thunderstorm, for when facing extinction life reveals its infinite attachment to the past. It was not just grief that I saw in the buffalo's expression but also a kind of despair, and there is no more shocking sight than that. Later I heard my big brother tell other boys that the buffalo's eyes reddened as soon as it was tied up. In the years that followed I would recall with a shudder the scene just before the buffalo's death: the tattered images of its polite surrender and its unresisting submission reappeared before my eyes, leaving me troubled and uneasy.

For a long time Granddad's passing was an enigma to me, its raw reality imbued with a mysterious ambience that made it impossible for me to ascertain the true cause of his death. "Joy at its fullest gives way to sorrow," they say, and no sooner had my grandfather delivered his fearless challenge to the heavens on that rain-swept morning than he was cast back into an abyss of misgivings, dumbstruck and lost. At the moment when he opened his mouth to yell, he felt to his astonishment that there was something inside him desperate to find an outlet, something that took wing with sublime, birdlike ease. He wheeled around in alarm, crying pitifully, "My soul! My soul has flown away."

Like a little bird, his soul had flown out through his gaping mouth. To me at thirteen this was something startling and bizarre.

That afternoon I saw on Granddad's face the look that I had seen on the water buffalo. By then the sky had cleared and the senior population in the village was marveling that Sun Youyuan's prediction had been fulfilled. My grandfather was in no position to enjoy his hour of glory, so grief stricken was he at the loss of his soul. Sun Youyuan sat tearfully on the doorsill, the returning sunshine in his face, and mournful whimpers came from his gaping mouth. He started crying after my parents went off to the fields and his tears were still gushing when they returned. I have never seen anyone cry for so long.

When Sun Kwangtsai came back home at the end of the day and saw his father's tears, he preferred to think they were being shed out of concern for himself. "I'm not dead yet," he muttered. "A bit early to mourn, isn't it?"

Later my grandfather rose from the doorsill and brushed past us, sobbing. He did not join us for dinner as usual but went into the cluttered storeroom and lay down in his bed. Soon afterward, however, in a voice of unusual force, Sun Youyuan called his son, "Sun Kwangtsai!"

My father ignored him, saying to my mother, "The old guy is giving himself airs. He wants me to bring him his dinner."

Granddad gave another shout, "Sun Kwangtsai, my soul has left me! I'm dying!"

At this my father went over to the door and said to him, "How can you be dying when you can yell like that?"

My grandfather started crying, his sobs punctuated by indistinct words. "Son, your dad is dying. I don't know what it's like to die. I'm scared!"

Sun Kwangtsai had had enough of this. "I don't see there's anything the matter with you," he pointed out.

Encouraged perhaps by his son's responsiveness, Sun Youyuan stirred himself to call, at even higher volume, "Son, I really have to die! You just get poorer with every day I live."

The loudness of his delivery made my father uncomfortable, and he said with annoyance, "Keep it down, will you? If people hear that, they'll think I've been persecuting you."

To my young mind, there was something unnerving about Sun Youyuan's premonition of death and his handling of this foreknowledge. It seems to me now that when Granddad sensed his soul leaving him, he must have genuinely felt that this was what had happened; surely he would not have concocted this story as some kind of subterfuge, when his own life and death were involved. But perhaps after he injured his back he had begun to plan for his own demise, and it may be that he magnified what was simply a normal physical reaction to his yelling at the sky, imagining it to mark the departure of his soul and a portent of his death. That afternoon when the sky cleared, as Sun Youyuan wept incessantly, he had already finalized his own sentence. For this old man in the twilight of life, there was no real choice to make when faced with the prospect of being reunited with his wife and departing forever from the world. For nine long years he had hesitated. Now, when he finally felt that death was inescapably approaching him, his tears demonstrated how tightly he still clung to this mortal life, despite all its hardships. His one request was that Sun Kwangtsai agree to make him a coffin and send him off with pipes and cymbals: "Make sure the pipes are blown good and loud, so the news carries to your ma."

I was stunned by the idea that Granddad would just lie down and die. The image of him in my mind underwent a fundamental change. No longer did I think of him as someone who sat in the corner recalling his past, for now he was intimately connected to death itself. He became unutterably distant from me, fusing with the grandmother I barely remembered.

My little brother showed a compulsive interest in Granddad's imminent passing. He stood by the door the whole afternoon, peeping at him through the crack and running outside from time to time to report to my big brother, "Not dead yet."

He explained to Sun Guangping, "Granddad's belly is still moving."

As far as my father was concerned, Sun Youyuan's resolve to

die was just empty posturing. As he left the house with his hoe on his shoulder, he had the unpleasant feeling that Sun Youyuan had simply found a new way to give him a hard time. That evening, however, after we had eaten and Granddad had still not emerged from his room, my mother took a bowl of rice in to him and we heard him whine, "I'm dying. I'm not eating."

Only then did my father take seriously Granddad's determination to die. With a look of surprise on his face he went into Granddad's room, and these two archenemies actually began talking to each other like devoted siblings. Sun Kwangtsai sat on Sun Youyuan's bed and talked to him in a good-natured tone that he had never used when speaking to him before. When he emerged, he was already convinced that his father would soon no longer be of this world. Beaming with joy, he made no effort to conceal his elation, indifferent to whether or not this would jeopardize his prospects of being seen as a proper son. He went out to spread the news that Sun Youyuan was about to die, and even from inside the house I could hear his ringing voice off in the distance. "How long can somebody live if they don't eat?"

Having lain in bed expectantly all night long, Sun Youyuan nimbly propped himself up the following morning when Sun Kwangtsai came in. "What about the coffin?" he asked.

It gave my father a shock to find that Sun Youyuan was not at his last gasp as he had been anticipating. He seemed a bit disappointed as he came out of the room, shaking his head and saying, "It looks like we're going to have to wait another couple of days. He still remembers about the coffin."

My father was perhaps concerned that when the next mealtime came around Sun Youyuan would emerge all of a sudden and humbly take his seat among us. Sun Kwangtsai did not rule out this possibility at all, so he felt compelled to give proper attention to the coffin that so preoccupied Granddad. That morning he walked in with two blocks of wood in his hand and with an air of exaggerated mystery instructed my little brother to knock the bits of wood together. I was taken aback to see my father, usually so careless and blatant, suddenly so stealthy and furtive. Then he stood erect, shoved open Granddad's door, and said to him in the tone of a filial son, "Dad, I've got the carpenter here now."

Through the half-open door I saw Granddad raise himself slightly and give a relieved smile. My little brother, who seldom performed any useful service, had now acquired a temporary occupation, and Sun Guangming brandished the two lengths of wood and knocked them together as though they were weapons in a lethal swordfight. But my little brother was a lover of freedom and could never accept space restrictions for very long. He soon became fully invested in these military operations and, like some general in ancient times, fought his way out of the house, perspiration pouring down his face. He had totally forgotten what his job was supposed to be, so carried away was he by the joy of fighting at close quarters. His wheezing war whoops gradually receded in the morning sunshine as he ran off who knows where, and he did not return until almost dinnertime, by which time his hands were empty. When my father asked him what he'd done with the pieces of wood, Sun Guangming looked baffled. He hemmed and hawed as though he had never seen them his entire life.

After my little brother disappeared, I heard a restive shout from my grandfather's gloomy room: "The coffin!"

With the silencing of the wood-tapping sounds that could appease his soul, a hungry rustle rasped in Sun Youyuan's flat and febrile voice. His last wish in life had been dashed by my little brother's insouciance.

Later it fell to me to carry on the construction of the bogus coffin. My older brother, fifteen by this time, saw this as quite beneath him. Sun Kwangtsai grabbed me by the shoulder, having realized all of a sudden that this morose son of his could occasionally do something worthwhile. As he passed me the blocks of wood his face was the very picture of disdain. "You can't just eat free meals all the time."

For the next two days I gave grandfather the reassurance he sought by beating out a monotonous rhythm with the wooden blocks. But I found myself in a hopeless trough of despond. At thirteen I was sensitive enough to wonder whether I was hammering nails in my own coffin. Although Granddad had not offered me understanding or sympathy after my return to Southgate, because his status in the family was so like my own, when he gave an indication that he felt sorry for himself—as he was inclined to do—I considered, from my perspective, that his sentiments also contained an element of compassion for me. My disaffection with father and home was aggravated by the tapping sounds designed to hasten Granddad's death. Now, so many years later, I still feel that this was a cruel punishment for my father to impose on me, however unwittingly he may have done so. My sense at the time was that I was like a convict on death row who is forced to carry out the execution of another hapless inmate.

The news of Sun Youyuan's impending death brought surprise and excitement to our normally torpid village. The old folks, who had regained a childish innocence after all their long years in the world, expressed an awed respect for Granddad's decision to die. His stance toward the bodhisattva gave them grounds to believe that he was most likely set on going home. According to one intriguing but far-fetched theory, at the time of his birth my grandfather had descended, like rain, from heaven; his foreknowledge of his own death proved that his assigned term in the dusty world had expired, and now he was returning to heaven, back to his true abode.

People of the younger generation, steeped in the atheism promoted by the Communist Party, viewed these ideas with scorn. Just as Sun Youyuan had been castigated by Sun Kwangtsai, these endearing seniors were flatly told that age had done nothing for them, that they were just getting more stupid all the time.

There I sat, in the middle of the room, the front door ajar, tapping out a monotonous rhythm. In the eyes of sundry spectators I was engaged in a ridiculous exercise. How did I feel about it? My fragile ego was hard put to keep shame and distress at bay, particularly with the village children pointing at me and giggling all the time.

All the commotion outside the house distracted Sun Youyuan as he made ready to depart this life, and a scene from his youth reappeared before him, the time he fled from a hail of Nationalist bullets. Agitated, unsure what was happening outside, he called Sun Kwangtsai. As my father entered the room, Sun Youyuan summoned the energy to sit up in bed, and he asked Sun Kwangtsai if somebody's house had caught fire.

When Granddad lay down in bed he had intended to die right away, but three days had passed and it seemed the longer he lay the more lively he felt. Even though Sun Youyuan yelled every dinnertime that his eating days were over, my mother still would wordlessly carry a bowl of rice in to him. Torn between an ideal death and all-too-real starvation, my grandfather hesitated agonizingly, but yielded in the end to hunger's authority. My mother always returned with an empty bowl.

Patience had never been Sun Kwangtsai's strong suit, and seeing my grandfather had not arrived at death's door as soon as he had expected, he lost confidence that he would die at all. When my mother, bowl in hand, prepared to enter Granddad's room and my grandfather repeated his old trick of insisting that he was on a fast, Sun Kwangtsai shoved my mother aside and yelled at him, "If you're going to die, don't eat! If you're going to eat, don't die!"

My mother found this rather shocking, and she whispered to Sun Kwangtsai, "That's going too far. The Lord will make you pay for that."

But my father couldn't care less. He stormed off and could be heard saying to people nearby, "Did you ever hear of a dead man eating dinner?"

In fact, Granddad was not behaving as willfully as my father imagined. Sun Youyuan had the genuine sensation that his soul had flown, and he was firmly convinced that he was about to die. On the mental level he had already died, and he was simply waiting for his physical being to reach that same point of no return. Just as my father was growing more and more exasperated, Sun Youyuan himself was vexed that he was taking so long to die.

At this final stage of his life Sun Youyuan employed his scattered wits to ponder the question of why he had not yet expired. As the rice swayed in the sunlight, soon to be harvested, an herbal aroma was carried in by the southeasterly breezes. I don't know if Granddad smelled it or not, but a peculiar notion persuaded him that death's delayed arrival was in some way linked to those heavy ears of grain.

That morning Sun Youyuan again called loudly for Sun

Kwangtsai. After venting so much rage, my father was now a bit despondent, and he walked listlessly into Granddad's room. Sun Youyuan told him in a conspiratorial whisper that his soul had not flown far away: it was still lingering in the vicinity, and that was why he had not died. (He said this so warily it was as though he feared his soul might overhear him.) The reason the soul had not flown far was that it was attracted by the scent of the rice field, and now his soul was mixed up with a flock of sparrows, the sparrows that were circling above the paddy at that very moment. Sun Youyuan asked my father to assemble some scarecrows and set them out in a circle around the house to frighten his soul away; otherwise his soul might reinhabit his body at any time. My grandfather opened his toothless mouth and said to Sun Kwangtsai with a mumble, "Son, if my soul returns, you'll be in the poorhouse again."

My father was beside himself. "Dad, forget about dying! Just get back to living, will you? First it's a coffin you want, and now it's scarecrows. Give me a break, for heaven's sake!"

When the old men of the village heard about this latest development from Sun Kwangtsai (now in high dudgeon), they did not share my father's view that Sun Youyuan was making a fuss for nothing. My grandfather's belief that his soul was hovering about nearby struck them as perfectly plausible. At midday—I had stopped my tapping then—I saw several old men walking over with two scarecrows in their hands, their pious expressions in the sunlight conveying a curious dignity. They propped one of the scarecrows against the wall next to our front door and set the other one down outside Sun Youyuan's window. As they explained to Sun Kwangtsai later, they did this to smooth my grandfather's ascent to heaven.

My grandfather's allotted span was truly drawing to a close, and in the three days following his condition rapidly deteriorated. Once, when my father went into his room, Sun Youyuan could talk to him only in a faint tone, like the hum of a mosquito. By now he was no longer at the mercy of his appetite, for he had lost even the most basic desire for food and at most ate two or three mouthfuls of the rice my mother brought him. This led my father to loiter outside the house for quite some time, eyeing the scarecrows suspiciously and muttering to himself, "Can it be these things really work?"

My grandfather lay unwashed in that summer room for many days, and he wet his bed in the final stages when he was scarcely breathing. The storeroom reeked.

Once Sun Youyuan truly looked as though he was close to death, Sun Kwangtsai began to calm down. On two successive mornings he went to Granddad's room to check on his condition, and when he emerged he was knitting his brows. Given to exaggeration as he was, my father asserted that Sun Youyuan had soiled a good half of the bed. He did not go into Granddad's room the following morning because, he said, he couldn't bear the stench. He told my mother to go in and see how Granddad was doing while he sat by the table and offered instruction to my brothers: "Your granddad will be dead soon." He elaborated. "People are like weasels: when you try to catch them they let loose a stinky fart to make you all groggy, so they can escape. Your granddad is about to make his getaway, so it's horribly smelly in his room."

When my mother came out of Granddad's room she was white as a sheet and was kneading the hem of her apron with both hands. She said to Sun Kwangtsai, "Quick, go and have a look!"

My father seemed to be launched off his stool. He scurried

into Granddad's room and after a few moments he came back out again, with a rapt expression on his face. Dancing with joy, he said, "He's dead, all right! No doubt about it."

In fact, Sun Youyuan was not yet dead; he was simply going in and out of shock. But my father, never very punctilious about small details, went off in a great rush to seek the help of people in the village, for it only now occurred to him that a hole had still to be dug. With a hoe over his shoulder and a mournful expression on his face, he went around the village calling people out of their houses, and then together with several locals he began to dig a resting place for Sun Youyuan next to Grandmother's grave.

Sun Kwangtsai was not easily satisfied, and when the neighbors had finished digging the grave and were about ready to go home, my father kept grumbling away in the background, saying that if they were going to help they should go whole hog, otherwise they'd do better not to help at all. He asked them to carry my grandfather out, while he stood by the doorway, opting not to join them in the room. When Wang Yuejin (the one who was later to get into a fight with him) screwed up his face and complained about the awful smell, my father said unctuously, "Dead people are like that."

My grandfather chose to open his eyes at the very moment that he was being lifted off the bed. He had no idea, of course, that they were just about to bury him, and he gave a little chuckle as he regained consciousness; the sudden appearance of a smile on his face gave them the fright of their lives. I heard a chaotic medley of shouts erupt inside the room, and the next thing I knew, every one of the neighbors bolted out in a panic. Wang Yuejin, the most strongly built of all, was white as a sheet, and he patted his chest and kept saying, "That scared the shit out of me!"

Then he started hurling curses at Sun Kwangtsai. "I screw your ancestors, all eighteen generations of them! You stupid bastard, what sort of joke is that to play on people?"

My father looked at them quizzically, not knowing what the problem was, until Wang Yuejin said, "Fuck it, the man's still alive!"

Hearing that, Sun Kwangtsai rushed into Sun Youyuan's room. On seeing him, my grandfather gave another titter, so infuriating my father that he started cursing even before he left the room. "All your talk about dying is just a load of shit! If you really want to die, then string yourself up or throw yourself in the river, don't just fucking lie in bed!"

Like a fine stream of water that just keeps on flowing, Sun Youyuan's life carried on unbroken, to the villagers' amazement. Practically everyone was convinced that he was about to die, but he had succeeded in making his passing a very protracted affair. The biggest surprise came that summer evening. It was stiflingly hot inside the house, so we moved the table out and set it down underneath the elm tree. We were eating there when Granddad suddenly appeared.

Though bedridden for some three weeks now, he had managed to clamber to his feet, and putting a hand against the wall for support he tottered outside like a child just learning to walk. We watched him in speechless astonishment. By now he was gripped by a deep unease about his inability to die properly. With difficulty he positioned himself next to the threshold and then lowered himself unsteadily onto the sill. He seemed oblivious to our reaction and sat as motionless as though he were a sack of sweet potatoes. We heard a dejected mumble, "Still not dead! What a pain!"

It was the following morning that Sun Youyuan died. When

my father went over to his bed, he opened his eyes wide and looked at him steadily. Granddad's look must have been chilling or my father would not have been so petrified. He told us later that Granddad's expression seemed to be saying that he wanted to take him along, so they could die together. But my father did not make a run for it, or rather he could not make a run for it as his hands were now held in his father's viselike grip. Two tiny tears fell from the corners of my grandfather's eyes, and then he closed his eyes forever. Sun Kwangtsai could feel his clamped hands gradually recover their freedom, and that's when he left the room all flustered and in a slurred voice told my mother to have a look. Compared with him, she was much more composed. She hesitated a little as she went in, but she came out with a steady step, telling my father, "He's gone cold."

My father smiled with relief, and as he headed outside he cried, "Finally, damn it! Finally!"

He sat down on the doorstep, grinning at some hens that strutted about nearby. But before long his face grew dark with grief, his mouth went out of shape, and he started crying; soon he was blubbering. I heard him murmuring to himself, "Dad, I let you down. Dad, you had such a hard life. I'm a lousy bastard, I didn't treat you right! But I really had no choice, you know."

When Granddad at last fulfilled his ambition and died, this failed to evoke the feeling that I had lost a real, living person. It left me in a strange state of mind, a combination of sorrow and disquiet. What was clear to me, however, was that one particular spectacle would fade from view and be lost forever. At twilight Sun Youyuan used to appear on the road into Southgate, shuffling along toward me and the pond. Even from a considerable distance I could always recognize the oilskin umbrella clutched to his chest and the blue bundle dangling over his shoulder. That tableau had so often brought me warmth and comfort, as reassuring as sunshine itself.

GRANDFATHER'S VICTORY

Sun Youyuan was no coward; at least inside he was not. If he was humble, this servility stemmed to a large extent from low self-esteem. In my fourth year away from Southgate, after my little brother had adjusted the table legs, Granddad's sorry predicament at home grew even more dire.

The table-leg episode did not mark the end of hostilities between Sun Youyuan and Sun Kwangtsai, for my father was a tenacious adversary and would not allow Sun Youyuan to rest easy for long. Soon he forbade my grandfather to sit at the table at mealtimes, insisting that he sit in the corner with a small bowl. My grandfather had to learn to put up with hunger. Although an old man, he had the appetite of a young newlywed, but now he was allowed only this one small bowl. Sun Kwangtsai's put-upon expression made it very difficult for him to request a second helping, and he could only watch with rumbling stomach as my parents and brothers dug into their meal with gusto. The only way of alleviating his hunger was to lick all the plates before they were washed, and now, through our back window, the villagers would often see

Sun Youyuan assiduously scouring the dirty dishes with his tongue.

My grandfather did not easily resign himself to suffering such humiliation, and given that he was no coward he had no choice but to go head to head with Sun Kwangtsai since it was impossible to outflank him. After a month or so, when my mother passed Granddad his little bowl, he deliberately failed to take a firm hold and instead let it drop and shatter on the floor. I can imagine how this would have infuriated my father, and sure enough he leapt up from his stool, and pointing a finger at Sun Youyuan cursed him loudly. "You old wastrel, you can't even hold a fucking bowl properly! How do you think you're going to eat now?"

By then my grandfather was already down on his knees, gathering up the bits of food off the floor. He put on an expression that seemed to acknowledge he had committed a terrible crime, and he said to my father, "Oh no, I shouldn't have smashed that bowl! Oh no, that family heirloom—it was supposed to be passed on to the next generation!"

This last sentence left my father nonplussed, and it was a moment before its implications sank in. Then he said to my mother, "You keep telling me the old man is so pitiful, but don't you see how devious he is?"

My grandfather did not look at Sun Kwangtsai. His eyes filled with tears while he kept crying stubbornly, "Oh no, that bowl was to go to my son!"

Sun Kwangtsai was now at the end of his tether, and he roared at Granddad, "Stop that fucking playacting!"

Sun Youyuan started to bawl, crying in an anguished voice, "Now that the bowl is broken, how's my son going to eat?"

At that point my little brother began to cackle. In his eyes Granddad looked so ridiculous that he burst out laughing, despite the inappropriateness of the occasion. My big brother Sun Guangping knew that this was not the time for levity, but Sun Guangming's mirth so infected him that he could not stop himself from joining in. My father now found himself under fire from all quarters: on the one side, Sun Youyuan with his ominous prediction of hardship late in life; on the other, his progeny seemingly savoring with their laughter the prospect of his future sufferings. Sun Kwangtsai glanced suspiciously at his darling sons and thought to himself: it's true I can't really count on these two guys.

My brothers' laughter served to buttress my grandfather's position, although that was not what they intended. My father, normally brimming with self-confidence, found himself at sea. Bereft of the rage he needed to deal with the still-wailing Sun Youyuan, he retreated feebly toward the door, at the same time waving his hand and saying, "Okay, I give in. Just stop all that wailing, will you? You win, all right? I'm no match for you, I admit. Just stop that damn wailing!"

But once he was outside the house Sun Kwangtsai flared up once again. Pointing at his family inside, he swore, "You're such sons of bitches, the whole lot of you!"

Chapter 4

THREATS

There was one lunchtime when I—an adult now—found my attention drawn to a charming performance by a brightly dressed little boy. He stood on the sidewalk in the full sunshine, stuck out a pudgy arm, and very intently executed a whole series of gestures that suggested a rich imagination, simple though they were. In the middle of this routine he suddenly stuck his hand into the crotch of his pants and scratched an itch, although his face continued to maintain a blissful smile. Undistracted by the din of the city streets, his mind still reveled in a fantasy world.

Later, when a troop of primary school pupils passed by, he discovered that he wasn't as happy as he thought. He watched agog as these older children walked off into the distance. Even without seeing the look in his eye I could feel his despondency at that moment. Satchels, slung casually over their owners' shoulders, swayed in a gentle motion as the class moved off, surely a dispiriting sight to a boy who had not yet reached school age, and the fact that the children were walking in pairs can only have sharpened his feelings of envy, leaving him vexed and dissatisfied with life. He turned and stomped off down an alleyway, wearing a long face.

Twenty or so years ago, when my big brother strutted off with his satchel and my father issued his parting injunction, I realized for the first time how unfortunate I was. A year later, when I went off to school with a satchel on my back myself, I was no longer in a position to listen to any advice that Sun Kwangtsai might have had for me, and received another kind of counsel altogether.

By that time it was six months since I had left Southgate. The burly man who escorted me away from Southgate had become my father, while my mother, a petite woman with a blue-checked headscarf who used to walk briskly across the fields, had been replaced by the pale and listless Li Xiuying. One morning my new father gripped the handles of a heavy wooden trunk, effortlessly shifted it to one side, and from the trunk underneath brought out a brand-new green military satchel, which he said was mine from now on.

Wang Liqiang's perception of country boys would have been amusing were it not so annoying. Perhaps because he was himself a peasant's son, he never altered his conviction that village children, like dogs, were liable to answer the call of nature wherever they felt like it. During his first full day of parenting he underscored repeatedly the importance of the chamber pot. His concern about my excretory functions remained uppermost in his thoughts even as I was putting the satchel on my back, a moment that to me was sacred. He told me that once I was at school I could not just go to the toilet whenever I felt like it; first I needed to raise my hand and secure the teacher's permission.

I felt proud to be so neatly dressed, green satchel dangling from my shoulder, escorted by Wang Liqiang in his army uniform. That was how I arrived at school on my first day. A man who was busy knitting a sweater chatted quietly with Wang Liqiang, but I dared not laugh at his incongruous hobby because this man was to be my teacher. Then a boy my age ran toward us waving his satchel. He and I exchanged glances, and a cluster of children nearby took a good look at me. "Why don't you go and join them?" Wang Liqiang suggested.

I walked toward those unfamiliar faces. They eyed me inquisitively, and I studied them with equal curiosity. I soon found that I had a significant advantage over the other children, for my satchel was bigger than any of theirs. But just when I was feeling rather pleased with my superior status, Wang Liqiang came across on his way out and delivered a loud reminder, "If you need to pee or drop your load, don't forget to raise your hand."

My nascent self-esteem instantly bit the dust.

My five years of town life were spent in the company of an ill-matched couple, one all muscle, the other frailty personified. I had not been selected by the town because I was so adorable, nor was I, for that matter, so enthralled by the town; the crux of the matter was that Wang Liqiang and his wife needed me. They were childless, the reason being, according to Li Xiuying, that she was not strong enough to breastfeed. Wang Liqiang put it differently, telling me categorically that if Li Xiuying, with all her ailments, were to give birth, this would kill her right away—a remark that seemed quite shocking to me at the time. Neither of them liked babies, and they opted for a six-year-old like me because I could do some work around the house. To be fair, they were expecting to be parents to me their whole lives through, for otherwise they could perfectly well have adopted a fourteen- or fifteen-year-old boy whose performance of chores would have been more satisfactory. The problem was that a fourteen-year-old would already have well-formed habits that might give them a lot of trouble. Having chosen me, they fed and clothed me, saw me off to school, scolded and beat me, just like other parents would. And so I, the product of another marriage, became their son.

During the whole five years I lived with them Li Xiuying went out of the house only once, and after that unprecedented excursion I never saw her again. It was always a mystery to me exactly what was wrong with Li Xiuying, but I was left in no doubt about her devotion to sunlight. It was as though, without exposure to sunshine, this second mother of mine was shrouded in a perpetual drizzle.

The first time Wang Liqiang conducted me into her room, I was astonished to see the floor dotted with little stools, on which were draped an immense number of undershirts and underpants, illuminated by the sunshine that came in through the window. She seemed completely unaware of our entrance. Her outstretched arm was groping for the sunlight, as though tugging on a slender cord. As the sun's rays shifted their position, she would move the stools so that her motley collection of underwear would always be bathed in sunshine. So absorbed was she in this monotonous and barren activity that I must have stood there for quite some time. When she turned around, I saw a large pair of eyes so hollow that I draw a blank when I try to picture their expression. Then I heard a sound so thin it was as though a thread was passing through my ear, the way it might pass through the eye of a needle. She was telling me what would happen if she wore damp underwear: "I'd be dead in a second."

I was startled to find this languid woman speaking about death with such finality. I had left the familiar and intimate surroundings of Southgate and parted from my parents and brothers who were all so full of life, and now, no sooner did I get here than the first thing this unnerving woman said to me was that she could die at any moment.

Later I came to feel that Li Xiuying's remark was not so exaggerated. During those periods when it rained day after day, she would run a fever and lie in bed mumbling. She looked so desperately ill at such moments that I often felt she was about to vindicate her own prognosis. But when sunlight shone through the window and illuminated her rows of stools, she accepted her survival with equanimity. She had an uncanny sensitivity to moisture and could even gauge the humidity in the air with her hand. Every morning when I pushed open her door and went to clean her window, she would extend a hand from her blue floral mosquito net and pat the air, just as if she was stroking something solid, in this way testing the dampness of the day that was just beginning. At first this scared me out of my wits, for her body was entirely obscured behind the mosquito net and all that could be seen was a white hand, its five splayed fingers in sluggish motion, like a severed limb floating in the air.

Sickly as she was, Li Xiuying naturally placed a high priority on hygiene. Her world was already narrow and confining, and if it was in a mess as well she would be hard put to sustain her fragile life. I was responsible for almost the entire job of keeping her room tidy. Window cleaning was the most important chore, to be performed twice a day so as to ensure that sunlight could reach her underwear unsullied by any impurities. The biggest challenge came when I opened the window, for I was expected to do a quick and thorough job of cleaning the outside of the pane, and it was a tall order for a child my age to perform this task with the requisite dispatch. Li Xiuying was truly too weak to withstand a gust of wind. She told me that wind was the worst thing in the world, for it blew dust, germs, and bad smells all over the place, making people sick, making people die. She made wind sound so dreadful that in my young imagination it almost took on the features of a green-faced, long-toothed monster, fastening itself to my window at night and rubbing the pane till it shook.

After concluding her vilification of the wind, Li Xiuying asked me in a conspiratorial hush, "Do you know where dampness comes from?"

Then she answered her own question. "It's blown here by the wind!" she exclaimed. The sudden fury with which she said this gave me such a fright that my heart started pounding.

Glass played a vital role in Li Xiuying's life, interposing itself in transparent form between her and the outside world, protecting her from the intrusion of wind and dust and at the same time safeguarding her special relationship with sunshine.

Even now I remember that in the afternoon, when the sunlight was blocked by the slope of the mountain opposite, Li Xiuying would stand in front of the window, gazing disconsolately at the red tint in the sky behind the mountain, as though she had been deserted and yet at the same time was unwilling to accept her abandonment. She told me softly, "The sun wanted to shine in my room, but on its way here the mountain abducted it."

Her voice traverses time and carries to my ears today, as though to remind me how long she and the sunlight had enjoyed cordial relations. The mountain, by contrast, was a despot that had forcibly appropriated her sunshine.

Wang Liqiang was a busy man, away at work the whole day, and he did not count on me simply to pull my weight doing chores: what he seemed to be hoping was that the noise I made around the house would alleviate the melancholy to which Li Xiuying was prone. In fact, however, Li Xiuying did not set much store by my presence, for she preferred to spend her time bemoaning her fate and seldom concerned herself with me. She would harp on about how this was sore or that was giving her trouble, but when I nervously appeared in front of her, looking forward to doing some little job that would make her life easier, she would act as though I wasn't there. Sometimes my astonishment at her health problems would simply have the odd effect of making her feel proud of them.

Soon after I moved into her house, I noticed that a newspaper had been spread out on the floor of her room; on top of the yellowing pages a pile of little white bugs had been laid out to dry. Li Xiuying was in the habit of seeking medical advice from a variety of authorities, and these fearsome little insects were a folk remedy that she had just acquired. When she boiled them in water and swallowed them one by one as calmly as if they were grains of rice, I paled at the sight. My horror actually rather pleased her: she flashed me a smile and said contentedly, "These things are good for you."

Li Xiuying could be terribly self-centered, but deep down she was ingenuous and kindhearted. If she was prone to suspicion, that's just a common failing in women. When I was new there, she worried that I would get up to no good, so she designed a trial. Once when I was cleaning the window of one of the other rooms, I found fifty cents on the windowsill. This was a startling find: for me at the time, fifty cents was a huge sum. When I took the money through and handed it to her, my surprise at the discovery and my honesty in reporting it took a big weight off her mind. She told me straightforwardly that this had been a test and praised me in a heartwarming tone of voice, complimenting me in such extravagant terms that I was almost moved to tears. Her trust in me never wavered throughout the whole five years, and when later I became the target of accusations at school she was the only person who believed in my innocence.

Strong and fit though he was, Wang Liqiang looked out of sorts when he was at home, and he often sat alone by himself with a frown on his face. But once during the first summer I was with them, he had me sit on the windowsill and told me about the river at the foot of the mountain and the wooden boats that plied its waters. His description, simple though it was, somehow managed to conjure up a clear picture in my mind. For the most part he was a mild-mannered person, but at times he would say shocking things. He had a favorite little wine cup, which was placed on top of the wireless and enjoyed the distinction of being the only decorative item in the whole house. So as to make sure I fully recognized its value he told me very sternly that if I was ever to break the cup he would wring my neck. At the time he was holding a cucumber, and with a sharp tearing sound he twisted it into two, saying, "Just like that." This scared me so much I felt a chill around my nape.

As I approached my seventh birthday, the change that I had just gone through seemed to have made me a different person altogether. At this stage I must have been at a loss to know what to make of it all. Drifting with the tide, too young to fight the current, I had transformed in the blink of an eye from the Sun Guanglin of the rowdy Southgate house into a boy who was easily spooked by Li Xiuying's groans and Wang Liqiang's sighs.

It did not take me long to gain a familiarity with the town of Littlemarsh, but in the early days I was consumed by curiosity.

Those spindly streets paved with stone slabs seemed to carry on forever, just like the river that flowed past Southgate. Sometimes at dusk when Wang Liqiang grasped my hand in a fatherly way and took me out for a walk, I would fondly imagine that if we just kept going we would eventually reach Beijing. But somehow, as my mind was following this train of thought, I would suddenly notice that we had arrived back home. For a long time I was perplexed by this enigma: though we seemed to keep walking in the same direction, we always ended up back at the house. Most of all I marveled at the pagoda that overlooked Littlemarsh, for out of one of its windows a tree was growing. Inspired by this sight, I once had the strange feeling that a tree might perhaps sprout from Li Xiuying's mouth, or if not a tree some grass at least.

The paving stones would often give a creak and rock to and fro when you stepped on them. Particularly on rainy days, if you stamped hard on one side, a spray of muddy water would shoot up from the other. For a long time I thought this was the most wonderful game, and whenever I had the chance to get out of the house it was the first thing I wanted to do. I was seized by an urge to splash the trousers of a passerby, but timidity made me resist the temptation, for I felt sure this would put me at the receiving end of some horrendous punishment. Later I saw three older boys walk along the street, picking up chamber pot covers propped up outside people's doorways. They tossed the lids up in a way that made them spin through the air delightfully. Outraged residents came rushing out of their houses, but could do little more than curse the boys while they ran off, laughing with glee. From this I realized the advantages of showing a clean pair of heels, for then punishment becomes unlikely and enjoyment is prolonged. So afterward, when I saw a girl walk by in a smart outfit, I stamped on a loose flagstone. As filthy water spattered her pants, I implemented the next phase of my plan—running away. Unfortunately, even though my desire had been satisfied, no pleasure ensued. The girl did not unleash a torrent of abuse nor make any effort to pursue me, but simply stood there in the middle of the street, crying her heart out. The longer she went on crying, the more I felt panic rising inside me.

The house on the corner was home to a teenager who wore a peaked cap. He could make music by blowing on a bamboo tube, something that seemed as wonderful to me in my early days in Littlemarsh as the tree that grew out of the pagoda window. I would see him ambling down the street, hands in his pockets, greeting grown-ups he knew, and I quietly attempted to imitate the way he carried himself. But when I stuck my hands in my pockets and did my best to strut around, the image that I had so proudly cultivated was spoiled by Wang Liqiang's rebuke. He said I looked like a juvenile delinquent.

Aside from his other tunes, the boy in the cap could also produce an amazing likeness of the jingle that the pear-syrup candy vendor used to play. When a few other greedy children and I dashed toward the source of the music, we found that it was not the street vendor at all, but this boy sitting in the window, laughing hard as could be. Our silly expressions provoked him to such mirth that he ran out of breath and ended up coughing.

No matter how often I was taken in, I couldn't seem to stop myself from heading over there every time. Summoned by those sounds, I ran with a blind and witless instinct, just so that he could have a joke at my expense. But once I was mortified to find that I was the only child to fall for the trick, and his gleeful laughter was a blow to my ego. I said to him, "The sound you make isn't like the candy seller at all." Thinking myself clever, I went on: "I knew it was fake as soon as I heard it."

To my surprise he laughed even harder, and asked me, "So why did you come running?"

I could think of no answer to this.

One lunchtime we crossed paths when I was out buying soy sauce, and he found a new way of mocking me. After walking past me in the street, he suddenly came to a stop and called me over. Then he bent down, stuck his buttocks in the air, and asked me to check if there was a hole in the seat of his pants, where two red patches had been sewn. Peering at his monkeylike bottom, I had no idea that I was falling into a trap. "I can't see any hole," I said.

"Take another look."

I did as he said, but still saw nothing. "Bring your head a bit nearer," he urged. As I put my face as close as I could get, he let out a resounding fart so foul I was practically gassed, and walked off laughing heartily. I couldn't help admiring him, even if he never missed an opportunity to tease.

Immersed in this new life, I often forgot the Sun Guanglin who had been tearing around the fields of Southgate not long before. Occasionally while I drifted off to sleep I could dimly make out my mother's blue-checked headscarf floating in the air. At such moments as these a sadness stirred, leaving me anxious and uneasy, but once I was asleep I forgot all about it. One evening, though, I did ask Wang Liqiang, "When will you take me back?"

He and I were walking hand in hand along the street as the sun was setting. He did not answer my question right away, but first bought me five olives. Then he told me, "Once you're grown up, that's when I'll take you back."

Wang Liqiang, always so harried by his wife's afflictions, ruffled my hair and told me gravely that I should be obedient and study hard when I went to school. If I met his standards, he said, "When you're grown up, I'll find you a strapping young woman to marry."

I had been wondering what kind of reward he would give me, and "a strapping young woman" came as a big disappointment.

After Wang Liqiang gave me the five olives, I no longer felt in any hurry to return to Southgate. This being a place where olives were provided, I had no wish to leave it any time soon.

Just once was I seized with a real urge to reclaim my old life. One afternoon I mistook for my big brother a boy who had hung his satchel over his chest and put his hands behind his back. At that moment I forgot that I was in Littlemarsh and thought I was back by the pond in Southgate, watching my big brother showing off on his first day home from school. I raced toward him, calling "Sun Guangping!" But my excitement drained away as an unfamiliar face swung around, looking baffled, and only then did I remember that I had left Southgate long ago. The jolt back to reality left me feeling bereft. Sobbing, I went on my way as the north wind whistled in my ears.

I made friends with a boy called Guoqing, whose birthday was October 1, and another boy named Liu Xiaoqing. When I think of them now, my heart tingles. Walking along those stone-paved streets, we would jabber and quack like three little ducklings.

Of the two, I was more fond of Guoqing. He was a boy who loved to run around. The first time he raced up to me he was pouring with sweat. Though I did not know him at all, he asked me warmly, "You're good in a scrap, aren't you? From the look of it, you really know how to fight." My bond with Liu Xiaoqing, on the other hand, was a by-product of his brother's delightful flute-playing. The fact that he was the brother of the boy with the peaked cap meant that my affection for him was colored by envy.

Guoqing was the same age as me, but already possessed leadership ability, and he won my loyalty by bringing spice and variety to my life. I'll never forget that time in the summer when he took me and Liu Xiaoqing down to the riverside to wait for the waves. Before that excursion I had no idea what wonderful pleasures were in store for me there. We stood in a row, evenly spaced along the riverbank, and after a steamboat passed its wake would lap over our bare feet and the waves would climb up our ankles. Our feet were like boats moored to the shore, swaying in the water. But soon I had to go home to clean the windows and mop the floor. As Guoqing and Liu Xiaoqing watched a boat in the distance steadily steaming closer, I had to leave, rushing home as fast as my legs would carry me.

Another unforgettable joy was going upstairs in Guoqing's house to view the countryside off in the distance. In those days, even in a town, not many people lived in a two-story house. When Liu Xiaoqing and I went to Guoqing's place, we were as excited as two twittering sparrows. Guoqing, for his part, displayed the poise one would expect from a host. Walking between us, he rubbed his nose with his hand, concealing his childish pride with a grown-up's smile.

Then Guoqing knocked on a door. The door opened only a little, revealing half a wizened face. Guoqing called loudly, "Hi, Grannie."

The door opened just enough to admit Guoqing, revealing the dim interior and the face of an old lady dressed in black. Her eyes were watching us with a brightness surprising for someone of such advanced years.

As Liu Xiaoqing started to go in, she swiftly pushed the door almost completely shut, leaving only one of her eyes visible. I heard her hoarse voice for the first time. "Let me hear you say 'Grannie.'"

Liu Xiaoqing said the magic word and was admitted; then it was my turn. Again the door opened just a crack and a single eye peered out at me. The old lady gave me the creeps. But Guoqing and Liu Xiaoqing were already pounding up the stairs, so I had no choice but to call out the required greeting, at the same time giving a shiver. I gained admission to the inner darkness, and after she had closed the door the only light came from the top of the staircase. As I climbed the stairs, I heard no sound of her steps moving away and realized with dismay that her sharp old eyes must be watching me.

In the two years that followed, my eagerness to visit Guoqing's house was always tempered with dread at having to pass the old lady's gloomy checkpoint. Her face and her voice, which often figured in my nightmares, began to haunt me. In order to work up the courage to knock on the door, I had to remind myself there was no greater pleasure than leaning out the upstairs window with Guoqing.

Unusually, on one occasion, she did not ask me to call her "Grannie" and instead ushered me in with a mysterious smile. It turned out that Guoqing was not at home, and as I nervously came back down the stairs the old lady pounced on me the way a cat pounces on a bird. She took my hand and led me into her room. Her moist palm made me tremble, but I was too petrified to put up any resistance.

Her room, as it turned out, was bright and spotlessly clean. Many framed pictures hung on the wall, black-and-white photographs of old men and women, not one of whom was smiling. She said to me in a whisper, "They're all dead."

She seemed to be speaking quietly for fear they might hear, and I hardly dared breathe. She pointed at a gentleman with a long wispy beard and said, "There's a good man. He came to visit me just last night."

A dead man came to see her? I started to cry. She was not pleased and told me disapprovingly, "That's nothing to cry about."

Pointing at another photograph, she said, "Now, her, she doesn't dare come to see me. She stole my ring, and now she's worried I'm going to ask for it back."

This old woman who cuts such a daunting figure in my childhood memory would not let me leave that spooky room of hers until she had introduced the people in the pictures to me one by one. I never dared visit Guoqing's home again. Even if he was there to keep me company, I didn't want to have anything to do with this eerie old lady. Only much later did I realize there was actually nothing to fear from her. She was simply immersed in an isolation unfathomable to me at my age. She straddled the boundary between life and death, forsaken by both.

How amazed I was to see things so far away, that first time I went up to the second story of Guoqing's house. It was as though distance had shrunk and I suddenly had the whole world at my feet. Like the hills in the distance, fields spread out as far as the eye could see, and the tiny moving figures made me chuckle with delight. For the first time I truly understood the meaning of the word *limitless*.

Guoqing was an organized child. His clothes were always clean, and the little handkerchief he kept in his pocket was folded into a perfect square. When we lined up for physical education, he would delicately remove his handkerchief and wipe his mouth. I was very struck by that well-practiced action of his, because if I had a runny nose I was more than likely to let my shirt get stained. What is more, he had his own medical kit, just like a doctor—a small cardboard box containing five vials in a neat row. When he took the bottles out and explained their various applications, this boy of eight was the embodiment of carefulness and gravity, and in my impressionable eyes he seemed more like a distinguished medical practitioner than a boy my own age. He took his vials everywhere, and sometimes, just as he was running across the school playground, he would come to an abrupt halt and gesture to me that it was time to take a pill. So I would go into the classroom with him and watch him take the medicine kit out of his satchel, extract a tablet from a vial, and put it in his mouth. He could swallow it dry.

Guoqing's father I found intimidating. If he wasn't feeling well, he would turn to his son for a consultation. My classmate was invigorated on such occasions: he spoke with eloquence, in his piping voice, quizzing his father on every aspect of his ailment. Only when his father interrupted him would he break off questioning and open his sacred box with an expert flick. His hand would hover above the five vials and select the medication required. As he handed the medicine over, he would lose no time in asking his father for five cents. On one such occasion, his father was about to go and get the money, but Guoqing quickly handed him a glass of water, considerately letting his father take the medicine while he went over and stuck a hand into the pocket of the jacket that his father had thrown on the bed. Taking his hand out, he showed his father a five-cent coin, which he then deposited in his own pocket. But then, as we set off together for school, he dug out of his pocket two five-cent coins. Guoqing was a generous boy; he told me that he had taken the other five cents for me. Then he carried out his promise to buy us both an ice.

I never knew Guoqing's mother. Once the three of us were playing on top of the old town wall, waving willow branches and running on the yellow earth, enacting an imaginary battle, war whoops and all. Afterward we sat down in exhaustion, and Liu Xiaoqing suddenly asked about her. "She went to heaven," Guoqing said.

Then, pointing at the sky, he said, "The Lord of Heaven is watching us."

At that moment the sky was so blue it seemed unfathomably deep. Heaven was watching us. We three children were enveloped in a huge emptiness, and deep within me I gave a deferential shudder, for the endless sky left me no place to hide. I heard Guoqing go on, "Whatever we are doing, the Lord of Heaven can see it as clear as anything. Nobody can put one over on him."

Xiaoqing's random inquiry about Guoqing's mother left me in awe of heaven—my earliest experience of a self-imposed constraint. Even now I sometimes have the sensation that I am being followed by a pair of eyes and have no safe haven, my secrets far from secure, but in danger of exposure at any moment.

In second grade Guoqing and I had a fierce argument triggered by the following question: if one tied together all the atom bombs on earth and detonated them, would the world be blown to pieces? It was Liu Xiaoqing who got us going on this, because he was the one who had the idea of roping all the atom bombs together, an idea that makes me smile when I think about it now. I clearly remember how Liu Xiaoqing looked when he said this: he broached the issue just after sniffing up a thread of mucus that was threatening to dribble into his mouth. He sniffed so loudly I could practically feel the snot slithering smoothly back inside his nose.

Guoqing agreed with Liu Xiaoqing, arguing that the world, or at the very least a big chunk of it, would surely be blown to pieces. We would be whipped all over the place by incredible gale-force winds, amid a terrible howling noise. Just like our physical education instructor, who had a hole in his nose—when he talked there was a wheezing sound, like the roar of the north wind.

I didn't believe that the world would be destroyed by the explosion; in fact I didn't even think there would be such a big crater. My reasoning was: atom bombs are made from things found in the world, and the world is bigger than atom bombs. How could something that's so big possibly be blown up by something that's so small? Carried away by the force of my argument, I put it to Guoqing and Liu Xiaoqing, "Can you beat your dads in a fight? No way! That's because you're their sons. You're small, and your dads are big."

Neither side could persuade the other, so we went to see Zhang Qinghai, the schoolmaster who knitted, hoping that he would serve as an impartial judge. This was during lunch break in the winter, and our teacher was sitting against the wall, sunning himself. His knitting hands flitted back and forth, as nimble as a woman's. Squinting in the sun, he listened as we presented our cases and then admonished us, "That's impossible. The peoples of the world are peace loving. How could they possibly tie atom bombs together and detonate them?"

We had been arguing about science, but he gave us an answer rooted in politics. So we had no choice but to continue our argument, which soon deteriorated into personal attacks. I said to them, "You don't know shit!"

"*You* don't know shit!" they fired back.

I was so angry I didn't know what I was doing, and I issued a most impractical threat. I said, "I am not going to have anything to do with you two from now on!"

"Who the hell wants to have anything to do with you?" they said.

After this, I had to bear the consequences of my reckless declaration. Guoqing and Liu Xiaoqing turned their backs on me as they said they would. But I found that I lacked the determination needed to carry through with my threat. There were two of them and only one of me: that was the problem. They could steadfastly ignore me, but I could give them the cold shoulder only at great expense to my nervous system. I was now a loner, standing at the doorway to the classroom, watching them running joyfully around the playground. I was green with envy. Every day I hoped that they would come over and propose reconciliation, for in that way I could both maintain my integrity and have my friends back. But when they walked past they would be rolling their eyes or laughing their heads off. It was clear that they were ready to carry on like this indefinitely, for it cost them nothing. But I was paying a heavy price: when I walked home alone after school, it was as though I had a chinaberry in my mouth, bitter and hard to swallow.

I was stubbornly resolved to preserve my self-respect, but at the same time my wish to be with them intensified. These two contradictory impulses canceled each other out, until I hit upon an alternative form of intimidation.

I chose a spot on Guoqing's regular route home for delivery of this new threat; I ran ahead as fast as I could to wait for him there. As Guoqing approached my observation post, he—true to his proud nature—defiantly looked the other way. But I shouted with all the ferocity I could muster: "You stole your dad's money!"

His confidence crumbled. He turned around and shouted at me, "No, I didn't! What a load of rubbish."

"Oh yes you did," I retorted. I reminded him of that time he asked for five cents from his father and took ten.

"I took those five cents for *you*," he said.

I didn't care about that. Instead I shouted out my most potent line: "I'm going to tell your dad!"

My classmate went deathly pale. He bit his lip and did not know what to do. That's when I spun on my heel and left, striding along with my nose in the air like a rooster at daybreak. My heart filled with a sinful joy, stirred to elation by the look of despair on Guoqing's face.

Later on I was to threaten Wang Liqiang in much the same way. What I realized was that if there is something you really want you have to be prepared to stop at nothing to get it. My threat allowed me to reclaim our friendship and still keep my self-respect intact, so I felt that practical results were being achieved, however underhanded the methods.

The following morning, Guoqing sidled up to me and asked in a conciliatory tone if I wanted to go to his house and look at the scenery from the second floor. I said yes right away. This time he didn't invite Liu Xiaoqing; it was just the two of us. On the way there, he begged me not to tell his father about that earlier act of deception. But by this time, of course, he and I were already friends again, and I no longer had any desire to reveal his secret.

ABANDONED

One morning when he was nine, Guoqing woke up to find that he held his destiny in his own hands. Though far from being an adult and still under his father's sway, all of a sudden he was independent. Premature freedom made him carry his fate on his shoulder the way he might carry a heavy suitcase, staggering along a busy street, not sure which way to go.

My poor classmate was wakened that morning by a chaotic din. It was early autumn, and when he went to the door, still in just his underpants, his eyes heavy with sleep, he found his father and a couple of other men busily packing up household effects.

Guoqing at first was thrilled, for he assumed they were moving to a brand-new house. His joy was much like mine when I was leaving Southgate, but the reality that he was about to encounter was far worse.

Guoqing asked his father, in a voice as fresh as the morning itself, if they would be moving to a place where he'd see white horses with wings. His father, always so stern, saw nothing charming about this flight of imagination; on the contrary, he thought his son's question too ridiculous to deserve an answer. All he said was "Don't block the hallway."

Guoqing returned to his room. He was the most worldly of the children in our class, but given his age at the time he could not possibly have anticipated what was about to happen. He set to work speedily organizing his possessions: his clothes, neither new nor old, as well as miscellaneous items like his screw nuts, his little scissors, and his plastic pistol. He was able to neatly pack them all into a cardboard box. He performed this task cheerfully against a background of bangs and thumps, often running out to the front door to watch with admiration as his father displayed his muscle power, shifting furniture. Then it was his turn. Although the box was about the same size as he was, he managed to lift it off the floor. He moved it slowly, edging along, brushing against the wall on the other side, for he knew the wall was a hand too, and a strong hand at that. Although he was fast running out of strength, there was a proud glint in his eye as his father came up the staircase. But his father said to him coldly, "Put that back where it came from."

My friend had no choice but to make the reverse journey, straining with effort, having achieved nothing. His hair was dripping with sweat, and even after he patted it down it was still a disorderly clump. At this moment he really did not know what to do, and he sat down in a little chair to ponder the question. But it was impossible for him to envision his future in bleak terms, for life had not trained him to think along those lines. His thoughts bounced around like a ball on the playground and did not stay fixed on his father for very long. As his mind wandered, he looked happily through the window at the sky outside. Perhaps he was still imagining a white horse as it sailed through the air, its wings outstretched.

Grunts and thuds descended the stairs time and again. Guoqing must have heard all this racket but he did not realize that the furniture had now been deposited on three flatbed carts, and he did not hear the wheels begin to turn. His thoughts had been whirring around like a bat, and when they finally stopped his father was in his room, and harsh reality faced him.

Guoqing did not give us a detailed account of what happened, and in any case Liu Xiaoqing and I were too young to understand. It was subsequent events that really drove home to me the fact of his abandonment. This was not the only reason I disliked his father. I had seen him on a number of occasions, and each time his manner was so severe as to give me the shivers. Now, as I try to recall him, I feel that there are some similarities between him and my grandmother's father. The first time I met him, he questioned me so closely about my background he might as well have been cross-examining me. When Guoqing tried to answer for me, he interrupted him, saying, "Let him speak for himself."

His aggressive stare made me quake. When he entered Guoqing's bedroom that day, I'm sure he fixed his son with the same stare. But his tone may have been calm, perhaps even gentle. He told Guoqing, "I'm going off to get married."

Guoqing had to understand the change this entailed, which was very simple: his father could not possibly look after him anymore. Guoqing was too young to appreciate all the grim implications, and he just looked at his father in bewilderment. The heartless bridegroom-to-be left his son ten yuan in cash and twenty pounds' worth of grain coupons, picked up a couple of baskets, and went downstairs. In the baskets he had put the last few items he was taking with him. My friend glued his face to the window, squinting in the sunlight as he watched his father saunter off.

It was when he went into the two rooms that had been emptied of belongings that Guoqing first began to feel sad. Even then he did not think his father had abandoned him forever; the sight of the deserted rooms alone was enough to prompt his tears. The pristine environment of his own room—which I had visited so often, whose window I so adored—helped Guoqing calm down, and he sat down on his bed to think things over. Only when he found me later that afternoon did he fully realize his predicament. I was busy cleaning Li Xiuying's favorite window when I heard him calling me from outside. I dared not leave the window before I had finished the job, but Li Xiuying could not stand Guoqing's shouts, which pierced the air like the sound of breaking glass. Sitting in bed, she said to me in dismay, "Oh, do tell him to shut up."

How could I tell him to be quiet when he was in such a fix? We stood in the stone-paved street while the power lines above us maintained a steady hum. I still remember how pale Guoqing looked as he told me what had occurred—all in confused fragments, for he was still not really clear about it in his own mind. He presented his story as a series of random impressions, like flies that buzz around and abruptly change direction—from the enormous strength his father displayed when moving furniture to the look on his father's face when he went out the door holding the baskets. I had trouble sorting out which things happened first and which later. As he told me the story, Guoqing suddenly realized what it all meant, and his narrative petered out. Tears gushed from his eyes, and he said something that he and I both understood perfectly: "My dad doesn't want me anymore!"

We went to find Liu Xiaoqing and found him running toward

the river, a mop over his shoulder. He was shocked by the sight of Guoqing's tears. I told him Guoqing had been abandoned. At first Liu Xiaoqing was as baffled as I had been earlier, but my wordy explanation, accompanied by frequent nods from Guoqing, eventually got the facts through to him. Right away he said, "Let's find my big brother!"

To consult the older boy in his peaked cap seemed an excellent idea, and for Liu Xiaoqing to suggest this so proudly struck me as quite natural. Who wouldn't want a brother like that? We went over to the window where he was sitting, and now it was Liu Xiaoqing's turn to tell the story. Toying with his flute his brother heard him out. He seemed very indignant. "This is outrageous!" he said.

He stuck the flute in his pocket, jumped out the window, and beckoned us. "Come on, let's go and sort him out!"

We three children walked along the damp street. A rain shower early that morning had drenched the trees. Leading the way was Liu Xiaoqing's brother—an older boy, to be sure, but rather skinny. He could play a fine tune on the flute, but could he get the better of Guoqing's father? The three of us followed him quietly, buoyed by his outrage. Reaching a tree heavy with rain, he seemed lost in thought, but when we caught up with him he raised his foot and kicked the trunk with all his might, at the same time darting off. Droplets showered down on us, soaking us to the skin. He ran off home, chortling.

His action, obviously, was most inglorious, for otherwise Liu Xiaoqing would not have turned red. Mortified, he said to Guoqing, "Let's go talk to our teacher about it."

Now sopping wet, Guoqing shook his head and said with a sob, "I don't want to talk to anyone about it!"

And he stalked off. This clever little boy could rattle off the names of all his maternal uncles and aunts, and when he got home he thought of them and sat down to write them letters—in pencil, on paper torn from his exercise book. At this point, when he was still struggling to find words to describe his plight to us, he must have found it even harder to write about it. When every one of his mother's siblings rushed to his side soon afterward, this showed how well he had put things.

Precise as he was, Guoqing recalled the workplaces of all his uncles and aunts and wrote their addresses on eight envelopes. But he wasn't sure just how to mail the letters. With his customary concern for order, he folded the eight sheets of paper into eight little squares. He clutched them to his chest and made his way to the forest green post office.

He found a young woman behind the counter. Guoqing timidly went up to her, asking in a pathetic tone, "Auntie, can you tell me how to post letters?"

Rather than answering, she asked him instead, "Do you have money?"

To her surprise Guoqing brought out a ten-yuan note. She did help him then, but she looked at him warily, the way one eyes a pickpocket.

Once the eight brothers and sisters of Guoqing's mother had assembled, they made an impressive party. Together they marched off toward his father's new house, Guoqing in the middle, the grown-ups surrounding him with determined looks on their faces. Guoqing had worn an expression of sheer misery the past several days, but now, pampered by his aunts and uncles, he walked among them with his confidence fully restored. At regular intervals he would turn back toward Liu Xiaoqing and me and call: "Be sure to keep up with us!"

It was late in the afternoon by then. Walking with this group of adults, I felt very important, almost as important as Guoqing; Liu Xiaoqing was also looking cocky. Guoqing declared jubilantly that his father would soon be moving back home.

It was my first outing after dark since I had come to Littlemarsh. When I asked Wang Liqiang's permission to leave the house I told him what had happened, and I was grateful to him for allowing me to go out so late in the day. While sympathizing with my desire to stand with Guoqing in his hour of need, he cautioned me not to open my mouth. In fact, however, Liu Xiaoqing and I would never have been allowed to enter Guoqing's father's new home; we had to wait outside. A squat little building stood before us, and we found it strange that Guoqing's father would leave the two-story house for such a modest dwelling.

"There's no view here at all!" Liu Xiaoqing and I agreed. We could hear the voices of the eight visitors from out of town. Their city accents evoked tall buildings and asphalt roads. At this moment two boys much younger than us came swaggering over and told us presumptuously to clear off. Only later did we realize that they were the darling sons of Guoqing's father's new wife. The idea that we could be driven away by two smaller boys was ridiculous, of course. We warned them that they'd better push off themselves. They spat at us then, and Liu Xiaoqing and I gave them each a punch in the face. These two little fellows were all bark and no bite, for they immediately burst out crying. But reinforcements arrived promptly, charging out of the house in the form of a woman as fat as a tub of lard. Guoqing's father's bride bore down on us with spit spraying from her mouth and such a murderous gleam in her eye that we fled in terror. She followed close behind, cursing us fiercely in language we thought only men were accustomed to using. One minute she threatened to toss us into the cesspit; the next minute she vowed to hang us from a tree, describing to us as we ran a whole series of awful fates. As I tired, I turned my head to look back; my scalp went numb when I saw the way her flesh wobbled as she ran. All she needed to do was sit on us and she would crush the life out of us.

Only after we ran across a stone arched bridge did we see her stop and turn around, still hurling curses. She probably felt that it was more vital that she go to the aid of her husband. After establishing that she was not waiting in ambush at some point along the road, Liu Xiaoqing and I fearfully edged our way back, vigilant as scouts in a movie who venture deep into enemy territory. By then the sky was dark, and when we returned to our original spot under the lamplight we still heard only the impassioned voices of the eight uncles and aunts. We wondered why Guoqing's father was saying nothing. After a long time we finally heard a different voice, the voice that had pursued us. His wife was saying to them, "Did you come here for a fight or for a discussion? For a fight you need a lot of people, but for a discussion one is enough. I want all of you out right now. One of you can come back tomorrow."

When this vulgar woman opened her mouth, somehow she projected power. She told them to leave just as arrogantly as her sons had told us to clear off. For just a moment the eight urbanites were silenced, and then they all burst into frantic protest. Liu Xiaoqing and I could not make any sense of what was said: with so many people talking at once, the hubbub that reached our ears was just a wall of sound. Then Guoqing's father spoke up, just as we were becoming convinced he wasn't there. He yelled angrily at the eight uncles and aunts: "Why are you all shouting? How irresponsible can you be? With you all making so much noise, how am I going to live this down?"

"Who's being irresponsible?" A quarrel erupted, as loud as a house falling down, and it sounded as though several men wanted to beat Guoqing's father and several women were trying desperately to stop them. Guoqing's mother's brothers and sisters were reduced to a state of helpless indignation, for after they had exhausted themselves explaining the rights and wrongs of the case, the obstinacy of the newlyweds made them suddenly realize that it was impossible to have a serious discussion with them. The oldest brother, the most senior figure of the eight, decided against leaving Guoqing in the newlyweds' care. He said to Guoqing's father, "Even if you wanted to raise him, we would absolutely refuse to let you. A man like you is just a beast!"

As the eight visitors came out the door, we heard a tumultuous expulsion of breaths. A traumatized Guoqing walked in the middle of the group, looking uncertainly at Liu Xiaoqing and me. I heard one of the men say, "How could Sis have married someone like that?" He was so exasperated that he had begun to think the fault lay with Guoqing's deceased mother.

The uncles and aunts assumed the responsibility of supporting Guoqing, and from then on they each sent Guoqing two yuan monthly. The forest green post office became the conduit for Guoqing's wealth. Several times each month he would announce to us proudly, "I have to go to the post office today."

When Guoqing began to receive his sixteen yuan for living expenses, I was to enter the most extravagant phase of my whole childhood, and the same was true for Liu Xiaoqing and a few other classmates. We stuck close to Guoqing, who often hankered for candy and olives. He was a generous boy, sharing with us the same pleasures that he allowed himself. He squandered his limited fortune as recklessly as a rich man's son, and on our way to school every morning we secretly looked forward to his big spending. The result was that by the second half of that month Guoqing was flat broke, and he was forced to depend on our charity to stave off hunger. But none of us could throw money around as freely as he, and we began to pilfer things from our homes: a handful of steamed rice, a piece of fish, a chunk of meat, some bits of vegetable, wrapped up in dirty paper and presented to him. Guoqing would open up the packages and spread them out on his knee, then eat their contents with gusto. He would smack his lips so loudly that even we who had already had a full meal found our mouths watering. This situation did not last very long, for soon our teacher, Zhang Qinghai the knitter, made himself responsible for managing Guoqing's living expenses and gave him only fifty cents a month as pocket money. That still left him the most affluent of any of us.

After his abandonment Guoqing gradually got used to handling his own affairs. But he never truly reconciled himself to his father's departure, and he did not follow his father's lead and repudiate him in turn. On the contrary, his father continued to exert control over his thinking. Our teacher tended to forget about the change in Guoqing's circumstances, and he would still sometimes threaten to inform Guoqing's father as a way of cowing him into submission whenever he did something out of line. It seemed never to occur to Guoqing that he was now free as a bird, that his anxiety was quite unnecessary. In his mind his father seemed still to be always watching him, and he was naive enough to be unsettled by the possibility that the man might appear in front of him at any moment. In fact, if his father did show up, it was only in a chance encounter. The man's standoffish attitude demonstrated that he had no plans at all to drop in on Guoqing.

I remember that the three of us were once standing on the side of the road, throwing pebbles at the streetlamps. It was Guoqing's idea, but we were all gung-ho, each hoping we would be the one to smash a light. When an adult came over to intervene, Liu Xiaoqing and I took to our heels, but Guoqing didn't budge an inch. He stood his ground and said defiantly, "Hey, it's not *your* light."

Just at that moment Guoqing's father appeared. Guoqing's nerve failed him; he went over, quaking, and called, "Hi, Dad."

He tried to clear himself of any suspicion of wrongdoing, insisting that he wasn't involved, and he even went so far as to defect completely from our camp, pointing at Liu Xiaoqing and me and saying, "They're the ones doing it."

But Guoqing's father said heatedly, "Who are you calling Dad?"

For him to forgo the right to punish his son was a much bigger blow to Guoqing than his refusal to look after him. How pitiful Guoqing now looked: when he crossed the street we saw that he had bitten his lip in a desperate effort to hold back the tears that were all ready to flow.

Even after this he still insisted that he would wake up one morning and find his father at his bedside. Once he told me with great conviction that when his father got ill he would "come and find me." He asked me to confirm that his father sought his help whenever he was ill; again and again he would say, "You saw that, right? You saw it." He no longer dipped into his little cardboard box, and even if he had a bad cough he wouldn't open one of his vials. Somehow he believed that as long as there was medicine in the pillboxes sooner or later his father would return.

Now when he talked about his mother, the past, though still remote, no longer seemed so hazy. He often used the expression "in those days": in those days, when his mother was alive, how good things were. He never gave us specifics of his happy life then, but heaved plenty of wistful sighs, making us wildly envious of "those days." He began to conjure up images of his mother; the imagination of this boy of nine was not focused on the future, but was connected—unusually for someone so young—to the past.

When we were small, we were fascinated by the horse on packs of Flying Horse cigarettes. The flatlands where we lived were traversed only by cows; the few sheep we glimpsed were always shut up inside pens. There were pigs, of course, but they left us cold. It was the white flying horses that we adored, for none of us had ever seen a horse. Later an army detachment came to Littlemarsh, and a horse-drawn carriage cut through the town in the early hours and rolled onto the high school grounds.

At the end of school that morning the three of us dashed toward the high school, waving our satchels. Guoqing ran ahead, spreading his arms wide like a huge bird. But it soon became apparent that I had misinterpreted his gesture, for he cried, "Hey, I'm a flying horse!" As Liu Xiaoqing and I ran behind, we followed his lead excitedly.

We were now a trio of flying horses, neighing with spirit and flying over the department store, the theater, and the hospital. But after sailing over this last building Guoqing let his arms drop to his sides, as though he had been shot; his ride was cut short. Looking miserable, he headed back in the direction from which we had come, hugging the wall. He did not say a word to us, and as we had no clue what had happened we chased after him seeking an explanation. But he just kept going, and when we tried to stop him he angrily pushed us aside and said with a sob, "Leave me alone."

Liu Xiaoqing and I looked at each other and watched in astonishment as he walked off into the distance. Then we put him out of our minds altogether. Liu Xiaoqing and I flapped our arms and set off at a gallop once more, intent on seeing the flying horses.

What we found in the little grove next to the high school were two chestnut horses. One was drinking water from a wooden trough while the other kept rubbing its behind on the trunk of a tree. They had no wings whatsoever and their coats were filthy. Their rank, horsey smell made us grimace. I whispered to Liu Xiaoqing, "Are those horses?"

Liu Xiaoqing went up to a young soldier and asked him timidly, "How come they don't have wings?"

"What? Wings?" The soldier waved us away impatiently. "Get out of here! Off you go."

We hurried away while the people around us tittered. I said to Liu Xiaoqing, "There's no way these can be horses! Horses should be white, surely."

An older boy said to us, "You're right, they're not horses."

"What are they, then?" Liu Xiaoqing asked.

"Rats."

Could rats be as big as that? We were shocked.

Guoqing had seen his father at the entrance to the hospital. This was why he was so upset: his final hope had come to nothing, so he was in no fit state to enjoy the flying horses.

It was the next day that Guoqing told us why he had turned around and left so suddenly. He said in anguish, "My dad is not going to come looking for me again!" Then he cried, "I saw him go into the hospital! If he doesn't come to see me when he's ill, then he'll never come at all!" Guoqing stood there under the basketball hoop, weeping loudly. Liu Xiaoqing and I angrily drove away the classmates who had begun to gather around.

Guoqing, deserted by the living, began to develop a close relationship with the old lady downstairs who had been deserted by the dead. In her black silk clothes, with wrinkles in her face as deep as waves, she gave me the willies, but Guoqing was unafraid. He spent more and more time with the lonely old lady. Sometimes I would see them walking hand in hand down the street, and Guoqing's features, normally so animated, seemed a little glum next to her. She was depleting Guoqing of his energy, and now when I think back on my childhood friend what I see in his young face are the dim shadows of decline.

I shuddered at the thought of them sitting together in that room, the doors and windows tightly closed, and felt convinced that they were headed for a collision with the spirit world. When the old lady talked about the dead, she spoke of them with a familiarity that I found chilling, but Guoqing was clearly intrigued, and now he often spoke of his mother with Liu Xiaoqing and me, of how she would come in silently before dawn to say a few words to him and then leave without a sound. When we asked him what she said, he told us gravely that this had to remain a secret. On one occasion his mother forgot that it was time for her to go back, and the cock's crow alarmed her. In her rush she did not leave through the door but went out through the window, taking off like a bird.

This final detail enhanced the authenticity of Guoqing's account, but it also left me bewildered: Guoqing's mother's jumping out the window made me anxious on her behalf, for they lived on the second floor, after all. I asked Liu Xiaoqing in a low voice, "Couldn't the fall kill her?"

His answer was, "She's dead already, so she's got no reason to worry about being killed in a fall." This sounded right to me.

When he talked about his reunions with his mother Guoqing was so earnest, so happy even, that we could hardly discount his reports. But I found his tone of voice disturbing, for the intimacy of his encounters with the dead reminded me so much of the old lady in the black clothes.

Another thing: Guoqing claimed often to have seen a bodhisattva as big as a house, as golden as the sun, who would appear suddenly in the sky above, then vanish like a flash of lightning.

Late one afternoon as we sat by the riverside I challenged him on this. I rejected the notion that such things existed, and to underscore my disbelief I heaped profanities on the bodhisattva's head. Guoqing sat there quite unmoved and after a moment he said, "It must be really scary to curse the bodhisattva."

If he hadn't said that, I wouldn't have worried, but as soon as he did all of a sudden I felt frightened. Dusk was falling, and I saw darkness spreading across the sky; so unsettled was I that my breathing became ragged.

"People who have no respect for the bodhisattva," Guoqing went on, "get punished."

In a quaking voice I asked, "How are they punished?"

Guoqing thought for a moment and said, "Grannie would know."

I did not find this reassuring.

Guoqing said softly, "When people are scared, that's when they can see the bodhisattva."

I opened my eyes as wide as I could and gazed intently at the ash gray sky, but saw nothing. I was practically in tears by now. I said to Guoqing, "You're not trying to pull my leg, are you?"

Guoqing then showed me what a good friend he was, with gentle words of encouragement: "Take another look."

I opened my eyes wide once more. By now the sky was completely dark. Through a combination of fear and zeal, I finally did see the bodhisattva, but I'm not sure if I really saw him or just imagined it. At any rate I did glimpse a bodhisattva as big as a house and as golden as the sun, though he disappeared in a flash.

The old lady, so close to the dead and so unconstrained in relaying their affairs, at the same time could not avoid contact with reality (for which she felt little affinity), because her life, much to her annoyance, showed no signs of ending. While she pacified Guoqing by means that I found unnerving, he for his part shielded her from the real world.

Her greatest source of anxiety was the brown dog that liked to sprawl in the middle of the alley. When she had no choice but to go out to buy rice or salt or pick up some soy sauce, the dog struck much greater terror into her heart than she had ever managed to instill in mine. Actually this ugly, unloved old dog barked at absolutely everyone, but she somehow got it into her head that she was its only enemy. As soon as the dog saw her it would put on a show of great ferocity, barking madly and threatening to leap at her, when in fact it was just jumping about in place. At moments like this the dead people on her wall were powerless to help her, and I saw her reduced to a quivering wreck. As she retreated headlong, her bound feet acquired an unexpected flexibility and her body swung from side to side like a fan in motion. This was before Guoqing's father moved out, and the three of us burst out laughing at the sight of her overreaction. As I walked to Guoqing's house that day, I had no need to fear her half face behind the door, for she was too busy crying to monitor our arrival. We glued our eyes to the door, admiring through the crack how she dried her tears with the hem of her jacket.

Later, through their common interest in the dead, she developed a special understanding with Guoqing and ended up benefiting from his protection. By having him accompany her every time she left the house, she relieved herself of a great deal of stress. When the brown dog barked and tried to block their passage, Guoqing would bend down and pretend to pick up a stone, and the dog would turn tail and dash off. As they proceeded on their way, the old lady would look at Guoqing adoringly and he would say to her with pride, "Even a dog meaner than that one would be afraid of me."

So acute was her phobia that she would kneel down daily in front of her clay Guanyin, piously begging the bodhisattva to bless the dog with a good long life. Every time Guoqing came home from school, the first question she would ask would be whether the dog was still outside. If he said yes, she would smile with pleasure, for her biggest fear was that the brown dog might die before her. She told Guoqing that it was a very long way to the underworld, and dark and cold to boot; she would need to wear a padded jacket and carry an oil lamp. If the dog died before she did it would wait for her on the way to the underworld. When she got to this point, she would tense up and shake all over. With tears welling up in her eyes, she would say, "You won't be able to help me then!"

This lonely old woman possessed the earnestness and obduracy that were hallmarks of the era. She had been using the same oil bottle for decades, its capacity marked with a line on the outside of the glass. She did not trust the shop assistants, for she said they were always looking somewhere else when they were refilling the bottle. If the clerk overfilled the bottle, she would not be the slightest bit pleased, but would pour some oil out with annoyance. If the clerk failed to fill the bottle all the way up to the mark, then she would not leave until they did. She would stand there for ages, not saying a word, just staring obstinately at the bottle.

It seemed that her husband had gone to his last resting place many years earlier. He had been a strong man, with a strange fondness for snails. He liked to sit in the courtyard in the summer, waving his fan and feasting merrily on snails. During her long widowhood her finest tribute to his memory was not the maintenance of her chastity but rather her punctilious tribute to this predilection of his. When he was alive he claimed all the flesh in the shell, and she happily consumed the unappetizing little muscle at the base. In the several decades since her husband's death she had never once helped herself to snail meat, but contentedly ate the remainders, leaving the flesh to the husband hanging on the wall. For her, habit and remembrance were fused into one.

Guoqing did not like snails, but the old lady would suck them out of their shells with a slurp and lick the juice off her lips afterward, and the more this carried on the more trouble Guoqing had keeping his mouth from watering. His appetite stirring, he tried picking up a piece of snail meat from the table, but the old lady was shocked. She quickly slapped it out of his hand and said menacingly into his ear, "He saw that."

It was true, in a sense: the dead man on the wall *was* watching them.

In the spring of the year that I turned twelve, the old lady at last was granted an unbroken slumber. She died in the street outside her house. She and Guoqing had gone out to buy soy sauce, and on her way home her legs seized up. She said she needed to rest a minute, and put her hand against the wall and sat down limply in the sun, clutching the soy sauce bottle to her chest. Guoqing stood next to her, and when she closed her eyes he thought she had fallen asleep. Bored, he looked around for distraction and noticed that grass was sprouting up next to the wall. The bright sun made him squint. At one point the old lady opened her eyes and in a faint voice inquired as to the dog's whereabouts. He saw it lying prone in the middle of the lane, observing them, so he said, "It's right over there." She gave a deep sigh and closed her eyes again. Guoqing stood for a while longer, watching with enjoyment as the sunlight played over the wrinkles on her face.

Guoqing told us later that she had lost her way and froze to death. According to him, she had been in too much of a hurry when going to the underworld, and had forgotten the padded jacket and oil lamp. She kept walking and walking along a road so dark you could not see the fingers of your hand, so she lost her way. A cold wind howled in her face, chilling her till she was shivering all over, and when she could not go another inch farther she sat down. That was how she froze.

When he was thirteen, Guoqing finally achieved a degree of personal liberation. He did not want to have to carry his satchel to school and put up with the teacher's endless dronings. When Liu Xiaoqing and the other classmates entered high school, he began to make a living.

By that time I was back in Southgate. As my wretched life at home began, Guoqing was fending for himself, working as a coal deliveryman. Like a real coolie, with a dirty towel hanging from his shoulder pole, his shirt open, grunting with effort, he would carry coal to the doors of his customers. Of his former habits, only the handkerchief in his pocket survived. When he set down a heavy load of coal, the first thing he did was to pull out the handkerchief and swab his lips. Even if sweat was pouring down his face, he just wiped his mouth. A little notebook and a pencil also took up space in his pocket. In his crisp voice, with naive courtesy, he would go from door to door asking if they needed coal. At first his age did not inspire confidence, and scanning his puny frame people would ask, "Can you carry coal?"

A canny smile would appear on Guoqing's face, and he would say, "If you don't let me try, how will you know?"

With his honesty and his careful arithmetic, it did not take long for Guoqing to win the trust of his customers. So vigilant was Guoqing that the shipper at the coal depot found it impossible to take advantage of him when weighing his consignment. In the end, Guoqing's innocent-looking appearance and his tragic circumstances (common knowledge to everyone) led the shipper to develop a soft spot for him, so he always slipped him a few extra pounds of coal. Of course it was the customers who reaped the greatest benefits, and their satisfaction in turn made Guoqing's career blossom. He practically put that rival of his out of business, despite his twenty years of experience in the trade.

I vividly recall Guoqing's fellow professional, for the simple reason that this little man was practically an idiot. Nobody knew what his name was, and he would answer to any name he was called. If he was walking by briskly with a load of coal on his back, he would not respond to our shouts; it was only when he was walking just as quickly, but with empty baskets hanging from his pole, that he would register our greetings earnestly, his head bowed, as we called him by any name we chose. I would call him "Guoqing" or "Liu Xiaoqing," while they would address him by my name. Off he would go, giving a grunt of acknowledgment, and he never raised his head to look at us. He was always rushing down the street as though he had a train to catch. Once we called him "Toilet" and he answered to that too, reducing us to paroxysms of laughter. Though cavalier about his name, he was meticulous where money was concerned. And his speed in making calculations was astounding: as his customers were just beginning laboriously to compute how much money they owed him, the total was already on his lips. Those figures were the only words that Littlemarsh residents ever heard him speak.

Guoqing made fun of him just like the rest of us, never imagining that he himself would wind up in the same line of work. Guoqing's entry into the trade knocked a big hole in the man's rice bowl, and he became less busy than before. This unfortunate fellow began to spend more time carrying empty baskets—still hurrying down the street, but looking more lonesome now that he was less in demand. He seemed not to be the slightest bit jealous of Guoqing, and I suspect he simply lacked the capacity to be so. Devoted to his job, he seldom let a smile appear on his face. After dumping coal into his customer's basket, he would take their broom and dustpan and scrupulously sweep up any coal slack that had fallen on the floor. Then he would lift up his empty pole and walk off, looking very solemn. But once when he saw Guoqing in the street, shouldering a pole identical to his own, he did break into a smile.

Nobody knew how these two became friends, but people began to notice how they would sit, still caked in coal dust, on the opposite sides of a table in the teahouse, drinking tea with smiles on their faces. The man of a million names—or of no name at all—sat like a servant, with both hands resting on his thighs, raising a hand only to lift his teacup to his lips. Guoqing cut a very different figure: he laid a handkerchief next to his cup, and would wipe his lips after every sip. In his tattered and dirty clothes Guoqing looked every inch the young gentleman down on his luck. Although they appeared to all the world like bosom pals, nobody had ever heard them have a conversation.

Not long after finding a career Guoqing found love as well. The girl that he fancied may have grown into quite a beauty later, but in those days it was too early to tell. I used to see the girl—Huilan, her name was—before I moved back to Southgate, and at the time Guoqing seemed to think her beneath his notice. Her house was down the same lane where Guoqing lived. Her hair tied into two perky pigtails, she liked to stand in the doorway, calling sweetly, "Brother Guoqing!"

The grapes that grew in her courtyard excited us to no end. One summer Guoqing, Liu Xiaoqing, and I developed an intricate scheme for stripping all the fruit from the vines under cover of darkness. Unfortunately their wall was too high for us to scale. That, however, was not the real reason we could not follow through; instead, it was the fact that none of us could leave our homes at night without the grown-ups knowing (this was before Guoqing's father had left him). When we thought of the fearful punishments lying in store for us, our plan, however sophisticated, remained only a fantasy.

As a result, when Guoqing ended up falling for this chit of a girl, Liu Xiaoqing, now in junior high, thought that he still had his eye on the grapes. He was so tactless as to ask Guoqing, "Shall we bring a few more people into it?" He told Guoqing that he could rope in some classmates from junior high and get hold of a ladder too.

Guoqing was furious. He said to Liu Xiaoqing, "How can you think of stealing my fiancée's grapes?"

Actually the seeds of their romance were sown before my return to Southgate. Now that there was nobody to oversee his activities, Guoqing liked to roam around at will during summer lunchtimes, barefooted, just wearing a pair of underpants. Huilan, two years his junior, joined Guoqing, and together they sneaked out to the countryside, where the two of them practiced skinny-dipping in a pond. Young though she was, Huilan already had an impulse to watch out for Guoqing's well-being. As they headed down the road out of town that day, the flagstones had been baking in the sun till they were scorching hot, and Guoqing could only hop desperately from foot to foot, like a frog. Huilan couldn't bear to see Guoqing suffering this way and took off her own little plastic sandals to offer to him. Guoqing was not yet aware of the importance of being nice to girls. He waved his hand in dismissal and said scornfully, "Who wants to wear girl's shoes?"

When at thirteen he came to court Huilan, Guoqing possessed the style of a more mature young man. Every afternoon Guoqing changed into a clean set of clothes and combed his hair so that it shone; then he waited outside the school gate at the hour that Huilan got out of class. This was the best possible reward he could give himself after a day of exhausting labor. The next thing one saw was Guoqing walking confidently in front with his hands in his pockets, while Huilan, her satchel on her back, trotted along behind.

At such times Huilan would pour out her woes, such as they were, telling him how such and such a boy had put a pinch of dirt in her textbook.

"Dirt? That's nothing." Guoqing waved his hand airily, like an adult, and told his little sweetheart with pride, "I once put a toad in a girl's satchel."

Their childish conversation made their romance seem innocent and artless. It was often only when they parted that Guoqing would take a piece of candy from his pocket—placed there carefully earlier in the day—and stuff it into Huilan's happy satchel.

From the look of it, Guoqing really did intend to marry Huilan and start a family; otherwise he would not have treated their relationship as seriously as he did. He was always trying to compensate for his still tender years, with the result that his gravity and earnestness took on comical proportions. Once these two children started going around together in the streets in such a public fashion, they gradually became famous in our little town. Guoqing misjudged grown-ups' perspective on their relationship. Believing the bond between them to be entirely natural, he thought that other people likewise would take it in their stride.

Huilan's parents were both pharmacists at the hospital. Although they had been aware from early on that their daughter and Guoqing were playmates, they felt that there was nothing untoward about children being close. When other people said that the two children looked as if they were in love, they found this suggestion preposterous. Later it was Guoqing's behavior which made them realize that such reports were well founded.

One Sunday morning, when Guoqing was still thirteen, he bought a bottle of spirits and a carton of cigarettes, inspired by a strange fancy to pay a call on his father-in-law. I have to take my hat off to him for the nonchalance with which he entered the house. When he set the gifts down on the table, he beamed deferentially. Huilan's father, of course, was taken aback and asked Guoqing what this was all about.

"These are for you," Guoqing said.

The pharmacist waved his hand in polite decline. "You have such a hard life. How could I possibly accept gifts?"

Guoqing had already sat down in a chair. He crossed his legs, but they were too short for his feet to touch the floor and dangled in the air instead. He said to Huilan's parents, "Please don't be so formal. These things are just a little token of respect from your son-in-law."

This last sentence came as a great shock. It took a few moments before Huilan's mother recovered enough to ask, "What did you say?"

"Mother-in-law." Guoqing addressed her in a dulcet tone and went on, "What I mean is—"

She did not wait for him to finish and was already screaming, "Who are you calling mother-in-law?"

Guoqing had no time to explain; the girl's father was now bellowing at him to leave their house immediately. Guoqing stood up, flustered, and tried to defend himself, using the formula so commonly recited by progressive couples: "We made this choice for ourselves."

Huilan's father was so furious his face went completely pale. Seizing Guoqing by his collar, he dragged him out and cursed him roundly. "You little hoodlum!"

Guoqing struggled desperately, repeating another mantra, "This is the new society, not the old one!"

Huilan's father shoved Guoqing out the door and a second later her mother tossed the gifts out after him. The bottle of spirits hit the ground with a crash and spilled everywhere. By this time quite a crowd had gathered outside, but Guoqing did not seem to feel that he had been at all disgraced. Pointing at Huilan's house, he told the onlookers with feeling, "Gosh, her folks have a really bad case of feudal thinking!"

Huilan's parents saw their innocent love as simply ridiculous. How could a thirteen-year-old boy and an eleven-year-old girl be engaged in a serious romance? Their daughter's conduct was an offense to public decency, and now they too had become a laughingstock. They could not tolerate this absurd liaison. They began to beat and scold their only daughter, and when Guoqing passed by their window and heard his sweetheart wailing, it is easy to imagine how upset he was. Huilan wilted under all the chastisement, but could not suppress her longing for those joyful moments with Guoqing, though I wonder if what she most hankered after was the candy in his pockets. They still had opportunities to meet, but all the pleasure was gone. Guoqing, moved now more by hate than by concern for Huilan, described to her, in a voice dripping with menace, the vengeance he was planning to exact from her parents. She listened with an expression of terror and tears tumbled from her eyes even before he had finished.

One afternoon Guoqing was passing by Huilan's house. He saw her leaning up against the window, her face dripping with blood, though actually it was just a nosebleed. Sobbing, she called to him, "Brother Guoqing!"

Guoqing was so angry he started shaking. At that moment he truly wanted to kill Huilan's parents. He ran home and then set off again for Huilan's house, this time with a kitchen cleaver in hand. A neighbor just happened to be coming out his door, and seeing Guoqing so strangely accoutered he asked him what he was doing. Seething with rage, Guoqing answered, "I've got some killing to do."

Guoqing had rolled up his sleeves and his trouser legs. With the cleaver resting snugly against his shoulder, he headed toward Huilan's house, a fierce glint in his eyes. His passage along the lane was completely unimpeded, because none of the adults who saw him took the full measure of his grim belligerence. When he told them he was off to kill people, his juvenile tone and callow manner made them chuckle.

Guoqing entered the courtyard of Huilan's house without difficulty. Huilan's father was busy lighting their coal briquette stove; her mother was squatting on the ground feeding the hens. When Guoqing suddenly appeared on the scene, cleaver in hand, they were dumbstruck. Guoqing did not immediately proceed toward his goal, but first pompously explained why he had to kill them. Then he moved forward, brandishing his cleaver. Huilan's father took to his heels, scurrying behind the house, where he yelled, "Help! Murder!"

Huilan's poor mother was frozen in her tracks and watched in horror as the cleaver approached. The chickens rescued her, for although most of these terrified creatures fled in all directions, two of them spread their wings and ran in front of Guoqing. This gave Huilan's mother time to recover her wits and flee out the courtyard gate.

Just as he was about to give chase, Guoqing noticed Huilan, who stood with her hand on the door frame, her eyes wide with alarm. Forgetting about pursuit, Guoqing hurried over to her, but it displeased him to find that she was shrinking back in fear. "What are you so afraid of? I'm not going to kill *you*!" he said.

His reassurance had no effect. She still looked at him in terror, her eyes so wide they almost looked artificial. Guoqing said heatedly, "If I knew this was how you were going to behave, I wouldn't have gone this far!"

By this time both entrances to the courtyard had been blocked by spectators, and before long police were on the scene. The news that a boy was bent on slaughter had spread through the town like wildfire; people came swarming from all directions. The first policeman to arrive stepped into the yard and said to Guoqing, "Put the cleaver down!"

It was Guoqing's turn to be petrified. He was already alarmed by all the noise outside, and the sight of the policeman made him grab Huilan and put the cleaver to her throat, yelling shrilly, "Don't you dare come in! I'll kill her if you do."

No sooner had the policeman issued his order than he found himself forced to retreat. Huilan, silent until now, burst out crying. Guoqing said to her fretfully, "I'm not going to kill you, I'm not going to kill you! I just said that to fool them."

But Huilan went on wailing as before. Guoqing said peevishly, "Stop crying! I'm doing this for you, you know." His face bathed in sweat, he looked around. "Now it's too late to run away."

Meanwhile, outside among the milling crowd, Huilan's distraught mother was reproaching her husband for being so selfish, fleeing for his life without the slightest thought for his wife's safety. Her husband, listening to Huilan's wails on the other side of the wall, said to her with tears in his eyes, "This is no time to talk about that when your daughter's life is hanging by a thread."

Just at this moment a policeman took a good grip on the eaves and in a single fluid movement sprang onto the roof. He planned to creep up behind Guoqing and jump down on top of him. This man enjoyed quite a reputation in Littlemarsh, for once he had succeeded in dealing single-handedly with five hoodlums, tying them up with their own shoelaces and marching them off to the Public Security Bureau like so many crabs hung from a string. The panache with which he leapt onto the roof won the appreciation of the assembled onlookers. He ducked down low and was making his way in catlike silence toward the other side of the building when he unfortunately slipped on a couple of loose tiles and tumbled off the roof, landing first on the grapevine trellis—the people outside heard a chaotic snapping of bamboo canes—before plunging down onto the concrete. Had the trellis not broken his fall, he might well have ended up a paraplegic.

The sight of someone suddenly falling from the sky scared Guoqing so much that he shouted again, "Get out, get out, or I'll kill her!"

The policeman pulled himself to his feet and said feebly, "All right, I'm going, see?"

The standoff lasted until the early evening, when a tall policeman came up with the solution. He changed into plainclothes and went in through the back gate. When Guoqing screamed at him to get out, he put on a friendly smile and asked in a gentle voice, "What are you trying to do?"

Guoqing wiped the sweat on his forehead and said, "I've got some killing to do."

"But it shouldn't be her that you're killing," the policeman said softly, indicating Huilan. Then he pointed outside the courtyard. "It's her parents you should be killing."

Guoqing could not help but nod. He was beginning to fall for the policeman's line.

The policeman asked, "Can a little boy like you kill two grown-ups?"

"I sure can!" Guoqing said.

The policeman nodded and said, "I believe you. But there are lots of other people outside, and they're going to protect the people you want to kill."

Seeing that Guoqing was looking unsure of himself, he stretched out his hand and said, "I'll help you kill them, how would that be?"

His tone was so friendly. Finally somebody was offering to help. Guoqing was now completely under his spell, and when the policeman extended a hand Guoqing instinctively passed him the cleaver. The man tossed it aside at once. But Guoqing failed to notice this, for after feeling so misused and so afraid at last he had found support, and he threw himself into the man's arms and burst into tears. The policeman seized him by the collar and shoved him—almost carried him—out the gate. Guoqing tried desperately to raise his head as the tall officer propelled him forward and the crowd parted to let them pass. Even now the fact of his bloodless surrender had not quite sunk in. The policeman tugged so hard on the back of his collar that Guoqing was practically throttled by his top button, and as he gasped for air his sobs turned into a succession of uneven whimpers.

SMEAR

Our teacher was soft-spoken but intimidating. With his glasses he somewhat resembled Su Yu's father, whom I was to meet later. He always looked at us with a smiling face, but he meted out harsh punishments at the drop of a hat.

His wife, it seemed, sold bean curd in a small market town in the countryside. This young woman would visit the school in the first few days of each month, wearing a floral-patterned outfit, sometimes with two brightly dressed little girls in tow. She had a funny habit of scratching her behind. But we all thought she was very pretty, and in her hometown, we heard, she was known as the Tofu Belle. Our teacher would wear a frown every time she came to stay, because he had to surrender to her the wages he had just been given, only a small portion of which she would return to him. At such moments she would admonish him in a sharp voice: "What are you scowling about? You're happy enough to see me in the evening, when you need me, but when I ask for money you look as though you're about to cry."

At first we couldn't work out why the teacher would smile so much in the evening. We gave his wife the nickname Imperial Army, because she made us think of the Japanese devils and their campaigns of loot and pillage: every month she would sweep in and clean out his money pouch.

I cannot remember now who came up with this name. But I'll never forget the time when Guoqing, then a second grader, ran into the classroom with a droll expression on his face. He tapped loudly on the dais with the blackboard eraser and solemnly announced that the teacher would be a little delayed, because "The Imperial Army is back . . ."

Guoqing was a real daredevil on that occasion, for he had the impudence to go on: ". . . escorted by the Chinese collaborator."

Guoqing had to pay for being a smart aleck. There must have been at least twenty classmates who reported him at the same time. When our teacher took his place on the dais, his face was livid, and Guoqing was so frightened he was sweating mightily. I too had my heart in my mouth, not knowing how the teacher would punish him; even the classmates who had ratted on Guoqing now felt uneasy. Given our age at the time we quailed at the prospect of punishment, even if it was inflicted on children other than ourselves.

This angry expression stayed on the teacher's face for a good minute, and then suddenly he was all smiles. There was something eerie about the way his manner changed. In a velvety tone he said to Guoqing, "I'm going to punish you." Then, turning to the rest of us, he said, "Now we'll start the lesson."

Throughout the whole period Guoqing's face was pale as he awaited with foreboding and a kind of perverse longing the teacher's retribution. But when class was over the teacher picked up his notes and left the room without even looking at him. I don't know how Guoqing managed to get through the day. He remained glued to his seat, watching us timidly like a new kid in class. He was no longer the same boy who loved to race around in the playground, but more like a skittish kitten. Several times his mouth twisted unnaturally as though he were about to burst into tears. Only when school finished for the day and he was completely outside the school gate did he dash about like a panther kept too long in captivity. We now felt that nothing was going to happen after all and confidently assured him that the teacher must have forgotten about it. Besides, the Imperial Army was still here, and the teacher was bound to have a smile on his face again tonight.

But when school began the following morning the first thing that the teacher did was to tell Guoqing to stand up. Then he asked him, "How do you think I should punish you?"

Guoqing had forgotten all about it, and his whole body trembled. He looked at the teacher fearfully and shook his head.

"You can sit down now," the teacher said, "and think it over."

When the teacher said to think it over, he was really telling him to not forget to torture himself. For Guoqing the next month was sheer hell. If he ever forgot about the punishment and looked his cheerful old self, the teacher would appear out of nowhere and quietly remind him, "I have yet to punish you."

This threatened but never-imposed sentence left Guoqing on tenterhooks every day. All it took was for the poor boy to hear the teacher's voice and he would quiver like leaves in a wind. Only when he went home after school did he feel more or less secure, but the feeling of apprehension would return on his way to class the next day. This life of anxiety did not really end until his father abandoned him, when it was superseded by far greater misery.

At that point, out of compassion perhaps, the teacher not only discontinued his intimidation of Guoqing but actually went out of his way to commend his achievements. Guoqing would get a perfect score for an essay even if he had written a couple of characters wrong, whereas I would get only ninety points for an essay with no mistakes at all. During the days before Guoqing's uncles and aunts arrived our teacher took him to see his father. In his kindly tone the teacher sang Guoqing's praises: such a respectful, intelligent boy, he reiterated—why, he was a favorite with every teacher in the school. After listening to these words, Guoqing's father said coldly, "If you're so fond of him, maybe you should adopt him as your own son."

Our teacher had an answer to that. Smiling broadly, he said, "Actually, I was thinking of adopting him as my grandson."

Until I myself was earmarked for punishment, I held our teacher in warm regard. When I went to school that very first time with Wang Liqiang, I was taken aback by the sight of him knitting, for I had never seen a man with a ball of wool in his hands. Only when Wang Liqiang brought me before him and told me to greet him as Teacher Zhang did I realize that this odd character was going to be my teacher. He seemed affable and considerate. I remember he put his hand on my shoulder and said something that I took as a compliment: "I'll make sure that you get a nice seat."

He was as good as his word, assigning me a place in the middle of the front row. Apart from times when he needed to go to the back of the dais to write on the blackboard, the rest of the class period he was standing right in front of me. He would lay his notes down, rest both hands on my desk, and lecture away, ejecting saliva with the force of his delivery. As I listened, my upraised face was fully exposed to his spit, as though I was taking notes in a drizzle. When he noticed that my face was flecked with saliva, he would stretch out a chalky hand to wipe it away, and by the end of class my face was often stained in gaudy colors, like a cotton print.

The first time I was punished by him it was about halfway through third grade. A big snowfall that winter gave us schoolchildren an opportunity to engage in a wild exchange of snowballs in the playground. Woe befell me when one of my snowballs, aimed at Liu Xiaoqing, accidentally hit the head of a girl classmate, whose name I no longer remember. This girl wailed as loud as if I had made her an indecent proposal. She complained to the teacher.

He called me up from my seat, where I had just sat down, and told me to go outside and make a snowball. I thought he was mocking me and just stood there, not daring to move. He continued to teach the class, seemingly having forgotten about me, and it was a few moments before he said to me in surprise, "Why are you still here?"

I left the classroom and went to make a snowball. When I returned to the classroom, the teacher was reading aloud a story from the textbook about the selfless courage of Ouyang Hai. It was a spirited recitation, sweeping high and dipping low like a road through the mountains, and I stood by the door, not daring to interrupt. At last he finished reading a long section of the story and walked toward the blackboard, but to my dismay he still did not pay me the slightest attention. It was disconcerting to find that he had forgotten about me, and as he wrote on the board I said to him timidly, "Sir, I made the snowball."

He shot me a glance and gave a grunt of acknowledgment, then continued to write. Finally he tossed the chalk into the box and turned to the girl. He told her to check to see if the snowball in my hand was as big as the one that had hit her. She, of course, had never seen the snowball, because it hit her on the back of the head and immediately disintegrated. Though some time had passed since she had been upset by the incident, she began to cry pitifully as soon as she arrived next to me, saying, "It was bigger than this one."

So I was ordered out of the classroom by the teacher once more, to make a bigger snowball. When I came in holding a jumbo-size snowball in my hands, he did not ask the girl to once again certify that it had the correct dimensions. He walked around the classroom a couple of times and formally announced my punishment: I was to stand there and could not return to my seat until the snowball had melted.

That winter morning a north wind howled through the broken windows of the classroom while the teacher, his hands in his sleeves, recounted in the cold the story of heroic Ouyang Hai. I stood by the door, clutching my icy snowball. Gradually I felt a peculiar scorching sensation in my hands, as painful as if they were being sawn off. But I had to be careful not to let the snowball fall from my grasp.

The teacher came up to me at one point and said to me solicitously, "If you hold it a bit tighter, it will melt more quickly."

The snow had not melted much by the time the class ended. After the teacher picked up his notes and slipped past me, my classmates gathered round. Their speculation about how long it would take for the snowball to melt simply intensified my distress, and I felt so misused I almost cried. Guoqing and Liu Xiaoqing marched over to the girl's desk in a rage, cursing her as a snitch and flunky. The poor girl collapsed in a flood of tears, and after putting her satchel in order she stood up and headed out the door, saying she was going to report them to the teacher. It had not occurred to Guoqing and Liu Xiaoqing that she would resort to this same tactic a second time; they rushed to restrain her, apologizing and begging forgiveness. By this point, my hands had gone completely numb—as hard as icicles—and the snowball fell from my lifeless fingers to the floor, where it broke up into slush. I was so horrified that I burst into slushy tears of my own, at the same time begging the classmates around me to bear witness: "I didn't do it on purpose! You saw what happened—I didn't do it on purpose!"

Our teacher's authority was not founded on correct judgments, but on draconian punishments that followed in the wake of the judgments that he did make. He was altogether too arbitrary in his decisions about right or wrong, and for that very reason his punishments would arrive suddenly and unpredictably. During my four years at the Littlemarsh elementary school he never once repeated a punishment. Because of his exceptional creativity in this area we were reduced to nervous wrecks at the very sight of him.

On one occasion a dozen of us were throwing a ball around in the playground, and by accident we broke a window in the classroom. In this case the penalty he imposed was light, but because I had not expected to be punished I performed a feeble act of resistance.

I still remember the look of misery on the face of the boy who broke the window. Even before the teacher stepped into the room he was already in despair, visualizing the awful punishment that awaited him. Then the teacher came in and stood beaming on the dais—I suspect that he was overjoyed every time there was an opportunity to punish a pupil. But as always he came out with a ruling that was not at all what we anticipated: he did not punish the guilty classmate directly but told all of us who had been playing ball to raise our hands. Then he said to us, "Each one of you is to write a self-criticism."

Although this decree was perfectly in keeping with his trademark style, at the time I was really shocked. I felt that I had done nothing wrong, so why should I have to write a self-criticism? The voice of resistance stirred in my heart: I would simply refuse to do it. For the first time in my life I would defy an adult—defy, moreover, the teacher who made every schoolchild quake in his boots.

I did my best to steady my nerves, though actually I was very unsure of myself. After class I tried to incite the other classmates affected to resist the teacher as well. They expressed their dissatisfaction just as heatedly as me, but they hemmed and hawed when it came to refusing to write the self-criticism. Guoqing shrugged it off, saying to me, "It doesn't matter if we write a self-criticism now, because there is no dossier on us yet. It's when you start working that you can't afford to write one, because then it goes into your file."

I was on my own, clearly, but I took the plunge anyway. Loudly I declared that I would not write a self-criticism, no matter what. My classmates looked at me in wonder. My voice shook, and I felt that I, a ten-year-old, had truth on my side. Yes, I was right. The teacher had said so himself, that it's impossible not to have weaknesses. "The teacher sometimes can be wrong"—that was what I told them.

I spent the whole day full of myself; here I was, just a child, but already I could recognize the defects of grown-ups! I imagined the following scene: the teacher and I would engage in a debate in class, and because I had justice on my side I would speak with great eloquence and brilliant witticisms would slip effortlessly from my tongue. Even though the teacher was an able debater, he could not call on truth to support him, so of course he would lose the argument. He would make a touching admission to this effect and praise me with fine words. The girls would all look at me with admiration—the boys too, of course—and they would praise me as well (by that age I already knew it was a pleasure to be liked by girls). At this point my imagination had to take a rest because tears filled my eyes. I wanted to savor this blissful scene.

While my emotions ran high, our teacher was cool and collected and paid me no mind. This made me nervous and I couldn't help but challenge my own judgment: could it be that the teacher was right? I *had* been involved in the game, after all, and if I hadn't thrown the ball to Liu Xiaoqing, who threw it to that other boy, how could he have broken the window? I ended up worrying myself sick, and the idea of debating the teacher in class seemed preposterous.

But then my confidence revived, courtesy of Li Xiuying. When cleaning the window, I could not stop myself from asking her if it was all right for me to throw a ball on the playground. Li Xiuying said that of course I could. Then I asked her whether I was at fault if one of my classmates broke a window. Her answer was even firmer: "If somebody else broke it, what has that got to do with you?"

Vindicated at last, I was no longer afraid of my own shadow. Nobody could alter my conviction that I was right.

In the face of the teacher's continued indifference, it was not long before this newfound self-possession began to wane, and dejection set in. At first I had been so looking forward to conducting a debate with the teacher. At night I would prepare feverishly, and in the morning give myself a pep talk. But at the sound of the class bell my heart would thump. My greatest worry was that I would have stage fright and be unable to say a word when the moment came. The teacher's lack of interest only fueled my insecurity. Eventually, however, my equilibrium was restored, as I put the incident behind me and began to forget about it. The teacher might well have forgotten about it ages ago, I told myself. The

Imperial Army was in town again and he would be wreathed with smiles at the end of the day.

It was as though I had simply been arguing with myself in my own mind, playing both the teacher and myself at the same time, and now at last I abandoned the game out of sheer exhaustion. I threw myself instead into playground activities, reclaiming my childhood, running and shouting without a care in the world. But then Guoqing came over to tell me that the teacher wanted to see me.

At once I was seized by anxiety, and despite the bright sunshine I gave a shiver as I headed off toward the teacher's office. The carefree shouts of Guoqing and the others sounded behind me, and I knew that the moment I had been anticipating and now dreaded had finally arrived. Although I tried desperately to retrieve the brilliant arguments that I had been rehearsing for so long, not a single one now came to mind. I could feel my lips trembling and was on the verge of bursting into tears, but I urged myself not to cry, to be brave. No doubt the teacher would scold me most harshly, and maybe he would come up with some outlandish way of punishing me, but I must not cry, because I had done nothing wrong. That's right, I had done nothing wrong—it was the teacher who was wrong. That's what I should say to him. I needed to speak slowly and not be browbeaten by a burst of rage or alarmed by a cheery grin. With these thoughts swirling in my head I entered the teacher's office, relieved that I had recovered my courage once again.

The teacher nodded to me amicably. He was talking to another teacher, a smile on his face. As I stood there, I noticed that he was fiddling with a sheaf of papers in his hand, the first of which was Liu Xiaoqing's self-criticism. While he chatted with his colleague, he slowly turned over the pages, exposing all the confessions one after another. At the bottom of the pile I saw Guoqing's self-criticism, written in very large characters. At this point the teacher turned around and asked me genially, "What about *your* self-criticism?"

That was when I fell to pieces. His display of my classmates' confessions had sapped my courage, and I said with a stutter, "I haven't . . . quite finished it yet."

"When will you have it done?" His inquiry was couched in a mild tone.

I replied eagerly, "I'll have it finished very soon."

In my last year in Littlemarsh I entered fourth grade. One Saturday afternoon I was downstairs lighting the coal briquette stove when Guoqing and Liu Xiaoqing ran up and delivered a sensational piece of news: somebody had written a slogan in chalk on the wall of our classroom, calling for the ouster of our teacher. "Down with Zhang Qinghai!" it read.

They seemed unusually excited, complimenting me, saying what guts I had, how that damned Zhang Qinghai should have been overthrown long ago, what fiendish punishments we had all suffered at his hands. I found their excitement infectious. By heaping such honor on me for having written the slogan, they made me really wish I had. But I knew I should be honest, and I told them with a trace of embarrassment, "I didn't do it."

The disappointment that I saw on their faces left me feeling bad. They seemed crushed to learn that I wasn't the fearless author, that there was no truth to Liu Xiaoqing's assertion of just a moment earlier, "You're the only one who would have the guts to do that."

To my mind Guoqing was more daring than I was, and I said

so, not at all out of modesty. Guoqing clearly accepted my tribute, because he nodded and said, "If you'd asked me to do it, I would have written it too."

Liu Xiaoqing quickly chimed in with an identical comment, forcing me to say the same thing. I hated to disappoint them a second time.

I had walked into a trap, never thinking for one moment that Guoqing and Liu Xiaoqing had come at the teacher's behest to probe into my involvement. When Monday morning came around, fool that I was, I went off to school as happy as a lark. But before I knew it I had been led into a small room, where Zhang Qinghai and a woman teacher named Lin began to question me.

Teacher Lin first of all asked me if I knew about the slogan. There in that little room, with the door shut tight, the two grown-ups stared at me aggressively. I nodded and said I knew.

But when she asked me how I knew, I hesitated. Could I tell them how delighted Guoqing and Liu Xiaoqing had been? If they too were called in, what would they think of me? Surely they would denounce me as a traitor.

I looked at them tensely, still unaware that they suspected me. The woman teacher inquired in a sugary voice if I had come to school on Saturday afternoon or Sunday. I shook my head. I saw her give Zhang Qinghai a smile. Then, quick as a flash, she swiveled around and asked me, "So how do you know about the slogan?"

Her sudden question startled me. Zhang Qinghai, who had said nothing up to this point, asked me softly, "Why did you write the slogan?"

I was quick to defend myself. "I didn't write it."

"Don't lie!" Teacher Lin thumped the table and went on.

"You know about the slogan, and if you haven't come to school, how else could you know?"

I had no option but to reveal the role played by Guoqing and Liu Xiaoqing, otherwise I had no hope of clearing myself. But they showed not the slightest interest in my explanation of how I heard the news, and Zhang Qinghai told me point-blank, "I have compared the handwriting, and there's no question that it's yours."

He said it with such confidence. Tears spilled from my eyes. I shook my head in desperation, pleading with them to believe me. By this time they were both sitting, and now they simply exchanged glances, paying no attention to my defense. My weeping was a magnet for my classmates, who clustered at the window to watch me cry—though the disgrace was the least of my problems. The woman teacher got up to drive them away and closed the window. First they had closed the door and now the window was closed too. Zhang Qinghai asked me, "Did you or did you not say that if you'd been asked, you would have written it?"

I looked at him, appalled. I had no idea how he knew this. Could he have eavesdropped on our Saturday-afternoon conversation?

The bell rang for the start of class, giving me a temporary respite. They told me to stand there and not move an inch while they went to teach their classes. After they left I stood alone in the small room; although there were chairs right next to me, I dared not sit down. There was a bottle of red ink on a desk, and I really wanted to pick it up and have a closer look at it, but they had said I was not to budge. All I could do was to look out the window at the playground. Children from higher grades lined up and then broke up into groups, to play ball or jump rope. Physical education was my favorite class. From the classroom opposite I could hear the faint sound of children reading aloud. I wished so much that I could be in among them, but I could only stand here in dishonor. Two older boys tapped on the window and I heard them calling, "Hey, why were you crying just now?"

More tears came, and I sobbed miserably. On the other side of the window they had a big laugh.

After the bell for the end of class I saw Zhang Qinghai leading Guoqing and Liu Xiaoqing over. I wondered how they had come into the picture and thought it must have been because I had implicated them. They saw me through the window, and their eyes rested on me for just a second before turning away in scorn.

I was devastated by what happened next. Guoqing and Liu Xiaoqing informed against me, testifying that on Saturday afternoon I had said, "If you'd asked me, I would have written it." Teacher Lin pointed a finger in my direction as she turned to Zhang Qinghai and said, "If this is the way he thinks, then he's certainly up to writing that slogan."

"But they said the same thing!" I protested.

Guoqing and Liu Xiaoqing quickly put this in context for the teachers: "We said that only to draw him out."

I looked at them in despair while they glared at me. The teachers told them to leave.

What a harrowing morning that was. The two grown-ups took turns attacking me, but I stuck to my story as the tears streamed down my face. They managed to cow me by yelling all of a sudden or banging the table impatiently, and there were several moments when I was so frightened that I trembled all over and could not say a word. Teacher Lin used every threat in the book, short of vowing to shoot me. In the end, she turned gentle and told me patiently that the Public Security Bureau had an apparatus used to analyze handwriting, and just a short test could establish that the writing in the slogan was identical to that in my homework notebook. This was the only ray of hope that came my way the whole morning, but at the same time I was worried that the device might make a mistake, so I asked her, "Could it get things wrong?"

"Impossible." She shook her head emphatically.

This was an enormous relief, and I said to them happily, "Then hurry up and do the test."

But they remained fixed in their chairs, looking at each other for quite some time. Finally Zhang Qinghai said, "You may go home for now."

The bell for the end of the session had already rung by then, and finally I could leave the little room. Though I had temporarily regained my freedom, I was still confused about everything that had happened. Somehow, in my dazed state, I managed to make my way to the school gate, and there I spotted Guoqing and Liu Xiaoqing. Tears spilled from my eyes at the thought of their betrayal, and I went up to them and said, "How could you do that?"

Guoqing looked ill at ease. His face reddening, he said, "You did something wrong, so we have to draw a clear line between us and you."

For his part, Liu Xiaoqing said smugly, "I'll tell you what happened: the teacher sent us to monitor what you said."

It had taken no time at all for adult authority to reduce to ruins what had been a beautiful young friendship. For many weeks following I did not say another word to them. Only when I was about to go back to Southgate and turned to Guoqing for help did he and I recover our closeness, but that was also the moment when we said good-bye. I never saw him again after that.

At the end of lunch break I was so silly as to sit down in the classroom in preparation for the afternoon's lessons. As soon as Zhang Qinghai came in, notes in hand, he saw me and asked me with a look of astonishment, "What are you doing here?"

What was I doing there? I was there to attend class, of course, but now that he had posed the question in this way I was no longer so sure. "Stand up," he said.

I stood up, flustered. He told me to leave, so I went out, all the way to the middle of the playground, where I looked around, uncertain where he wanted me to go. After some hesitation I plucked up the courage to go back to the classroom, where I nervously asked Zhang Qinghai, "Sir, where do you want me to go?"

He turned and asked me in his gentle voice, "Where were you this morning?"

I looked back at the little room on the other side of the playground, and now I understood. "I need to go to that little room?" I asked.

He nodded approvingly.

So that afternoon I continued to be shut up in the little room, and my stubborn refusal to confess made them angry. The result was a visit to the school by Wang Liqiang. Dressed in his uniform, he listened attentively to their accusations, glancing at me several times with a reproachful look on his face. I was hoping that he would listen just as seriously to my side of the story, but after hearing the teachers out he showed not the slightest interest in learning what I had to say. He reminded them in an apologetic tone that I was adopted, and already six when I came under his charge. He said to them, "As you know, once a child reaches that age, it's hard to change his character."

This was not at all what I wanted to hear. On the other hand, he did not press me to confess, as the teachers had done; in fact he said nothing along those lines whatsoever. Soon he stood up and said he had something to do and left, perhaps as a way to avoid causing me more distress. If he had stayed longer he would have found it difficult not to toe the teachers' line, and now he could get clear of this embarrassing situation. Still, I was seething with indignation, for he had listened so earnestly to the teachers and never once asked me whether there was any truth to their allegations.

Were it not for Li Xiuying's expression of confidence in me later, I really don't know what I would have done. At this point, after being so misunderstood, I had sunk into deep despair, a sensation that left me constantly struggling for breath. Nobody believed me; everyone in the school was convinced that I was the author of the slogan. I had become a mendacious child simply because I had refused to confess.

When I got out of school that afternoon, I felt doubly tormented. Already I was oppressed by the feeling that my words had been twisted against me, and now I had to brace myself for another ordeal once I got home, for Wang Liqiang would surely have informed Li Xiuying. I had no idea how they would punish me and walked back to the house in hopeless gloom. As soon as she heard my footsteps, Li Xiuying called me over to her bed and asked me in a severe tone, "Did you write that slogan or not? Be truthful."

The whole day through I had been peppered with questions, but not one had been couched in these terms. Tears rolled from my eyes, and I said, "No, I didn't write it."

Li Xiuying sat up in bed. She called shrilly to Wang Liqiang, "There is no way that he wrote it, I can vouch for that. When he first arrived here I left fifty cents on the windowsill, and he handed it over to me like an honest lad." Then she turned to me and said, "I believe you."

From the next room, Wang Liqiang expressed some displeasure with the teachers, saying, "It was a dumb thing to do, but they shouldn't make such a big deal out of just scrawling some graffiti."

Li Xiuying was irked by this remark and reproached Wang Liqiang. "How can you say that? That's tantamount to saying you believe he did it."

However pallid her face, however eccentric her behavior, Li Xiuying at that moment touched me so deeply that my tears would not stop flowing. Perhaps because she had been shouting so vigorously, she fell back onto the bed in exhaustion, saying to me gently, "Don't cry, don't cry. How about . . . you clean the window now?"

I may have gained support at home, but this did nothing to alleviate my predicament at school. I spent another whole day in that dim room. Isolation exacerbated my fears. Although I came to school just like my classmates and went home just like them too, in between times I was here in this little cubicle, questioned in turn by two grown-ups who held a position of total superiority. How could I withstand such pressure indefinitely?

In the end they described for me an absorbing scenario. In tones of great admiration they told me about a child my age, just as smart as me (an unexpected compliment, this), who committed a misdeed. Angry no longer, they began to tell me his story, and I listened with rapt attention. This boy my age had stolen something from a neighbor, so he was reproached by his conscience, for he knew he had done wrong. Finally, after a series of mental struggles, he returned the item to the neighbor and confessed to the errors of his ways.

Teacher Lin asked me warmly, "Now guess whether he was criticized."

I nodded.

"No," she said. "On the contrary, he was commended, because he had already recognized his crime."

That is how they worked on me, inducing me gradually to come around to the idea that to admit error after committing error is more praiseworthy than not to have erred at all. Having been made the target of such extreme criticism, I was all too eager for approval. Now fired with zeal and hope, I at last confessed to something that had nothing to do with me.

Having achieved their goal, the two grown-ups could finally relax. They leaned back in their chairs wearily and gave me an odd look, neither praising me nor scolding me. In the end Zhang Qinghai said, "You can go to class now."

I left the little room, crossed the sun-baked playground, and walked toward the classroom, my heart drained and empty. When I got there many of my classmates turned their heads to stare at me, and I felt my face getting red.

Some three days later I went to school a little earlier than usual. I got a fright when I entered the classroom because I found Zhang Qinghai sitting by himself on the dais, with his lecture notes spread out in front of him. He beckoned me, and when I went over he asked me in a low voice, "You know Teacher Lin?"

How could I not? Her sweet voice had cursed me and intimidated me in that claustrophobic room, and she had told me I was smart too. I nodded.

A little smile played on Zhang Qinghai's face. In a conspiratorial tone he said to me, "She's been locked up. She's from a landlord family, but she always kept this hidden. They sent someone to conduct an investigation, and the truth came out."

I was stunned. Teacher Lin locked up? Just a few days before she had joined Zhang Qinghai in interrogating me. How stern and righteous, how forceful and eloquent she had been! And now she was behind bars.

Zhang Qinghai went back to his notes while I left the classroom. I looked over at the little room in the distance, mulling over the revelation that Teacher Lin was now in confinement. Other classmates went inside, and I could hear Zhang Qinghai quietly sharing the news with them too. The teacher's smile was chilling. In the little room he and Teacher Lin had seemed to be united in a common purpose, but now he was showing a different face altogether.

RETURN TO SOUTHGATE

My memories of Wang Liqiang and Li Xiuying, it is fair to say, remain fresh even now. I have often had it in mind to go back to Littlemarsh and have another look at the town that for five years I called home. What I wonder is whether Li Xiuying managed to keep herself going after the loss of her husband, and whether she is still alive today.

Although they did make me toil away at household chores, my adoptive parents often showed a touching concern for my welfare. When I was seven Wang Liqiang decided I was old enough to go on my own to the teahouse to fetch boiled water. He said to me, "If I didn't tell you where the teahouse is, how would you know where to go?"

I came out in a sweat trying to figure this out, but in the end came up with the answer, saying brightly, "I would ask somebody else."

Wang Liqiang laughed just as brightly. When I picked up their big two-liter thermos bottles and got ready to leave, he squatted on his haunches, trying to shrink his height to my level. He kept emphasizing that if I found I really couldn't carry the bottles an inch farther, I should toss them aside. I found this an extraordinary idea, because to me two thermos bottles were colossally expensive items, and here he was telling me to throw them away.

"Why should I do that?"

He told me that if I really couldn't carry them and just dropped them on the ground, the hot water might splash, and I would get scalded. Now I understood.

With two cents in my pocket I proudly headed out, a thermos in each hand. I walked along the flag stones, asking people ostentatiously where the teahouse was. I didn't care whether further inquiries were redundant and kept on asking directions all the way down the street. My little stratagem worked like a dream, for my shrill queries elicited looks of surprise from grown-ups all along the street. When I entered the teahouse I placed my order in an even louder voice, and the old lady at the cash register gave a start. Patting her chest, she said, "You gave me such a fright."

Her mock alarm made me chuckle, but soon her expression

changed to one of genuine astonishment. As I left with my two brimming thermos bottles, I heard her saying anxiously to my retreating back, "You can't carry those, can you?"

How could I ever think of throwing the thermos bottles away? All these doubts about my capabilities served only to boost my self-importance. Wang Liqiang's injunction as I left the house was converted on the way home into a hope, conjuring up the following picture: when I arrived home with the bottles of water, Wang Liqiang would be so thrilled that he would give a shout to Li Xiuying, and she would get out of bed specially to witness my achievement, and they would shower me with praise.

That was my goal as I carried the bottles home, one in each hand, gritting my teeth with effort. I kept telling myself: no throwing, no throwing! I made only one rest stop.

But when I got home, Wang Liqiang disappointed me by showing not the least surprise and taking the bottles from my hands as though I had done only what he expected. As he bent over to put them on the floor, I still clung to a final shred of hope and gave him a little hint: "I stopped to rest just once."

He stood up with a smile, as if there was nothing wonderful about that. I was so crushed that I went off by myself, thinking, "Where did I get the idea that he would congratulate me?"

One night I was so foolish as to interpose myself between Wang Liqiang and Li Xiuying, and the outcome was a beating. The nighttime interactions between husband and wife had always left me anxious and unsettled. When I first came to live with them, every few evenings after I had gone to bed I would hear the voice of Li Xiuying: pleading at first, and then with time her entreaties would change to moans. I found this quite frightening, but the next morning I would hear them chatting cordially enough, and their calm exchanges reassured me that nothing untoward had happened.

One evening I had already undressed and got into bed when Li Xiuying, who had lain in bed listlessly all day, summoned me sharply. Shivering in the cold winter air, I put on my underpants and pushed open their bedroom door, only to see Wang Liqiang in the process of taking his clothes off. He flushed bright red and kicked the door closed, telling me angrily to get back to my room at once. I did not know what was wrong, but I dared not return to my bed because Li Xiuying was still calling me desperately. I lingered just outside the door, cold and scared, shivering from head to toe. Later Li Xiuying must have squirmed out of bed; though wearing just a slightly damp item of underwear could easily make her run a fever, she was now throwing caution to the winds. I heard Wang Liqiang calling in a low voice, "Are you crazy?"

The door was flung open, and before I knew what was happening Li Xiuying dragged me into bed with her. Panting from her exertions, she said to Wang Liqiang, "Tonight we'll sleep together, all three of us."

She put her arms around me and tucked her face so tightly against mine that her hair fell over one of my eyes. She was all skin and bones, but her body was warm. With my other eye, I saw Wang Liqiang glaring at me. He said furiously, "Get out of here!"

Li Xiuying put her lips to my ear and said, "Say you won't."

I was like putty in her hands. I hated the thought of leaving her cozy arms and said to him, "No, I won't!"

Wang Liqiang seized me by the arm, yanked me out of Li Xiuying's embrace, and shoved me to the floor. There was a fearsome bloodshot gleam in his eyes, and when I just sat there, unmoving, he yelled, "Get out, I said!"

This provoked my stubborn streak, and I yelled back, "No, I'm not leaving!"

Wang Liqiang stepped forward and grabbed me with both hands, but I clung for dear life to the leg of the bed and refused to loosen my grip no matter how he tugged. He then seized me by the hair and knocked my head against the bed. I could hear Li Xiuying screaming in the background. Pain finally made me relax my hold, and Wang Liqiang picked me up and flung me out the door, then locked it. By now I was in a frenzy too: scrambling to my feet I pounded on the door, wailing and cursing, "Wang Liqiang, you bastard! Take me back to Sun Kwangtsai!"

I wept pitifully, hoping that Li Xiuying would come to my rescue. At first I could hear her arguing with Wang Liqiang, but after a while all was quiet inside the room. Still I cried and wailed, still I shouted abuse, until I heard Li Xiuying call my name and say in a faint voice, "You go off to bed now. You'll freeze to death staying there."

Suddenly I felt forlorn and had no choice but to make my way back to my room, sobbing as I went. On that inky winter night my heart seethed with hatred for Wang Liqiang as I slowly fell asleep. When I woke up the following morning, I knew that my face was aching painfully, but I did not realize that I had been beaten black and blue. As he was brushing his teeth, Wang Liqiang saw me and reacted with alarm. I ignored him and picked up the mop from the wall. He stretched out a hand to stop me, and through foamy lips said something unintelligible. I shoved his arm aside and carried the mop into Li Xiuying's room. She too gave a start and muttered a reproach to Wang Liqiang: "You didn't have to hit him so hard."

Wang Liqiang bought a couple of dough fritters that morning—just for me, he said, and he laid them on the table. It was then, just as I had an appealing breakfast in front of me, that I chose to launch my hunger strike. I refused to eat a bite, no matter how they tried to persuade me. Instead I burst into tears and told them, "Take me back to Sun Kwangtsai!"

This was more a threat than an entreaty. Wang Liqiang knew he was at fault, and his efforts to appease me simply strengthened my resolve to remain at odds with him. As I went out, satchel on my back, he followed quickly on my heels and tried to put his hand on my shoulder, but I jerked away out of reach. When he dug in his pocket for ten cents' snack money, I refused the bribe with equal determination, shaking my head and saying obstinately, "I don't want it."

I insisted on savoring hunger to the fullest. Wang Liqiang's consternation at my fast had inspired me with the confidence to continue, and by inflicting hardship on myself I would get my revenge on him. At this stage I was proud of the stand I was taking. I vowed never again to let any food of his pass my lips, and at the same time I knew I would perish as a result; my eyes welled up with tears at the thought of my splendid martyrdom. My death by starvation would be the greatest retaliation against Wang Liqiang that there ever could be.

But when it came down to it I was simply too young to carry this through: my will was indomitable only so long as I had a full stomach and a warm set of clothes. When I was later to reach the point of practically fainting from hunger, I would find I just could not resist the temptation to eat. In fact, I was not then—and am not now—the kind of person willing to die for a conviction, so much do I value the sound of life flowing through my veins. Apart from life itself I cannot conceive of any other reason for living.

That morning my classmates noticed my bruised and swollen face, but they did not realize how much more painful was the hunger I was now experiencing. I had left home that morning on an empty stomach, and by the third period I was paying the price. First I was overcome with a vacant sensation: my insides felt as lonely as an alleyway late at night, windblown and desolate. Then the emptiness spread to all extremities, leaving my limbs powerless and my head groggy. Finally I came down with a stomachache, a pain more unbearable than the contusions on my face. Somehow I managed to make it to the end of the period, and then I dashed to the line of water faucets, put one to my mouth, and swallowed a whole bellyful of water. This gave me a short-lived respite from hunger. I leaned weakly against the water pipe and practically melted in the sunshine. The chilly winter water was so quickly absorbed into my system that I had to keep gulping it down right until the bell rang for the start of the next period.

After I left the water faucets, I found myself facing an even worse ordeal, for when hunger returned I had no resources to combat it. I collapsed on my chair like a sack of rice. Soon I was hallucinating that the blackboard was a cave and the teacher was pacing back and forth at the entrance to the cave, his voice booming as it echoed off the cave wall.

While my stomach was enduring one kind of pain, my expanding bladder inflicted a different sort of discomfort. It began to retaliate for my excessive fluid consumption. I had no choice but to raise my hand and ask Zhang Qinghai's permission to go out for a pee. We were only a few minutes into the period and he scolded me in very bad humor. "Why didn't you go during the break?"

I made my way gingerly to the toilet, not daring to run, because as soon as I tried that I could feel the water in my bladder sloshing back and forth. After finishing in the toilet, I grabbed the opportunity to drink another bellyful of cold water.

The fourth period that morning was perhaps the most trying hour of my whole life. Not long after I had been to the toilet, my bladder again became bloated and my face began to turn purple. When I really could not hold it another minute, I raised my hand a second time.

Zhang Qinghai eyed me suspiciously and asked, "You need to pee again?"

I nodded in embarrassment. Zhang Qinghai called Guoqing over and told him to go with me to the toilet to check whether I really had to pee. This time I didn't dare drink any more water afterward. On Guoqing's return, he loudly reported, "He passed more water than a cow!"

I sat down red faced amid my classmates' titters. Despite my self-restraint during the last toilet break, it was not long before my bladder again became distended. Hunger had now become a matter of secondary importance; it was the bulging bladder that was my concern. I wanted to avoid raising my hand if at all possible and tried to endure the agonizing pressure, hoping that the bell would ring soon. I didn't dare adjust my position even slightly, feeling that the dam could burst at the least provocation. But later I just could not wait: time was passing so slowly and the bell would not ring. Timidly I raised my hand for the third time.

Zhang Qinghai was exasperated. "Are you trying to drown us?" he said.

The class erupted in laughter. Zhang Qinghai didn't let me go to the toilet again, but told me to go around by the window and pee on the outside wall of the classroom, because he wanted to see for himself whether I really had a call of nature to answer. When I splashed the wall with a powerful jet of urine, he was forced to accept the evidence. He walked a few steps away from the window and continued to conduct the class. It must have taken me a long time to empty my bladder, because Zhang Qinghai suddenly broke off from instruction and turned to me in surprise. "What, still not finished?"

Blushing hotly, I gave him a bashful smile.

I did not go home at the end of the morning session like the rest of my classmates, but continued my hunger strike. That whole lunchtime I lay underneath the water faucets, and when hunger pains gnawed I would raise myself up and consume a bellyful of water, then go back to lying there and feeling sorry for myself. By that time my pride was just for show; I was actually looking forward to Wang Liqiang finding me. I lay in the sunshine as the grass happily grew around me.

When Wang Liqiang did find me, it was afternoon, and classmates were arriving for classes. He discovered me sprawled next to the water faucets. I learned later from Li Xiuying that he had been anxiously waiting for me to come home ever since finishing his lunch. He helped me up, and when his hand grazed the bruises on my face I burst into tears.

He set me on his back, holding my thighs firmly with both hands, and set off for the school gate. My body swayed from side to side, and my feelings of pride, so dominant earlier that morning, gave way to dependency. Now I did not hate Wang Liqiang in the least, and when I rested my face on his shoulders I was thrilled to have a protector.

We entered a restaurant, and he set me down on the

counter. Pointing at a blackboard that listed all kinds of noodle dishes, he asked me which I wanted. I scanned the menu but said nothing, for the remnants of pride were still circulating through my system. Wang Liqiang ordered a large bowl of noodles with three toppings—the most expensive option—and we sat down.

I will never forget the look in his eyes. Even now, so many years after his death, I feel a pang whenever I recall this moment. He gazed at me with such shame and affection that I say to myself: yes, I did have a father like that. But that was not how I responded at the time: it was only after he died, when I was back in Southgate, that I gradually became aware that Wang Liqiang was much more of a father to me than Sun Kwangtsai. Now, when it is all so far away, I realize that Wang Liqiang's death for me has been a lasting sorrow.

When the dish arrived, I did not start eating right away, but just looked at the steaming noodles—greedily, to be sure, but also with some reserve. Wang Liqiang read my mind: he stood up, saying that he had to get back to work, and walked out. As soon as he left I laid into the noodles with gusto. But my small belly was satisfied all too soon, and then I could only dejectedly pick up pieces of chicken and fish with my chopsticks, stare at them, and drop them back in the bowl, then dredge them up again; sad to say, I just could not eat any more.

By now I had recovered my normal energy and my unhappiness had vanished. I noticed an old man in tattered clothes across the table from me, who was eating a small bowl of the cheapest noodles. He watched attentively as I played around with my chicken and fish, and I could sense that he was looking forward to my leaving, so that he could help himself to the tasty morsels that I couldn't finish. This brought out my mean streak: I made a point of lingering over my meal and poked at the food in my bowl time and again. The old man, for his part, seemed to be making a point of eating very slowly. A silent struggle had developed between us. Soon I grew tired of this game and an entertaining new variation occurred to me. I chucked my chopsticks to one side, stood up, and swaggered out. As soon as I was out the door, I crouched down next to the window so I could observe his next move. He glanced toward the exit, and then speedily dumped his noodles into my bowl and placed his bowl where mine had been, after which he immediately resumed eating as though nothing had happened. I abandoned my place at the window and strode cockily back into the restaurant and over to the table where I had been sitting. I stared at the empty dish with feigned astonishment and was tickled to see the look of shame that spread over his face. Then I left in the best of spirits.

Once I reached third grade, I spent more and more of the day playing outside. By this time I was more familiar and comfortable with Wang Liqiang and Li Xiuying, and the trepidation that I felt early on had waned. Often I would be having so much fun that I would lose all sense of time, until suddenly it would occur to me that I needed to be home and I would race back to the house as fast as I could. I would be scolded, of course, but it was not so severe a reproof as to really scare me, and if I applied myself to chores and made a point of working up a good sweat, the reprimands died on their lips.

For a time I was especially fond of fishing for shrimp in ponds, and with this activity in mind practically every afternoon after school Guoqing, Liu Xiaoqing, and I would run off into the country. One day we had just put the town behind us when to my alarm I saw Wang Liqiang walking slowly along a path between the fields, a young woman just behind him. I quickly turned around and started running in the other direction, but Wang Liqiang had already spotted me, and when he called out, I had to stop and watch uneasily as he came walking up with his long strides. I should have been home by this point. Guoqing and Liu Xiaoqing hurriedly explained that we were out to catch shrimp, not to steal melons. He smiled and to my surprise did not rake me over the coals, but put his big hand on my head and simply said that he and I would go home together. All the way he asked solicitously about things going on at school and showed no sign of trying to find fault with me, so I gradually relaxed.

Later, in what was for me a happy boyhood moment, we stood under the ceiling fan in the department store and ate ice pops. In those days there was no electric fan in Wang Liqiang's house, and I watched with fascination as the ceiling fan, so perfectly round, spun in a circle and glimmered like water in motion. I stood at the edge of the fan's draft and walked in and out, enjoying the contrast.

That time I ate three ice pops in a row. Wang Liqiang was seldom as generous as this. When I'd finished the third, Wang Liqiang asked me if I wanted another and I nodded. But then he hesitated and disappointed me by saying, "Better not. You might have a tummy upset."

He compensated by buying me some candy instead. On the way home, he suddenly inquired, "Did you know that young lady?"

"Which young lady?" I didn't know who he was talking about.

"The one behind me."

Only then did I remember the young woman on the path. I had no clear impression of when she had vanished from the scene, so intent had I been on putting distance between Wang Liqiang and me. I shook my head, and Wang Liqiang said, "I don't know who she was either."

He went on, "It was only after I called you that I looked around and realized there was someone there." He opened his eyes wide in such an exaggerated expression of surprise that it made me laugh out loud.

As we got close to home, Wang Liqiang got down on his haunches and said to me quietly, "Let's not say we went to the country, but say instead that we met in the alley. Otherwise she might be annoyed."

I thoroughly approved, for I was not keen on Li Xiuying knowing that I had gone off to play again after school.

But six months later I saw Wang Liqiang and the young woman together again, and this time I found it hard to believe that they were strangers to each other. I made my getaway before Wang Liqiang could see me, and later I sat down on a rock to puzzle things out. At eleven I could put two and two together, even if it took a bit of effort. Understanding now the improper relationship between the woman and Wang Liqiang, I thought, with a sudden shock, what a wicked man he was. But when I got home I kept quiet about it. I cannot fully recall what led me to keep quiet, but I remember that when I contemplated reporting the matter to Li Xiuying I found myself quaking with dread. Years later I would still wonder naively what would have happened if I had told Li Xiuying, and whether the sight of her pale and powerless outrage might have had just enough impact on Wang Liqiang to forestall his death.

The fact that I kept silent on this matter later enabled me to blackmail Wang Liqiang into not punishing me when I should have been punished. Despite all my best efforts the little wine cup that rested on the wireless finally came to a bad end. As I swiveled around while mopping the floor, the handle of the mop knocked the cup from its perch, and it fell to the floor and shattered. Of the property owned by this humble household, this cup was the only decorative element, and its destruction left me a bundle of nerves. Wang Liqiang would wring my neck with the same crisp snap with which he broke that cucumber.

That had been my fear when I first moved in, and I now knew he would not really do that, but I certainly anticipated a towering rage and severe punishment. I needed to do everything in my limited power to avoid this unhappy fate, and a preemptive threat seemed the best approach. Li Xiuying was in another room, unaware of the accident, so I quietly swept the fragments into the dustpan. By the time Wang Liqiang came home from work, I was so keyed up that I began to sob. Puzzled, Wang Liqiang crouched down and asked me, "What's wrong?"

In a quaking voice I delivered my threat, "If you beat me, I am going to tell about you and that lady!"

Wang Liqiang paled. He shook me and said, "I won't beat you. Why should I?"

That's when I told him, "I broke the wine cup."

Wang Liqiang looked blank for a moment, but then he realized what had triggered my threat and broke into a smile. "That wine cup means nothing to me," he said.

Not sure whether to believe him, I asked him, "So you're not going to beat me?"

He promised he would not, putting me completely at ease. To reciprocate, I whispered in his ear, "I won't say anything about the lady."

After dinner that evening Wang Liqiang took my hand and we went for a long walk. Often he would exchange greetings with people he knew. I did not know that this would be my last stroll with Wang Liqiang, and I was enchanted by the glow of the setting sun as it lingered above the eaves. Infected by my boyish enthusiasm, Wang Liqiang talked a lot about when he was small. The thing he said that most stands out in my mind was that until he was fifteen he was so poor he often had no pants to wear. As he told me that he said with a sigh, "Being poor's not so bad; it's other things that make you miserable."

Later we sat down by the bridge. He studied me and said worriedly, "You're a little devil, aren't you?" Then he changed his tone. "You're a smart boy, that's for sure."

That autumn when I was twelve, Liu Xiaoqing's big brother—the musician I so admired—died of hepatitis.

By then he was no longer an idle teenager, for after graduation from high school he had been sent off to labor in the countryside. But he still wore his peaked cap and carried his flute in his jacket pocket. I heard that two boatmen's daughters had been assigned to work in the same village, and these two sturdy girls both fell in love with him. He played the flute so beautifully, it was no surprise they fell under its spell on those lonely nights in the countryside. But he found life there a trial and often sneaked back into town, playing the flute by his window, conjuring up the pear-syrup candy tune on our way home from school. He got a kick out of our silly faces and was loath to return to the village, even if there were two girls awaiting him there, poised with the love nets they had woven.

The last time he came back, he must have stayed a little too long. His father was on his case the whole day through, badgering him to hurry back to the village. Several times I heard him sobbing as I passed his window. He had no energy at all, he told his father pitifully—he could hardly eat, much less work.

None of them knew he had hepatitis. In the end his mother talked him into going back and boiled him a couple of eggs for the journey, but just two days after his return to the village he collapsed and lost consciousness. His admirers took turns carrying him home on their backs. After school I saw two sunburnt girls with mud on their legs and stricken looks on their faces come out of Liu Xiaoqing's house. His brother died that same evening.

I still remember his dismal expression when he left home that last time. He shuffled toward the steamboat jetty with a bedroll over his left shoulder and the eggs in his right hand. At this point almost all the life had been squeezed out of him, and he walked with the tottering steps of an old man not long for this world. Only the flute, jutting out of his jacket pocket, swung back and forth and projected a certain air of vitality.

Though death was lurking just around the corner, he still tried to tease me when he ran into me in the street. He asked me to see if there was a hole in the seat of his pants. Having fallen for that trick once already, I shouted back, "No way! You want me to smell your stinky farts."

With a chuckle he released a tepid fart, then shambled off toward extinction.

In those days people had an exaggerated idea of how contagious hepatitis can be, and when Liu Xiaoqing came to school with a black armband the other children shunned him like the plague. With an ingratiating smile on his face the bereaved boy walked toward a bunch of classmates who were playing underneath a basketball hoop, but they instantly swarmed to another hoop, cursing him for all they were worth, while he kept smiling stiffly. I was sitting on the steps outside the classrooms and watched as he stood beneath the hoop, a lonely figure, his hands dangling by his sides.

Then he slowly walked toward me. He came to a halt not far away and pretended to be looking in another direction. After a moment, seeing that I had made no effort to put more distance between us, he sat down next to me. We had not spoken to each other since the graffiti episode—or even sat close to each other. His sudden isolation had brought him back to me, and he was first to break our long silence. "Why aren't you running away?" he asked.

"*I'm* not afraid." I replied.

We were both a little embarrassed. We buried our heads between our knees and snickered. We had been ignoring each other for quite some time, after all.

I was to suffer two losses in as many days, for the death of Liu Xiaoqing's big brother was immediately followed by the death of Wang Liqiang. It's hard to judge just how much this combination of events was to affect my future, but my life undoubtedly took a new turn with the passing of Wang Liqiang. I had only just repaired my friendship with Liu Xiaoqing and still had not had time to make up with Guoqing when, that very night, Wang Liqiang was gone forever.

He and the young woman were doomed. With their hearts in their mouths they made it through two happy years, only to be caught in the act that evening.

The wife of one of Wang Liqiang's fellow-officers was a staunch guardian of the morals of the age. This mother of two made herself responsible for monitoring other people's love affairs, and according to her Wang Liqiang and his mistress had long been on her list of suspects. When the wife's husband was out of town on business, Wang Liqiang would take his young lover at night to the office that the two men shared. They cleared the desk and then used it as a bed, savoring their bittersweet happiness.

The officer's wife quickly unlocked the door with her husband's key and with equal speed turned on the light. Exposed, the couple stared at her in openmouthed horror. As she began to launch into a denunciation of their misconduct, Wang Liqiang and his desk partner did not bother to dress but threw themselves on their knees before her, pleading desperately for leniency. Wang Liqiang, so awesome and forbidding in my eyes, was reduced to tears and moans.

But after keeping them under observation for so long and now at last with such splendid results to show for it, how could their nemesis let them off so easily? She made it clear to them they were wasting their time begging for mercy. "It wasn't easy catching you," she said.

Then she went over to the window and threw it open, clucking like a hen that has just laid an egg.

Wang Liqiang knew that the damage was done. He and his lover got dressed and seated themselves. When his colleagues from the security section arrived, he spotted the political commissar and said to him shamefacedly, "Sir, I've committed a lifestyle error."

The commissar instructed several soldiers to keep Wang Liqiang under guard and told the young woman to go home. She was sobbing too much to speak, and when she got up to leave she shielded her face with her hands. The snoop was reveling in the moment. "Put your hands down!" she barked. "I didn't see you blushing when you were doing it with him."

Wang Liqiang walked up to her and slapped her across the face.

I do not know much more about what happened then, but one can imagine how it must have made her blood boil to be struck by Wang Liqiang just when she was giddy with success. She lunged at him with fingers spread but stumbled over a chair and fell to the floor. Her fury gave way to humiliation, and she burst into tears. The commissar had the soldiers hustle Wang Liqiang away and told a few others to stay with the woman, who was now sitting on the floor and refusing to get up. The commissar himself went back to bed.

Wang Liqiang sat in a pitch-dark room until late in the night. Then he stood up and told the soldier guarding him that he needed to get something from his office. The bleary-eyed guard felt awkward in front of his superior; as he hesitated, Wang Liqiang said he would be back shortly and left without further ado. The soldier did not follow, but stood by the door and watched Wang Liqiang walk across in the moonlight toward the offices, until his sprawling shadow melded with the larger shadow of the office block.

Wang Liqiang did not go to his office: instead he unlocked the door to the armory. He picked up two hand grenades and went down the stairs. Sticking close to the wall, he walked quietly over to the dependent housing, climbed the stairs to the second floor, and came to a stop outside a window on the west side. He had visited this apartment on a number of occasions and knew where his colleague's wife slept. He pulled the pin on one of the grenades and then smashed the window and tossed the grenade inside. As he dashed toward the staircase, the grenade detonated, and a huge roar shook the old building so that it swayed back and forth, throwing up clouds of dust that settled on Wang Liqiang as he ran. He fled all the way to the perimeter wall and squatted in the shadow there.

The security department was thrown into such uproar it was almost as though war had broken out. He heard the commissar, now awake for the second time, heaping curses on the negligent soldier, and he heard someone crying for a stretcher. To Wang Liqiang, straining his eyes to see, the chaotic scene might as well have been a churning mass of locusts. Later he saw three stretchers being carried out of the building and heard someone shout, "Still breathing, still alive!"

He gave a start. When the stretchers were carried into an ambulance and driven out of the compound, he clambered over the wall and jumped down the other side. He knew he had no time to waste.

In the early hours a man with a grenade in his hand and a look of raw menace on his face appeared at the town hospital. The surgeon on duty when Wang Liqiang entered was a northerner with a beard. As soon as he saw the visitor, he knew that he must have something to do with the three patients who had just been carried in, and he fled down the corridor in panic, crying, "Help! The killer!"

The doctor was too flustered to express himself clearly, and it was a good half hour before he had calmed down. Now he stood next to a trembling nurse, and they watched as Wang Liqiang moved from room to room, grenade in hand. A sudden spark of courage led the doctor to propose that the two of them jump him from behind, and part of this idea certainly registered with the nurse, for as Wang Liqiang came ever closer she turned to him fearfully and implored, "Quick, you grab him now!"

The doctor thought for a moment and said, "Maybe I should report to the leadership first." So saying, he opened a window, jumped out, and made his escape.

Wang Liqiang moved along the corridor, searching room by room. The shouts of panic grated on his nerves. When he pushed open the door to the nurses' station, it snapped back and dealt his left wrist a stinging blow, pinning it against the jamb so painfully that he grimaced. By throwing all his weight against the door, he succeeded in knocking it open, to find four nurses weeping and wailing inside, but no sign of his quarry. He tried to calm the nurses, promising not to harm them, but they just continued to shriek, oblivious to everything he said. Wang Liqiang shook his head helplessly and withdrew. Then he went into the operating theater, abandoned long before by the terrified staff. He saw two boys lying on gurneys and recognized them as the woman's sons. They were dead, their bodies mangled. Wang Liqiang gaped in shocked disbelief that this could have happened. He retreated from the operating theater; with the deaths of the two boys, he had lost interest in searching for their mother. He slowly made his way outside and lingered momentarily by the hospital entrance, thinking that he ought to go back home, but then he said to himself, "Forget it."

Soon he found himself surrounded. As he leaned back against a power pole, he heard the commissar yell, "Wang Liqiang, drop your weapon! Otherwise, you're a dead man."

Wang Liqiang called back, "Sir, when Lin gets back, please tell him for me, I know I did him wrong. I didn't mean to kill his sons."

The commissar thought this beside the point. Again he shouted, "Put down your weapon. You're a dead man if you don't."

A wry answer came back. "Sir, I'm a dead man already."

Wang Liqiang, who had shared his house with me for five years, who had loved me and disciplined me like a true father, suddenly found the pain in his injured wrist almost too much to bear, and in the moments before his death he pulled a handkerchief out of his pocket and meticulously dressed his wound. No sooner had he finished than he realized this made no sense and muttered to himself, "Why bother?"

As he looked at his neatly strapped wrist he forced a smile, and then he detonated the grenade. The force of the blast snapped the power pole behind him, and the brightly lit hospital was plunged into darkness.

The woman whom Wang Liqiang had been so determined to blow to pieces had emerged from the explosion with just some cuts and bruises. On the afternoon following Wang Liqiang's suicide, she left the hospital weeping and sobbing, still badly shaken. But before long she recovered her former self-confidence, and six months later, when she left the hospital once more, she was positively jubilant. The gynecologist's examination had confirmed that she was pregnant again, with twins to boot. During the next few days her standard greeting was, "He thought he'd got rid of my sons, but now their replacements are on the way!"

Li Xiuying was left to cope with the calamity of Wang Liqiang's death. Frail though she was, at first she seemed untouched by the enormous strain this placed on her. When one of Wang Liqiang's colleagues came to break the news on behalf of the security section, she managed to weather the initial blow. Keeping her composure, she simply scrutinized her visitor, so he was the one who was thrown off balance. Then she gave a piercing shout: "You people killed Wang Liqiang!"

The man had not anticipated this, and he began to repeat the story of how Wang Liqiang had taken his own life. Li Xiuying waved her slender arm dismissively and came out with an even more awful accusation. "You people—all of you—killed Wang Liqiang, and that's a fact. But it's me you really want to see dead."

Her bizarre logic made the visitor realize to his dismay that it was going to be impossible to conduct a normal conversation with her. But there was a practical matter he needed to attend to. He asked her when she would like to collect Wang Liqiang's body.

Li Xiuying took her time to answer this. Then she said, "I don't want it. If he'd committed another kind of error, I'd say yes, but since he committed this kind of mistake, I'm not interested."

That was the only thing she said that one could imagine an ordinary person saying.

After the man had left, Li Xiuying turned to me—I was still dumbstruck—and said resentfully, "They took a live man away from me, and now they're trying to fob off a dead one on me!"

She tilted her head up and said defiantly, "I refused."

What a trying day this was—a Sunday, too—when I could only stay at home, whirled around in a jumble of emotions: bewilderment, anguish, and fear. I found it hard to accept that Wang Liqiang was dead; the whole episode had the unreal quality of a secondhand report.

Li Xiuying spent the whole day in her room, carefully attending to her underwear and adjusting the little stools' positions in the shifting sunlight. But from time to time she would issue a scream so bloodcurdling it made me quake—the one way she could express her sorrow and despair. So piercing were her screams, they conjured up images of shards of glass whistling through the air.

Though it was daytime, I was petrified by the sound of these wild cries. Later I could not restrain my curiosity and surreptitiously opened the door to her room, to see her figure crouched over her underwear. Every so often her body would straighten, and she would raise her head and scream, "Aaaah!"

Early the next morning Li Xiuying set off for her maternal home. The sky was still dark when I was shaken awake. In the bright lamplight I saw a face mask looming over me, the body attached to it tightly encased in thick layers of clothing, and I was so startled that I gave a wail. Then I heard Li Xiuying's voice emerge from the mask. "Don't cry, don't cry. It's me."

Li Xiuying must have been pleased with the effect achieved by her disguise, for she said to me triumphantly, "You didn't recognize me, did you?"

In my five years in Littlemarsh, this was the first time Li Xiuying had left the house. On a morning before the advent of winter Li Xiuying walked off in her winter clothes toward the steamboat wharf, and I struggled along in her wake, lugging one of her little stools.

Before daybreak the streets were quite deserted, apart from the occasional old man coughing heavily on his way to morning tea. Li Xiuying was not strong enough to walk more than a hundred yards at a time, and when she stopped to catch her breath I promptly set the stool down underneath her bottom. Thus we proceeded through the damp morning breeze, walking and stopping in turn. Once or twice I was about to say something, but she would cut me off with a quick "Shh!" and whisper, "Not a word, or you'll give me away."

Her cloak-and-dagger manner gave me the jitters.

It was in this atmosphere of simulated mystery that Li

Xiuying left Littlemarsh. What seemed to me then an interminable walk to the wharf is now reduced in my memory to just a few brief scenes. As this strange woman in her bulky clothes cleared the ticket inspection, she turned and waved. I pressed up against the ramshackle waiting-room window and watched as she stood uncertainly on the bank. She needed to cross a narrow gangplank to board the boat, and now she abandoned all precautions, heedless of whether this might blow her cover, and called out, "Can someone help me across?"

When she stepped inside the cabin, that was the last I saw of her. I stayed glued to the window until the boat sailed into the distance, where the river disappeared out of sight. It was only then that I confronted a terrible reality: what was I to do?

Li Xiuying had forgotten me. Through sheer grief, she had put everything apart from herself out of her mind. At the age of twelve, as dawn approached, I was an orphan.

I didn't have a penny in my pocket; my clothes and satchel were locked inside the house, and I did not have a key. My sole possession was the little stool that Li Xiuying had left behind. I slung it up on my shoulder again and left the wharf, sobbing.

Out of habit I went back to the house, but when I pressed my hand against the unyielding door all I succeeded in doing was making myself more miserable. I slumped down outside the door, crying as though my heart would break, and then sat there in a daze, my mind drained of thought, until Liu Xiaoqing came along on his way to school, when I burst into tears again. Our relations now mended, I held nothing back: "Wang Liqiang is dead and Li Xiuying has gone away! There's no one to look after me."

Liu Xiaoqing was still wearing his black armband. "Come

and stay at my house!" he cried with impulsive generosity. "You can sleep in my brother's bed."

He ran back to his house, quick as a flash. But after a couple of minutes he returned, wearing a hangdog expression. Not only had his invitation been vetoed by his parents but he had received a tongue-lashing as well. He gave me an embarrassed smile. That's when I decided I would go back to Southgate, to be with my parents and my brothers. I told Liu Xiaoqing my plan, but added that I didn't have money for the boat fare.

His eyes lit up as he cried, "Borrow the money from Guoqing!"

We found Guoqing on the school playground. When Liu Xiaoqing called him, he said, "I'm not going over there—you've got hepatitis."

"How about if we come over where you are?" Liu Xiaoqing said pitifully.

Hearing no objection, we walked over to the boy with the deep pockets. Were it not for Guoqing's beneficence, I don't know how I would have made it back to Southgate. My two childhood playmates saw me to the boat that would take me away from Littlemarsh, and as we walked to the wharf Guoqing said to me airily, "If you're short of money in the future, just drop me a note."

Liu Xiaoqing trailed along a step or two behind, an uncomplaining porter, the stool propped against his shoulder. But in the end I forgot to take it along, just as Li Xiuying had forgotten to take me. When the boat pulled away I saw Guoqing sitting cross-legged on the stool, waving to me, while Liu Xiaoqing stood next to him, saying something into his ear. The wharf and the embankment on which it rested quickly disappeared from view.

Late that autumn afternoon I stepped onto my native soil. Returning after five years away, I asked directions to Southgate in an outsider's accent. As I began to walk toward the little road that would take me there, a child much younger than me stuck his nose against an upstairs window and called, "Kid! Hey, kid!"

To my ears, these words sounded like an exotic dialect. Fortunately I still remembered Southgate, and my parents' and siblings' names, and my grandfather's too. Memories from when I was six helped me sense which way to go, stopping occasionally to check with passersby. That was when I met my grandfather Sun Youyuan, with his bundle on his back and clutching his oilskin umbrella to his chest. He had just spent a month at my uncle's and was on his way back to Southgate. Now in his final years, my grandfather lost his way on the one road that should have been most familiar to him, and it was there we met, although neither of us recognized the other.

At this point I had put the county town behind me, and the countryside lay ahead. At a crossroads I was unsure how to proceed. But I did not immediately feel anxious, because I was entranced by the sunset. Rolling black clouds were gradually flooded with crimson light; a red globe had settled on the distant horizon and was beginning its luminous descent. I stood in the glow of the setting sun, yelling, "Down, down!" A huge black cloud was moving toward the western sky, and I didn't want to see it swallow up the setting sun.

Only after the sun obligingly sank from view did I notice my grandfather Sun Youyuan. He was standing behind me, just a few inches away. He looked at me imploringly, and when I asked him, "Which way to Southgate?" he shook his head and mumbled, "I forgot."

He forgot? I thought this a curious answer and said to him, "If you don't know, then why don't you just say so? What do you mean, you forgot?"

He smiled apologetically. The sky was now beginning to darken, so I chose one road at random and hurriedly set off. After a while I realized that the old man was following me, but I paid him no attention. A little farther on, I saw a woman with a scarf on her head bent over in a field and asked her, "Is this the way to Southgate?"

"You're going the wrong way." She straightened herself and said, "You should have taken that other road."

By now it was almost dark, so I turned around abruptly and headed back. The old man did the same, and his eagerness to stay with me began to get on my nerves. I took to my heels and ran, and when I looked back I could see him staggering along in a desperate effort to keep on my tail. This made me angry, and when he came a bit closer I said to him, "Hey, stop following me! Go some other way."

When I got back to the intersection, it was now completely dark. I could hear thunder; there was not even a hint of moonlight at this point. I groped my way to the other road and took several quick paces in that direction, only to find the old man still behind me. I turned around and yelled, "Stop following me! My family's got no money, and we can't afford to support you."

Rain began to fall, and I ran ahead as fast as I could. Suddenly I saw flames in the distance. The rain grew heavier, pitting its strength against the fire, but the blaze, far from weakening, was crackling with even greater fury. It had asserted itself in the rain like an unstoppable cry, and now it was burning with a vengeance.

By the light of the fire I could make out the wooden bridge that led to Southgate, and memories from the past gave me the happy sensation that I was already home. As I dashed through the rain, a hot breeze swept over me and a tangle of voices reached my ears. By the time I arrived, the flames had died down, and now they were just licking the ground; the rain had dropped off. I entered the village of Southgate amid clamor and commotion.

My two brothers stood there in shock, sheets wrapped around them; I didn't recognize them as Sun Guangping and Sun Guangming. Nor did I realize that the woman kneeling on the ground and wailing was my mother. Next to them, in an untidy heap, were items rescued from the flames. Then I saw a man naked to the waist, his scrawny chest exposed to the chilly autumn wind. In a hoarse voice he was telling the bystanders how many things had been lost in the inferno. Tears rolled from his eyes. He smiled at them desolately and said, "You all got to see a big fire, didn't you? It was a grand sight, that's for sure, but it's cost me a right bundle."

I did not know that he was my father, but something drew me to him, so I went up and loudly announced, "I'm looking for Sun Kwangtsai."

ALSO BY YU HUA

"A rare achievement in literature. . . . [Xu Sanguan is] a character that reflects not just a generation but the soul of a people."
—The Seattle Times

CHRONICLE OF A BLOOD MERCHANT

One of the last decade's ten most influential books in China, this internationally acclaimed novel by one of the mainland's most important contemporary writers provides an unflinching portrait of life under Chairman Mao. A cart-pusher in a silk mill, Xu Sanguan augments his meager salary with regular visits to the local blood chief. As he struggles to provide for his wife and three sons, his visits become dangerously frequent. And when he discovers that his favorite son was actually born of a liaison between his wife and a neighbor, Xu Sanguan is shattered, while his wife is publicly scorned as a prostitute. In the face of such soul-destroying indignities, Xu Sanguan ultimately finds strength in the blood ties of his family. A novel of rare emotional intensity, grippingly raw descriptions of place and time, and clear-eyed compassion, *Chronicle of a Blood Merchant* offers us a stunning tapestry of human life in the grave particulars of one man's days.

Fiction/Literature/978-1-4000-3185-6

*"Immensely moving. . . . Artfully constructed, beautifully written, and stealthily consuming—[*Chronicle of a Blood Merchant*] repeatedly stops you in your tracks."*
—The Boston Globe

"*A work of astounding emotional power.*"
—Dai Sijie, author of *Balzac and the Little Chinese Seamstress*

TO LIVE

An award-winning, internationally acclaimed Chinese best-seller, originally banned in China but recently named one of the last decade's ten most influential books there, *To Live* tells the epic story of one man's transformation from the spoiled son of a rich landlord to an honorable and kindhearted peasant. After squandering his family's fortune in gambling dens and brothels, the young, deeply penitent Fugui settles down to do the honest work of a farmer. Forced by the Nationalist Army to leave behind his family, he witnesses the horrors and privations of the Civil War, only to return years later to face a string of hardships brought on by the ravages of the Cultural Revolution. Left with an ox as the companion of his final years, Fugui stands as a model of flinty authenticity, buoyed by his appreciation for life in this narrative of humbling power.

Fiction/Literature/978-1-4000-3186-3

ANCHOR BOOKS
Available from your local bookstore, or visit
www.randomhouse.com